*Books by Jill Gregory
from Jove*

THE WAYWARD HEART
PROMISE ME THE DAWN
MY TRUE AND TENDER LOVE
MOONLIT OBSESSION
LOOKING GLASS YEARS

JILL GREGORY

LOOKING GLASS YEARS

JOVE BOOKS, NEW YORK

LOOKING GLASS YEARS

A Jove Book / published by arrangement with
the author

PRINTING HISTORY
Jove trade paperback edition / November 1987
Jove mass market edition / February 1989

ISBN: 0-515-09930-9

Jove Books are published by The Berkley Publishing Group,
200 Madison Avenue, New York, New York 10016.
The name ''JOVE'' and the ''J'' logo
are trademarks belonging to Jove Publications, Inc.

PRINTED IN THE UNITED STATES OF AMERICA

10 9 8 7 6 5 4 3 2 1

To Larry, Rachel, Dad, Barbara, Stuart, and the rest of my wonderful family, with all my love.

To my mother, whose memory shines brightly in my heart.

And to my "other" family: Marianne, Ruth, and Elly, who are so dear and special to me.

❧ Prologue

Kentucky, 1861

ON THE DAY that Abraham Lincoln took his oath of office to become the sixteenth President of the United States, Boone Walker won his first fight.

His battleground was a deserted crossroads beneath a sloping hillside half a mile from home, his adversary a stocky nine-year-old named Caleb Dunne who had bloodied the nose of every smaller boy in the school. Only Boone had been spared so far, and that was simply because his older brother Clay looked out for him.

Boone was eight years old and small for his age, and he enjoyed everything about the one-room schoolhouse outside Hickoryville except sharing it with Caleb Dunne and his bullying companions. So far, Clay had been able to protect him from Caleb and the other boys who liked to fight. Boone was glad of that, but he lived in dread of the day when he would have to defend himself. Ma didn't allow any fighting at home—not the punching, kicking kind, at least. The four Walker boys did their share of wrestling and yelling and scuffling among themselves, but if ever one raised a fist against his brother, Ma gave them a licking they didn't soon forget. So Boone, the youngest, had as yet no experience in boyhood combat of the gouging, no-holds-barred variety— until that chilly March day when Caleb Dunne attacked him as he trudged home from school. It was one of those bitter spring days when the air bit right through trousers and jacket. The Kentucky hills were damp and green with rain. Clay was home sick with a fever, and the other boys had gone on to their own farms after school. Boone had his chin tucked into the frayed brown collar of his jacket as he turned into the winding road that skirted the Walker farm.

Caleb caught him by the crossroads where the giant elm tree had been mangled by lightning the summer before. He ran at Boone from behind, and before Boone even knew what was coming, knocked the younger boy face down in the dirt. Boone lay stunned, his cheek stinging from the gravelly dirt. As he lifted his head, he heard jeering laughter behind him.

"Git up, you chicken-hearted little toad. Git up and fight me iffen you dare!"

Boone scrambled to his feet. Caleb Dunne sauntered forward in front of him, his hands planted on his hips, his scraggly red hair hanging down into his round, cherubic eyes.

"Come on, boy. Don't be no sissy. Your ugly old brother ain't here to protect you today. Come on and fight!"

Boone swallowed back the panic in his throat. Part of him was scared, part of him furious. He wanted to fling himself at Caleb and pound the other boy's face with his fists. But Caleb was bigger, stronger. He outweighed Boone by at least twenty pounds.

"Get outta my way, Caleb." Boone's chin jutted out as he tried to sound tough and determined. "I'm goin' home."

Caleb laughed. Then he lunged forward and knocked Boone to the ground again. This time he pounced on top of the smaller boy and began to pummel his face. Boone cried out, struggling, trying to protect his face from the onslaught of blows. He tried to throw off the boy atop him, but Caleb dug his knees into Boone's ribs. In desperation, Boone's fist shot upward. He struck Caleb in the chin. Caught by surprise, Caleb reeled back. Boone took advantage of the moment by lurching aside with all his strength, rolling free of the older boy. Then both youths scrambled to their knees, closing in on each other with flailing fists.

The world exploded with pain and grunts. Boone was terrified. He fought frantically. He was strong for his age and size, and he surprised Caleb by the forcefulness of his blows. But he was seeing the worst of the fight. His nose was bloodied, there was a cut on his lip, and every rib in his body screamed out in agony under the frenzied punches of his enemy. But Boone was determined not to let Caleb knock him down again. Suddenly, one blow sent the red-haired boy spinning down into the dirt. For a moment, shaken, Caleb lay still. Boone stood over him, fists at the ready, blood trickling from the corners of his mouth. Caleb stared up at him.

In that instant, Boone saw a flash of uncertainty, of fear, in Caleb's eyes. A surge went through him, something hot and sweet and powerful as liquor. Caleb was scared, thought he might get beat, and in that second, Boone knew he could win the fight. He smelled Caleb's doubt and fear as a hound dog smells blood. He threw himself down on the older boy with a kind of wild joy and drove his red-scraped fists into Caleb's eyes, his nose, his jaw, his chin, until Caleb Dunne lay sobbing beneath him.

Boone heard his sobs through roaring ears. His arms froze in midair, and he peered down, dazed, at Caleb. He was shocked at the bloodied mess that was Caleb's face. His arms dropped, and he got to his feet, his own knees shaking. Caleb hadn't moved.

"Can you git up?" His voice was a croak.

Caleb was still sobbing.

"Caleb, take my hand."

"Git out! Git away from me!" Caleb shouted in a voice that was hoarse and raw with pain and fury.

Boone wiped his bleeding nose on his sleeve, sniffed, and hesitated.

"Git out before I lick you good!" Caleb rasped, and staggered to his feet.

Boone was silent. He watched as Caleb threw him a glance of hatred, then stumbled off in the direction of his family's farm, two miles from the Walker property. Boone watched him go, steadiness slowly returning to his trembling legs. Caleb Dunne would never bother him again, he thought with sudden elation. Not after today.

Boone hurt all over as he walked home. He'd have a black eye come nightfall, and bruises enough to make sleeping near impossible. But he'd beaten Caleb Dunne! The pride and wonder that filled him almost blotted out the pain of his injuries. He felt a new independence, a new freedom, no longer having to rely on Clay to look out for him. He could take care of himself. It was the first time in his life he had known such power, such wonderful self-assurance, and he gave a whoop. But something inside him nagged at the happiness that wanted to pour out of his soul. Shame. Shame dug at him, needling past his hurts and his victory. He wasn't

ashamed of having battered Caleb in a fair fight, a fight not of
his making. No, that wasn't it at all. He was ashamed of the
joy he had felt when he pounded and pounded at Caleb. That
strange, shameful, uncontrolled joy that had flooded through
him when he realized that he was winning, that the victory
was his. He dropped his head as he walked. He didn't like
that feeling. It was unfamiliar and somehow dangerous. Ma
wouldn't have liked it either, Boone was sure. He wondered
uneasily what she would say when she saw his bloodied face
and filthy clothes. His steps dragged as he reached the path
that led home, and he saw the gray, two-story frame farmhouse ahead, silhouetted against a rain-washed sky.

His fears were unfounded, though, for there were other
matters to occupy his mother's attention. Clay's fever had
worsened, and she was too busy tending him to spare Boone
more than a cursory glance.

"What in the world . . . Boone, you've been fighting!
Land sakes, child, clean yourself up and get outside to your
chores. We need kindling for the fire, and it'll be up to you to
see to the cows and chickens all by yourself, for Clay's took
real sick and you'll have to do his chores, too. Ezra'll want
supper in a while, and you'll have to come here and set with
Clay while I fix it. Now, scoot, boy. Hurry, or I'll have Ezra
take the switch to you!''

Clay's fever broke that night, and the relief that swept
through the weather-beaten farmhouse warmed and softened
every corner of the plain, spotless rooms. Ezra Wells celebrated by imbibing half a jug of whiskey, which he generously shared with the two oldest boys. Their mother had
come downstairs to tell them the good news, looking weary
and happy as she sank into the hickory chair by the fire. The
bright orange flames sent flickering shadows across her lined
face, softening the circles beneath her brown eyes, touching
her wispy gray hair with amber light. The mantel clock
showed eight o'clock, near Boone's bedtime, but he put down
his spelling slate and crept from the rug by the fire to rest his
head on his mother's lap.

"I'm glad Clay's better, Ma," he mumbled.

She gazed down at him almost as if seeing him for the first
time all day.

"Boone, look at you. You're a rascally sight, if ever I saw
one," she scolded, but her hand smoothing his hair was

unexpectedly gentle. "What in heaven's name happened today?"

Ezra answered for him in his raspy voice. "He told us all 'bout it whiles you were tending Clay. The boy licked Caleb Dunne, Hannah, licked him real good."

"I did!" Boone exclaimed, lifting his head. "He was whupped, I tell you!"

"I b'lieve you, Boone. You're tough, like all the Walkers. We don't give in easy, never have." Henry grinned at him and reached for the whiskey jug again.

Ezra shook his head and snatched it away. "You've had enough, boy."

They all caught the note of irritation in Ezra's voice, and Tom and Henry exchanged knowing glances. Ezra hated it when they spoke of themselves as Walkers. It was a continual reminder to him that he was an outsider, the man married to their ma, but not their father.

Jeb Walker had died in a hunting accident three years ago, and Ezra had married Hannah a year and a half later. He was a small grizzled man from the backwoods, a cousin to the Slades, the Walkers' nearest neighbors in this isolated Kentucky valley. Ezra was far different from the enormous gentle-tempered Jeb. He was quick, nervous, always fretting about something or other. He was constantly worried about the tobacco crop, the weather, the barn door latch that needed fixing. He was sharp and demanding with Hannah's boys, but clearly fond of the slight, small-boned woman who oversaw the household with such martial efficiency yet always had a kind word for those who needed it. Ezra liked that about Hannah, but he felt in some ways she was too soft on her boys. He resented the fact that all four still refused to call him Pa or to take his name. Out of respect for him, Hannah ought to insist that the younger ones consider him their rightful father now. Clay had been eight when Jeb died, and Boone had been only five. What in hell did they remember about Jeb Walker? He was their pa now, Ezra reasoned, and would be for longer than Jeb had known them. He felt insulted every time they referred to the Walker pride, the Walker spirit. Why should he have to listen to praise of a dead man right in front of his wife?

"I'll teach you how to fight, Boone, iffen you really want to learn," he said, wheeling toward the boy who still knelt

beside his mother's chair. An eager light showed in his dark
eyes, but when he saw the stiffening of Boone's thin young
shoulders, saw the animation leave the boy's face, he scowled.
Boone dropped his head and muttered an indistinguishable
response.

"What's that you say, boy?" Ezra's tone grew goading.
He lifted the whiskey jug, took a swig, then smacked the jug
on the mantel so hard one of Hannah's decorative cups rattled
on its saucer. "You'll have to speak up iffen you want to be a
man! No more whimperin' from your mama's knee."

"I'm not whimperin'!" Boone shot back. "And I already
know how to fight." Ezra always seemed to find pleasure in
baiting him. Boone felt resentment quivering through his
slight frame.

"You do, do you? Well, mebbe you can beat a young'un
like Caleb Dunne, but the day will come when you want to
beat a real man. Scrawny little thing like you, you'll need all
the help you can get. Iffen you ask me, I'll show you a few
things that'll keep you on top. There never yet was born a
man who could whup Ezra Wells."

"My pa coulda beat you." Boone stuck out his chin. "My
pa was a lot bigger'n you."

"Boone!" Hannah exclaimed, her hands gripping the arms
of the hickory chair. She glanced at Ezra's reddening face,
saw the anger glazing his dark eyes. "That's no way to talk
to your step-pa! Ezra's tryin' to be nice."

That don't come easy to him, Boone thought, but aloud he
muttered, "Sorry, Ma."

"You apologize to Ezra."

Boone lifted his head and met his stepfather's hard stare.
"Sorry."

Ezra grunted. "That young'un don't respect me the way he
should," he began, his voice slightly slurred from the whiskey, one finger jabbing the air. He took a step toward Boone,
who was still kneeling beside his mother, but Tom headed
him off.

"Easy, now, Ezra." Eighteen-year-old Tom put a calming
hand on the older man's arm.

"Get your hands off me, boy!"

"I'm only tryin' to—"

"I know what you're tryin' to do! And I'm tellin' you that
this is between me and that young'un."

"I won't have arguin' in this house." Hannah spoke quietly from her chair, and Ezra and the boys fell silent. "Boone, you go on up to bed now." Hannah's fingers squeezed his shoulder, and she pursed her lips. "With all this talk about fightin' and whuppin', we clear forgot that our Clay is gettin' well." She sent a reproving glance around the firelit room. "We oughta be sayin' our prayers of thanks to the good Lord, 'stead of arguin' among ourselves."

"You're right, Ma." Boone listened to Tom's apologetic voice as he climbed the stairs. "Do you think Clay'll be up and around in the mornin'?"

"Hope so," Ezra snapped. "There's enough work around her as it is, without losin' out on one more pair of hands."

Boone glanced down from the landing and saw Henry grin. "Well, Ezra," his brother drawled, "jest hope war don't break out between Lincoln and the Confederates, or Tom and me'll be off fightin' and you'll be stuck with just Clay and Boone to keep up the farm. Then you'll know what a peck of work is like."

"Shush, Henry," his mother cried with unaccustomed fervor. "Don't talk about war!"

"But, Ma—"

"There's not goin' to be any war!" Hannah's face had gone pale. "Leastways, not for you. No matter what the fool government does and those damned Confederates, you're stayin' home and work the tobacco patch, and that goes for you, too, Tom. I don't want to hear any more about it."

"Sorry, Ma," Henry muttered. Boone crept away.

When the boys had all gone up to bed, Ezra and Hannah sat a little longer by the fire. Hannah was exhausted from worrying about Clay and nursing him all day long. She had been forced to neglect some of her household chores in order to tend him, and the resultant disarray, although it would scarcely have been noticeable to most women, grated on her sensibilities, for Hannah was an immaculate housekeeper, and anything less than complete cleanliness and order in her domain irked her. And then there was all this talk about a war. Henry found it exciting, she knew, and she suspected Tom did, too. But she was terrified. None of her boys would go to war. She wouldn't allow it. She thanked the Lord that Clay and Boone were too young to even think about it. It was bad enough that Boone had had to fight Caleb Dunne today.

But war . . . She shuddered and closed her eyes, blocking the terrible thought from her mind.

Upstairs, it was quiet. Boone slept on a pallet on the floor, curled up with his straw-filled pillow, thinking again about Caleb Dunne. He hadn't liked fighting, but he liked knowing that he *could* fight—and win. Boone relived the moments when he had struck Caleb over and over, but this time, it was Ezra's face he pictured—Ezra's face, bleeding and pulpy, terrified and defeated. He didn't know exactly why he hated Ezra so. He supposed it would be disloyal to Pa to feel any other way. Boone remembered Jeb all too well. His father had had easy ways—a kind, drawling Kentucky voice, a booming laugh that made everyone around him smile. He was nothing at all like Ezra. Boone flipped onto his back and stared at the moonlit shadows on the beamed ceiling, wondering why Ma had married Ezra anyway, and why Pa had had to die. It wasn't fair, he thought, biting his lip against the threatening tears. No one wanted Ezra, except Ma. Because of her, they all had to put up with him.

Boone envied Tom and Henry. If there was a war, they'd get to go and fight. He and Clay would be stuck here on the farm with Ezra. Boone could remember when the farm had seemed like heaven to him. Ma had kept it cozy and neat, and they'd always had clean, mended clothes to wear and plenty of Ma's good cooking. Pa used to tell them stories at night about Grandpa Gil and Gramma Elsie coming over from Virginia. There were summer nights when Boone just sat on the porch, listening to the crickets and Pa's voice and thought he'd never want to leave the farm, never want to go farther than Harrodsburg, for all that was good and pleasant and familiar was right here at home. Now he thought of war, of rifles and uniforms and distant battlefields, and shivered with envy. Tom and Henry might be lucky. They might escape Ezra, become fighting men, heroes. They might be free.

He heard footsteps on the stairs. Ma and Ezra were coming up at last, and so he turned on his side and shut his eyes, pretending sleep in case his mother should come to look in on him. He heard a hand on the doorknob, and the creak of the door. Then came Ezra's voice, gruff and low.

"Don't trouble yourself, Hannah. You baby that young'un too much."

"He's only eight, Ezra. Boone had a rough day."

Boone heard his mother sigh. She sounded tired, more so than usual. Then Ezra's voice came again.

"When you goin' to tell them about the baby? They'll be seein' for themselves 'fore you know it."

Baby?

"Soon, Ezra. I'll tell them soon."

"Hell, woman, all they have to do is take a good look at you to see." Ezra's voice took on a petulant note. "I want to be there when you tell them. You hear? I want to see their faces."

Boone couldn't hear his mother's reply. He strained to catch the softly spoken words, but the door had shut, and the footsteps retreated down the hall. He lay, breathing hard, his throat aching.

His mother was going to have Ezra's baby.

He balled his hands into fists and rubbed them hard against his eyes. He wanted to hit someone. He wanted to cry. He wanted to wake Tom and Henry and Clay and tell them. Instead, he flung himself over on his back again and squeezed his eyes shut.

It started to rain outside, a soft Kentucky rain pinging against the roof and windows. Thunder rumbled low in the distance. Boone fell asleep to the sound of it, but he woke once after an unexpectedly loud crack of thunder, thinking it was cannon fire. He'd been dreaming about war, but there was no war. Only spring thunder and the deep breathing of his brothers and the creakings of the old farmhouse, built by his father and grandfather more than thirty years ago. He fell back asleep, dreaming of a baby lying in the tobacco patch and soldiers shooting from the roof of the barn, dreaming of Henry running toward a fire in the hills and Ma rocking on the porch, with her hair turned all to white. And he dreamed of Ezra Wells, grinning as he uncorked a jug of Kentucky lightning and spilled the contents on Jeb Walker's grave.

But it wasn't whiskey that flowed from the bottle in Boone's dream, staining the headstone and burial plot where Pa lay beside Grandpa and Gramma. In the white gauzy light of his dream, Boone stared in helpless horror as Ezra poured out a gushing bottle of blood.

❧ One

SOMEWHERE ON THIS earth, Elly Forrest believed, there was a place of beauty and golden tranquillity. The trouble was, she reflected with a scowl, pulling her shawl closer about her shoulders and hurrying through the gray October fog, she didn't know where it was or how to get there, and chances were this Paradise, if indeed it existed, was impossibly far from Emmettville.

Twilight drifted over the factory buildings and stores as she made her way through the center of town, past the bakery and the post office and the livery stable to the gravel road that led home. The other girls from the cotton mill had taken the usual shortcut after the shift ended, but Elly had walked first to town to buy peppermint candy for her brother Timothy's eighth birthday. Overhead, the leaden sky threatened rain, and in the distance, gold- and amber-cloaked hills half hidden by clouds added to the gloom of the fading day, exactly mirroring Elly's mood. Her shoes pinched her feet, and a cold mist sprayed her cheeks as she clutched the stick of candy in her hand. She had promised Timmy a special treat tonight in addition to the knit cap and mittens Mama had made him, but somehow, she couldn't muster much enthusiasm for the celebration ahead—all because of the argument she had overheard last night, when her parents were alone in the parlor, thinking that she and Caroline and Timothy were fast asleep. The words kept drumming in her head. As she approached the lanes of "company" row houses where Emmettville's working families lived, she saw neither the rotting planked sidewalk where she set her feet nor the unpainted frame houses with their muddy yards and sagging porches. Instead of hearing the barking of Mrs. Alexander's mongrel dog, she heard the words her mother had flung at Papa in the golden light of the kerosene lamp.

"I won't have it, Samuel. I won't have my baby slaving in that mill."

Her mother's words rang in Elly's ears, clamoring like alarm bells. Until that moment, she'd had no idea their circumstances were so bleak. Timothy working in the mill? The cotton mill, her mother had meant, where Elly herself worked twelve hours a day, six days a week, and where eight-year-old bobbin boys had to stand on boxes to reach the whirling spindles, their fingers always in danger of being caught.

"You think I want that? You think I want my son working in that stinking place?" Papa had groaned, limping back and forth before his wife. "Bess, I just don't know what else to do. We're in debt up to our shoulders now."

"It's all your fault." Mama had thrown down her sewing and glared up at him. She had looked thin and pale in the big slipcovered chair whose once-vivid print had now faded to blurred patches of yellow and blue and green. "You and your ridiculous ideas about organizing the workers. All you've done is antagonize Silas Emmett further. We'll be lucky if you don't lose your job completely."

"I know you want Timothy to keep on with his schooling until he's twelve. But a job as a bobbin boy will make the difference of putting food on this table in the winter months or not."

Elly saw again the anguish on her mother's pallid, still elegant face. Even poverty and struggle had not been able to erase the patrician beauty Elizabeth Stevenson Forrest possessed. The lines and creases of care and worry only accentuated her finely chiseled bone structure and the crystalline luminosity of her blue-gray eyes. At that moment, Elly had wished she were huddled in her bed instead of witnessing her parents' despair. She had knelt on the upper landing in her nightdress, too frightened to move. The helplessness and desperation in her father's voice, as well as her mother's distress, caused a lump to rise in her throat. She swallowed, listening as her mother's voice rose.

"It's bad enough that Caroline and Elly have to work like

common drudges. Elly, at least, is strong like you, and she's sixteen now. But Caroline is delicate. . . ."

"Bess, please." Through the pine railing, Elly had watched her father try to touch her mother's shoulders. Bess had flinched away. "I know nothing's turned out the way we planned. Too many things got in the way. I can't blame you if you regret marrying me after all."

"Samuel, don't!" Mama had covered her face with her hands. "I still love you. I don't regret defying my family to be with you. But . . . our children. I want more for our children."

"So do I."

"Then stop fighting Silas Emmett and let us live in peace. Maybe he'll raise wages again if you're not trying to pressure him to do it. Maybe we can get by without sending Timothy to the cotton mill yet."

"Maybe." Her father's tone had been doubtful. As Elly had gazed at him from the landing above, his handsome, craggy face had seemed suddenly haggard and old, and the glinting, intelligent blue eyes she loved to stare into were shadowed by untold pain.

Samuel Forrest was a big, dark-haired man with solid shoulders, a square jaw, and a dimple in his strong chin. His limp, the result of a knee wound incurred at Gettysburg, would be with him for all of his days, but it did not detract in any way from his powerful masculinity. As Elly watched, he sighed and went to her mother. He tried to draw Mama into his arms, but she pulled back in her chair.

"I'm going up to bed." Mama had stuffed her sewing into the wicker basket beside her and carried it to the stairs, avoiding touching him as she passed. Elly, alarmed, had crept silently along the hall to her room to avoid discovery. "I'm tired, Samuel," she had heard her mother murmur as she came up the darkened, narrow steps. "I'm exhausted. Good night."

All day at the cotton mill, Elly had been haunted by their words. Lately Mama had been more on edge than usual, but Elly hadn't known why. Now that she knew, she wondered what she could do to make things easier. Timothy mustn't be allowed to work in the mill. It was too dangerous, too taxing. He was only a child. She sighed, thinking of his delight over the birthday supper Mama had planned: her special stew, potato dumplings, and applesauce, with blueberry pie for dessert. She couldn't remember when they'd last had such a dinner. It was a feast in honor of Timothy's eighth birthday, but Elly wondered if she'd even be able to swallow a bite.

Her fingers tightened on the peppermint candy in its paper wrapping. She loved no one in the world more than Timothy. Caroline was a spoiled, pettish brat, but Timmy was a little dear. Perhaps because she knew herself to be her father's favorite and Caroline to be Mama's pet, she loved Timmy more than all the rest, even Papa. She'd work a double shift at the mill herself, she thought fiercely, before she'd let Timmy set foot in there.

Suddenly, a gust of wind sent a flurry of crimson and mustard-colored leaves flying into her face. She brushed them aside, then heard, from the glade of woods beside the road, a familiar trilling laugh.

Caroline. There was no mistaking that high fluting sound. It floated through the wet and dreary afternoon, and Elly turned in surprise, for Caroline should have been home long ago to help Mama with the birthday supper.

As Elly watched unseen, her sister emerged from the wood, accompanied by a tall, well-dressed young man.

Elly recognized him at once, but could scarcely believe her eyes. Jason Emmett. The son of Emmettville's titan, Silas Emmett. Elly stared as he helped Caroline over a spreading tree root, his hand cupping her elbow.

Silas Emmett had begun his rise to fortune as a cantankerous iron forger who had turned out railroad axles with his father and brothers in their modest forge. Through the war years, making brilliant use of keen business sense, ruthless maneuvering, and a considerable degree of arm-twisting, he had built his forge and his community into a booming personal empire. The once-sleepy little town of Mayfair, nestled thirty-five miles from Pittsburgh, had become a thriving industrial center bearing his name and manufacturing everything from iron to beer to gentlemen's boots. Silas Emmett now owned everything in Emmettville, from the iron mill to the company stores to the brewery and glass works and company row houses where the workingmen's families lived side by side in drab little boxlike hovels. Caroline, much to Papa's displeasure, worked in Hyacinth House, the mansion Silas had built, serving as companion and nursemaid for his wife, an invalid. She enjoyed the lavish surroundings and the gentle nature of her mistress, but as far as Elly remembered, she had never even mentioned Jason Emmett. Probably because until recently he'd been away much of the time at a university in New York. No one knew exactly what had happened, but there were rumors that he had gotten into trouble at the beginning of the fall term and had been suspended for the remainder of the year. So he was home now, bossing the brewery workers, and trifling with Caroline, from what Elly could see.

She compressed her lips, experiencing a sudden spasm of anger, clear and cold in the chill October day. She didn't know who infuriated her more: Jason Emmett for dallying with her sister, or Caroline for giggling like a stupid ninny at his attentions. She gathered her gray calico skirts in her hand and started across the muddy grass toward them.

Caroline was laughing up at Jason, her golden curls bobbing in the breeze, her beautiful, childish face alight with pleasure. At fourteen, she was already blossoming into a breathtaking, buxom young lady, a fact of which Jason Emmett had apparently taken good note. He picked up a handful of crimson leaves and tossed them in her hair, grinning as she gave a screech and brushed them aside with a dainty, graceful hand.

Then she saw Elly coming toward her and turned with a little cry of surprise. "Elly! Why, we never even saw you. You're late getting home." The foolish smile still lit her face. "Oh, is that candy for Timothy? What a good idea. Elly, this is Jason Emmett. He very kindly offered to walk me home. Jason, this is my sister, Elinore."

"You girls are sisters? Amazing. I've never seen two females less alike."

Tall, slim, and handsome in a narrow-faced, patrician manner, Jason looked Elly up and down. With wavy chestnut hair parted in the center, aristocratic features including pale blue eyes and a high-bridged nose, and a dandy's flair for clothes, Jason looked every inch a high-born prince, but his manners left Elly cold. He sneered at her, as if to doubt that she could be related to the petite golden creature at his side. It was true that Elly was tall, thin, and dark compared to Caroline's blond daintiness, but Jason Emmett behaved as though he'd been confronted with the ugly duckling alongside the delicate swan.

"Amazing," he repeated, and shook his head.

Caroline giggled. "Yes, Elly is the smart and serious one. Papa just adores her. I'm too silly and frivolous for him to bother with."

"Caroline . . ." Elly began, but her sister waved a hand.

"It's true, Elly. Papa always *talks* to you. He merely smiles at me and pats me on the head."

"Oh, yes, your father." Jason Emmett crossed his arms in his tweed sporting coat and tilted his head at a raffish angle. "That Communard."

Elly's gaze riveted on him. She tried to suppress the anger that surged within her, but some of it showed in the smoldering blue-gray depths of her eyes.

"My father is not a Communard, Mr. Emmett," she said as quietly as she could.

"Of course he is." Jason flicked a fallen leaf from the sleeve of his jacket. "What do you call those little meetings he tries to organize among the workers? Ice-cream socials? He's a member, isn't he, of that bastard Sylvis's National Labor party? Dirty anarchists, all of them. And he's one of 'em."

"He merely believes in an eight-hour workday, the abolition of child labor, and a fair wage for workers. That's all. He's a patriot, Mr. Emmett. He loves this country."

"He loves it so much he wants it taken over by those Communards he worships. Well, let me tell you, he's lucky his pitiful attempts to organize the other workers only ended with rocks being thrown through the windows of the dramshop. Next time the place might be set afire."

"Oh, Jason, no!" Caroline clutched his arm. "Let's not argue. If you only knew Papa, you'd understand that he's a brilliant man—the smartest man in the world—and he merely wants what's fair for the workers."

"The workers ought to consider themselves fortunate to have jobs at all, little one." Jason tousled her curls with one gloved hand and gave a short laugh. "But you're too pretty and sweet to be worrying over such matters. Go home to your supper now."

"Yes, yes . . . I really ought to." Caroline appeared so

overwhelmed by the compliment he tossed at her that she quite forgot to move.

Grinning down at her pink cheeks and glowing blue eyes, Jason laughed again.

"Come along, Caroline." Elly grabbed her sister's arm and pulled, not gently. "Mama expected you long ago."

"But, Elly, it wasn't my fault. Mrs. Emmett was feeling especially poorly today and kept me past six, and then Jason offered to walk me through the glade, and—"

"Well, come on." Elly tugged harder as Caroline hung back, her gaze fixed longingly on Jason Emmett as he lounged near the stand of oaks. Elly dragged her toward the lane of grimy row houses. "Stop making a ninny of yourself," she hissed.

"Elly, Mama won't mind if we're just a few minutes longer. . . ." Caroline whispered, but Elly kept a firm grip on her arm.

"Better not argue, Caroline," Jason Emmett called from the edge of the glade. He was chuckling. "Your sister looks ferocious."

"Oh, no, Jason." Caroline waved back at him. "Don't mind Elly. It's just that she has no sense of humor. She takes everything seriously. She—"

"Caroline, shut up!" Elly derived great pleasure from the outraged shriek her sister emitted at having her flesh pinched. "Stop talking to that obnoxious, self-satisfied oaf. Come along!"

"Let go of my arm! Elleeee!" Caroline changed abruptly from flirtatious young woman to whining adolescent. "You're hurting me, Elly! Good-bye, Jason!" she called over her shoulder as Elly propelled her away. Behind them, Elly heard Jason Emmett's rumbling laughter.

When she glanced back, he had disappeared into the wood that led toward Hyacinth House. She scowled, thinking of his smirking, arrogant face and the insults he had hurled at Papa. Like her father, she hated the Emmetts. She considered them rich, selfish bastards who made their fortune off the poverty and suffering of others, but she couldn't afford to show her feelings, for the Forrests were already outcasts of a sort in the town. Most people were afraid even to think about the National Labor party, to which Papa belonged, much less consider joining it. Papa's job seemed constantly to hang on a thread. And Elly's work in the cotton mill could be cut short, too, if Jason Emmett took it into his head to have her fired. It had taken all of her will not to glare at him or slap his face for the things he had said about Papa and the liberties he had taken with her sister. She had wanted to tell him to leave Caroline alone, but she had not dared to say anything or even to let him see her outrage.

"Elly, let go of me or I'll kick your shin. What's wrong with you? Can't I even talk to a boy without—"

"Oh, shut up!" Elly scowled, releasing her sister as they neared their own shabby row house, which rose like a lump of gray clay from the earth. For a moment, she struggled for control of her temper, telling herself that Caroline was only fourteen, and stupid at that. No, not stupid, she corrected herself. Frivolous. Careless. Unthinking. But that was no excuse.

"How could you?" Elly turned on her sister furiously, anger turning her thin white cheeks a bright rose. "Caroline Forrest, how could you flirt so shamelessly with that boy?"

Before Elly's rage, Caroline shrank, but her tone was defiant. "What's wrong with Jason Emmett? He's perfectly nice. He's handsome, and he's rich. Why shouldn't I—"

"Silas Emmett is a tyrant. He rules this miserable town like a pharaoh. And Papa is trying to fight him, remember?"

"Papa's wasting his time, just as Mama says. Silas Emmett will never allow the workers to unite. He'll never raise wages or shorten the shifts to below twelve hours a day. All Papa is doing is causing trouble, and if he's not careful, I might even lose my job taking care of Mrs. Emmett, and then where will we be? Timothy would have to go to work in the mill, and Mama would never forgive that, and—"

"And you think that by being friendly with Jason Emmett you are helping matters? Believe me, if Papa finds out, he'll forbid you ever to go back to that house again."

Dismay filled Caroline's beautiful blue eyes. "Oh, Elly, no." She clutched Elly's arm. "You won't tell him, will you?" Then she pushed her soft pink lips into a pout. "You and Papa don't seem to mind my working for Jason's mama. You don't care if I work in her house, taking care of her and accepting her husband's money, just as long as I don't talk to her son?"

"That's right." Elly shivered in the wind and pushed a

strand of dark hair back from her eyes. "Your work for the
Emmetts is a job, and it saves both you and Timothy from the
mills. But don't ever think that you can trust the Emmetts."

I can trust Jason, Caroline thought defiantly, but she dared
not say it to Elly. Instead, she just sniffed, and hid her
thoughts to herself. She was half frightened by the wonderful
dreams floating through her mind, dreams about the worldly
and wealthy young man who paid such delicious attention to
her when his mama wasn't nearby. Jason wasn't really worried about what his mama would say, of course, for he was a
man already at eighteen years old, but there had been that
problem she had heard whispered around the house, something about trouble at the university, and that was why Jason
was home now for the entire year, and tiptoeing around on his
best behavior. Caroline could sympathize with him. She was
certainly in Papa's black book often enough to understand,
and she could see why Jason wouldn't want to do anything to
further upset the family. If Jason chose not to let his mama
see that he had a liking for her—a particular liking, she
thought ecstatically—it was only because he knew that his
family would object, just as her own father would erupt like a
volcano if he suspected she was being courted by Jason
Emmett. She and Jason were like Romeo and Juliet, she
realized suddenly, her mouth forming a pink O. And Juliet
was right: parting *was* such sweet sorrow.

Elly scowled at her as they reached the door of the house.
"I won't say anything to Papa about this if you promise to
stop sneaking around with Jason." Her face was shadowed
and forbidding in the windswept dusk overtaking the sky.
Caroline couldn't help thinking how like Papa she looked.

"I wasn't sneaking," she protested, but her voice was
weak.

"See that you don't." Elly turned on her heel and went
into the house, leaving Caroline to follow in resentful silence.

Bess Forrest did the best she could with the cramped,
shabby rooms of the row house, and Elly often thought with
pride that no one else working in Emmettville had a neater,
more pleasant home. The parlor was cozy with its overlap-
ping strips of tartan-checked carpet, its slipcovered armchairs
and plump sofa. The kerosene lamp on the center table rested
on a crisp doily, and the assortment of seashells, fans, and
other little treasures, which Bess had collected over the years,

and which were displayed on the whatnot in artful profusion, were always kept dusted and polished with loving attention. Elly's favorite piece of furniture, though, was the bookcase with its shining glass doors, inside which reposed the wondrous books her mother and father had gathered in their lifetime, books every bit as treasured as the conch shells and figurines. There was *William Shakespeare's Works*, along with a worn copy of *Ivanhoe*. The family Bible stood between *The Arabian Nights' Entertainment* and *The Rise and Fall of the Roman Empire*. For her birthday in June, Caroline had received a copy of Louisa May Alcott's *Little Women*, but this gem she kept in her room, tucked under her pillow, while Elly gladly placed her own birthday gift—an inexpensive edition of Mark Twain's humorous satire of European customs and institutions, *Innocents Abroad*—in the bookcase with the other volumes, and took turns with her father reading it to Timothy on occasional nights. There were many things on which the members of the Forrest clan disagreed, but they all shared a reverence for books, and it was something that helped draw them together even when other problems would have kept them bitterly divided.

Elly was struck today, though, by the silence in the little house and by the unaccustomed darkness. Only the clock on the mantel interrupted the odd stillness, which seemed even deeper because the lamp had not been lit against the falling dusk outside the curtains. From the kitchen came the acrid odor of something burning.

"Mother? Timothy?" While Caroline tended to the lamp, Elly hurried into the kitchen, where she found the stew burned on the stove, the meat and dumplings shriveled in the blackened pot. She seized a dishrag and removed the pot from the stove.

Caroline ran in behind her, wrinkling her delicate nose. "Where are they?"

"I don't know." For some reason, Elly suddenly felt nervous. Something important must have called her mother away; otherwise she never would have let Timothy's birthday supper burn, nor would she have disappeared without even a note of explanation. She had known that both girls would be home soon and that Papa would arrive shortly. The table was not set; in fact, the plates were stacked on the wooden counter as though her mother had been about to lay them out. Only the good white linen, which had been a wedding gift from Aunt Adelaide in Chicago and which her mother reserved for special occasions, covered the carved rectangular table.

"Let's check upstairs," Caroline suggested, and this time Elly followed her sister, both of them half running up the narrow uncarpeted steps to the two small bedrooms and tiny attic room above. Elly tried to keep from running, because that would somehow be an admission of urgency, and would open the way to fear, but the fear was there anyhow, sneaking in and touching her with its cold, biting fingers. There was no note in the yellow-painted room she and Caroline shared, or in her parents' blue-papered bedroom, or in the little attic room where Timothy insisted on sleeping, claiming that he was too old now to stay on the cot in Mama and Papa's room. Everything was neat and polished and clean, as Bess always kept it, but the unnatural silence, tonight when the house should have been alive with festivity in honor of Timmy's birthday, was unnerving and made pinpricks of fear rush up and down Elly's arms.

"Maybe Willa Brown had her baby and Eben sent for Mama," Caroline suggested quite reasonably, and then both girls heard the banging on the front door. They left the attic room and hurried downstairs, their feet clattering on the steps.

"Elly! Caroline!"

They halted midway down as they saw that Billy Moffett had pushed open the outside door and charged into the parlor.

"What is it, Billy?" Elly clutched the railing, and tried to speak with calm. She was trying to tell herself that the odd feeling she had encountered the moment she'd stepped into the empty house was nothing, that this was all about some minor emergency like Willa Brown having her baby or old Mr. Phipps down the lane needing a hand with his firewood, but she had already seen Billy's flushed face, his stocky chest rising and falling rapidly as he gulped for air, and the fingers of fear grabbed her harder. Billy was the son of her mother's closest friend in Emmettville; he had begun courting Elly in the past few months, a development Elly had endured with chagrin. Just now, though, courtship seemed the furthest thing from Billy's mind. He looked upset and scared and more like a frantic hare than a suitor, and his big ears stuck out even more noticeably than usual from a head shaggy with wild red hair.

"What is it, Billy?" she demanded again, more harshly, as he merely stood staring at her, and panting.

"Your mama sent me to . . . bring you."

"To bring me where?"

"Oh, Elly, I wish I didn't have to be the one to tell you. . . ."

"Tell us what, Billy?" Caroline interjected at Elly's elbow. Her voice was a frightened, high-pitched squeak.

"You must come to the rug factory. . . . It's—"

"Papa. Something's happened to Papa."

Caroline turned slowly and stared at her. Elly sounded so calm. She couldn't believe it. Billy was staring at her, too, and nodding unhappily.

"There was an accident. I was near him. One of the looms—"

Elly stood frozen as his voice broke. He squinted his eyes and wiped his nose with his sleeve. She felt her muscles tightening. It couldn't be. No, it couldn't be. Nothing truly bad had happened. She refused to think it, despite the stricken expression on Billy's face, despite the hard pounding of her heart, which seemed to beat out a dreadful staccato: *Oh, no. Oh, no. Oh, no.*

"Come, Caroline. We must go to Mama." She spoke firmly, hoping to silence the awful drumbeat inside her. Her voice still had that deceptive overlay of calm. Without waiting for Billy to explain further, without allowing Caroline to delay them with questions, Elly went to the door. She was remarkably composed, her oval face pale and still, her tall, thin body moving forward with even strides.

Dark hair flew wildly as she opened the door and the wind caught her in its gust, sending the ends of her shawl flying. Caroline and Billy followed, noisy with questions and answers, tears and words of comfort. Elly quickened her pace, not listening to them. She wanted to leave them behind, to get there, to see for herself that there was, after all, nothing to be upset about, nothing to justify Caroline's stupid, sickening tears. But when she did reach the rug factory—a long, low windowless building set among a dozen other structures exactly like it just beyond the smoke-belching iron works at the north end of town—the first thing she saw was her mother coming through the double doors into the gloom of the autumn dusk, and she knew from the stunned grief on her

mother's face that the truth was much worse than she had
permitted herself to think.

Timothy Forrest clung to his mother's dark green calico
skirt. His face was red from crying. At sight of him, ludicrously, considering the moment, Elly remembered the candy,
melting on the wooden counter in the kitchen beside the
charred stew and the stack of dinner plates. There would be
no birthday celebration tonight.

Her mother was leaning heavily on Bob Giles's arm as she
came out of the factory. Bob Giles was Papa's friend. He
worked in the rug factory, too, like Billy. Other men, with
drooping shoulders and grave faces, milled about as Bess
Forrest saw her daughters approaching.

The stunned look vanished from her face, and she gave a
cry of sheer, heart-wrenching pain.

"Elly!" She left Bob and stumbled forward, throwing her
arms around her elder daughter. Tears poured down her grief-
torn face. "Elly, he's dead! My poor, poor girl, my darling
children. Your papa is dead!"

❧ Two

EVEN CONFRONTED WITH the truth, part of Elly still wanted to
deny it.

"What happened?" Her voice was harsh, almost disbeliev-
ing as she addressed her mother, Bob Giles, all of them.
Then, before they could even answer her, she said, "I want
to see him," and she started to brush past Mama and Timmy.
Behind her, Caroline had started to cry, and she couldn't bear
to hear the sobs. She darted forward, past Bob Giles, but he
caught her arm.

"No, Elly. Don't go in there. It's an awful sight. Let the undertaker fix him up first."

"Let me go!" Elly shook free furiously and dodged past those filing from the factory, shaking their heads in pity. She ran past the silent machines and hushed workers, and ignored Seth Johnston, the foreman, who called for her to stop. But when she glimpsed her father, lying on the floor in a pool of blood beside the big machine loom where he toiled every day, she blanched and could go no closer. Half a dozen people still standing around partially obstructed her view, but Sam Forrest's tall, fierce frame was unmistakable. Only now, instead of strong and whole, he was broken and bloodied, with one arm torn cleanly off and blood still spurting from the open cavity. His face wore an expression of excruciating pain, even with his eyes closed, and that look ripped at Elly's heart.

No, no.

She must have said it aloud. The workers turned to look at her, and their silent sympathy unleashed a terrible agony inside her chest.

"Come on, Elly." Billy Moffett suddenly appeared beside her and took her arm. "You don't need to see him like this." His voice was unexpectedly firm. "You remember him the way he looked this morning at your breakfast table, or last night when you saw him at home. Not like this. Come on, now, away from here. Your ma and sister and brother need you."

She almost laughed with hysteria. Imagine Billy Moffett talking such sense to *her*. Elly—the practical one, the intelligent one, the one whom everyone else could always count on to remain serious and calm—getting advice from the plodding and quiet boy who rarely even met her eyes. But he was right. She looked at Billy's freckled, homely face and allowed him to lead her out of the factory and away from Papa's mangled body. Away from the whispering workers, and the great steel loom that had killed her father.

She went to her mother and kissed her cheek, feeling numb. Bess was clinging to Caroline. Elly took Timothy's hand. It was icy, and she squeezed it, kneeling down to draw his small, shuddering form against her. While her mother enfolded Caroline to her breast and their tears and sobs mingled, Elly stroked her brother's fine, pale hair.

"It's all right, Timmy. It's all right."

"Papa's dead," he blurted, through his sobs. Her shoulder grew damp as he buried his face in it.

"I know, Timmy. I saw him."

"Can't he come back?" His voice held a desperate plea.

"No, Timmy." She moistened her lips. "It's like Mr. Atkins, when he was killed on the railroad car. He can't come back." She choked down her own tears. "But he would want us to be strong."

"I—I can't. . . . I want Papa!"

"I know. I do, too."

She disengaged herself and came slowly to her feet. She put a hand to Bess's elbow.

"Come home, Mama. It's time. The road is no place for exhibiting our grief. Papa wouldn't like it. And it's starting to rain."

The dun sky drizzled chill drops down on the desolate group. Bess blinked at her through swollen eyes. "Elly, the undertaker. We must arrange for the casket. For the funeral."

"I'll do it, Mama, after I've taken you home. Caroline, hold Timothy's hand. Watch the puddles, now." She put an arm across Bess's shoulders. "Come, Mama."

"I'll help." Bob Giles supported Bess from the other side. Billy Moffett walked behind.

Elly bent her head against the falling rain.

Eventually they reached home, a huddled, grieving entourage, led by the sixteen-year-old, tall and willowy like her mother, dark like her father. Elly refused to cry. There was too much to do, and everyone needed her too much. She couldn't let them see how weak and broken she was inside.

They sat up all night with the body, the closed casket resting on old crates before the window in the parlor. Timothy fell asleep in the chair where Mama did her sewing. Caroline drifted off around midnight, curled on her mother's lap on the sofa. Bess's eyes, too, eventually closed, and by the time the clock chimed three, she lay exhausted and still. Elly had chosen the straight-backed chair that her father had favored, the one beside his desk and the bookcase. She sat rigidly, staring at the coffin, listening to the tick of the mantel clock, her face a shadow of pain illuminated by the single candle burning in the house.

Had it truly been an accident, Papa's death? Or had Silas

Emmett tired of Sam Forrest's efforts to unite the workers against him? She couldn't be sure. Accidents were commonplace in the factories and mills, on the railroads and in the mines, and every workman knew that his life was at daily risk, but still . . .

Elly's innate hatred of Silas Emmett and all he stood for made her all too ready to believe that he was responsible for her father's death. Even if he hadn't engineered the mishap, he had set up the demonic working conditions and frantic pacing of the machines that had led to the accident which had severed Papa's arm and left him to bleed to death in a matter of minutes. Rage filled her as she remembered Caroline walking home beside Jason Emmett. *Never again,* she vowed. Her sister would never spend another moment alone with him, even if it meant forcing Caroline to leave Hyacinth House and take a job in the mills.

But what were they going to do now, without Papa? Her meager wages from the cotton mill wouldn't support the family, even with the sewing Mama took in, even with Caroline working for Mrs. Emmett. They couldn't possibly replace Papa's wages, unless she could find another job, after her shift at the mill—in one of the shops, perhaps, sweeping up or tidying the shelves. But still, it wouldn't be enough. An aching tension filled her as she glanced over at Timothy, asleep in the chair.

Like her mother, she found the thought of his working in the mills unbearable. Bess had always vowed that her children would not go to work until they had finished school, and she had not permitted Elly and Caroline to do so until they reached the age of fourteen. Timothy was so bright, so adept at his schoolwork. He wasn't like the other boys, always fighting and scrapping. Elly shook her head, unable to imagine him shut up all day in the suffocating factory, constantly at risk of losing his fingers to the whirring bobbins. That's what had happened to little Davey O'Cullen. And Ephraim White. But it would not happen to Timmy, Elly vowed, her own hands clenching on the arms of the chair. She would find another way to bring in enough money. She would have to think of something else.

If only Papa were here, he could advise me. She froze on the thought, a wave of indescribable sadness rolling over her.

If Papa were here, things wouldn't be so desperate. If Papa were here, they could endure anything. . . .

But he was gone.

She closed her eyes tight, trying to blot out the awful memory of him lying on the factory floor. That image had kept coming back to her all evening. Billy was right; she should remember Papa as he had looked here in this very room last night, reading aloud from *Macbeth*, his deep, resonant voice filling the tiny parlor. It didn't seem possible that Papa, who had always been so vigorous, so vibrant and alive, dominating every room he entered, commanding the attention and respect of all who knew him, was lying dead now in that coffin, his strength and wry humor and steadfast dignity snuffed out.

The parlor clock ticked on. Timothy snored gently in his chair, and Caroline lay peacefully in her mother's arms while Bess dozed and every so often whispered in her sleep. Yellow candlelight flickered in the cool, shadowy darkness. Elly watched and listened to it all. She didn't sleep all through the night, and didn't cry until the first glimmers of light signaled the beginning of dawn. Then tears filled her eyes. She realized that on this day they would bury her father, that he was really gone for good. And she knelt by the coffin and ran her fingers over the smooth wood and cried deep, silent sobs that shook her chest and left her aching and cold and hollow in the gray, bitter dawn.

By the time her family wakened and stirred, she had washed and changed her dress to the good blue linen, combed her black hair, and put on the oatmeal for breakfast and the kettle for tea. She was determined to be her father's daughter, strong and reliable, a rock to which others could cling in the face of disaster. She put aside her pain and behaved as Samuel Forrest would have wanted her to behave, taking comfort in the knowledge that he would have approved her outward self-possession, finding solace of a sort in her own forbearance.

❧ Three

THAT WINTER WAS the most difficult of Elly's life. She missed her father terribly, and everything around her suffered from his absence. The once cozy row house on Third Street was not the same, and neither was Mama. Instead of listening with a smile, as she always used to do while Elly or Caroline read aloud in the evening, Mama now worked feverishly at the sewing she took in for extra money, accepting more and more garments as each week passed and getting less sleep as each night went by. She grew short-tempered and irritable. When one of the girls would try to read to Timothy or when he would play at marbles near her feet, she would crossly push her hair back from her face, scowl, and chide them for disturbing her concentration. They all understood what it was. Mama grieved for Papa. They often heard her crying in her bed at night. And she was worried, badly worried about having enough money to pay the rent and buy the groceries. She looked older, care worn, and frail, and even the once-beautiful fair hair, which she always wore in a smoothly braided coronet, now seemed to lack luster and fullness, wisping around her wan face in thin pale strands that defied the braids and seemed to mock her former perfectionism.

Worst of all, the loving atmosphere Elly had so cherished dissipated as each winter day passed. Mama was too wrapped up in her sewing and her own desperate grief to pay even Timothy much attention, and it fell upon Elly to care for him and help him with his lessons, to read to him from *Ivanhoe*, and tuck him into his attic cot when bedtime came. She continued to work in the cotton mill by day and had obtained extra work for one hour each night before coming home to

27

supper. This hour she spent sweeping out the druggist's shop and helping him add up his receipts. Though she was young and strong, the added labor and additional responsibilities at home proved exhausting, and she grew increasingly impatient with Caroline's lackadaisical behavior.

Against Elly's better judgment, her sister continued to work for Virginia Emmett. This occupation was approved by Bess, who staunchly maintained that Caroline could never hope to earn such high wages in the mill and that it was more healthful and dignified to be a companion and helper to Mrs. Emmett than to toil in a factory for less than three dollars a week. Elly didn't tell her mother about Jason Emmett's attentions, but she kept an eye on her sister. Outwardly, Caroline gave no indication of interest in her employer's son, but she continued to behave like a lazy, preening child, with no time for her younger brother and little inclination to help out with the chores around the house. All of this irked Elly no end. But whenever she took her to task, Caroline would run tearfully to her mother, and Bess would sigh and look so overburdened by their bickering that Elly just gave up in the end and took everything upon herself. The days were cold and cheerless, the nights frozen and glum. The house never seemed warm enough, no matter how much wood Elly fed into the stove, and at night when the wind howled down from the hills, Elly would huddle in her bed beneath the thin, patched blankets and shiver like a mouse burrowed in the snow.

One day in January, when an ice storm had left treacherous silver patches glittering on the streets of Emmettville, Elly returned home from the druggist's shop to find her mother weeping at the parlor table. She threw off her cloak and went to kneel beside her. In her mother's hand was a letter spattered with tears.

"What is it, Mama? Not Aunt Adelaide?"

"No."

"Who is the letter from?"

"It's from the devil!" Bess's vehemence startled Elly, and she stared into her mother's face in alarm. Bess was pale and angry, her lovely blue eyes swollen with tears. "It's from my father, Elly, and never again will I call him by that name!"

Elly felt wonder as she knelt there. To her knowledge, there had been no correspondence between Mama and her parents since Bess had married Sam Forrest more than seventeen years ago. Bess had come from a prosperous Boston family. Her banker father had been appalled when she married a common cabinetmaker. Her family had cast her off, and she and Sam had left Boston and settled in Pennsylvania, where for a while he had made a good living plying his trade. Then the war had disrupted their lives in violent and lasting fashion, wrenching Sam from his wife and young daughters, plunging them all into poverty and fear. He had returned from the battlefield after Gettysburg, with a permanent limp and a lasting abhorrence of violence. But that had not been the only effect wrought by the war. The economy of the country had undergone a drastic change. No longer did the individual craftsman matter in a world that had become accustomed to the wonders of machine production. During the war years, factories had churned out guns and goods at an incredible rate, and the nation had become accustomed to mass production and vast quantities of machine-made products. The movement toward mechanization was as unstoppable as a runaway locomotive. Craftsmen like Sam Forrest, who labored long and lovingly over each piece they built, could not compete with the factories that turned out identical goods with such cold-blooded speed and efficiency. Those had been hard times for the Forrest family, and Elly was just old enough to remember vaguely the comfort of the prewar years and how different their lives had become afterward. It had taken a while for Sam to accept that he would have to give up his trade and find work in one of the hated factories, but he had done it in order to keep his family clothed and fed. In all the long years of struggle that had ensued while her parents toiled to make ends meet, Elly had never once heard either of them mention Bess's Boston family. Now she stared at the letter in her mother's hand as though it were an object flung down from the moon.

"May I read it?"

"No!" Bess snatched it out of her reach, then ripped it into shreds and crumpled the pieces in her hands. She was shaking. She whirled on her daughter tearfully, the little pieces of paper still clutched between her fingers. "I'll tell you what it said, Elly. My father and mother have refused to help us, even though they know now that Samuel is dead."

"I didn't know you had written to them. I thought you only wrote to Aunt Adelaide in Chicago."

"I've been frantic because I fear Timmy might have to go to work in the mill. I'm willing to do almost anything to prevent that, even beg my family for money." Trembling, Bess hurled the pieces of the letter into the wicker wastebasket beneath the table. She turned and started pacing the room, her hands fluttering nervously to her hair, her skirt, her throat, reminding Elly of a bird trapped and caged, unable to be still on its perch. "That was something I had promised your father I would never do. But I had no choice. I wrote to them a few weeks ago, informing them that Samuel had died and that our circumstances were desperate." She stopped before Elly, who had come to her feet and stood with her back to the parlor table. Her eyes were filled with rage and sorrow. "My darling, I'm sorry you must be burdened with this. But I simply don't know what to do. Our debts are growing each day. I'm a month behind on our rent, and our account at the company store is getting out of hand. I'm afraid that Mr. Lester won't be able to extend our credit any further until we settle it. And"—her voice quavered slightly as she continued—"there is simply not enough money to settle it. I'm going to have to find work in the mills myself, and Timothy will have to stay alone when he comes home from school until one of us gets here. Or maybe Willa Brown or Katie Moffett will take him in until we can call for him. That is the only answer. I'll have to make inquiries at the cotton mill and the glass factory tomorrow."

Elly's stomach twisted sickeningly. *No,* something in her protested. Mama didn't belong in the mills. She had always worked so hard to make their shabby home clean and pleasant, to bring a glow of coziness and refinement to the crude surroundings. She didn't deserve now to be thrust into the roaring, dehumanizing pit of the factory. Mama had once worn the finest Belgium laces and danced the minuet at a governor's ball. She had enjoyed the opera from her father's private box, ridden prize horses, and drunk tea from exquisite Limoges cups. All of this she had given up when she married Papa, and she had never complained, not a word, until Timothy, too, was threatened. Only then had she allowed the shadow of defeat to settle over her elegant features and to lurk furtively behind her eyes. And only because she loved her children more than herself, and feared for them. Everything in Elly cried out against her mother working in the mills, and, her heart sinking, she watched Bess press her lips together and turn toward the kitchen as if the matter was settled.

"Wait, Mama." She followed Bess into the kitchen. A watery soup bubbled on the stove. It smelled good, despite the pitiful lack of meat and vegetables in the iron pot. Steam rose in a fragrant vapor, filling the scrubbed kitchen. "Do you mean that your father refused all manner of help? Isn't he willing to advance you even a small amount of money as a loan that we could pay back?"

"Oh, he made an offer of sorts." Bess whirled a spoon around the simmering pot, splashing the scorching liquid dangerously about her forearms without even noticing. Her voice was as bitter as a medicinal draft. "One I will never accept. He most patronizingly offered to take in my son—to raise him in Boston as a Stevenson should be raised." Her features hardened, and her voice rose. "I'll never give up my son, Elly, or any of my children. We'll stay together as a family even if I must work double shifts in the mills to do it."

Elly was stunned by the very idea of sending Timothy away to Boston. It was unthinkable. "We'll find a way, Mama," she agreed quickly. "By the way, where is Timmy?"

"Helping Willa with some chores. She has her hands full with the baby. And she's offered to pay him five pennies a day to help with the cleaning and laundry."

"Does he know about Grandfather Stevenson's offer?"

"No. It would terrify him. And don't say a word to Caroline either." She sighed and set down the spoon, staring at the light snow starting to fall beyond the kitchen curtains. "She would dearly love the chance to live in a fine house in Boston and have the luxuries of a lady, and it would hurt her to know that her grandfather is only interested in the male child of the family. He couldn't care less about the rest of us."

"Don't worry, Mama. It'll all work out."

"Of course it will. There's bound to be something a strong, able-bodied woman can do to earn a good wage in this town. Now, not another word about this, Elly. I don't want Caroline or your brother burdened. It's bad enough that you know exactly how bad things are, but at least you're strong enough to handle it. They're only children. We have to protect them as much as possible."

It seemed to Elly that the letter from Boston had invigorated Bess in a way that nothing else had since Samuel's death. Some of the sparkle and determination returned to her face and her step that evening, and she served their humble supper of soup and bread and tea as though it were a feast, spreading the table with the best cloth, the one Aunt Adelaide had sent. She even placed lighted candles on the neatly set table, as if asserting her confidence that the family would emerge whole and victorious from their trials. Caroline caught her mother's deliberately festive mood, and her self-absorption abated enough for her to laugh and chatter quite in her old way during the little meal, while Elly smiled and prayed inwardly that this new cheerfulness would endure. Their mood had a magical effect on Timothy, who grew as animated and lively as Caroline, and they all sang loudly and with spirit as they cleared away the dishes, swept the floor, and tidied the kitchen after supper was done.

That night the parlor had something of its old glow as the family sat together, and Bess stole time away from her sewing to smile as the children took turns reading aloud. But the gaiety of that night did not endure, for in the next few days, Bess found work in the cotton mills, and the orderly home she had always maintained was forced to suffer.

She grew more weary as each day passed. Struggling to work in the mill, keep the row house clean, manage her sewing, and tend to the family's meals, she grew thin and tense and wasted. The children pitched in to help, but the strain affected them all, even Timothy. As if sensing that his mother's grueling schedule was a sacrifice made on his behalf, he retreated into a guilty shell, his once-merry blue eyes growing dim and somber as the winter progressed.

In April, Billy Moffett came calling again, and Elly found herself obliged to sit with him on the row house steps after supper. Night after night, as spring deepened into summer, he came to her, and they listened to the bullfrogs and crickets, and watched the stars bloom in the lavender sky. She would stare at the stars and lift her face to the sweet spring breezes, trying to forget where she was and who was beside her.

"What're you thinkin', Elly?" he asked one night. It was mid-August and the summer was nearly gone. Billy shifted closer to her on the steps and fidgeted with his pocket knife. She could feel him beside her, and the contact made her stiffen uneasily. She wished Mama hadn't fallen asleep inside over her sewing. Billy wouldn't be getting so close if Mama had her eye on him through the window.

"Just . . . thinking, Billy."

"What?" he pressed, and she sighed.

"I'm wishing I were far away from here—in Egypt or Vienna or Rome." She took a deep breath of the sultry summer air and braced herself for his laughter. Surprisingly, it didn't come.

"Do you always think things like that?" He gazed at her in awe. "That's so interesting, Elly. You're a very interesting girl."

"Don't you ever imagine things, Billy?" She turned her head and met his rapt brown gaze with sudden curiosity. Drops of perspiration shone on his ruddy face, like tiny glimmering mirrors. "Don't you wonder what it would be like to leave Emmettville—to go far away and see exotic, beautiful things?"

"Nope, never do." He shrugged. "Where else is there to go? My ma and pa are here, and Peter and Lora Mae. I'd have no reason to leave. Besides, Elly, Emmettville ain't so bad."

"Maybe to you it isn't. I hate it." She had to struggle to keep the vehemence out of her voice. How could he not hate Emmettville? She despised everything about it. The row houses, the factories, the brewery, and the ugly, smoke-belching iron foundry. She hated the company stores where Silas Emmett regulated every price and item sold, the sawdust on the plank sidewalks, the sooty, smoky air. Mostly, she hated the grime and the tedium and the hopelessness of it all, and dreamed more and more of leaving, of finding a place of beauty and peace.

"I'm going away from here one day, Billy. Far, far away, and I'm never coming back." She stood, brushing out her skirts, restless suddenly, as if she wished she could strike out right now on her journey. Billy jumped up beside her. He stuck his pocket knife in his belt.

"Elly, no. Don't say that. I was going to ask you . . ."

"What?"

"Well . . . I was going to ask you if . . ." Billy gulped air suddenly as if it were courage that he could swallow whole. "I know things are hard for you and your ma and all now, and I was going to ask you if you would marry me. I been working steady in the rug factory for four years now, and I can take care of you, all of you. . . .''

There it was. The solution to their problems. Billy's wages would make up for the loss of her father's earnings. Mama could quit the mill.

Billy talked on, but his words were a blur. He said something about marrying her right away, moving into the row house, taking care of the others. Timothy would be safe, Elly realized—at least for a little while. She bit her lip, frantically wondering what to say. She didn't want to marry Billy; she didn't even want to sit out here on the steps with him. But it had been in the back of her mind for the past few months as a possibility, an answer to her problems.

"What do you say, Elly?" Placing his hands on her shoulders, he turned her and forced her to look at him.

She was as tall as he, though gangly still, lacking her mother's willowy grace. Her dark hair was braided back from her face, and she wore a plain gray challis dress and warm, heavy shoes. The strong, distinctive features that marked her were not yet beautiful, but they were striking, lovely in the summer moonlight. Her mouth was full and generous, her dark eyebrows arrestingly arched. Hypnotic blue-gray eyes burned above chiseled cheekbones. In the faint milky light that shone down on the porch, Billy thought her the most perfect girl in the world.

"Marry me, Elly," he begged.

She ducked her head. "I can't, Billy."

"Why not?"

She raised her head and gazed at his ruddy, perspiring face. "I'm not ready to marry anyone yet. And I'm not sure we're suited for each other."

She felt years older than he, and wiser. But they were the same age, and they'd grown up in the same town. How could they be so different? Billy was satisfied with his lot in life. She burned with resentment. She wanted so much more! More than Billy Moffett and Emmettville could ever give her. "The trouble is," she said slowly, hating to hurt him, and hating to think of Mama having to continue at the mill, "you're not in love with me, Billy, and I'm not in love with you. Getting married would be convenient and practical, but it's not a good idea. Not now, anyway."

Not ever, she thought, but she didn't say that. She couldn't completely close the door.

"But I do love you, Elly." Billy smiled shyly. He was so earnest and eager that she flinched. Suddenly, he took a step closer and pulled her to him. He kissed her, pressing his full, moist lips to her face, almost missing her mouth and kissing part of her chin. He smelled of sweat and potato pudding. "See?" He started to kiss her again, his flabby palms sliding up her arms, but she twisted back, pushing him away.

"No, Billy, don't. Caroline will be home soon. You'd better go."

"Caroline? Isn't she inside?"

"No, she had to work late at the Emmetts' tonight. They're having a dinner party or something, and Mrs. Emmett wanted her to stay. I'm tired anyway. You'd better go."

"But Elly . . ." Beet red, he started to follow her onto the porch. "Look, I'm sorry if I—"

"It's not your fault, Billy. Don't feel bad. I'm just very tired, and I know Caroline will be coming along in a minute. Good night."

"But . . ."

She fled inside, unable to look at his hurt face and listen to the feeble protests he tried to utter. She closed the door behind her and leaned against it. She had handled that badly, but then, she always handled people badly. She was too blunt, too abrupt, like her father, but without his wisdom and strength to temper her directness. And she didn't have Bess's soothing, softening ways, either. She clenched her fists and closed her eyes as frustration welled within her.

Inside the house, the heat was oppressive. Flies buzzed around the kerosene lamp. A wilting humidity blanketed everything. Mama was still dozing in her chair, a common occurrence of late, even though it wasn't yet eight-thirty. But she had to be at the mill in ten hours. Elly roused her gently and helped her up to bed, trying not to think about Billy or about her life in Emmettville. She would finish the sewing after Mama was tucked in bed. Mrs. Alexander, whose husband was the foreman at the brewery, wanted her tea gown hemmed by tomorrow; it would only take an hour or so to stitch the lace. When Caroline got home, she could work on some of the other garments in the sewing chest. Maybe, Elly thought, as she took out a nightdress and helped slide it over her mother's head, the effort of sewing would keep her mind off Billy and what he had offered her—and how she had ruined her chances of rescuing her family from their quagmire.

Elly had finished Mrs. Alexander's gown and three other minor repairs when the mantel clock struck eleven. Again, as she had been doing for the past hour, she put down her sewing and went to the window to stare out at the dark lane of row houses, lit only by a handful of stars and a silver half-moon that kept gliding from behind shifting clouds. Caroline had never been this late before. The dinner party must have lasted longer than expected, and she must be busy helping Mrs. Emmett prepare for bed. Though it still grated on her that Caroline was employed in the house of her father's nemesis, the man responsible for their poverty, she accepted the fact that Caroline's wages were an important contribution to the family income, and she had to admit that Mama was right about Caroline being far more suited to a position as a companion than to a job in the mills.

Though Caroline was too young to remember much about the comfortable life that they had known before the war, she had never been able to endure the strictures of poverty with the tolerance that her mother and sister managed. Perhaps because she was so pretty and vibrant, she yearned to be surrounded by bright and lovely things, to wear satin dresses and to tie silk ribbons in her hair. Bess had always shielded her from suffering, even spoiling her a little. While Elly and Timothy received plain and practical gifts on their birthdays, somehow Mama always found a way to buy some extra frippery for Caroline, as if sensing that her need for the beautiful trinket or small bit of luxury was greater than the others'. She indulged her as Mama herself had been indulged as a young girl. Perhaps, Elly thought, Mama could see in Caroline a mirror image of her own youthful beauty. Elly didn't mind, for she knew there was a bond between her mother and Caroline that she would never feel. She had felt that kind of closeness with her father, sharing his idealism and his cynicism, his passion for justice and his contempt for greed. Yet she wished that Caroline was not quite so empty-headed and self-centered. Only this morning she had cajoled their mother into letting her wear a gown that was Bess's own. It was old, true, a remnant of her Boston days, but still soft and fine, made of old Brussels lace. Caroline had worn it to Hyacinth

House, and Bess had watched her go with a smile, as if remembering the days when she herself had been young and lovely and carefree, and had worn the fairy-lace gown. Now Elly stared out into the night-gloom, wondering why Caroline was not yet home, searching the darkness for some glimpse of that ivory lace. When the clock struck the quarter-hour, she replaced the sewing in the chest and straightened the room and fidgeted with the doily beneath the glowing kerosene lamp.

Where was Caroline? she wondered, with the beginnings of unease. Billy Moffett had all but faded from her mind. She went to the door and stood on the porch, peering up the dark, deserted street. Surely she should have been home by now.

Though it was still sultry and hot, a slight breeze now stirred the old yellow curtains at the window and she went back inside to wait. The minutes ticked by. Elly paced between the slipcovered chair and the window, between the mantel and the stairs. She made herself a cup of tea, drank it, and poured another. She perched on the edge of the sofa and watched the porch through the open door. All to no avail.

The mantel clock chimed twelve midnight, and still Caroline did not come home.

❦ Four

JASON EMMETT WINKED across the glittering dinner table at his friend, Richard Henderson. He was enjoying himself immensely. Richard and Thaddeus James were his guests for the evening, and the captivating daughter of his parents' friends, the Rhodeses, sat directly across from him, fresh from her summer in Newport. Miss Sarah Rhodes was spectacular. A silver-haired little goddess, she was dainty and elegant, with a charmingly pert nose, huge china-blue eyes, and a mouth he longed to kiss. Too bad Father hadn't let him go to Newport this summer, instead of forcing him to stay in Emmettville and work in that damn awful brewery. He could have been with *her,* sailing, dancing, riding. The thought of it burned like acid through his chest. He'd never laid eyes on Sarah Rhodes before yesterday, but now he couldn't tear his glance from her. Her pink tulle evening dress, trimmed in malines and puffed to the waist, exhibited a most tempting figure to his discerning eyes, and like his companions, he was doing his best to win her attention, trying to devise a way of seeing her alone. Unfortunately, she was ignoring him, and appeared totally serene as she spooned turtle soup into her delectable little mouth.

At the head of the huge oval table, which was draped in snowy linen and ablaze with candles in tall silver sconces, Silas Emmett tried to conceal his displeasure. Jason's behavior was abominable. The boy was making a fool of himself, as were his two idiotic friends. One would think they had never met an eligible young woman before, with all the winking and ogling that was going on. He could only hope that Horace and Amelia would not notice. He would have to give Jason a stern talking-to the moment he got him alone.

Silas Emmett was a shrewd little mole of a man, with quickly darting ferret eyes and thinning gray hair brushed back from his brow. He was marked by unusual energy; his hands were always busy tapping or waving a cigar or scribbling furiously on a tablet. His black broadcloth evening suit was superbly cut, his linen crisp and spotless, but his fingernails were dirty. As he raised his soup spoon swiftly to his lips, they drew the notice of Sarah Rhodes, who shivered inwardly at their unkempt appearance, but gave no outward sign of her revulsion. Silas wouldn't have noticed anyway. All he could think about was Jason and his clumsy, fawning attempts to engage the Rhodes girl in conversation. The boy was engaging in the most inane banter, and his sallies were crude and immature. If he hoped for a match with Horace's daughter, he would have to polish up his performance considerably. Silas was embarrassed by him, and Sarah was plainly put off.

It certainly wasn't easy having all these houseguests at once, Silas thought, smearing his napkin across his lips as the

servant removed the soup bowls—especially with Virginia's
failing health. When Jason had returned from New York
unexpectedly with his two former college chums yesterday at
the same time that Silas had welcomed the Rhodes family,
who were en route to Pittsburgh, Silas had been none too
pleased. Fortunately, the house was grand enough to accommodate them all in comfortable style, but Silas wished his
wife were well enough to fulfill all of her duties as hostess.
Virginia's ill health left most of the burden of entertaining in
his own hands, which irked and bedeviled him. Horace Rhodes
was too important a business associate to neglect in any
manner, and Silas resented having to maintain his pose as
genial host when he wanted to get his hands on his shipping
records and production books and work far into the night, as
was his habit. That was another thing that bothered him. If
Jason would only show half as much interest in business as he
did in gallivanting around with his friends and whoring around
with shopgirls, the amount of work would not be so gargan-
tuan. Sometimes Silas felt buried by the mountains of paperwork
constantly awaiting his attention, but secretly he enjoyed it,
relishing the maintenance of his empire with the zeal of a
king in his countinghouse.

After enjoying a dinner of capon and roast beef and mutton, accompanied by mushrooms and wild rice, asparagus in
butter sauce, sweet corn, and mashed potatoes, the diners
selected their desserts from a rainbow array of tiny iced
cakes, miniature tarts, and mint wafers. Coffee and tea were
poured, sugared, and drunk, and platters laden with fruits and
cheeses were presented for the guests' enjoyment. Then, for
once postponing the gentlemen's indulgence in their brandy
and cigars, Silas suggested they all repair to the music room,
to be entertained by Sarah, whose father had boasted at length
about her musical abilities. That was when Virginia Emmett
begged to be excused.

"Of course, my dear." Silas nodded. He had been expecting this, for she rarely left her bed for more than an hour or
two at a time. "Shall I walk you up to your room?"

His tone and expression plainly indicated that the question
was just a formality. He had no intention of doing any such
thing.

"No, no, Silas, do see to our guests," Virginia murmured,
sending an apologetic smile around the dining salon. She was

a small, frail woman—pretty in a pale, fluttery way—who almost always wore pink or lavender and who suffered from a chronic back problem that made it painful for her to move about or even to sit or stand for long periods. "Caroline will help me, you know," she added with a wave of her fan. "I do so depend on her these days. I do beg your pardon, Amelia and George, and Sarah dear, for I hate leaving you like this. Jason, I do hope your friends understand . . ."

"Certainly, ma'am," Richard said instantly.

"I wish you a good evening, ma'am," added Thaddeus with a short bow.

Jason watched indifferently as his mother left the room. All he could think about was Sarah Rhodes. Unfortunately, she paid neither him nor Richard nor Thaddeus the least bit of attention. In the music room, she played the piano coolly for the assembled guests; sang in a clear, sweet voice that sent waves of illicit desire through Jason's loins; and then, before he could engage her in any further conversation, begged prettily to be excused.

"So soon?" Jason strode forward as she rose from the piano, her pink tulle skirts rustling. "The evening is only beginning."

"I have a headache, Mr. Emmett." She turned to his father. "Will you forgive me, sir, if I retire early?"

"Of course, my dear, of course. This heat is the thing. Makes everyone feel like the devil."

"Darling, I'll come along and see you comfortably settled." Her mother took her arm.

Horace Rhodes accepted a demure peck on the cheek from his daughter, bidding her a good night, but the younger men were silent and filled with disappointment as the two ladies left the room. They drifted toward the mantel and tugged at their shirt collars, which were damp with perspiration in the humid night air. While Silas and Horace Rhodes rang for brandy and lit up cigars, Jason scowled at his friends.

"That was a damnable failure. She's leaving in the morning, and the whole time she's been here she hasn't given me a second glance."

"Stuck-up," Thaddeus grumbled. "Needs a swift kick in the ass." He was a paunchy eighteen-year-old with squinting eyes and a mop of dark unruly hair. Despite the finest suits of wool and gabardine crafted by all the best tailors, he always

looked somewhat rumpled and disreputable. He had a wicked
sense of humor, though, and Jason liked him for his never-
ending practical jokes.

"Or a few days in bed—my bed." Richard grinned and
stuck his hands in his trousers pockets. A slim, debonair
young man with sharp features and fair hair always curled and
brushed meticulously, he shook his head at Jason. "You'd
think she was royalty or something, the cold little bitch, the
way she looked down her nose at us."

"She's twenty," Jason reminded him. "She thinks she's
older and wiser." Glumly, he studied the toes of his polished
boots.

Richard Henderson laughed softly, glancing toward the
older men to be certain they weren't within hearing. They
were safely embroiled in a business discussion, comfortable
on the jade damask sofa with their snifters and cigars. He
turned to Jason. "We could teach her a few things of our
own, if that's what she's looking for," he said slyly.

Thaddeus plunked down into one of the gilt-armed chairs.
"I wouldn't mind."

"Forget about that, damn you." Jason's pale blue eyes
narrowed on Richard as he realized what his friends had in
mind. "I was the one who got kicked out of school. You're
both damned lucky I covered for you. The least you can do is
never mention that little tramp again." He smoothed his
brown hair in a nervous, irritated gesture. His lips were a thin
slit in his sweat-glistening face. The gas jets that illuminated
the music room seemed to burn with an intense heat, magni-
fying the broiling August temperature. "Besides, how can
you even compare Sarah Rhodes to her? Sarah is a lady, not a
common, stupid shopgirl. Anyone could see that."

"Ah, I think you're truly smitten, my boy." Richard
sprawled in the chair beside Thaddeus, stretching out his long
legs. "But your sudden onslaught of scruples surprises me."

"Why?"

"Sarah Rhodes may well be a virgin, but so was that
shopgirl. That fact didn't deter you then."

"That was different. She wanted it. She was cheap and
common right from the start—or she never would have come
up into the carriage with us."

"He's right," Thaddeus put in. "She wanted it all along."

"Too bad she kicked up such a fuss afterward," Jason

grumbled, remembering how she had summoned the authorities, how they had come for him later and taken him to the police station. It had been a bad mistake, getting involved with a girl he knew, a fatal mistake. She had worked at Hailey's department store, where he occasionally bought small gifts for girls of his acquaintance and items for himself, and she had helped him with his purchases once or twice and had known his name.

That evening as he and the others were driving uptown in a hack, they had noticed her on the street. He had recognized her but had been unable to place her. She had been knocked over by a freight wagon and had hurt her ankle. Half drunk already, and passing a bottle of rum among them in the carriage, he and Richard and Thaddeus had noticed her picking herself up on the congested sidewalk as their hack was stalled in traffic. They had called to her, and Richard had jumped down and offered her a ride home. The girl had accepted. Only they hadn't taken her home.

They had shared the bottle of rum with her, and taken her to a deserted park on the outskirts of the city. She had argued and cried and begged, he remembered in disgust, a ridiculous pretense of virtue. He had been surprised to find she really was a virgin, but it hadn't made much difference. She was still a slut at heart, or she wouldn't have come along with them in the first place. Afterward, she had remembered his name and had sent the police down upon him. She had shown them the bruises on her arms and face, and they had locked him up.

Jason had refused to give out Richard's and Thad's names, and for that, his friends owed him dearly—a debt they would have to spend the rest of their lives repaying. For he alone had been the one to suffer the indignities at the police station, to be forced to send frantic telegraph messages to his father, to suffer the humiliation of the rumors and scandal that had forced him from school. He had had to listen to his father's stupid lectures about how much money it would take to buy the damned girl off and how close he was to finding himself in jail. But of course Silas *had* bought her off, and the charges had been dropped, and by now, nearly a year later, the talk had died down. He would return to Alfred University next month, and life would get back to normal. It suddenly occurred to him, chillingly, that perhaps Sarah Rhodes had heard rumors about that incident, even up in Pittsburgh. Then reason intervened, and he realized that her aloofness was merely due to her being spoiled, sophisticated, and too damned beautiful for her own good. There wasn't much he could do about any of those things.

"Well, it's no use thinking about the past," Jason muttered. He went to the brandy decanter and filled glasses for his friends. "But it's a pity Sarah's leaving in the morning, along with the two of you. If I had a few days more to entertain her, I just might make a dent in the lady's icy heart."

"You're dreaming, Emmett," Richard said. "From what I saw tonight, she'd rather kiss a skunk than spend a quarter of an hour with you."

Angry, Jason clenched his fists. Visions of Sarah Rhodes floating down the stairs toward him in a voluminous gown, with her pale hair shimmering and her arms reaching out toward him, appeared in his mind. His loins ached. He had never wanted any woman so badly. She was everything a girl ought to be. Deep down, a fear nagged at him that she was indeed superior to him. She was so graceful and elegant, so composed. And he *had* felt like a clumsy fool tonight when he'd dropped his coffee spoon and when he'd tried so miserably to engage her in conversation. She had made him feel like a fool. But he refused to be angry with her. It was Richard's words that antagonized him now, and he suddenly blamed his friend for the evening's failure.

"If you hadn't been sitting there leering at her all night, I might have had a sporting chance," he growled, his fingers tightening on the stem of his snifter.

Thaddeus, glancing from one to the other, hastily intervened. "Now, now, no woman is worth quarreling over," he began, but at that moment, Silas approached the little group.

The young men all stood.

"Jason, would you and the boys care to join us in a game of billiards?"

"No, we would not." Jason slurped the last of his brandy and set his brandy snifter on the black marble mantel with a clatter. "We're going for a walk."

Silas Emmett frowned at his son's surly tone. "Afraid of losing again, Jason? A little practice will sharpen your skills."

"I said we're going for a walk!"

"A little respect, please, when you address me!" Silas snapped.

Silence fell in the room, except for the soft hiss of the gas jets. Horace Rhodes coughed. Thaddeus groped around in the pockets of his dinner jacket, pulled out a wrinkled handkerchief, and patted his dripping brow. Then he burped and tried to disguise it as a hiccup.

Silas Emmett's piercing eyes never left his son's face. "Your conduct was shameful enough at dinner," he said slowly, bitingly. "But I'll never tolerate open rudeness—not to me. Now apologize."

"I'm sorry, sir." His cheeks crimson, Jason forced himself to speak the hated words. He stared straight ahead like a soldier. "My friends and I prefer to go for a walk about the grounds, sir. If that is all right with you."

Silas nodded, relaxing. "Just don't forget that I expect you at the brewery first thing tomorrow morning. Merely because your friends are vacationing doesn't mean you are also, Jason."

"Yes, sir."

"Half the time the day is nearly gone before he rousts himself from bed," he said to Horace. "In my time, a young man knew the value of a full day's work. I never would have gotten where I am if I had stayed awake drinking and playing cards all night and then slept half the morning away."

Horace nodded agreement, stroking his goatee. "It's different with these young men. Imagine how I feel, Silas, knowing I must see my daughter safely settled in another man's care. I do hope Sarah will choose well from among her beaux." He chuckled ruefully. "There are certainly enough of them."

Richard and Thaddeus glanced at Jason, whose face felt as if it were on fire. "Let's go," he muttered, and stalked toward the hall. "Good night, Father." He forced each syllable from between tightly clenched teeth. "Good night, Mr. Rhodes."

Richard and Thaddeus stayed to shake hands with the older man, then caught up with Jason at the front door.

By that time he was in a towering rage. The whole evening had been a series of disasters. First, Sarah had ignored him, spurned his every attempt at conversation. Then Richard had brought up that shopgirl fiasco. And finally, his father had humiliated him in front of his friends and Sarah's father.

Frustration surged through him, transforming his pale blue eyes into slits of icy fury. He didn't even look back as he struck out across the lawns in the direction of the wooded glade at the north end of the house. Damn Richard and Thad for witnessing that little scene. He wished they'd go away and leave him alone; he wished the whole damn world would go to fiery hell.

"Wait, Jason," Thaddeus puffed as he tried to match strides with the taller boy, who spurted ahead as if driven by a demon. "Don't mind your father, dear boy. He's like all the rest. Why, mine talks to me that way all the time."

"They all do," Richard added, inhaling the pungent sweetness of the wildflowers that carpeted the starlit glade. "Say, slow down, Jason. This is rough going. Where are we headed, anyway?"

Jason was about to retort that he didn't know where in hell he was headed but wished to go there alone, when an unexpected sound caught his attention. He cocked his head and halted so abruptly that Thaddeus bumped into him.

"What the devil . . . ?"

Jason held up a hand for silence. Then all three of them heard it—soft feminine singing from deep within the glade.

"Who's that?" Richard whispered.

From the trees ahead drifted the melody again. Stephen Foster's "My Old Kentucky Home." It was a young girl's voice, sweet and lilting and faint in the hot, mossy darkness. Jason suddenly smiled to himself, recognizing it. An odd excitement licked through his blood.

"Come on, I'll show you," he said. He led them through the hickories and sycamores toward the faint wisps of song.

All in all, it had been a most pleasant evening, Caroline thought, as she picked her way through the shadowed wood in a happy daze. Her life, if not exactly the way she wanted it, at least not yet, was agreeably satisfying, and she had no complaints about her work. She loved being at Hyacinth House, surrounded by lovely, luxurious things. Tonight Mrs. Emmett had even given her a gift for her extra hours of service: an exquisite handkerchief edged in Venetian lace.

Caroline let the handkerchief flutter between her fingers as she walked home, feeling elegant in her mother's fine gown with the bit of lace in her hand and Virginia Emmett's French perfume mingling in the glade with the scent of honeysuckle. If only Jason were beside her, she thought dreamily, everything would be perfect. If only Jason were here to take her in his arms and kiss her lips, she would be blissfully, totally content.

Caroline never minded when Mrs. Emmett asked her to stay late, and tonight had been no exception. While Mrs. Emmett was downstairs at dinner, Caroline had waited in her bedroom suite to help her retire for the evening. She had spent her time daydreaming most enchantingly about what it would be like to live in Hyacinth House, not as a servant but as Jason's wife. She had even dared to dab on a bit of perfume from one of the crystal bottles on the dressing table, and had examined all the powders and brushes and creams. She had admired her reflection in the silver-handled mirror for quite some time, picturing herself as the lady of the manor. Then she had inventoried all of the silks, satins, and taffetas in Mrs. Emmett's wardrobe, running her fingers over the soft, pale fabrics, imagining what it would be like to wear such magnificent gowns, throw splendid parties, and ride in a fine new carriage.

It had been a delightful way to spend the evening. The only dark spot had been her regret that she herself could not dine downstairs with Jason, in place of that snooty little ice-princess, Sarah Rhodes. But she knew that Jason would much rather have been in her company; she was sure of it, and this certainty gave her a shivery satisfaction as she walked home alone. As she thought about the way Jason was always catching her alone, kissing her in that quick, teasing way, and putting his arms around her waist, she felt shivers of excitement coursing through her. Caroline knew that one day his feelings for her would overcome the considerations of family and position that she knew must weigh with him.

She considered herself most patient and understanding, and felt that time was on her side. Jason's mother already liked her; the handkerchief was proof of that. It would not be difficult to win her to their cause once Jason took it upon himself to make a declaration. Caroline's face glowed in the darkness of the trees as she thought of all she could do for her mother, and for Elly and Timothy, too, when she became Jason's wife. Mama would never have to set foot in the cotton mill again, and she would sleep in a silk-canopied bed and wear gossamer dresses and have a maidservant to wait on her, just as she had during her girlhood in Boston.

So happy was she that Caroline began to sing as she made her way through the wood toward home. Beneath her feet the earth was soft and fragrant, and glimmers of stars flickered occasionally between the intertwining branches of the soaring trees.

Her heart jumped in fright, though, when a voice disturbed the nocturnal sounds of the forest. She dropped the lace handkerchief, and one hand flew to her throat.

"I do beg your pardon, Caroline." Jason stepped from the shadows, followed by two other young men, whom she recognized as his visiting friends from the university. They were all in their evening dress, with their collars loosened against the heat.

Caroline's heart began to beat with sudden happiness when she saw Jason, elegantly handsome in his black coat and white linen, his chestnut hair ruffled attractively by the faint stirring breeze. She laughed aloud, and clapped her hands together. "Why, Jason—Mr. Emmett—you startled me! I never expected to meet anyone at this hour of the night."

"It is late, isn't it, Caroline? One of the grooms should have driven you home."

"Oh, no. Mrs. Emmett offered to summon one, but it's such a lovely evening that I wanted to walk." Her voice trailed off, and she smiled shyly at him, wondering if he knew she had been thinking of him, imagining what it would be like to stroll with him through these quiet midnight woods, with only the birds and wild creatures rustling in the shadows around them. Glancing at his companions, she wished them far away. "I thought you'd be with Miss Rhodes tonight," she chattered, aware that all three young men were watching her closely. Their scrutiny embarrassed her, and she started talking faster. "I saw her gown before she went downstairs. It was truly lovely, though pink is not her color, exactly. Still, it became her well enough. I always wanted a pink gown. Don't you think it would look well on me, Jason—uh, Mr. Emmett?"

"Very well."

Jason surveyed her buxom figure and golden hair. Her eyes were the color of violets against her milky, delicate skin. A

smile of appreciation twitched at the corners of his lips,
encouraging Caroline to prompt, "Lovelier than Miss Rhodes?"

Richard's brows shot up. "That's a damned impertinent
question."

"Caroline didn't mean anything by it." Jason's gaze flickered over her indulgently. "Did you, Caroline?"

"No, no, of course not." Flushing, she tried to redeem
herself. "I was wondering, that's all. I didn't mean to compare myself with her. Miss Rhodes is *such* a pretty girl, even
if she is as sour as a lemon. I would never think of . . ."

She broke off, realizing she had made matters worse. Far
worse. Gone was the tolerance from Jason's pale blue eyes.
Now a dark angry flush suffused his face. His friends were
staring at her in disapproval. She began to stammer. "I'm
sorry. I shouldn't have said that."

"You're damned right you shouldn't have said it."

Could that be Jason, lashing out at her that way? She
stepped backward at the sharpness of his voice.

"Richard's right, you are impertinent." His lip curled. "I
think you have some of your father's Communard blood in
you after all."

"Communard?" Thaddeus gaped. He peered at her from
beneath his scraggly brows. "Who the hell is she, Jason?"

"Nobody. My mother's servant."

Jason was watching Caroline's face lose its color. He found
a cruel satisfaction in her dismay. How dare she impugn
Sarah, who was so much finer than she could ever dream of
being? Sarah Rhodes was a goddess, a true aristocrat. Caroline Forrest had better learn her place. "I think you owe Miss
Rhodes an apology," he said. "Right now."

"But . . . she's not here. . . . I mean, how can I . . ."

"Lord, she's stupid," Thaddeus groaned. "Apologize to
us, nitwit. Your effrontery is an insult to all three of us, not
only to Miss Rhodes."

"If you were a man, you'd have to fight a duel with us,"
Richard pointed out, moving in closer to her. "Lucky for
you, you're not."

"You're certainly not," Jason murmured, his gaze pinned
now to Caroline's breasts, which were rising and falling
rapidly beneath the ivory lace gown. In the moonlight, he saw
her wide, violet eyes fill with tears. Her distress both excited
and disgusted him, reminding him of that dreadful shopgirl

pleading and sobbing in the deserted park. How he hated
these weak, ignorant, common women. So stupid, they were.
So fearful and pathetic in their whimperings. He stepped
closer and grabbed her arms. As he did so, his boot squashed
the fallen handkerchief into the earth. But Jason was unaware
of everything but the girl now sniveling before him.

"Shut up," he ordered.

"J-Jason . . ."

"Stop crying. You're annoying me."

"I want to go home."

" 'I want to go home!' " Thaddeus mimicked her high-
pitched squeak, and then snickered.

"Should we let her go home?" Richard asked, almost idly,
his gaze, too, flicking over her delicate face and blossoming
woman's figure.

"I don't think so," Jason drawled, watching the pupils of
her eyes widen with fright. Starlight beamed down through a
web of tree branches, falling directly upon Caroline's panic-
stricken face. "You must pay a penance, dear Caroline," he
said slowly. "A penance for maligning the fair name of Sarah
Rhodes. She is my father's guest, after all. Unlike you, she is
a lady, a paragon. I'm sure Richard and Thad both agree."

"Absolutely." Thaddeus bobbed his head, but Richard was
starting to look worried. He ran a hand through his well-
combed fair hair.

"Are you sure about this, Jason? Won't she talk?"

"Not if she knows what's good for her."

"Jason, let me go!" Terrified now, Caroline began to
struggle against his grasp. Oh, to have her dreams around her
once more, draping her like layers of silken gauze. She felt
panic choking her as the three men pressed in around her,
blocking off her air, hemming her in with their bodies, their
liquored breath, their gleaming eyes.

What had happened to change everything so quickly, so
horribly? Why was Jason's expression so distant and cold?
She searched his face for some glimpse of her beloved prince,
her dashing Romeo, but could find none. This man was a
stranger who gazed at her with hatred. She looked ahead
toward the clearing that led home and, with a wrenching cry,
began to plead with him to let her go.

He stepped back only when the others had each taken an
arm and were holding her imprisoned between them. Then

Jason simply stood there, smiling down into her terrified face. "You've been wanting it, Caroline—you know you have. This is what you've been dreaming about."

"I don't know what you're talking about! You have to let me go! Jason, I'm sorry I said those things about Miss Rhodes! I'll never do it again. Tell them to let me go. They're hurting me!"

But he wasn't listening. He was studying the soft curves of her young body as it twisted and writhed in the enticing lace dress. His gaze lingered on her breasts, her rounded hips, and his tongue slowly licked the corners of his mouth. "Hold her down," he directed the others. "Under that tree there. I'm going first."

Caroline began to scream.

🌿 Five

ELLY HAD FALLEN asleep on the sofa and didn't hear Caroline cross the porch. But the soft click of the latch roused her, and she sat up with a start. In the golden light of the kerosene lamp, the mantel clock read one-fifteen.

"Caroline? I was worried about you. You've never been this late before. What in the world kept you so long?"

Her sister was a shadowy silhouette in the doorway.

"Did Virginia Emmett have you sing her a lullaby before she went to sleep? I hope she paid you extra for your time."

Caroline shuffled toward the stairs without answering. Yawning, Elly rose and regarded her in faint surprise. Caro must be tired. She usually came in bubbling with talk of Virginia Emmett's finery, of Hyacinth House's grand appointments. She looked exhausted, her shoulders sagging, her hair a shapeless tangle. Then, suddenly, as Caroline edged along the railing, the light touched her at last and Elly caught sight of her dress.

"It's ripped! Mama's gown, you've ruined it." She hurried closer to get a better look, but Caroline gave a great, gasping sob and fled upstairs before she could reach her.

Elly stared after her in dismay. Then she pounded up the stairs in pursuit. "Caroline, what happened?" It was too dark to see anything in their room, but she heard Caroline's sobs as she fumbled with the lamp. Then, when the muted yellow glow swept the darkness aside, she looked down at the girl huddled on the blue-counterpaned bed near the window.

Shock struck as she saw the dirt and twigs embedded in her sister's hair, and the lace gown torn and soiled by earth and grass. Caroline's stockings were ripped; her hands were filthy and covered with scratches. Fear knifed through Elly, like a slashing, white-hot blade. With it came horror and a terrible dread.

"Oh, Lord, Caroline, what happened? What happened to you?"

"N-nothing! Go away!"

Caroline's sobs filled the tiny, spotless room. They seemed out of place between those cheerful yellow walls, echoing back and forth between the three-drawered pine bureau, the little cherrywood chair, and the two blue-counterpaned beds where the girls had slept nearly all their lives. The blue and yellow gingham curtains seemed to shudder at the sound, and the breeze that wafted through the room carried the mingled scents of horse manure from the street and azaleas growing wild in the garden, smells as contrasting as the sight of the bedraggled, weeping girl in the middle of that pleasant, peaceful room. Elly sank down on the bed beside her. She put a hand on Caroline's shoulder. A shudder ran through her sister's body.

"Oh, Caroline, what happened?" she whispered. No answer, merely a shake of the head, which sent the fair hair, now matted with dirt, flying around the crying girl's face. Gently, she lifted Caroline in her arms, turned her around, then caught her breath when she saw the purpling bruise on her sister's face.

"Who did this?" Elly cried, her blue-gray eyes round with horror.

"Go away!"

"Who did this?"

Hysteria consumed the girl on the bed and she wrenched free, burying her face in her pillow again. Tears burned Elly's eyelids and fell slowly down her cheeks. Grief, not unlike what she had felt for her father, entered her soul. Not knowing what else to do, she gathered her sister in her arms and held her, rocking back and forth on the bed. Caroline dissolved against her, trembling, sobbing. Elly spoke quietly, not even knowing what she said, using the tone she reserved for Timothy when he awakened from a nightmare. She smoothed the tangle of pale hair and stroked the quivering back, wondering with dread exactly what had befallen her sister, and by whose hand. After a while, the storm of grief subsided, and Caroline collapsed against her shoulder, spent and gasping and broken, like a doll battered beyond what its frail construction could withstand.

"Was it Jason Emmett?"

Caroline went rigid. Her head shot up, terror shining in her eyes. She clutched Elly's hands in her damp, filthy ones.

"Don't tell Mama! Don't tell anyone!"

Pain stabbed Elly, and with it came rage, boiling, blinding rage. She fought it down, keeping her voice calm with supreme effort. "We have to tell, Caro. Whoever did this must be punished. Was it Jason?"

"Yes. *Yes.* He and two of his friends. They were in the woods when I was walking home. They . . . Elly, how could they do this to me?"

Elly's arms trembled; she bit her lip to keep from screaming and forced herself to continue speaking calmly. "Did they rape you, Caroline?"

Caroline covered her face with her hands. *"Yes."*

A broken whisper, simple, soft, hideous.

"They took off my clothes. They touched me—everywhere. They held me down and . . . and . . ."

Elly squeezed her eyes tight shut, as if to block out the images brought to life by Caroline's words. This was a nightmare, a living nightmare. How could something so awful have happened to Caroline? She was only a child. A silly, dreaming child. Elly moaned and shook her head. Then she heard Caroline's voice, pathetic in its desperation.

"Elly, we can't tell anyone or do anything. Jason threatened me . . . He hit me and said that if I told, he'd see us starve, our entire family. We'll all lose our jobs, and the company stores won't sell us food and . . ."

An ice-cold fury stronger than any emotion she had ever known surged over Elly. That pig had dared to do this to Caroline and then had followed it with threats. What would her father do if he were here? She knew the answer.

"Don't worry, Caroline. It'll be all right."

"I mean it, Elly. No one must know! I'd die if anyone knew!"

"Shh, don't worry about it now."

"Elly." Caroline was shaking again. Her blue eyes were still swimming in tears. "I want a bath. I must get clean. Somehow I must get clean."

An hour later she dragged Caroline from the washtub in the kitchen. Caroline had begun to sob again after soaping and scrubbing her bruised flesh in the cool water, and she had refused to leave the tub, claiming she wasn't clean, not yet, not nearly. Elly wrapped her in a towel, slipped a nightgown over her head, and bundled her up to bed. She heard Timothy's voice as she picked up the hairbrush to comb out Caroline's hair. He called to her from the attic room.

"What is it?" She was breathless, having run to him, the hairbrush still in her hand.

"I heard noises."

"Go to sleep."

"Is Caroline home?"

"Yes."

"Is Mama all right?"

"Yes! Timothy, go back to sleep." She didn't even take time to blow him a kiss, and without looking back at his sleepy, bewildered face in the little bed, she hurried back to Caroline, praying that her mother wouldn't also awaken. She didn't think she had the strength to tell Mama everything tonight.

She brushed out Caroline's hair and reassured her that everything would be fine as she tried not to stare at the bruises on her sister's arms and wrists. Those savages had been anything but gentle in their attack. When Caroline put a hand to her swollen cheek and whispered that she had fought them as best she could, Elly had to swallow back her own tears.

"Don't think about it anymore, Caro."

"I can't stop thinking about it. There were three of them, Elly—all three of them did those things to me. And then Jason, he . . . he got on top of me again. He told me he wanted to be first and last."

"Oh, Caro, Caro." She enfolded the crying girl in her arms again. Caroline's nightgown was damp with tears, but she didn't seem able to stop reliving the horror in the glade. Elly held her, stroking her hair, murmuring soothing—and, she knew, inadequate—words while Caroline wept and shuddered on her bed. It was dawn when she at last fell into a fitful sleep, and Elly covered her with the sheet, staring blearily down at her red, swollen face before creeping to her own bed. Each time Caroline moaned and awoke, Elly went to her and held her hand and lulled her back to sleep, and in the morning she sat on her own bed, limp with exhaustion, yet filled with a nail-hard determination.

"Don't tell Mama," Caroline begged, when she opened her eyes and stared across the yellow-painted room at Elly. Bleak sunlight fell on the faded blue coverlets, spattered the polished wood floor, illuminated the ugly bruise rising to a welt on Caroline's delicate face. "Promise me you won't, Elly."

"Mama must know."

"No one must know!"

"Leave it to me, Caroline. Don't worry about anything."

"I can't go back to that house ever again." Caroline sat up, her little shoulders looking pitifully thin beneath her white nightgown. "I can't work for Mrs. Emmett anymore, or go near Hyacinth House."

"Absolutely not. You're never going to set foot near that house again."

"I'll work in the cotton mill with you and Mama, Elly. We'll all be together every day. I want to be with both of you every minute. That way we'll all be safe."

The frantic fear and desperation emblazed on Caroline's face spurred Elly's rage anew. There was no sign now of the breezy, frivolous fifteen-year-old who had so often infuriated her with foolish daydreams. The girl who peered at Elly from the other bed was a terrified shadow of her former self. She had Caroline's silky, golden hair and ivory skin, her softly ripening figure and wide-set blue eyes, but there was an ugly mark on her face, her eyes were swollen and bloodshot with crying, and devastation stamped her like a blight on all that was young and hopeful in her soul. Elly wanted to scream and weep, but she held her emotions in tight check and reminded herself that it was up to her to take care of all this. Mama was not strong enough, not anymore. Elly dreaded having to tell her and hoped to put it off at least until tonight. This morning there was business to take care of.

Elly left Caroline lying silent and drained in her bed. She was terrified of being left alone in the house for the day, but even more unnerved at the thought of facing her mother and admitting the truth. With an agonized nod, she watched Elly leave the room and go downstairs to find Bess with a story they had agreed on.

Bess was preparing breakfast, looking frail and worn in her gray cotton dress with the thin ribbon of white lace around the collar and waist. She smiled wanly at Elly, and asked if Caroline was dressed yet. Elly shook her head. She went to the shelf where the breakfast plates were stacked and, without looking at her mother, told her that Mrs. Emmett had given Caroline the day off and that the girl was still asleep. She suggested that they let her rest, for it had been a late night.

"I'm going in early to the mill," she lied as she set out two plates and Bess stirred corn-cake batter with a long wooden spoon. "Mr. Finch asked a few of us girls to come in ahead of the shift today and help him catch up with some paperwork in the office."

"Elly, you work so hard. I wish I could provide a better life for you." Bess's eyes misted with tears. Already the August heat was oppressive in the kitchen, and her mother's freshly scrubbed skin looked wilted and old. "You're a dear to have finished Mrs. Alexander's tea gown for me. I don't know what I'd do without you. My eyes get so tired at night; I just can't keep up with all the sewing, but heaven knows what would become of us if it weren't for the extra money it brings."

Her mother sounded so discouraged that Elly renewed her determination not to tell her the truth about Caroline just yet. Not until she had taken steps to resolve matters. At one time, Bess might have been able to cope with any ordeal, but not anymore. The buffeting winds of poverty and grief had robbed her of the strength she had once possessed, and since Papa's death she had grown more and more fragile, more and more dependent on Elly.

"I'm glad to help, Mama. I wish I could do more. But I don't have time to eat breakfast. I have to get to the mill. You and Timmy will have to keep each other company."

She kissed her mother's cheek and fled into the blistering morning sunshine. Already it was humid, the heavy air nearly unbreathable, and her skin grew moist under her calico gown as she walked with long, quick strides toward the main junction of town. Beyond the row houses and the planked sidewalks of Emmettville loomed misty blue mountains, rising majestically against the shimmering lilac sky. They looked beautiful and imperious in the distance, through the haze of sunshine and factory smoke that filled the sultry August air. Nearby, the surroundings were grimmer—gray stores, dust, an old wagon with creaking wheels pulled by a pair of horses clopping along in dismal fashion. The pair, brown heads drooping already, left their droppings on the cobblestones like a fetid trail for the swarming flies that pursued them. Elly was immune to the stench; it was no worse than the fumes of coal and smoke and soot that spouted from the chimneys of the mills day after day.

It was still early; the main bulk of workers had not yet started for their morning shifts, nor had the evening laborers been released. Elly glanced into the bakery, where fresh loaves of bread and rolls of countless variety overflowed the wooden shelves. She strode past the Emmettville Hotel and the courthouse, past the druggist's shop and the blacksmith's stable, until she reached the two-cell jailhouse at the corner of Second Street. There she found Sheriff Greeves sitting with his feet propped up on his desk, the *Emmettville Gazette* held inches from his bespectacled eyes, and a half-filled cup of black coffee set amid the litter of cigar ash on his desk.

"You got a problem, Miss Forrest? It *is* Miss Forrest, isn't it?"

He squinted up at her, a wiry man with dirty gold hair worn long, a drooping mustache, and whiskers. Spectacles framed tiny blue eyes set deep within brown weathered sockets. He had come to the house to harass her father often enough over his union activities to remember their family. The threats and arguments had been long and frequent, unsettling Bess more with each visit. That didn't make it any easier for Elly to begin now.

"Sheriff, I've come to swear out a complaint. My sister was attacked last night, and is badly hurt."

"That so?" He swung his feet off the desk, put down the newspaper, and stared at her. "Why ain't she here herself?"

"She's badly hurt," Elly repeated, "and in no condition to leave her bed. The men responsible for this atrocity belong in jail."

"Atrocity, eh? She know who done it?"

"Jason Emmett and two of his friends."

Sheriff Greeves stared at her, then gave a loud guffaw. "What are you blabbing at me about, girl? Go home."

"Not until you fill out a complaint against Jason Emmett and act on it."

Sheriff Greeves picked up his cigar stub and twiddled it between his tobacco-stained fingers. "No way I'm going to do any such thing, missy. You can stand there all day if you want."

Every nerve in her body was taut. "Don't you believe me?"

"Believe you? Daughter of a rabble-rousing Communard who did nothing but stir up trouble in this town? Why wouldn't I believe you?" he taunted.

The threads of anger snapped inside her. She leaned forward. "I demand that you act on my complaint!"

Sheriff Greeves came slowly to his feet. He was not much taller than Elly, but the look he gave her made her step back involuntarily. "Silas Emmett didn't raise no wild boy," he said coldly. "I know Jason Emmett, and I know he wouldn't hurt your sister—lest he had a good reason. Which maybe he did."

"He had no reason. Nor did his friends. They raped her in the woods, Sheriff!"

"That's pretty strong talk, missy."

She nearly shouted. "Sheriff, are you going to fill out a complaint and arrest those men or not?"

"Not." He picked up his cup and started to drink his coffee, then made a face and spat the brown liquid onto the floor. It dribbled over the sawdust and the ants. "Cold and bitter as hell," he muttered, before glancing at Elly again. She hadn't moved, but watched him in disgust, as frustration mounted inside her. "I'll tell you what I'm going to do, Miss Forrest. Since you're so worked up, I'll go over and have a little chat with Mr. Emmett and see what he thinks about all this. I'll let you know what he has to say when I'm all done. Meantime, you'd best get to the mill yourself. You Forrests got enough trouble—you don't need to get yourself fired for bein' late to work.''

Her chin quivered with indignation. Instead of arresting Jason, Sheriff Greeves intended to "chat" with him? Bitterly, she realized she should have expected as much. Silas Emmett controlled everything and everyone in this town, the sheriff's office included. But she wasn't going to let the matter drop.

"You do that, Sheriff Greeves. You let me know what happens—this evening. I expect some action on your part—or by tomorrow, everyone in this county will know what that animal did to a decent young girl of this community. All of the mill workers, all of the factory workers, everyone. You tell that to Mr. Jason Emmett.''

She glared at him a moment, letting the words sink in before she spun on her heel and walked away without a backward glance. It was a relief to be out of that unkempt place, away from the sheriff's icy, piercing stare. But she had a nagging feeling of regret, wondering if she had been wise to make that threat and demand that it be delivered to Jason Emmett personally. An uneasy foreboding prickled at her as she made her way across town to the cotton mill.

That day was one of the longest, hottest, and most miserable Elly had ever spent. The stifling air and broiling heat soon had her soaking in perspiration, and her thick hair, tightly coiled in a braid atop her head, seemed to weigh upon her like an armored helmet. She saw her mother at lunchtime when they shared the sandwiches Bess had packed into a pail. Bess looked as though she was about to faint. Her flushed face and too-bright eyes indicted how intensely the heat was affecting her. Elly urged her to ask permission to go home and rest for the remainder of the day, but Bess refused. She returned to work with the others, and the afternoon dragged on. When the shift-ending whistle finally blew, they walked home together, too tired to talk. Elly's mind was spinning with thoughts of Caroline and how best to help her, and how she was going to break the truth to Mama tonight.

She was startled when they arrived home to hear raised voices through the open front window. It was Caroline's cry, high-pitched and hysterical, answered by a man's harsh rasping tones. Her throat dry, Elly dashed up the steps and into the hall ahead of her mother.

Caroline shrieked and rushed forward when she saw her. Elly hardly noticed her tear-streaked face with the red-rimmed bruise, or the old print calico her sister had donned haphazardly, the buttons improperly done up and the sash askew. She was staring hard at Sheriff Greeves, who stood with legs planted firmly apart near the sofa.

"What did you say to upset her so, Sheriff?" she fumed. "How dare you use that tone? I heard you clearly through the window."

Greeves pushed his soft-brimmed hat back from his brow, and looked at her through eyes like tiny blue stones. Those eyes made her shiver. Elly saw the brown tobacco stains on his whiskers, the mole beneath his right ear. He stroked his gold mustache and took his time answering.

"I've got a warrant here for your sister's arrest, missy. I'm taking her in to the jailhouse where she belongs."

"No, you're not! She's not leaving this house!" Timothy hissed with valiant boyhood bravado from the middle of the parlor, where he had placed himself between Caroline and the sheriff. Caroline clung to Elly and sobbed in her arms.

"Don't let him take me, Elly! Don't let him, please! I can't go to jail, I can't! You've got to do something."

Elly went cold. This was her doing, she realized. She had brought this on them by asking the sheriff to arrest Jason Emmett. Before she could speak, her mother hurried forward, her face pinched and worried. "Sheriff Greeves, what is all this talk about jail? My daughter has done nothing wrong."

"Beg to differ with you, ma'am. She's stolen something from Mrs. Virginia Emmett. She—"

"Caroline—your face! What happened to your face?"

Bess had at last caught sight of the bruise. She stood stock still, her skin whitening to a ghastly pallor as she stared at her younger daughter.

Caroline began to shake her head wildly. "I fell, Mama. I fell and hit my cheek on a rock—in the glade last night when I was walking home. Don't let him take me to jail, Mama! I fell down, that's all." She threw herself into Bess's arms, weeping again. "Don't let him take me away!"

"Of course not, darling, of course not." Stunned, Bess looked at Sheriff Greeves. Beneath the calm, refined tones, there was panic in her words. "Sheriff, if you'll kindly explain. I don't understand."

"No doubt your daughter fell down when she was running away from the Emmett house last night. Can't blame her for running. If I'd stole a valuable necklace like that, I'd have run too, and hid it real good, just like she's done."

"What necklace?" Elly demanded harshly.

"Mr. Silas Emmett informed me today that the diamond and pearl necklace his wife wore to dinner last evening is missing. Your sister, missy, was there in the room when Mrs. Emmett took it off. She helped put Mrs. Emmett's things away. She was the only one who could've taken it."

"This is ridiculous." Elly spat the words at him, her eyes flashing her contempt. "Jason Emmett is the one you should be arresting."

" 'Fraid not, Miss Forrest." Greeves smiled thinly at her, and took a folded paper from his shirt pocket. "I asked a few questions about that little matter and came up with some satisfying answers. Right here is the sworn statements of Mr. Silas Emmett and Mr. Jason Emmett and Mr. Richard Henderson and Mr. Thaddeus James, testifying that those three young men never left Hyacinth House last night. Mr. Emmett vouched for the fact that Jason and his friends spent the evening playing billiards with him and a Mr. Horace Rhodes. Seems Mr. Rhodes and his family left early this morning for Pittsburgh, so I couldn't speak to them, but Mr. Emmett's word is good enough for me."

He stuffed the paper back in his pocket. "Now, you'd best calm your sister down and tell her to come with me peaceful like. Unless, of course, she's ready to 'fess up and give back that necklace. Then I might be able to persuade Mr. Emmett to drop the charges."

"I don't have any necklace!" Caroline shrieked, and Bess, stroking her daughter's hair, lifted her head to glare at him.

"This is totally absurd, Sheriff. My daughter has never stolen anything in her life, and she never, ever would."

"Looks like she'll have to prove that in a court of law, now, don't it, Miz Forrest?" he replied with a grin, taking a step forward. He jerked his head in Timothy's direction. "That young'un better get out of my way. And you, too, missy," he warned Elly. "I don't want no trouble leaving here with your sister."

Suddenly, Elly's self-control cracked. Her shoulders started to tremble. Sweat poured down her face. So this was what you got when you fought against money and power. This was what happened when you dared to tell the truth, to seek justice in the aftermath of a heinous crime. Now she was beginning to understand firsthand some of her father's frustration in dealing with the bosses of industry, and she was starting to comprehend the great, passionate bitterness she had often glimpsed in his face. There was no triumphing over people like the Emmetts and the lapdogs who depended on them. There was no winning against the ruthless, powerful few. She had tried to protect Caroline from further hurt, she had tried to see the men responsible punished, and now it was Caroline who had to suffer, Caroline who would go to jail.

"Don't let him take me! I can't bear it if he takes me." Caroline was pleading with her mother, and Bess's tears mingled with her own.

"Sheriff, please, let her stay tonight and . . . and I'll speak to Mr. Emmett about settling this . . . misunderstanding," Elly said in a rush of breath, not knowing what else she might do or say to persuade him. Pride no longer mattered; dignity could be cast aside. If she had to beg to protect Caroline, she would.

But Greeves's smile merely widened, and he shook his head. "I've got my orders, missy. She goes tonight."

"This is your fault, Elly. It's all your fault!" Caroline shrieked, whirling on Elly. "You told Sheriff Greeves—even though I warned you, I begged you, not to tell a soul. Jason told me what would happen if anyone found out, but you wouldn't listen, you had to tell him!"

"What is she talking about, Elly?" Bess glanced back and forth between her daughters, more distressed than ever. "You told Sheriff Greeves about what?"

"Don't tell her!" Caroline grabbed Elly's shoulders and shook her wildly, tears streaming down her cheeks. "I can't bear it if you tell her!" Suddenly, she collapsed on the floor, sobbing. Bess moved to her as if in a dream.

Outside the window, the gold sun sank in the pink and mauve western sky, gilding the distant Alleghenies. A dog barked in the street, the shrill sound echoing in the sizzling night. A train whistle sounded. From down the lane came the slamming of a door and the sound of a man's voice raised in anger. Then there was silence, except for Caroline's weeping and Bess's vain attempts to comfort her.

Elly stepped forward, unable to listen to her sister's pain another moment. She faced Greeves, as pale and shaken as the others, but her blue-gray eyes were vibrant and dark with determination.

"Leave our house, Sheriff. Let my sister be."

His pebbly eyes blinked at her. "Maybe after she spends the night in jail and has a chance to think about things, she'll feel sorry for what she's done. Could be Mr. Emmett'll drop the charges then."

He strode over to the rug where Caroline sat huddled on the floor, Bess's arms around her. "Come along, miss. Time to go."

"No, Mama, don't let him take me." Caroline clung to her mother's shoulders, while Bess gaped at the sheriff helplessly. Timothy, confused by all the adult babble, had backed himself into a corner and now stared at Sheriff Greeves as if the devil himself had come into the house amid a spiral of flames.

Only Elly continued to talk rapidly and desperately, unable to believe Greeves would really go through with the arrest. "Let her stay here tonight, Sheriff," she urged, putting a hand on his grease-stained sleeve. "You know she's done nothing wrong. I'll drop the charges against Jason Emmett. I'll apologize to the Emmetts, and we'll straighten this all out. Only let Caroline stay here."

"Outta my way." He hauled the sobbing girl to her feet and started for the door.

Bess ran beside them to the sheriff's wagon. "Stay with Timothy," she called over her shoulder. She dragged herself up into the wagon behind Caroline and Greeves. "I won't leave her, and we'll be home as soon as we can straighten this out. Keep some supper for us—Caroline will be hungry when we get back."

Elly knew her mother was talking to keep Caroline's spirits up. There was no possibility of straightening this out with Sheriff Greeves. Only one man could settle this matter. She didn't waste any time once the wagon had rumbled out of sight. She took Timothy to the Moffetts' house and left him in Katie's care.

"I can't explain now, but he hasn't had supper, so if you can spare some food, I'd be grateful."

"We're just about to sit down, and he's more than welcome. But what's this about, Elly? Is your mama sick?"

"I'm sorry, I can't explain." Gazing suddenly at Timothy's ashen face, she knelt down and whispered, "Don't worry. Be a good boy. Caro will be home tonight."

Then she left, avoiding Billy's questioning gaze. She ran up the lane past rows of houses where, inside, families ate their meager suppers in hot, dingy rooms. She ran past clouds of summer gnats swirling in the sunset sky, past an amber cat stalking mice in Willa Brown's garden. When she reached her own house once again, her breath was coming hard and fast, making her chest ache as though she'd been struck by a two-by-four. Her hair tumbled into her eyes, and perspiration dampened her neck and breasts. She went straight to the desk by the window. The main drawer was always locked, but Elly knew where the key was. She opened it and removed the battered Colt revolver her father had brought home with him from the war. It felt heavy in her hand. She liked the feeling. She didn't know how to use it, but she knew Papa had always kept it loaded, and she remembered that once he had shown her the safety mechanism and how it worked.

That was enough to know, Elly decided as she hid the revolver in the pocket of her skirt. She left the house again and headed toward the glade where her sister had been ravaged the previous night. As twilight fell and the birds twittered in the whispering leaves of the treetops, she strode through the wood, knowing she was acting as her father would have acted, had he been here, as anyone of decency would act if a loved one had been hurt and endangered. She stepped over a bit of lace trampled into the earth without noticing it; her thoughts were on the grand house ahead. Something cold and hard settled in Elly's stomach as she drew nearer and nearer to it, leaving the musk-scented glade behind for the manicured jade lawns of Hyacinth House. If the Emmetts didn't care about morality or law or reason, maybe they would care about the Union Colt. Maybe there was only one way for justice to be served, after all. She would show them at last the limits of money and power and influence, remind them of the vulnerabilities they possessed beneath the armor of their tainted wealth.

☙ Six

"A YOUNG PERSON calling herself Miss Elinore Forrest is here to see you, sir."

The disdainful English butler Silas Emmett had imported during his last trip to London spoke in clipped tones from the doorway of the dining salon. "I told her you were dining, but she insists—"

"Yes, yes, I'm certain she does." Silas Emmett took a huge bite of his roast duckling, licking his lips over the currant jelly that oozed over the skin. "It's all right, Duncan." He waved a hand in the air. "I've been expecting her. Put her in the gold salon and let her wait."

"Shall I offer her a refreshment, sir?"

"No." Silas regarded his son from beneath frowning brows and spoke slowly. "Don't offer her a damned thing. I certainly don't intend to."

Jason's fork had paused in midair at the butler's announcement. Now he set it back on his plate with the morsel of asparagus untouched.

"Lost your appetite, eh?" Silas noted, chewing his own food with relish. "Show some gumption, boy. You're not afraid of that Forrest girl, are you?"

They were alone at the enormous oval table. Virginia had felt too ill to join them, and Richard and Thad had left at four, but not before being treated to a roaring dressing-down, which ended with Silas sending telegrams to their fathers, detailing their exploits in Emmettville and explaining how he had been informed of their actions by none other than the sheriff. Jason still seethed as he remembered his father's rage, the way he'd cussed and reviled them for well over an hour in his library, lecturing and shouting at them as if they were schoolboys. But at least this time, he reflected with some small satisfaction, Richard and Thad had shared the blame; they, too, faced the fires of parental wrath.

When Duncan left them to their repast, Silas continued to fork mouthful after mouthful between his lips, but Jason sat staring darkly at his gold-rimmed plate.

"Damn it, boy, never let the lower classes get the better of you," Silas snapped, taking his son's silence for nervousness. "We've got that Forrest girl exactly where we want her. I know what I'm doing. She's not going to make another ounce of trouble for us, but that's no thanks to you. This could have been a disaster." Anger throbbed anew in his voice as he leaned forward across the table. "If I didn't pay Greeves as well as I do, and if he wasn't loyal to me, we might have had a tidy scandal on our hands and possibly a major workers' revolt. Caroline Forrest's own father failed to unite them with his Communard ideas, but something like this could stir up all kinds of trouble, could turn the workingmen against us once and for all. Fortunately, I don't think matters will come to that now."

"It was a brilliant plan, Father," Jason conceded. A grudging smile touched the patrician lines of his face. They were making the slut pay for opening her mouth. She and her whole troublemaking family were paying dearly. Caroline was not only jailed but discredited as well. By tomorrow the story would be all over Emmettville that she had stolen from her employer.

"Watch me handle the Forrest girl and you might learn something." Silas sampled a bit of the plum pudding before him. "Whatever happens, don't admit to one damned thing. The sister stole your mother's necklace and tried to seduce you. Perhaps, in time, if she's penitent, we'll do her a favor and drop the charges."

"Not for quite a while, I hope," Jason muttered, wiping his mouth on his napkin. "I think it would do her and her scum of a family good to let her mold away in that cell awhile."

"It might do you and your friends some good as well!" Silas replied, leveling a disgusted glance at the surly chestnut-haired young man opposite him and watching Jason's cheeks flame at his words. "I hope you've learned something from all this, because I've gone to a hell of a lot of trouble for you today, and I'm not going to make a habit of it. I think you'd better find yourself a complaisant wife and leave the servant girls alone. I've had enough of these tawdry incidents, Jason, and your behavior ill becomes a man who hopes to be respected in the world. You've been groomed to take over my enterprises in Emmettville, to increase the holdings of this family, and to enter into partnership with your Uncle Louis. He's a notable man in Pittsburgh, you know, and if he ever got wind of your exploits, he'd refrain from doing any business whatsoever with the Emmett side of the family. That wouldn't do at all. Louis Whitcomb can help us double—no, triple—the empire we now rule. Are you willing to throw all of that away?''

"No, sir." Jason gulped, thinking of his straitlaced uncle and aunt, and what they would say if they knew he had raped his mother's servant. "I'll try to remember," he pledged.

"Find yourself a girl like Sarah Rhodes, marry her, and settle down!" Silas banged his fist on the table for emphasis, making the wineglasses jump. "Then you can turn your full attention to the worthwhile enterprise of making money so you can have something to leave *your* children when you're gone—it's a damned sight better than leaving behind a parcel of bastards of women who didn't want anything to do with you.''

The servants cleared away the empty platters and soiled china and cutlery. They brought coffee, mince pie, and assorted cakes. Taking a cue from his father, Jason took his time over dessert. *Let her wait,* he thought viciously, imagining Elly Forrest's impatience, her anxiety and fear. He smiled suddenly at the image of Caroline Forrest at this very moment locked in a jail cell. It served her right for opening her mouth, he thought, banishing with only a slight twinge of conscience the memory of the sweetly adoring golden-haired girl he had found so amusing in the past months. It was her own fault, he reminded himself, his fingers clenching on his coffee cup. He had given her fair warning to keep silent.

When they finally removed to the gold salon, a deep emerald darkness had fallen over the grounds of Hyacinth House. The immense gaslit chandelier winked from the ceiling of the room where Elly Forrest sat so still on the white silk sofa. It was a stunning room. The black-haired girl in the sprigged calico dress seemed out of place amid the gold-inlaid tables and heavy velvet draperies; surrounded by gold-framed masterpieces and priceless Chinese vases. Her scuffed, too-tight shoes rested quietly on the magnificent Aubusson carpet, and she seemed to be staring hard at the marble swan sculpture set on its ivory pedestal in the corner of the opulent white and gold room. She looked up when Silas and Jason strolled in.

"So you're Elly Forrest, eh? Well, speak up girl. This is about your sister, is it not? The one who stole from my wife. Have you come to return the necklace?"

Elly struggled to control her temper. The sight of Jason Emmett's handsome, smirking face made her long to whip out the Colt and wipe that superior expression from his eyes once and for all. A bullet in the brain would do it, she thought, though one between his legs would be more fitting justice. She came to her feet and deliberately refrained from glancing at him again, lest she lose track of what she hoped to accomplish. The Colt was a last resort. She turned her attention to Silas Emmett and gazed into his molelike face with a calm she was far from feeling.

"This is about your son, Mr. Emmett. We both know what he and his friends did to my sister. They're the ones who belong in jail."

Silas turned his back on her as he took a seat in a Louis XVI chair, resting his hands on the arms of it like a monarch in his throne. "Young woman, I have no idea what you're talking about. It's true that the sheriff told me of your allegations, but they're totally ridiculous. Jason and his friends spent last evening with me, playing billiards. Why, the boy even won a game."

At this remark, and the sardonic tone in which it was uttered, Jason flinched. The old man never lost an opportunity to rub in the fact that Jason had never once beaten him at billiards, or at any other undertaking.

"Your sister is nothing but a common tramp and a thief!" Jason unleashed his anger at Elly Forrest. "She's been chasing me for months! Instead of daring to stand there insulting me with these accusations, you ought to be persuading her to return my mother's necklace."

"She didn't steal your mother's necklace or anything else." Elly stepped past him, speaking to Silas. She tried to make her voice as soft and persuasive as she could, like Mama's. Papa had often said that Mama could talk a fish into a frying pan if she felt like it. "Mr. Emmett, I ask you to reconsider what you've done here. My sister doesn't belong in jail."

"That's precisely where she belongs."

Elly bit her lip. "Perhaps we should ask your wife if she is missing any of her jewelry."

The look of superior, bemused tolerance vanished from his eyes. Silas Emmett's voice hardened, and coldness clamped over his features. "My wife is too ill to be disturbed any more than she has been already. She was upset enough when she told me of the theft—for some reason, she was fond of your sister, and the girl's betrayal has hurt my wife quite enough."

A new voice spoke gently from the open doorway. "You're correct about one thing, Silas: I am fond of the girl. But as for the betrayal, I am completely in the dark—as I told Elinore in my room a few moments ago."

Virginia Emmett came slowly and painfully into the room. The scent of musky rose perfume accompanied her, and she wore a cloud of a pink dressing gown, trimmed in layers and layers of rose-colored lace. Her hunched shoulders and measured gait attested to the fact that she was in pain.

At the sight of his wife's frail figure and questioning face, Silas's neck reddened; he sprang to his feet and lashed out at Elly: "You dared to disturb my wife!"

She thought he was going to strike her. "I had nothing better to do while you kept me waiting," she responded swiftly. "Mrs. Emmett, thank you for coming down."

She hadn't counted on his fury at this maneuver. The ugly contortions of his face frightened her, but he quickly smoothed them out as he turned to Virginia.

"My dear, I forbid you to make yourself ill over this nonsense." While Jason and Elly watched, he went to her and took her arm. "Duncan will take you straight back to your bed."

Jason pulled the gold-tasseled cord that would summon a servant. "Father is absolutely right. This is nothing that you should involve yourself with, Mother."

Virginia Emmett weakly shook her head. "Let me sit down—I want to talk to you, Silas. About Caroline. Is it true you had her arrested? But why?"

Silas and Jason exchanged quick looks. So, she didn't know about the accusations against Jason. Elly Forrest hadn't gone so far as to repeat the rape charges to Virginia, and Silas didn't mean to give her the opportunity to do so, for Virginia would be destroyed if she knew. He kept hold of her arm, but instead of helping her reach the sofa, guided her back toward the door.

"Caroline Forrest is a thief, my dear. It grieves me to tell you this, but the girl has no morals whatsoever. She has no business in this house, or in any other decent place. I had wanted to spare you the truth but—"

Elly broke in. "Mrs. Emmett, you assured me that my sister stole nothing—not a single item is missing from your belongings. Isn't that true, ma'am?"

"Yes, yes, it is. Caroline is a sweet girl. She wouldn't steal from me."

"That's enough, Virginia!" Silas's voice boomed, startling the woman beside him. Her fragile, powdered face seemed to shrivel at the intensity of her husband's anger. "You're too ill most of the time to understand half of what goes on around you. There's a great deal you don't know. Now, I refuse to listen to another word on the subject. I'll explain it all to you when you're feeling up to it, but right now I insist that you return to your bed and rest. A sleeping draft is in order. You're upset and exhausted."

Duncan appeared in the doorway in response to Jason's summons.

"Duncan, help Mrs. Emmett to her room."

Virginia flung a helpless look toward Elly.

"Please, ma'am, wait," Elly begged, but Jason suddenly bore down on her.

"Shut up, you." He flung her backward onto the sofa, and hurried to his mother, taking her blue-veined hands in his. "Go along now, Mother. This is an ugly business. I'd hate to see you upset yourself and make yourself ill. Father and I can handle it."

"But, Jason dear, I don't understand . . ."

"Duncan, have Mary fix my mother a potion and attend to her until she falls asleep. She is not to be left alone for the rest of the evening. Is that clear?"

The butler held out his arm. Virginia glanced uncertainly

from Silas to Jason to Elly, who jumped up from the sofa and
rushed toward her, only to be blocked by Jason's tall form.

"Please, Mrs. Emmett, listen to me. Your husband has
invented charges against Caroline because of what Jason did
to her. He—"

Jason grabbed her wrists so hard she gasped in pain. Tears
filled Elly's eyes.

Virginia did not see; she was already retreating on the
butler's arm. "I'm sorry, my dear." She was murmuring the
words almost to herself. "I suppose I don't fully understand
the circumstances. I'm certain Jason and Silas will do what's
right . . ." Her voice trailed off as she left the room, and
Silas Emmett closed the door firmly behind her. His expression when he turned around was one of barely contained fury.

"Damn you to hell!" His boots crashed on the parquet
floor as he stalked toward her.

Helpless in Jason's grasp, Elly stared wildly from one
Emmett to the other.

"I ought to have you horsewhipped, young woman. Daring
to disturb my wife with your stupid complaints! Going to the
sheriff with these ridiculous stories about my son. You're as
much a troublemaker as your father was! Let her go, Jason. I
don't know how you can stand to touch the dirty little bitch."

Elly rubbed her wrists as Jason stepped back. He was
smiling with arrogant satisfaction. "If there was any justice,
you'd be horsewhipped—or hanged!" she cried. With these
words she remembered the pistol in her pocket. She drew it
out, her hands shaking, and before Jason Emmett had even
comprehended what she was doing, she released the safety
mechanism and held the Colt pointed at his face, the barrel
only inches from his nose. "Shooting's too good for you,"
she said, "but it'll have to do."

Horror inched across his face; it started in his eyes, lit them
with a shining terror, then stiffened the muscles of his jaw
and cheeks and finally flared his well-formed, aristocratic
nostrils until they looked as if they would explode. Silas, too,
stood frozen and silent, except for the sound of his breath
whistling from his lungs. The exquisite mantel clock made
the only other noise. Its measured ticking resounded through
the white and gold salon like the ominous prelude to a bomb.

"You're crazy!" Jason's voice was a hoarse croak. "You'll
hang if you shoot me. Is that what you want?"

Suddenly, Silas shouted. "Grab it, Jason. She won't shoot," and Jason flung his arm out toward the gun.

Elly squeezed the trigger, but it was too late. Jason knocked the Colt aside, sending the bullet across the room where it shattered a Chinese vase on the mantel and buried itself in the thick oak paneling above the mantelpiece. The explosion crashed in her ears, nearly deafening her. At the same time, Jason wrenched the gun from her grasp, snapping her wrist. She screamed in pain as he stepped back, holding the gun in his right hand. With his left, he hit her hard across the face.

She went down on the Aubusson carpet like a toy soldier felled at play. Pain seemed to envelop her body, from her gunpowder-scorched fingers to her broken wrist to the agonized throbbing of her jaw. Mists of pain floated around her, touched her, burned her, then left her lying cold and floating, like a corpse on a buoyant sea.

From a distance, she heard the sound of running feet, a door opening. Voices inquiring if everything was all right. Silas Emmett's barked reply sent the voices away. Then there were more words, drifting over her.

"She was going to kill me, Father."

She would have laughed at Jason's amazement if she had been able to move her mouth, to lift the terrible fog of pain under which she lay.

"We're damned lucky she didn't. By the devil, I'd like to finish her here and now, but we don't need the trouble. Lord knows, she's caused enough already. The whole damn lot of them have. Troublemakers, every single one. I think, Jason, we'll be better off in Emmettville without any of the Forrests."

"The sooner they're gone, the better." The younger man agreed, his voice filled with contempt.

Tears blurred Elly's vision as she lay listening to them, her cheek pressed against the carpet. Worse than the roaring pain in her jaw or the splintering needles in her wrist was the knowledge of her defeat. She ought to have known better than to try to win out against the Emmetts. They could do just as they pleased, and no one could stop them. Now they would probably throw her in jail, too—and it was all for nothing, because she hadn't even succeeded in shooting Jason, or in winning Caroline's freedom. She was a failure. And what would her failure bring to Mama and Timothy and Caroline? More pain, more uncertainty and unhappiness.

"Get up, you."

She felt the tip of someone's boot in her ribs. The pressure increased. "Get up, damn you. My father has something to tell you."

She began to move slowly to a sitting position. Each movement of her head made her jaw throb with new intensity. Her broken wrist hung limply as she used her other hand to hold the arm of the sofa and drag herself to her feet. Jason and Silas Emmett watched her without a word.

"As of this moment," Silas said at last, "you and your mother are dismissed from the cotton mill. I can't and won't have murderesses, even would-be murderesses, employed in my factories. Or thieves, or Communards. You can pick up your remaining wages from Joe Finch after the day shift tomorrow. Your sister, of course, is no longer employed in this house. And as for pressing charges against her . . ."

Elly lifted bleary eyes to his face.

Silas's lips smiled mirthlessly; his feral eyes gleamed beneath the graying bushy brows. "If you apologize to my son for the false accusations you lodged against him, I'll allow the theft of the necklace to go unpunished. Provided that you leave Emmettville within the week and never set foot in my town again."

Apologize to Jason? Elly felt faint. She swayed and put a hand on the arm of the sofa to steady herself. She glanced at Jason, who was still holding her father's gun, dangling it from the crook of his finger. Smug satisfaction was written in the set of his lips, in the cold lines of his face. Her throat had gone dry. He deserved death for what he'd done to Caroline. Yet nothing bad would befall him; he would suffer no punishment for the unspeakable act he had committed. And she must apologize.

"I . . . can't . . . I won't," she croaked from swollen lips.

"Then your slut of a sister will rot in jail," Jason said.

She wanted to fly at him, to scratch his eyes out, but she held herself motionless before him. He was too large for her. She could not win, could not even inflict any significant injury on him; she would only give him an excuse to strike her again or fling her aside.

"If you can't bring yourself to utter a civil apology, girl, then go on." Silas waved a hand at her, then went to the bellpull and summoned his servant. "We've wasted enough time already. I, for one, am ready for a glass of port. Will you join me, Jason? Good night, Miss Forrest. I'm certain Sheriff Greeves will allow you a quarter-of-an-hour daily to visit your sister.''

"Wait." She croaked the word as the butler appeared once more in the doorway. Silas Emmett appeared not to have heard.

"I trust Mrs. Emmett is well?'' He addressed Duncan brusquely. ''Her maid is with her? Good. Show this young woman out, and then bring us a bottle of port.''

Duncan held the door wide for her, but Elly turned away from him, holding her broken wrist in her good hand. She faced Jason and swallowed back the bile in her throat.

"I apologize.''

"Do you, now? For what?''

"For . . . accusing you.''

"Falsely and maliciously," he prompted.

"Falsely and maliciously.''

"Of harming your tramp of a sister.''

"Yes, yes! Now will you drop the charges tonight and let Caroline come home?''

"I think,'' Silas spoke deliberately, like a judge passing out sentence, ''it would do her good to spend the night in that cell. Tomorrow will be soon enough; let her think meanwhile about the consequences of trying to smear scandal on decent young men. Maybe it will help her in the future.''

"I'd like my father's gun back, please.''

Jason shook his head. ''Consider it a forfeit of war.''

"It's mine!''

"You can't be trusted with a weapon like this. And if you intend to complain that I stole it from you, I'll let it be known that you brought it to my home in order to kill me with it. Now get out before my father changes his mind and decides to press charges against both you and your sister.''

Leaving the house was a blur, as was the long walk home in the gloom of the wood. Elly had never known she could feel so much hate. The hate was there, beneath the numbing daze of pain and humiliation with which she struggled through the glade, hiding herself in the trees, sheltered from the lights of Hyacinth House. Strong and searing as flame, hate burned the depths of her soul, and with it, another emotion: terror. Terror of all the Silas and Jason Emmetts of the world, of her own Grandfather Stevenson, of all the wealthy, powerful men who ruled the fate of the pitiful masses. They were all alike, all the titans who with the sweep of an arm could destroy a life, a family, a future. A deep, abiding rage filled her, rocked her, changed her forever.

One week later, with no jobs, no money, no food, the Forrests loaded their bags into Billy Moffett's wagon and left Emmettville for good.

The Union Depot was a beehive of tumult and activity on the rainy August day when Elly and her family struggled to find their train to Chicago. Billy had driven them to the Emmettville trunk line, which had reached Pittsburgh late in the morning. It had drizzled all day, a hot, humid drizzle that made clothes sticky and damp, and frayed tempers. Elly was grateful to Billy, who had remained their friend despite all that had happened. Most of the people in Emmettville had steered clear of the Forrests after word had gone around, fearing that they too would incur the enmity of the Emmetts if they associated with the outcast family. But Billy, dogged and determined to do the right thing, had insisted on driving them to the railroad station, and he had looked sad and miserable when Elly had impulsively kissed him good-bye. Now he was gone from their lives forever, for he would never leave the town where he had been born, and Elly had vowed never to return. Casting anxious glances about her to be certain that they didn't become separated from one another, she fought hard to herd her family toward the Chicago-bound train.

"This way, Mama," she shouted, then winced as a stout woman in a purple-feathered hat elbowed her in the ribs. She held tightly to Timothy's hand, ignoring the pain of her broken wrist, pulling him this way and that as she tried to steer through the jabbering throng. In her good hand, she clutched the suitcase that held the few clothes and belongings she had brought with her. The furniture—what little hadn't been sold—would be shipped later when they could afford it. For now, they had three trunks stuffed with clothes, books, and the few sentimental objects Bess couldn't bear to part with.

By the time they reached the correct track and turned their baggage over to a porter, Elly's hairpins had come loose and the hem of her brown merino dress was soaked and torn. Behind her, she saw her mother shepherding Caroline, who looked terrified of the crowds and noise. Tooting whistles, belching black smoke, a roar of shouts, and the great hiss and thunder of the trains themselves created an atmosphere of bedlam. The odors of perspiration, rain, and horse manure from the street resulted in an almost overwhelming stench. Elly gritted her teeth and hung on to Timothy's hand as she neared the boarding steps, jostled on every side. Her arm ached from lugging the heavy suitcase, but she kept her eyes on her destination and, at last, reached it.

"Careful on the steps, Mama," she called breathlessly over her shoulder, then realized that Timothy's hand was no longer in hers.

"Timothy!" She spun about on the top step, and scanned the bobbing crowds frantically. "Timothy!"

"You're blocking the way."

"Move! We want to board the train!"

"Get out of the way!"

Angry passengers thrust her aside. Bess's face registered her panic.

"Where is he?"

"I don't know. He must have let go of my hand when we started up the steps—oh, there he is."

Relief flooded through her, and she almost laughed as she saw Timothy, perched atop a man's shoulders, point to them with an excited shriek. The man began walking toward them.

"Oh, thank goodness," Bess murmured, and leaving Caroline with Elly, she threaded her way toward the boy. Elly turned her attention to getting herself and Caroline aboard. This time they made it inside and worked their way down the narrow aisle until they found four seats together. Before long, Bess joined them.

"What happened to you?" Elly scolded Timothy, as he slipped into the seat across the aisle from her. The train was crowded and thick with dust.

"Someone stepped on my toe, and I let go of your hand. Then I couldn't see you. I was lost. But a nice man picked me up and put me on his shoulders so I could find you."

"Next time, don't let go of my hand, no matter what." Elly pushed a wisp of hair from her eyes and let out a long sigh. She settled her rain-spattered skirts more comfortably around her. ''Well, at least we're safely on the train. We'll be in Chicago with Aunt Adelaide before we know it.''

A dark-haired man working his way up the aisle peered at Caroline and smiled. She looked strikingly pretty, if wan, in her blue, puffed-sleeve dress, her hair tied back with a blue ribbon. She paled when she saw him looking at her. With ice-cold fingers, she clutched Elly's hand. Her eyes dropped to her lap until he moved past.

''It's all right, Caro. He was only being friendly.'' Caroline's fingers squeezed hers so tightly it hurt. ''Everything's all right now,'' Elly said quietly. ''We'll make a new beginning in Chicago. You'll see. You'll be happy again when we're away from Pennsylvania.''

Privately, Elly wondered if her sister would ever be happy again. She guessed that Mama suspected what had truly happened in the woods that night, but that she didn't want to know the whole truth and was content to accept the story of a fall to explain Caroline's bruises. The truth would have been too much for her to bear. The events of the past week had marked her even more drastically than Papa's death. She now seemed a ghostly imitation of the once strong and dignified woman who had borne her life's lot with such grace. Elly felt a huge responsibility as the train chugged its way out of Pittsburgh amid smoke and fumes. Not only did she have to look out for Caroline and Timothy, but she had to care for Mama, too. Her mother needed her protection and her strength.

She stared through the mist of rain at the crammed, factory-dotted city as they left Pittsburgh behind, then at the rolling blue-green hills of the craggy Pennsylvania countryside. Despite what she told the others, she gained little peace of mind in running away. There were rich men and bosses in Chicago, too. The powerful and cruel were everywhere, and they would take advantage of anyone in their path. She could think of no protection against them, save one. She had to become equally powerful, equally wealthy. Then men like Silas and Jason Emmett would not be able to harm her or her family ever again.

But how? How? Closing her eyes in exhaustion, she leaned back in her seat, vowing deep in her heart to find a way.

❧ Seven

O'MALLEY'S SALOON WAS noisy, hot, fetid, and crawling with flies. Old scarred tables and wobbly-legged chairs crowded the soot-blackened floor, while lanterns cast a yellowish light on beamed walls and ceiling and illuminated the sticky grime coating the wooden serving bar. The stench of sweat and tobacco fumes choked the place. A rat, fat and wary, nibbled at a crust of bread that had fallen behind a crate. Still, despite the filth and squalor, O'Malley's was one of the less vile dramshops in downtown Pittsburgh. The men from the iron mills and foundries who frequented the place were not evil or dangerous transients, like many who filled the saloons near the factories and river. They were just workingmen who had come off a shift or were about to report for one, and who sought solace and refreshment in the spirits Michael O'Malley so gladly provided.

A dozen or so men from the Mason Iron Works, finished with the day shift, hunched over their beer tankards, intent on squelching the thirst brought on by twelve hours in the sweltering factory. It was nearly nine o'clock, and outside, the sun had already set over the river in a swirl of orange flames. Windows had been thrown open, but barely a breeze stirred in the taproom to relieve the oppressive heat that tormented the men.

The two workers who sat at a small square table in the rear of the saloon had scarcely touched their brew. One of the men talked in a swift, steady stream, while the other, leaning on his elbows, listened, intent and thoughtful.

The speaker was the handsomer of the two. A tall, muscular young Irishman with black hair and blue eyes, he exuded an aura of energy, animation, and confident charm. The listener, a strapping, sandy-haired giant who appeared to be in his early twenties, had a quieter air. He seemed caught up in the words of his companion, yet a cool and skeptical expression remained on his face.

"Wait, Con." Boone Walker interrupted, as Connor Maguire leaned forward in his excitement and nearly knocked over the tankard before him. Boone waited until the Irishman had grabbed it and set it to rights before saying carefully, "Do you know for a fact that Louis Whitcomb wants to buy land on the Monongahela or is this some of your Irish whimsy?"

"Fact." Connor's blue eyes blazed with excitement. He gripped the edges of the table. "He wants to start an iron foundry. It's perfect, Boone, perfect! He already owns one of the largest blast furnaces in Pittsburgh and a rolling mill in Beaverton. Now he is expanding. This is it, Boone, I tell you—the chance we've been watching for."

"The servant girl told you this—the one whose brother drives Whitcomb's carriage?"

"Susan, yes. I was with her last night." Connor leaned forward and banged his fist on the table. "We're going to do it, Boone—we're really going to make our fortune!"

"Maybe." Slowly, a smile spread over Boone's face. He was beginning to catch some of Connor's excitement. For the first time in months, a promising opportunity lay before them, a chance to start their joint climb to success. There had been many times in the past months and years when Boone had wondered if it was his lot to wander the earth forever, never anchored to any one place, never making anything of himself. He had even wondered if that was his penance, his punishment for past offenses. But something inside him had always driven him on, seeking, wanting something more and better, yet never understanding what it was he sought. Success, maybe. Money, power. Every man wanted those things, didn't he? Yet few got them. He wanted to be one of those few, and he meant to make it happen. Already he had a plan.

Maybe, he thought again, as Connor took a quick gulp of his beer. Maybe this was the time when it would begin, when things would start to fall into place for him. Maybe Louis Whitcomb would provide the answer.

Yet caution still kept a rein on his enthusiasm. Over the years, he had learned to be wary. "We'll have to handle

Whitcomb just right,'' he warned, tapping a finger absently against the rough table. ''If he's as shrewd a businessman as I suspect—and he must be, if what they write about him in the *Gazette* is true—he won't be easy to convince.''

''Susan says he drives a calash—and right dashing it is, too. Maybe this time next year, I'll have one of my own, and a grand house to go with it and as fine a suit of clothes as . . . What are you laughing at?'' ·

Boone stopped chuckling long enough to take a long draft of his beer. ''You and your highfalutin ambitions, Con,'' he retorted. ''We haven't even approached Louis Whitcomb yet, and already you have our fortunes made and spent.''

Maguire threw up his hands, exasperated. ''Not every man is as damned practical-minded and cautious as you. Some of us know how to dream, Boone Walker.''

Boone stared at him, his cool gray eyes hard and level. ''I share your dream, Connor. You know that. Or have you forgotten?''

For a moment, the Irishman looked abashed. After all, it had been Boone's idea to buy the land on the river. He had foreseen its value as a site for the steel plant they one day intended to build, had foreseen the need of a partner with wealth enough to undertake such a formidable project, and had foreseen the need to start with something smaller, like a foundry or a rolling mill. Boone had planned it all out. Steel was the metal of the future, he had decided, back when they had first come to Pittsburgh and started working in the Mason foundry. He had made up his mind to become a part of it—somehow, anyhow—and Connor, sensing the possibilities in the plan, had eagerly thrown in with him.

At nineteen, Boone Walker was a year younger than Connor Maguire, but he had the look and maturity of a man in his twenties. He stood well over six feet, having outgrown all of his brothers in the years following his thirteenth birthday. He was broad-shouldered and immensely strong, his muscles hardened by railroad work and the succession of other jobs he had undertaken since leaving home six years ago. His sandy hair, piercing gray eyes, and aggressive features combined to give him a look of toughness, yet there was about him an air of discipline, strength, self-control, and shrewd intelligence, which distinguished him from most of the other workmen and had helped him rise to his present supervisory position at the iron foundry. For all his height and rugged demeanor, and despite his air of quiet determination, his appearance lacked the flashiness that the more dramatically handsome Connor Maguire exuded naturally. Boone knew this, but didn't care. Connor attracted women the way a dish of cream drew purring kittens, but Boone hadn't the time for, or the interest in, courting and wooing. When he felt the need of a woman, there was always a plentiful selection of whores to choose from in the working district of any city. Boone, steady and commanding in the presence of men, found himself abominably awkward among the female sex and was glad to leave that pursuit to Connor. It was work that interested him, but no longer merely as a means of making enough money to get by. He meant to do more than that. He would find his place, *make* his place—no matter what it took.

Their friendship had sprung up when they were working on the Union Pacific Railroad, breaking their backs day after day laying track across Wyoming and Utah. When the last rail had been laid in Promontory, and Leland Stanford, had drive a golden spike into a silver tie to think, and sometimes to dream about what he meant to achieve. Connor brought him here to O'Malley's frequently, though, injecting some of his own high-spirited congeniality into Boone's more serious nature.

Their friendship had sprung up when they were working on the Union Pacific Railroad, breaking their backs day after day laying track across Wyoming and Utah. When the last rail had been laid in Promontory, and Leland Stanford, had driven a golden spike into a silver tie to officially complete the railroad, everyone had rejoiced in a triumphant celebration. But for Boone and Connor and the other men who had worked so furiously to finish the project, a letdown had followed. What next? Where could they turn their energies, which for so long had been entirely consumed by the tremendous challenge of laying track across empty prairie, bridging the civilized East with the untamed West?

The morning he and Connor had left the railroad camp, his supervisor had summoned Boone to his office.

"Well, Walker, where you aiming to go now?" Ed Burrows—five feet two, barrel-chested, and shrewd—had eyed him from across a paper-strewn desk. "You're too smart to spend your life laying rails, Walker. It's backbreaking and too damn dangerous. You're young, and you have a good way with men. I haven't told this to many fellows in your shoes, but you've impressed me. You're not afraid of hard work, and you have a way of inspiring others to join in with you. Those could be valuable qualities.''

"Thank you, sir.'' Boone had stared at him in surprise, a pleased flush spreading up his neck. "I don't know where to go or what I'm looking to do, but I'd appreciate any suggestions.''

Ed Burrows had leaned forward, resting his elbows on the sea of papers covering his desk. "There's a fellow in Pittsburgh name of Cal Yates. He's foreman at the Mason Iron Works. If you need a job and you don't mind the stink and the soot of Pittsburgh, go see him and tell him I sent you.''

"An iron works?'' Boone had considered the idea quickly, trying to recall all he had ever read or heard about Pittsburgh. It was the indisputable center of the iron and steel industries; that much he knew for certain. With all the changes in the country—the expansion of the railroads and the settling of the West—the metals used for laying tracks and building bridges were in greater demand than ever. If the boom continued, as Boone guessed it would, there would be a need for more and more iron, for steel, and for the coke and ore and limestone needed for their production. A man could get rich being in the center of all that industry, Boone had reflected with a flickering of excitement. A man could make a place for himself. Boone had reached swiftly across the desk to shake Burrows's hand in genuine gratitude. "Thank you, Mr. Burrows. I appreciate this. I'll think seriously on your idea. It's kind of you to suggest it.''

In the months that followed, he and Connor had both found work at the Mason Iron Works, he in the foundry department, and Connor in the rolling mill. Over the past two years, Boone had been fascinated by the frenzied tumult of the mills, by the soot-spouting smokestacks, the roaring blast furnace, the hundreds of men working night and day in the fiery pit that was Pittsburgh's industrial core. But Boone had not been content merely to work and learn and take home his dollar-fifty a day. He had talked to people in the mills themselves and in the taverns; he read the *Gazette* eagerly and with scrupulous thoroughness, and he became convinced early on that there was a fortune to be made in the mills of Pittsburgh, but that that fortune would be earned not through iron, but through the manufacture of a superior metal, stronger, greater, more costly, and infinitely more durable: steel.

"Sorry, Boone," Connor said now, in genuine contrition as he recalled how much of their plan they owed to Boone. "Sometimes my Irish tongue gets away from me, and I sound like a damned idiot. I know you want to make your fortune every bit as much as I do."

"Forget it." Boone responded with his ready smile, the moment of tension dismissed. "We'll go to see Whitcomb tomorrow after the shift ends. And we'll . . . damn!"

"What's the matter?"

"I haven't got a decent suit of clothes and neither have you. We can't call on Whitcomb in these." He grinned, with a wry glance at his sweat-soaked flannel work shirt and the overalls that hung from his big shoulders and fit loosely over his lanky frame.

"There's only one answer for it, my lad," Connor said. "We'll both of us have to visit Jonas McDowell's dry goods store. We'll need some finery if we're to impress Whitcomb."

"We can't afford finery." Boone swallowed the last of his beer, wiped his mouth on his sleeve, and frowned.

"We can't afford anything less." Connor eyed him with an air of sagacity. "You've got to look like a swell if you want to become a swell, my lad. Mark my words."

"Maybe only one of us should go to see Whitcomb. We could pool our money and buy one good set of clothes. The only problem," Boone went on, pursing his lips thoughtfully, "would be in deciding which of us should put the plan forward."

"You can do that," Connor conceded with a grin. "It's your plan, after all. My silver tongue might do us some good, but when it all comes down to it, you're the one men tend to trust. Now, if there was a woman involved, it'd be a different story . . ."

At that moment there was a shout at the other end of the barroom. Boone and Connor swung around. Two men were engaged in an arm-wrestling match at a table in the center of the floor. Half a dozen customers had clustered around to watch.

"Connor," Boone began, knowing what his friend had in mind even before he came to his feet and stood staring at the struggling contestants. "Forget it. Save your money. We'll need every dollar, especially if Whitcomb agrees to our proposal."

"Aye, we will, Boone, and this is my chance to win a bit extra to put behind us," Connor replied with a confident laugh, his gaze never leaving the combat taking place near the bar. "Maybe we'll both have new suits of clothes after all." He grinned, showing handsome white teeth.

Boone shook his head as the Irishman strode away. He couldn't suppress a sigh. His friend loved a wager more than any man he'd ever met. Connor Maguire might be many things, but he was never dull company.

Boone put money down to pay for their beers, then got up to join the men surrounding the other table. A huge, red-faced German had just wrested an equally large opponent's burly arm to the table.

The moment the loser of the contest rose from his seat, Connor stepped forward. He tapped the victor on the shoulder. "I'm next, lad. Ten dollars says I can best you quicker than the bartender can pour ale for a dozen men."

The red-faced man peered in surprise at Connor's slim, well-muscled physique and his merry smile. "Why, you're on, Paddy." His German accent was as thick as his middle. A big grin spread across his features as the onlookers made room for Connor to take his seat.

An ironworker from the Mason plant waved his money in the air. "I'm with you, Connor Maguire!"

"Moose, Moose!" A chant rose up from the pushing, eager men who worked at the Blakely mill.

"Moose?" Connor's gaze met his opponent's grinning countenance.

"That's what they call me, Paddy. But my name is Fritz Bruiner." The German must have been close to forty, with straight, pale hair and a bushy mustache. His jowly cheeks were the color of ripe tomatoes, and he had a one-inch scar alongside his nose. But it was his eyes that drew Connor's attention and elicited a small shiver within him. They were small, pale blue, and cold as ice. Something that could only be described as malicious pleasure shone from those frigid blue depths. "They say I'm strong as a moose," he went on in his guttural voice. "And it's true, you know. I am. But you'll be finding that out for yourself, now, won't you?"

"I suppose I will," Connor replied with great cheerfulness, but for the first time he seemed to take in the gigantic proportions of the red-faced man who was now rolling up his sleeves to reveal thick, hairy arms with muscles the size of melons. Jeering laughter circled through the crowd as Connor stared at him and then gazed boldly about the room. "Anyone care to bet against me now?"

Shouts of assent filled the smoky air. "Sheep ready for the shearing!" Connor announced, and everyone laughed as he rolled up his sleeves. He glanced pointedly at the corded muscles of his own arm and then at Bruiner's giant physique. "Twenty dollars! I'm wagering twenty dollars on my own self to beat this Moose fair and square. Fair and square, my lads! A Mason man against the Blakely mill's Moose! Come, come, lads, what will it be?"

He sounded like a damned barker at a county fair, Boone thought with a grimace. Count on Connor to stir up the simmering rivalry between the two plants. Excitement buzzed through the taproom after his words.

"Win or lose, all drinks are on me!" Connor shouted suddenly, as he plunked his elbow on the table. He raised his arm to wrestling position with slow, dramatic flourish and laughingly turned to Fritz Bruiner. "Get ready, my lad, and let's go on with the battle, before the bell clangs summoning you and your fellows to your shift at the mill. I wouldn't want to lose the opportunity of defeating you before this fine throng!"

Even Bruiner laughed. It was impossible not to respond to Connor's affably outrageous statements and confident charm. Only Boone watched in silence, trying to control his irritation that Connor continued to risk his hard-earned pay on foolish wagers even though they had decided to pool every extra penny toward the formation of their company and the eventual building of their own steel mill. Well, Boone had known what he was getting when he had allowed Connor to throw in with him on the Monongahela land deal. Yet for all his gambling stunts and occasional daredevil antics, Connor understood both money and people, a trait that made him good material for a business partner. Boone also knew that Connor had ten younger brothers and sisters who were crowded into a Lower East Side tenement in New York, and that he sent money home to them with regularity. Beneath the affable devil-may-care exterior was a man who had suffered a miserably impoverished boyhood and who was determined to climb from the stench and filth of the slum pits and to pull his family up after him. Boone only hoped that Connor wouldn't gamble away every precious cent they needed to build their future.

Boone watched Connor and the monstrous German grip hands and lean toward each other over the table. With a grunt from both men, the contest began. Connor lasted longer than Boone expected. Sheer determination kept his fist in the air as he battled against the German's superior strength for agonizing moments. Edging past the ring of onlookers, Boone noticed the sweat shining on Connor's reddened face, saw the tight cording of the Irishman's muscles as he exerted every ounce of his energy trying to force Bruiner's arm back and down. Yet, slowly, painfully, the German overpowered him, grinning broadly all the while, his head bobbing.

"I win, eh? Pay up, Paddy Maguire."

Cheers from the Blakely men greeted his triumphant declaration.

Connor was gingerly flexing his crushed fingers. "I'm afraid there's a bit of a problem with that," he began, and Boone groaned inwardly.

Fritz Bruiner's grin faded. "Problem? What problem?"

Connor shrugged. "I'm short on cash—temporarily, of course. I've no more than a few dollars in my pockets tonight. But I'll pay you . . ."

"Damned right you will!"

". . . tomorrow," Connor finished quickly, licking the sweat off his upper lip.

Fury descended over the German's face, and a rumble of disapproval spread around the room. The previous goodwill of the saloon's patrons was vanishing; their mood had changed the moment Connor lost the match.

"No! Not tomorrow! You will pay me tonight, you filthy Irish welsher!" Purple blotches now stained Bruiner's puffed cheeks as he lunged across the table and grabbed Connor's worn shirt. "If there's anything I hate," he bellowed, "it's a mick who won't pay his debts!" He shoved his huge fist against Connor's nose. "Twenty dollars now, Maguire, or I'll mop the floor with you."

The onlookers had all backed off when the trouble began.

Only Boone still remained near the little square table. *Damn it*, he thought to himself. Why did Connor always get himself into these situations? Boone hesitated, tempted to step back like the others and let Connor get out of this himself. Maybe it would teach him something.

He waited and watched.

"Let me go, you damned kraut!" Connor wrenched free of the German's grasp, his shirtfront ripping in the process. His blue eyes shone with wrath. "I said you'll get your money and you will!"

"I want it now." Fritz Bruiner shook his fist, his entire body trembling. "You will give it to me now, Maguire, or I'll fix you so you never arm-wrestle another man! I'll break both your arms, and your legs, too."

Connor had paled at the German's threat, but he couldn't back down now. Doing so would label him a coward. He stuck out his chin. "You're free to try."

Oh, hell. Boone stepped forward, disgusted with Connor and with himself. "There's not going to be any fighting," he said.

Immediately, silence fell over the rowdy ring of onlookers.

"Who the hell are you?" Bruiner turned on him angrily, taking in the large proportions of the sandy-haired young man who spoke with such quiet authority. "Stay out of it, or you'll get the same as him."

"I'm the man who's going to pay you, Bruiner. At least, I'll pay you part of what he owes."

Boone saw the relief in Connor's eyes. Then he heard Fritz Bruiner's jeering laughter. "What's this, a friend? So. Your friend is going to pay your debt for you, eh, Maguire? And you're going to let him, aren't you, you chicken-hearted little mick?"

Connor flushed and clenched his fists. Boone knew what was going through his friend's mind. Part of him wanted to accept Boone's help in settling the debt peaceably, but his pride, and the German's taunts, demanded that he face Bruiner alone.

"Never mind, Boone," Connor said hurriedly. He gritted his teeth, forcing himself to say what honor required of him. "I'll settle this myself."

"The hell you will." Boone locked gazes with the German. The man was a bully, no doubt about it. Boone had

always hated a bully. This one was no different from Caleb
Dunne or Ezra Wells. And experience had taught him that
there were only two ways to handle a bully: you could meet
him head on, or you could run like hell. Running didn't
always work—Boone had discovered that. He shifted his
shoulders, ignored the ache in his stomach that always as-
sailed him before a fight, and took out his wallet. Contemptuously, he slapped some bills on the table in front of the
German. "You said you wanted payment tonight, Bruiner, so
here's eleven dollars. You can get the remainder tomorrow.
Take it or leave it."

For a moment Bruiner just stared at him. Then renewed
fury broke over his face like waves crashing against a rock.
This big sandy-haired bastard dared to speak to him like that!
To him! *Take it or leave it*. He was accustomed to men
scurrying out of his way, apologizing if he happened to
collide with them, laughing nervously at his jokes. But not
this! Especially in front of an audience. His muscles bunched,
tightened, and a cord twitched in his thick neck. He opened
his mouth and bellowed, "I will leave it, you sniveling son of
a bitch! I'll take it out of your hide as well as your friend's!"

With this, he seized the table on which Boone had placed
the money. He hefted it high in the air.

"Look out!" Connor yelled, just as Bruiner heaved the
table with murderous force right at Boone's head.

🌿 Eight

BOONE DODGED TO the right just in time. The table crashed and
splintered against the floor where he had been standing.
Bruiner rushed at him, and Boone swung his fist. He hit the
German square in the eye.

All about him fighting had broken out as the men from the rival mills turned on one another. Boone had no time to notice, for Bruiner wasted not a moment recovering from the blow. He charged in on Boone, his huge fists flying, and hit him hard in the face and then the stomach and then in the face again. Before Boone could escape, Bruiner grabbed him and hurled him against the serving bar. Pain and blinking light exploded in Boone's skull.

Dazed, he glanced up in time to see the German running at him yet again. He rolled aside, came to his feet in a smooth motion, and delivered a cruel right punch to Bruiner's midsection. The German doubled over in pain.

The din in the saloon was incredible. Everywhere men swore and screamed and grunted, furniture crashed against wood or human bone, the bartender yelled for order. The place reeked of spilled beer, and puddles of it soaked the floor. Suddenly, above the uproar, the clatter of hooves and the shriek of whistles from the street signaled the approach of the police wagon.

Bruiner's head jerked up from his chest. His hands were still splayed on his middle, and he was gasping for breath after Boone's punch, yet with surprising alacrity, he made a dive for the scattered money on the floor, scooped up the bills, and stuffed them into his trousers pocket. "I'll collect the rest next time, Maguire!" he shouted, as he hurtled toward the door in an effort to escape before the police burst in. He flung men right and left out of his path as he ran, before lunging through the saloon door.

"Come on," Boone yelled as Connor ducked a flying chair, which landed on the bar and sent a dozen pewter tankards skittering to the floor. "If we don't get out of here quick, we'll be spending the night in the lockup."

Jumping across flailing men and broken table legs, they picked their way behind the serving bar and through the rear of the tavern. As Connor pushed open the alley door, they heard the clamor of police whistles and boots stomping through the tavern.

Outside, the air was hot and stifling, the sky lit with flame and smoke from mill furnaces and chimneys all over the city. Noise from the factories and blast furnaces, the river and its boats clamored all around them. Pittsburgh never slept. It was an inferno, a continuous sweatshop of toiling men, black smoke, and molten heat. The smokestacks belched dark plumes all through the day and night, the factories crawled with workers during every hour. The skyline, with its iron bridges and tortuous hills, its endless rows of drab industrial buildings, resembled a drawing of hell rather than a city, and the narrow, filthy streets, workers' hovels, and dramshops all crammed into the factory district reinforced the impression of ugliness and squalor.

Boone and Connor pulled themselves up onto a passing horsecar, which would take them to their boardinghouse in old Allegheny. The car was nearly empty, and they staggered eagerly toward seats. Blood smeared their work shirts, and Boone had a purpling bruise on his jaw. Connor's left eye was swollen and already discoloring. Both men were soaked with perspiration.

"We're a sight, my lad," Connor laughed, examining his raw knuckles and torn shirt with amazing cheerfulness. He noticed a horrified shopgirl staring at them from across the aisle. She turned scarlet as he grinned and winked at her.

"We're getting too old for this, Con." Boone wiped his sweating face with his sleeve. His jaw ached like the devil. "Next time you want a suicide fight with a mad German, count me out of it."

"I can't understand why you had such a hard time of it tonight," Connor said amiably. "I've seen you handle two, three men at a time. You must be slipping."

Boone ignored his friend's teasing. He was noticing the shopgirl. Her figure was full and lush, yet without plumpness. "I'm not slipping, Con," he said almost absently, smiling tentatively at the girl. Her eyes slid away from his to study the toes of her heavy dark shoes. "It's just that I've learned fighting's not always the answer."

The girl glanced up again, her eyes shifting from Connor to Boone, then back to Connor again. Boone sighed as Connor gave her a devastating smile, which she returned, shifting the weight of her parcel to her other arm. He was accustomed to the effect his friend's dark good looks had on women, and he knew it was the one area in which he couldn't compete with Con.

Connor stood as the car reached the outskirts of Pittsburgh. "Promised Susan I'd come by tonight and take her for a stroll. She can bandage up my hurts for me and give aid and comfort. And, Boone,'' he said, turning back briefly on his way to the door, ''thanks for helping me out back there. I'd have been done for without you.''

''I know it.'' Boone laughed. ''You were almost done for *with* me.''

Their eyes met for a moment, and they stared at each other. Understanding and friendship passed between them then without spoken words. Then Connor stepped from the car.

Boone settled back in the seat, feeling his muscles throb. Through the car window, the shopgirl watched Connor saunter away, her face reflecting her disappointment. Glancing at her, Boone tried to think of something to say. At the next intersection, the girl rose and walked down the aisle. Suddenly in the midst of the August night, Boone felt indescribably lonely. He watched the shopgirl get off the car, her brown hair brushing her cheek. In the darkness below the flickering gas jet of the corner lamp, she slipped as she descended. Then she straightened and, without a backward glance, began to walk down the street. Boone knew that Connor could have caught her attention with a single word. But the horsecar rolled on, and the shopgirl disappeared behind him.

By the time he left the horsecar in old Allegheny, the tenderness of his jaw had worsened. It hurt with every step he took. Clenching his teeth against the pain, he pushed his hands into his overalls pockets and turned down Rebecca Street toward the roominghouse he and Connor called home. His footsteps lagged as he reached the little wooden house with the sagging porch and small rear yard. He shouldered past the front door, nodded to the landlady, Mrs. Shepherd, as she passed him in the hall, and took the narrow steps up to his second-floor room two at a time. There he stripped off his sweaty work shirt, flung himself down on the bed, and stared morosely up at the cracked plaster of the ceiling.

No breeze disturbed the torn curtains at his open window. Even this late at night, the air remained hot and stifling, and Boone felt the sweat gather on his brow and his chest, running in rivulets as he lay with his arms crossed beneath his head. The little room was plain and cheerless, and seemed far too tiny for his massive frame. Newspapers littered the floor, and flies buzzed at the curtains. Soiled laundry lay in a heap in the corner. Yet it was home, the one place that belonged to him. He had no other.

As he lay there, Boone thought back on the fight in the tavern. A faint tang of disgust soured his mouth as he remembered. Fighting, always fighting. Ever since that first battle with Caleb Dunne, it seemed that violence had dogged him. In the years since he had left home, he had been forced to make his way in the world of men and to earn their acceptance. He had mingled with lumberjacks and dockworkers and had learned rough ways. But he had long ago forgotten the joy that came with victory. Now he felt only weariness when he looked down at a man he had beaten. It always reminded him of . . .

Boone broke off his thoughts, unable to complete the sentence, even in his mind. All that was behind him now. He could never go home to Kentucky again, never see his mother or Clay or little Rose, so there was no use thinking about it. The past was done. But the future—the future was open to him, and anything could happen. There was one thing of which Boone was certain: he sure as hell wasn't going to spend the rest of his life in squalid roominghouses and smoky taverns. And he wasn't going to spend it taking orders and bringing home less than two dollars a day while the iron- and steelmasters lived like kings. The way Boone saw it, he would end up either washed out and beaten and old before he turned forty or, like Andrew Carnegie and Louis Whitcomb, vigorous and wealthy, planning, building, controlling his own life and destiny. He had made his choice years ago, and buying the land on the Monongahela had been the first step toward achieving his goal. Now it was time to implement the next step. That's where Louis Whitcomb came in.

Boone got off the bed and went to the bureau, sticky with the sweat that ran down his armpits and dampened the sandy hairs of his chest. He felt better after pouring a pitcherful of tepid water into the washbowl and splashing it over his face, arms, and chest. He winced when his fingers brushed against his injured jaw, and he blinked the pain from his eyes. Then he strode to the window and took a deep breath of the suffocating summer air. Staring out into the darkness at the outlines of the shabby houses and scraggly yards, he leaned an arm against the window frame. The night was thick with stars, the heavens deep blue and lovely above the dreary Allegheny street. But he didn't see the crowning starlit spectacle above or the pitiful desolation of the scene below. All of his thoughts and his will were bent upon one man. He had to persuade Louis Whitcomb to take him and Connor on as partners, to invest in the project he envisioned. But how? How could he interest a man of Whitcomb's wealth and power in accepting two partners with little of tangible value to bring to the deal? How could they begin to move up in the world of industry without someone on top giving them a toehold with which to begin the steep climb that would lead them to the summit of power?

Boone's head ached by the time he lowered the gas jet and got ready to turn in. But he was smiling as he stripped and then tossed back the green quilt. He could sleep now. His mind was at rest.

Once again, he had a plan.

🌿 Nine

DURING THE NEXT week, as usual, Boone and Connor went each day to their jobs in the Mason foundry and rolling mill, but their minds and hearts were full of hope, brimming with anticipation for the future. They stopped one night at O'Malley's, when a cloudburst hit just as they left work, but though they stayed long at the tavern, drinking and talking excitedly, they didn't run into Bruiner or anyone else from the Blakely mills, and Boone, at least, hoped they had seen the last of the fat German. Connor, typically, was unconcerned and even bragged that he would relish the opportunity of shutting Fritz Bruiner up once and for all, but Boone snorted and shook his head, then changed the subject. What most concerned him was the plan for winning Whitcomb's support. Together, he and Connor worked over the details. By the time he had visited McDowell's dry goods store and purchased a new single-breasted frock coat, a waistcoat, checked trousers, and a pair of patent leather button boots, along with a black felt bowler McDowell's clerk assured him was necessary to a gentleman's attire, his excitement had mounted still further. He waited only long enough for the bruise on his jaw to subside, and then, on a humid Monday evening after finishing his shift at the foundry, eating a hurried supper, and washing up and changing at the roominghouse, he set out for Penn Avenue in his fine new garments.

Ready as he was for the challenge that lay before him, he was doomed to be disappointed. The Whitcombs were entertaining guests that evening. His arrival outside the grounds of the estate coincided with the depositing from various carriages of elegantly clad guests at the mansion steps. Boone watched in sharp disappointment. He couldn't interrupt a dinner party—Whitcomb would be furious. He returned home, swallowing back his disappointment. It was no matter, Connor assured him, after Boone explained the situation. Tomorrow he could try again.

The same thing occurred the next night. Only this time it was carriage after carriage that swept along the grand drive, each splendid vehicle filled with magnificently attired passengers. The lights of the mansion on Penn Avenue winked out at the star-sprinkled night, seeming to mock him with their warmth and gaiety. Boone groaned and banged his fist on the iron fence bounding the property. Did Whitcomb entertain every evening of the week? Did the man never sit home with his paper and his wife and go to his bed at a normal hour?

Once again, he returned to the roominghouse in defeat, and this time, Connor shared his frustration. On Wednesday, Boone once more donned his new suit of clothes and fixed his bowler on his head. This time he vowed to see Whitcomb even if it meant interrupting a ceremonial ball.

It was a fine house, Boone noted, as he stood on Penn Avenue shortly after nine-thirty and stared at the white-columned stone mansion where Louis Whitcomb lived. A very fine house. Set in its own private fenced park, it rose gracefully from among the surrounding trees and shrubs like a great elegant swan in still waters. The full moon, aided by glowing lanterns set along the sweeping circular drive, permitted him to glimpse the perfectly clipped shrubs, the well-placed chestnut and maple trees, and the blooming flower beds, which created a lovely setting for the magnificent home nestled within. That home, and its immaculate grounds, seemed to Boone a splendid monument to one man's achievement. Unlike some of the mansions in and around Pittsburgh, it had not been built in the currently popular vogue, which called for a profusion and mixture of styles, with mismatched spires and towers, porches, and cupolas all combined in one home, often with garish results. The Whitcomb house had a classical simplicity that was as pleasing to the eye as it was impressive. Standing outside the grounds, he studied the mansion with interest and some nervousness. That could be his house someday, he told himself. Or one like it. But it wasn't the sumptuous luxury of the mansion that appealed to him. He had never known anything of the sort, so he didn't hunger for something that was beyond his imagination or even his need. It was what the home represented that caused him to regard it so raptly. Success. The man who lived in that house had success, and the wealth and power that went along with it. He knew from newspaper accounts that Louis Whitcomb hadn't been born wealthy. He had inherited a forge from his father and had gradually built it into a major ironmaking business. Of course, it hadn't hurt that his wife had inherited a small glassworking factory upon her father's demise, but it was still Whitcomb himself who had managed those two businesses, building and nurturing them into the giant, thriving successes they were today. *I can do it, too,* Boone told himself. *And I will. If ever I find the gumption to walk up to the door and ask for Whitcomb, that is.*

For the third evening in a row, Whitcomb was apparently hosting a party. During the time Boone had stood outside the intricate wrought-iron fence that surrounded the grounds of the estate, he had seen three carriages roll up the drive and deposit their passengers at the base of the stone steps leading up to the mansion doors. Light shone from the windows of all the rooms on the first floor, as it had for the previous two evenings. Boone didn't care. This night, the third he had come, was going to be his last. He was rapidly reaching the conclusion that Louis Whitcomb and his family did indeed entertain every evening, so that there might never be a time when he wouldn't be disturbing them. He refused to return to the boardinghouse in defeat one more time.

Still, he hesitated, hating to interrupt the dinner party or whatever the hell was going on inside. That would only anger Whitcomb, and Boone wanted to win his confidence and approval. At last, staring at the lighted windows, while carriages and horsecars whooshed by in the street behind him, he decided to wait—however long it took—for the party to break up. When the guests had gone and the house was quiet, he would walk up that grand path, climb the steps of the mansion, and ring the bell.

The guests didn't depart until nearly midnight, and by then Boone's legs ached, and he felt tired and uncomfortably rumpled. He had put in a full shift at the mill today, and tomorrow he had to report for work at eight. His immaculately polished black boots were now caked with dust, and the new waistcoat and jacket were sticking uncomfortably to his large, perspiring frame. Yet he was determined to see Louis Whitcomb before the night was over.

He moved quickly, before he could lose his courage. So much depended on this meeting. His future and Connor's rode on the outcome. Resolutely, he crossed the long drive and approached the house.

Light poured out onto the porch as a uniformed servant opened the carved mahogany doors.

"Yes?" The man—small, mustached, and punctilious—stared at him in astonishment. Boone could well imagine how infrequent were such late-night calls by total strangers. The inappropriateness of his behavior struck him yet again, but he knew that this was the only way he'd get to see Whitcomb. Working at the foundry six days a week left only Sundays free, and he suspected that calling then would be an even worse offense against Whitcomb's privacy. So he ignored the disapproving hauteur on the servant's face and asked to speak to his master.

"Mr. Whitcomb has retired for the evening," the man informed him with a sniff, and began to close the door.

Boone blocked it with one arm and held it ajar. "But his guests left only a moment ago."

"Mr. Whitcomb has retired."

"Listen to me. I must speak with him. It won't take long."

The portly little man eyed him coldly. "Do you have a card, sir?"

"A calling card? No."

"Then there is no point to this discussion. Good night,

sir." Once again he attempted to close the door, and once again Boone prevented him from doing so.

"This won't take long. Just tell him it's a business matter."

"I will do no such thing. Mr. Whitcomb does not conduct business at such an hour of the evening."

And not with riffraff like you. He didn't say it aloud, but Boone read the sentiment in the man's small black eyes. He felt anger coursing through him and tried to restrain himself. What he really wanted was to fell the haughty little bastard with a punch, but instead he said again, with growling patience, "I must speak with him tonight. Tell him Boone Walker is waiting to see him."

"That is out of the question—"

Boone, much stronger than the other man, suddenly pushed the door open and strode across the threshold. He walked quickly into the high-ceilinged hall, elegant with its blue and gold flocked wallpaper, a marble floor, and a fine crystal chandelier that tinkled with the movement of air that accompanied his entrance. He glanced about, started to speak to the outraged and babbling servant, then broke off as he saw the broad and sweeping marble staircase in the center of the large hall and, on the uppermost step, the man he had come to see.

Louis Whitcomb was an imposing figure, with his curling brown hair, mustache, and whiskers, his tailcoat and evening shirt, his gleaming half boots and white silk gloves. Standing on the staircase with his monocle lifted in surprise, he placed a hand on the ornately carved balustrade and snapped at the servant, "Humphreys, what the devil is going on?"

"I tried to stop him, sir. He insisted on seeing you."

"He did, eh?" Whitcomb dropped the monocle and glared at Boone from beneath bushy brows. He was not a tall man, but he was stout, with a thick neck and a face which, behind the reddish brown whiskers, resembled a fox. He spoke in a sharp, commanding voice.

"Young man, get out of this house before I summon the police. You have no business here."

"I do, sir. My business is with you." Boone, under that piercing, unfriendly scrutiny, tried to forget his dusty appearance and concentrate on winning a few moments of Louis Whitcomb's time. If he was thrown out of the house now, he would never have another chance to speak to the man. He spoke quickly, his words rushing together, "I'm sorry for the rude way I came in just now—"

"As well you ought to be."

"—but I've been waiting all evening for your guests to leave so we could talk." Boone plunged on, desperate. "I have an urgent business matter to discuss with you, Mr. Whitcomb. It will be for your own good to hear me out. I won't take more than ten minutes of your time, I guarantee, unless you ask me to stay, which I'm sure you will, sir."

He paused and drew breath, during which time Louis Whitcomb studied him curiously.

The young man before him had obviously gone to great pains to see him, Whitcomb reflected. Against his will, he was intrigued. The fellow was respectably dressed, right down to his bowler, though he looked a bit hot and mussed. But then, if he'd really been waiting outside all evening, that was to be expected. He looked clean, nevertheless, and spoke politely, despite the alarming manner in which he had made his entrance and the slight drawl that tainted his voice. Whitcomb didn't like that drawl. But there was about the fellow an aura of purpose and determination that caught his interest. He was about to utter his consent when his wife's voice distracted him.

"Louis, what is it? Is everything all right?"

Victoria Whitcomb had come to the head of the stairs, still attired in her sage-green gown with the heart-shaped basque waist and demitrain. Her enormous sky-blue eyes widened as she anxiously surveyed the intruder in the hallway. She was a handsome woman, taller than her husband, with a strong chin, a long, thin nose, and finely shaped lips. At forty-five, her figure was still good, her features strong and pleasant to behold, and her bearing was becomingly graceful. Louis Whitcomb, having married her twenty-six years ago, loved her as much this day as he had the day they took their vows.

"Nothing to worry about, my dear," he assured her, and saw her relax.

The young man snatched his bowler off his head at the first sight of the woman, and Whitcomb heard him say, "I didn't mean to scare you, ma'am."

Victoria stiffened at the soft drawl of his voice. She frowned. "Louis?"

"It's all right, my dear. This young man has come to see me about a business matter."

He turned back to Boone. For a moment, hesitation showed in his face.

Boone spoke swiftly, knowing this would be his last chance. "Mr. Whitcomb, after ten minutes I'll wager you will thank me for having come to your door this evening!"

The butler made a derisive sound. Boone tensed. He heard a clock ticking somewhere, heard the quiet movements and talk of servants in the parlor and dining room to his left. They were clearing the rooms after the evening's entertainment. He felt three pairs of eyes fixed on his every move, and he silently prayed the outcome would be in his favor. For a moment, standing there, with the butler staring at him coldly and Louis Whitcomb's sharp gaze examining him and the woman's cool scrutiny from above, he wished that he had let Connor do this damned thing. Connor would have charmed Whitcomb's wife, at the very least. His entrance would have been graceful and polished. Deep down, Boone had believed that he could present a more solid and practical proposal and that he was right not to risk everything on Connor's glib tongue. But just now, pinned by those three pairs of disapproving eyes, with everything riding on the decision made in the next few seconds, he wished he were anywhere else but in Louis Whitcomb's hallway. In fact, he wished he had never heard of the man and his iron company.

His stomach started to hurt. He felt sweat gathering at his temples. Then Louis Whitcomb's voice broke the silence.

"What did you say your name was, young man?"

"Walker—Boone Walker."

"Humphreys, summon Davies and Phipps. Prepare to assist them in ejecting Mr. Walker from this house in ten minutes—unless I order you otherwise."

"Yes, sir." From the butler's tone, it was obvious that he was shocked by his employer's decision, but Boone felt euphoric. At least he would be given a chance to air his proposition.

The woman spoke again. "Louis, are you quite certain . . . ?"

"I'm curious to hear what the young man has to say, Victoria. I'll join you shortly, my dear."

Victoria Whitcomb gave Boone the briefest of nods before

turning with a sweep of her bustled skirt and disappearing along the upper corridor.

Whitcomb descended the stairs, and Boone followed him into his library. He had never seen so many books. Volume after volume filled the glass-fronted bookcases that lined two full walls of the room. Engravings and oil paintings hung above the mantel and on every available space of wall. Boone recognized one popular lithograph. It had been made the year before by Otto Krebs, and depicted a panoramic vision of Pittsburgh and its surrounding cities, Birmingham and Allegheny. On the large walnut desk Boone saw books, a few papers, an inkstand, and a framed photograph. Above, a gas chandelier hung from the muraled ceiling, and suspended from this was a shaded desk lamp. The marble fireplace, whose empty hearth was decorated by an ironwork fan during this season, boasted a marble clock and a pair of brass candlesticks. There were some armchairs set about the Oriental carpet, a few of cane, the others upholstered in maroon leather, which matched the draperies. Whitcomb seated himself in one such upholstered chair behind the desk and motioned Boone into another. Then he eyed the younger man from beneath those intimidating, bushy brows.

"I believe nine minutes remain, Mr. Walker."

Boone grimaced. Whitcomb wasn't going to make this easy on him. With his fingers crushing the felt brim of his bowler, he began to talk.

"I'm the day foreman at the Mason Iron Foundry, Mr. Whitcomb. I've held that position for eight months now, since Cal Yates retired and recommended me as his successor. I know nearly everything there is to know about the manufacture of iron, and what I don't know, my partner, Connor Maguire does. He works in Mason's rolling mill. Together we'd like to join you in a business venture on the Monongahela River."

"I'm certain you would." Whitcomb gave a bark of laughter. He tugged at his mustache, drawing it between the tips of his fingers. "What kind of venture would I be interested in pursuing with a couple of workmen from the Mason mills?"

"An iron foundry. You're planning one on the river, aren't you?"

Whitcomb blinked. "How the blazes did you know that?"

"That's not important." Boone wasn't about to give away

Susan or her brother. "What matters is that Mr. Maguire and I own considerable acreage on the Monongahela, and we'd be willing to contribute the land to a partnership."

Whitcomb sat up straight in his chair and stared at Boone incredulously. "Are you proposing that I invest my capital in the foundry while you supply the river valley land on which to build it?"

"Yes. But—"

"By George, that's rich." Whitcomb gave another snort of laughter, cutting off Boone's words. This time there was anger as well as scorn in his face. "Do you realize, Walker, that what you're suggesting is a vastly unequal partnership?"

"I know it sounds that way, but—"

"You expect me to invest the many thousands of dollars necessary for the construction of the foundry while you contribute a few acres of river valley land? No doubt you and your partner expect fifty percent of the company in exchange!"

Boone flushed. "Of course not." He went on cautiously, "We were thinking of fifteen or twenty percent."

Whitcomb's face grew red. "You ignorant young jackass. What kind of a fool do you take me for? I can buy my own land on the river and find my own partners—men who can put up forty, fifty percent of the capital needed for an investment of this kind. You have nothing of value to offer me. Anyone but a simpleton would see that. You have wasted my time and your own. Good night." He rose and stalked toward the door.

Boone struggled to hide the panic rising in him. He followed the other man, talking quickly all the while. "Mr. Whitcomb, I haven't finished. Our land on the Monongahela is prime property. The location is ideal—near the Pennsylvania and the Baltimore and Ohio railroad tracks—and right on the river. We'll have easy access to Pittsburgh proper and to the Ohio River, and from there to Connellsville and the coal fields. And in addition to that, my partner and I are willing to put up four thousand dollars of our own money for the venture."

"Four thousand . . ." Amazed, Louis Whitcomb stared at the tall young man before him, wondering if the boy had any idea how ludicrously small such a sum was when compared with the huge investment needed to build an iron foundry. Whitcomb was a shrewd man and a hard one when it came to business, but he was not without feeling. Boone Walker was obviously in earnest, almost touchingly so. He was throwing every desperate appeal he could into the proposition, yet his mention of the four thousand dollars only served to emphasize how pitifully unsuited he was to embark on such a large project. "My boy . . ." Louis began, searching for a tactful way to explain.

"It's everything we've got between us, Mr. Whitcomb. Connor and I believe so much in what we're doing—as a first step, of course—that we're willing to put in everything we have in the world, all we've accumulated in these past years. How many partners have you found willing to contribute everything they possessed?"

Whitcomb's mouth fell open and then shut quickly. "Why, none," he replied slowly. He met Boone Walker's direct gray gaze, liking the blunt, sensible openness of this strapping young man, sensing something of his determination as he watched him and listened to his words. "Go on, Mr. Walker." Whitcomb nodded for him to continue, though he remained near the library door.

In jubilation, Boone realized that he at last had the financier's attention, perhaps even his interest. Despite his excitement, he forced himself to speak in calm, measured tones.

"Besides contributing the land and the four thousand dollars, Connor Maguire and I are willing to work as foremen during the construction of the foundry and for one year thereafter at half-wages—in exchange, of course, for our twenty percent ownership of the company. And," he went on, reading the skepticism still flickering in Whitcomb's eyes, "should you have any doubts of our abilities to work with both iron and men, we'd like to suggest a way in which we could prove ourselves."

"Would you, now?" Whitcomb shook his head, almost dazed. He waved Boone back to his chair. "Sit down, Mr. Walker, and tell me all about it."

Whitcomb sent his henchmen scurrying when they appeared as directed, to throw Boone out of the house, and he listened, calculating, thinking as the boy spoke. His proposal was interesting, very interesting. It showed thought and willingness to take a risk. And it couldn't have been made if he and his friend didn't have a solid belief in themselves. If Walker was this persistent and thorough about everything he did, he just might make a good business partner, after all, Whitcomb reflected, stroking his mustache and gazing appraisingly at the young man before him.

Boone tried not to fidget with his hat as he waited, watching Whitcomb's bewhiskered face. Suddenly the idea, which had seemed so sound a few hours ago when he'd gone over everything with Connor, now sounded feeble and unconvincing. He had told Whitcomb that he and Connor would give up their jobs and work for Whitcomb in any capacity he chose for three months to prove their competence and their value as business partners. If they didn't convince him of their worth in that time, the deal would be off. *He'll never accept the proposal,* Boone thought, dismay creeping through him. *He'll laugh me out of this house.*

Whitcomb's fingers strayed to his monocle, and he toyed with it as he sat in the leather chair, considering. At first, Walker's proposition had sounded absurd, but after hearing reason upon reason added on as to why he should allow two unknown young men into his foundry venture, he found himself wavering. He liked the fact that they were willing to prove themselves by working for half-wages as foremen until the foundry had had a chance to become profitable. And more than that, he liked Boone Walker. Whitcomb felt he had an instinct for people, and his instinct about Walker was very favorable indeed. But he needed to know more.

"You a family man, Walker?"

Startled by the abruptness of the question, Boone dropped his bowler on the floor. He retrieved it, using the few seconds that passed to refocus his thoughts. "No, sir. At least, I've not got a wife."

"Where do you hail from? Down south somewhere, lest I miss my guess."

The slight drawl in his voice gave him away every time, Boone reflected silently. Was it his imagination, or did Whitcomb sound troubled suddenly? Aloud, he replied, "Yes, sir. West Virginia."

He hoped Whitcomb couldn't tell that he was lying. It was the one fact about his past he'd been forced to alter after leaving home. He couldn't afford not to. Even Connor thought he'd been born and raised in West Virginia. Boone added, "My family owned a small farm there. It wasn't much to begin with, but after my two oldest brothers went off to the war, we couldn't keep it up nearly well enough. Then Henry and Tom—my brothers—were killed, and I went to work in a lumber camp, hoping to send enough money home to help out." It was close enough to the truth so that he felt no qualms saying it.

"You still send money home and keep in touch with your family?"

"Yes, sir." Another partial truth. He sent money home whenever he could through an elaborate system that hid his location from the recipients. He hadn't had any direct or written contact with his mother or Clay since the icy December night he had run off.

"Which side did your brothers fight on in the war?"

So that was it. The reason for all these questions. Suddenly, Boone understood. Though Louis Whitcomb asked the question so quietly he had to strain to hear the words, he knew that this was the one that mattered. Bitterness came over him. Now he knew why his drawling voice disturbed Louis Whitcomb. Now he knew why the state where he was born made a difference. The last battle in the war between the states may have been fought seven years ago, but the war itself was still not over, and might never end. Hate and rancor still divided this country. And though Pittsburgh had thrived during the war—*because* of the war—Louis Whitcomb wanted to know if he was a reb.

"My brothers fought on different sides, Mr. Whitcomb," Boone replied, unable to keep the harshness from his voice. "Henry fought with the Confederates. He was captured at the Battle of Perryville and died in a Union prison camp. Tom, my oldest brother, died at Vicksburg. He fought for the Union under Grant, and got a musket ball in his head. Does that answer your question?"

Louis Whitcomb's almond-shaped eyes were remote. "Must've been pretty rough, having the family divided." His voice was flat, expressionless.

"We survived." *Barely.* Boone thought of Ezra. Suddenly, a shiver chased down his spine. The past, always the past. Would he never escape the war and what it had done to his family? Would he never escape the memories of his own violence and guilt?

He shifted in his chair, suddenly angry. "I was twelve years old when the war ended, Mr. Whitcomb. I can't see that any of it makes any difference now. Judge me as I stand before you, man to man. Not as a Reb or a Yank. If you can't do that, we have nothing more to talk about.''

Whitcomb leaned forward suddenly and turned the photograph on his desk so that Boone could see it. "That's my son, Walker. His name was Philip. He died in the war, too. Gettysburg.''

Boone gazed at the photograph of a young man in the blue uniform of a Union infantryman. The man had darkish hair, a narrow face, and solemn eyes.

"Victoria still hasn't quite gotten over it. Maybe she never will. You can see why we don't take kindly to southerners.''

Connor won't believe this, Boone thought in disgust. *The deal scotched because I'm from the South.*

"Apparently we have nothing more to discuss,'' he said aloud, and rose from his chair.

Louis Whitcomb stared at him a moment as if in a daze, then slowly rubbed his hands across his eyes. "Sit down.''

"What, sir?'' Boone thought he must have heard wrong.

The financier scowled. "I said, sit down! When I'm finished with you, Walker, you'll have no doubt about it. Till then I'm going to overcome my dislike of your reb accent and give your proposal some thought.''

He inked a pen and drew a ledger before him. While Boone tried to think clearly, Whitcomb fired questions at him. It was one o'clock when he finally put down the pen and leaned wearily back in his chair.

"That'll do for tonight, Walker. I must say you seem to know a great deal about what you're getting into. And your knowledge of Bessemer steel is . . . impressive.''

Boone hadn't actually admitted that his real interest lay in steel, but in answering Whitcomb's questions it had become clear that his knowledge of the converter developed by the Englishman, Henry Bessemer, was more than casual. Boone felt that the Bessemer process of purifying iron by blowing air on it while it was molten might revolutionize the iron and steel industry, and despite his tiredness, he sensed that Whitcomb agreed. His questions had been particularly keen on the subject, almost as if he guessed Boone's dream that one day the Monongahela River foundry might be expanded into a plant producing Bessemer steel.

Boone felt a burning hope as he stared at Louis Whitcomb

across the lamplit library. The interview had not gone badly. He had stayed far longer than he had thought possible. And despite Whitcomb's confessed dislike of southerners, he had listened long and hard to Boone's ideas.

"Well, Mr. Whitcomb? What do you think? My partner and I are going into the iron business with or without you. We're going to build on the river, and we're going to turn out more iron than you ever dreamed about. Maybe steel, too, someday—tons and tons of steel. I need your answer, sir. Are you going to take advantage of our offer, or should we make another man rich—richer," he amended, with a pointed glance around the well-appointed library. "The decision is yours."

Louis Whitcomb came slowly to his feet. "You're an arrogant son of a bitch, Walker. But I like you for it." A gleam entered his eyes. "I'm interested in your land and in your proposal. But I'm going to have to think about it." He stroked the tips of his brown mustache. "I'll need to consult with my wife's brother-in-law, who would be the fourth partner in our venture. His name is Silas Emmett; maybe you've heard of him?"

Boone certainly had. Silas Emmett had built up an entire town from a single forge. Emmettville was an industry unto itself, with its founder controlling every aspect of the town's life and economy.

"I'll see what Emmett thinks about your proposition, Walker, but one thing is certain. If we do go ahead and work something out, there is no way in hell you and Maguire will get more than ten percent of the company between you. If you insist on more, we can end the discussion right here."

Boone had to restrain himself to keep from smiling. He had never hoped for more than that. The figure of twenty percent, which he had thrown out earlier, had merely been a bargaining chip to be reduced later. Even at five percent apiece, he and Connor would be well on their way to financial independence—especially since this project was only the beginning of what Boone had in mind. "Fine, providing that the deed to the land remains solely in Maguire's name and mine," he countered.

Whitcomb stood. "We have plenty of time to reach agreement on these details—if Emmett and I decide to go ahead with the deal."

Boone followed Whitcomb out of the library and through

the hall. When they shook hands beneath the crystal chandelier, Boone met the other man's gaze directly.

"When will I hear from you?"

"When I've made a decision, young man, and not a moment before." With these words, Whitcomb showed him out into the broiling August night.

Ten days later, Boone came home from his shift to find a letter awaiting him under his door. He hollered for Connor, forgetting in his excitement that most of the other boarders were already retiring for the night. Connor came running. Both young men put their heads together over the expensive monogrammed sheet: "Mr. Silas Emmett and I have decided to further explore your business proposition and wish to meet with you and Mr. Maguire to discuss it in further detail."

Connor shouted and threw an arm across Boone's shoulders. "You did it, Boone, my lad," he chortled, and followed this with another loud whoop and a series of hops that evolved into a graceful jig. Boone kept reading, a grin on his face.

"But listen to this, Connor," he interrupted Maguire's exuberant gyrations, holding up one hand. His eyes had grown sober and thoughtful as he read aloud.

" 'If you or Mr. Maguire fail to prove your abilities in the three months under my employ, as agreed to in our discussion, the foundry deal will go no further. And in addition' "— and here Boone raised his head a moment to meet Connor's intent stare—" 'in addition, you and Mr. Maguire will find yourselves out of work and out of luck, for between us Silas Emmett and I will see to it that you never work in any Pennsylvania iron or steel mill again.' "

Connor stopped dancing. "If we fail to prove our abilities? Whitcomb plays tough, doesn't he, lad?"

"He's a millionaire, Con. He takes his money and his investments very seriously."

"Well, so do we. We're not going to fail; that's all there is to it."

"I agree." Boone grabbed his friend by the shoulders and shook him excitedly. "We're going to do it, Connor. We're going to build ourselves a future no one can tear down."

That night he slept soundly and woke with a feeling of optimism. A business partnership with two of Pennsylvania's most successful men was no mean accomplishment. "It's the beginning,'' Boone told himself as he got out of bed and strode to the window, watching the dawn color the sky above Rebecca Street. ''But there will be more—much more.''

It was a promise he made to himself.

❧ Ten

Chicago, 1874

THE WINDOWS OF the Wabash Avenue boardinghouse rattled with the wind as Elly stood before the ormolu mirror brushing her hair. February was a brutal month in Chicago—bitter, snowy, and swept by fierce winds—but the two-story gabled house had been snugly built by Aunt Adelaide's husband almost forty years ago. It had survived Uncle Jarvis's death from typhoid fever in 1869 as well as the great fire two years later, which had claimed nearly three hundred lives and thousands of buildings. Though moth-sized snowflakes whirled against the windowpanes on this icy morning, seeming to beat against the glass like furious wings, and though the wind moaned ghostlike in the gray light of early morning, the heavy velour draperies in the cozy bedroom barely stirred, and the potbellied coal stove hissed and gurgled in its corner, sending forth lovely bursts of heat to combat the icy temperatures. Comfortable in her crisp white shirtwaist and navy wool skirt, Elly took pleasure in the sturdiness and warmth of the house. She felt safe here, protected. The howling of the wind only made her smile as she pulled the brush through the heavy black silk of her hair. She paused in midmotion as a knock sounded at the door.

''Come in,'' she bade, setting the hairbrush down on the cherrywood bureau and tying a neat white apron about her waist. Aunt Adelaide bustled through the door, her plump pink face even more agitated and wrinkled than usual.

"My dear," she began, her heavy shoes clopping on the scrubbed pine floor, "it's a positive blizzard out there, a positive blizzard! And I don't know how it's happened, but we've run clean out of potatoes and barley, and I haven't enough vegetables to boil a decent soup. Whatever are we going to do?"

"Don't worry, Aunt Adelaide, I'll stop by the market this afternoon," Elly soothed. "Has Jeweline begun changing all the bed linens this morning? She might need some help with the washing; her back was aching terribly yesterday."

"Not to worry, Caroline is with her at this very moment. And your mama is putting the finishing touches on breakfast." Adelaide's fat little hands waved the air like twittering birds. "I fear that Bess is too expert a cook, you know," she frowned. "Elinore, we've never gone through so many muffins and griddle cakes before. The amount we spent on food last week was enormous!"

Elly plaited her hair into a neat braid down her back, tying it with a ribbon. "We may have to ask more for room and board to compensate for the additional grocery costs," she mused. "I'll go over the figures tonight."

"Dear me." Aunt Adelaide bit her full, moist lips, set above a bouncing double chin. Though she was Samuel Forrest's sister, the two could not have been less alike. Her brother had possessed an oaklike strength and a dedication to ideals. Aunt Adelaide, younger than he by four years, had always been the chatterer of the family, prone to gossip and social posturing, but warmhearted and generous for all of her peevishness and anxieties. "Don't think I'm not grateful, Elinore, for all you've done in this house," she said now, facing her niece a trifle nervously. "Why, I've never had every room taken before, you know, and I'm just tickled about it! But it's turning my hair white before it's time. There's so much to do now, and the boarders have come to expect everything to be so nice, the way you always arrange it." She shook her head. "You have such good ideas. I never would have thought of offering them the chance to have their rooms cleaned and the slop jars emptied for them, and laundry and sewing services. Amazing how some people will pay extra for such things. And we're certainly getting a nicer quality of boarder, too. Decent people, yes, indeed. Why, it makes going in to dinner a real pleasure."

Elly's eyes danced. "I'm glad you approve, Aunt Addie. I have more ideas, too."

Her aunt gasped, to Elly's amusement. "More? I don't know that I can bear any more. You've turned this house into a prosperous place in precious few months, my dear, but . . . I'm so frightened."

"Frightened?" Elly repeated, staring at her incredulously. Behind her, the large bedroom—with its two beds and matching yellow counterpanes, its doily-covered trestle table, and the little cane-backed chair with the red and gold embroidered seat cushion—sparkled like a gem in the gray-white light reflected in from the snowstorm. To Elly's mind, there was absolutely nothing in the world to be frightened of. For the first time in ages, she felt safe. She was in control of her world, far from Emmettville, far from Silas and Jason Emmett and their stinking corruption. The Forrest family's lives had improved tremendously since they'd come to Chicago, and she knew, with pride, that much of it was due to her own efforts. Through Elly's management, the decaying boarding-house on Wabash Avenue, which Aunt Adelaide had struggled alone to maintain after her husband's death, had been revitalized and redecorated until it was now a cozy, spotless haven with boarders filling every gleaming room. The four Forrest women, along with Timothy and Jeweline—the former slave who had run away to the North and had worked for Aunt Adelaide since the close of the war—kept the house running as smoothly as a bright flowing stream. It was pleasant and cheerful—and prosperous. Timothy, now an inquisitive ten-year-old, was enrolled in public school, which made Mama happy, and there was food aplenty on the table. The mortgage was paid off, so Aunt Adelaide owned the house free and clear, and the rooms were filled with paying boarders. What could Aunt Adelaide possibly fear?

"It's you," the woman blurted, wiping her hands on her embroidered apron and meeting Elly's startled gaze with wide, imploring eyes. "Without you, Elinore, this place would fall apart, just as it had before you came." She took out a handkerchief and loudly blew her nose. Tears filled her eyes. "I certainly don't have your talent for managing things, my dear, that I admit, and your mama, well, she's content in the kitchen, cooking and cleaning her own little domain, with a bit of sewing on the side. Much as I'm fond of her, I know she hasn't the energy to do what I see you accomplish each day. And Caroline, she's scared of a flea. So we're all relying on you, Elinore. And I just keep thinking that one day you'll come waltzing in here with a young man on your arm, marry him, and run off to your own house to start a family of your own. Now, you've got a perfect right to do it, mind you, but what'll become of us? This poor house has become too busy—too successful—to get along without you. You started the whole thing, and I'm just afraid we'll lose you and it'll all come falling down around our ears.''

Elly hugged her, not knowing whether to laugh or cry. "Aunt Adelaide, *that* is something you need never fear,'' she said. "I wouldn't desert you any sooner than I'd jump off a mountain. We're a family, and we'll stay together always, no matter what else happens. Besides,'' she added, and her thin, serious face lit with sudden laughter she couldn't contain, "what young man would want a bossy bluestocking for a wife—someone, as Caroline once said, with no sense of humor? Someone who thinks she knows the best way to handle every situation and, if I do say so myself, is invariably right?'' A gurgle of laughter burst from her throat as she hugged her aunt tightly. "There is no such man, I assure you, so your fate is sealed. You're stuck with me for the rest of my days, until I can't do anything but sit like Mrs. Malloy in my rocker and mutter about the dogs barking down the street and the racket made by the trains. Then, I daresay, you'll be glad to be rid of me.''

"Never, child.'' Adelaide's watery blue eyes fixed themselves on the tall, dark-haired girl before her, taking in the neat, high-breasted figure, the delicate, striking features set in the oval face. "I think for once you're wrong, Elinore,'' she said slowly. "There are many young men who would be eager to take up with a girl like you. Your problem is you work so hard you don't have an opportunity to meet them.''

"Or any desire to do so. Come,'' Elly said, changing the subject as she took her aunt's arm and led her toward the door. "I am going to town this afternoon, and I will be glad to shop for whatever you wish. Only write out a list for me, and I will see to it.''

It gave her pleasure, as they descended the broad oak steps, to glance around the house and reflect on its current splendor. Oh, it was hardly a marble palace with costly rugs and gilded cornices, but gone were the cobwebs and layers of dust that had lurked in the corners, banished like the faded curtains and torn quilts that had made the rooms look so shabby. Upon arriving in Chicago, Elly had set to work with a vengeance, washing and scrubbing and mending, borrowing and buying, until the boardinghouse had begun to take on the glow of a well-cared-for home. Now the newel post at the bottom of the stairs shone with beeswax polish, the floors gleamed like warm honey in the sun, and new throw rugs, bought with the money she had saved by going over the household accounts and cutting out all needless expenditures and waste, brightened the main parlor and dining room floors. The boarders' rooms, too, had benefited from her efforts, as had the small sewing parlor near the stairs. She couldn't help but feel satisfaction every time she surveyed the pleasant handsomeness of the house and heard the compliments the boarders offered to Mama after one of her fine meals. Oh, the luxury of money to spend on good wholesome food! The delight of modest yet dignified surroundings, hard work, and knowledge that one could enjoy the fruits of one's own labor! Now, as Aunt Adelaide left the room to take her place at the head of the table, Elly slipped down the back stairs into the kitchen so as not to disturb the boarders at breakfast. Her nostrils widened in appreciation as the fragrant smell of fresh, warm bread and sizzling sausages greeted her, filling the kitchen with tantalizing aromas. Her stomach growled its hunger, but there was much to do before she could allow herself the time for a meal.

Timothy sat on a three-legged stool at the kitchen table, forking alternate mouthfuls of boiled eggs and griddle cakes into his mouth. Her heart warmed at the sight of him.

"Guess what!" he exclaimed, his cheeks nearly bursting with the contents of his breakfast. "Mrs. Garrett's daughter is getting married to a schoolteacher in St. Louis because she's going to have his baby!"

Elly halted, one arm in midair as she reached for a pitcher of milk. She spun toward her brother, her face filled with dismay. "Shh! For heaven's sake, Timothy, they'll hear you!" she gasped, with a glance toward the dining room. She left the pitcher and came to stand beside him. "What a thing to shout across the room," she scolded. "However did you hear something like that?"

"When I swept out her room yesterday, there was a letter on the table from Missouri. I read it."

He grinned, obviously proud of himself. Timothy, whose job it was to keep the boardinghouse and its porch and walkway swept clean of dust and debris, had an unfortunate habit of eavesdropping on every conversation within earshot and gathering up gossip and information about the boarders. He didn't understand half of what he heard, but he repeated it indiscriminately to the members of his family, much to Bess's horror and Aunt Adelaide's rich amusement. Timothy was sprouting into a tall, thin boy with hair the color of wheat, and almond-shaped eyes of a translucent blue beneath pale, arcing brows. He was losing some of the childish sweetness Elly had always loved in him; he was still good-tempered, but mischievous and bright, sometimes too bright for his own good. When he wasn't stealing muffins from the pantry, he was scribbling secrets in his journal, arguing Civil War strategy with old General Willis, or beating the poor man at chess. He had few friends his own age, preferring the company of his elders, but was outgoing and happy and bursting with curiosity. Far too much curiosity, Elly reflected disapprovingly, as she lectured him this morning on the impropriety of reading other people's mail.

The scolding was interrupted, however, by Bess, hurrying in from the dining room and muttering distractedly. "Elly, bring that pitcher of milk to the table, there's a lamb. And would you boil another pot of coffee? Abner Joseph dropped the entire platter of sausages on the floor and that mongrel you brought home yesterday, Timothy, gobbled them up before anyone could stop him! I want that dog tied up outside during meals—even if it is colder than an icebox today." She sighed and scooped more butter into the frying pan, which immediately began to sizzle. "If I don't bring out some more in a flash, I fear Mr. Peters will hit him—Abner Joseph, that is, not the dog—for those sausages are his wife's favorite, you know, and she's refusing to eat anything else. Why," she asked Elly, as the girl started for the door with the pitcher in hand, "are people so peculiar?"

"Because they haven't yet learned to be perfect like you and me, Mama," Elly said gravely over her shoulder.

"And like me!" Timothy shouted, dropping his fork onto his plate with a clatter. With the energy reserved for the very young, he lunged toward his wool coat, which hung on a peg near the door.

The next few minutes were filled with a feverish bustle as Elly and her mother served the eight boarders a generous breakfast, Timothy bundled up in his brown woolen coat and knitted cap and trudged off through the snow toward the school five blocks away, and the boarders one by one left the house for their various jobs in the city. By the time Elly had helped Aunt Adelaide clear and polish the carved oak table in the dining room and had assisted Jeweline and Caroline in making up all the beds with fresh linen, shaking out the rugs and draperies, and dusting the brass lamps and knickknacks in the parlor, it was time for luncheon, the first meal of the day she allowed herself. They consumed a quick repast in the kitchen, and then Elly abandoned her apron, tucked her dark curls into a snug wool cap, and slipped her navy corduroy coat from its peg near the kitchen door. Taking care that no one should see the contents of her reticule, Elly tucked Aunt Adelaide's grocery list inside, beneath the heavy brown packet she had placed there earlier. Then she set out on foot toward the horsecars.

The snow had lightened to a soft, wet sprinkling as she made her way, head bent, along the glistening streets. Every once in a while, a ferocious gust of wind sent icy snowflakes fluttering onto her lashes and settling deep inside the collar of her coat, making her regret that she hadn't bothered to wear her scarf. Even her fingers felt frozen inside her gloves as she thankfully boarded the horsecar at last and settled into a seat.

As the car rumbled northward toward the newly rebuilt business district of the city, Elly peered out the window at the limestone and brick buildings, the railroad tracks of the Illinois Central, and the snow-covered, traffic-crowded streets. Buggies and wagons were everywhere, crammed with goods and passengers, all hurrying toward some unknown destination. Buildings, large and small, were at various stages of completion on every block. Train whistles shrilled, horses snorted, sirens clanged, and children threw snowballs at passing horsecars and freight drays. Emmettville seemed small and distant now, a mere worm compared to the giant, fire-breathing dragon that was Chicago. But the men who had ruled the sooty Pennsylvania town and imprinted their tyranny on her family still stood out in bright relief in Elly's mind.

She could never forget what they had done or the feelings of helplessness they had raised in her. Though Mama and Timothy had recovered from the ordeal and now seemed content enough in Chicago, Caroline still bore the marks of it. Poor, broken Caroline, Elly thought, her mouth tightening in lines of sadness. Caroline rarely spoke to anyone outside the family; she never even raised her eyes when addressed by a man. She grew agitated if one of the male boarders so much as wished her a good day. And her hands, her ugly, sore-covered hands, were rough and bloody from incessant washing. No amount of salve could heal them, for she almost immediately scrubbed it off again. It was a sickness, Elly recognized, this constant washing of the hands and interminable bathing, stemming from Caroline's belief that she was permanently soiled. Only unlike Lady Macbeth, it was not the stain of guilt Caroline sought to cleanse, but the memory of her own debasement. It was time she got over it, Elly thought, edging closer to the window as a fat woman with bushy red hair and garlic on her breath squeezed onto the seat beside her. For her own good, Caroline had to face what had happened and resume her life. But Elly wasn't sure how to bring this about. In all this time, Caroline had never once shown any sign of her former gaiety or zest, no interest in the world outside the boardinghouse. Like a caterpillar, she was content to curl up in her safe cocoon, retreating from all the brilliant color, fragrance, and melody of life.

Perhaps it would be better if Caroline were forced to venture outside the boardinghouse, where she would have to deal with other people. Maybe daily contact with others would help her to throw off the terrible anxiety that riddled her, to smile and speak normally again, to remember that people could be good and kind and friendly as well as vile and treacherous and cruel.

Deciding to speak to her sister about it soon, Elly rose as the horsecar neared her stop.

Elly mingled with the crowd as she walked past the grand entrance of the First National Bank at State and Washington streets. Those inside that building would never even listen to what she had in mind. Instead, she approached the far less imposing structure down the street, a respectable three-story brick building housing the Hamilton Bank of Chicago.

All around her the city hummed. It had sprung back from

the fire of 1871 with astonishing speed and resiliency. Despite massive destruction, many of the factories, rolling mills, meat-packing yards, and railroads essential to Chicago had survived. The businesses and homes that had been ruined were being feverishly rebuilt: bigger, better, and finer than before. A financial panic had gripped the nation since October, many Chicagoans were forced to stand in breadlines, and public buildings had been housing the poor over the long, bitter winter, but somehow the rebuilding continued. Hotels, banks, theaters, railroad stations, and office buildings rose on every street corner, but where, before, the business district had been centered on Lake Street, now, thanks to the influence of Potter Palmer, it had regrouped on State. Like a beacon to light the way, the newly rebuilt Palmer House at the corner of State and Monroe streets stood in all its opulent splendor. Aunt Adelaide had told Elly that Potter Palmer had lost ninety-five buildings in the fire and had been almost unable to pay the taxes on the charred rubble to which his land had been reduced. Although he was $15,000 short, he had been rescued by an insurance company whose confidence in his ability to rebound had earned him a loan of $1,700,000, with only his signature for collateral.

If only Mr. Ross would grant her the merest fraction of that amount, with the boardinghouse as collateral, she would be able to carry out her plan, Elly thought as she entered through the glass-plated doors of the Hamilton Bank and found herself in a handsome, dark-paneled lobby.

Engulfed by moss-green carpeting, rows of ornately carved desks, and an army of dark-suited men, her confidence suddenly wavered. There were no other women in sight. The male clerks in their business suits and spectacles, and the well-dressed bank customers, outfitted with walking sticks, top hats, and fur-collared coats, all seemed to know exactly where to go and what to do. Elly had never been in a bank before; such establishments generally serviced the wealthy few. Most of the people she knew kept their money in boxes or pouches hidden away in a mattress or a bureau drawer. She felt out of place, shabby, and small in her corduroy coat and fuzzy cap. Too bad she didn't have an elegant cloak and ermine hat with which to impress Mr. Edward Ross, she reflected ruefully. She had never met the account manager, though she had written to him and arranged this meeting, but

she suspected he would be far more open to her request for a
loan if she looked as if she didn't need it. Well, at least she
had nothing to be ashamed of in her crisp shirtwaist and wool
skirt. They were practical and neat, qualities much more
desirable in an aspiring businesswoman than fashionable
splendor.

She squared her shoulders and crossed the lobby with an air
of confidence greater than she truly felt. The very air of the
bank seemed stiff and crisp, like new hundred dollar bills. It
smelled of money, rich leather, and the mingling of a variety
of male colognes. A masculine domain, she realized, as one
after another, heads swiveled curiously to stare at her. Was
she mad to try to breach it?

In a cubbyhole almost too small for the immense walnut
desk that nearly filled it, she found Mr. Edward Ross. He had
a face like a mongrel dog and a long, gangly body encased in
a prim black suit. Square-lensed spectacles, a long, thin nose,
and black hair receding from a high, pale forehead gave him
the look of an undertaker, Elly decided with a little inward
shudder as she appraised him from the doorway briefly before
he glanced up and saw her.

"Yes? Is there something I can do for you, ma'am?" he
inquired in a surprised, nasal tone.

"Mr. Ross, we have an appointment," Elly said with her
best smile. "I am Elinore Forrest."

His droopy brown eyes widened and blinked behind their
spectacles. He came to his feet, stumbling a little in his
astonishment. "Elinore . . . Forrest? E. Forrest? You? But I
thought . . ."

She nodded, hoping he couldn't see her nervousness. "Yes,
I know. You thought E. Forrest was a man."

"I merely assumed . . . from the tone of your letter . . ."

"A natural misunderstanding," Elly murmured. "May I sit
down?"

"Of course, of course." Flustered, he indicated the high-
backed chair opposite his desk. "I beg your pardon; I'm not
usually so thoughtless, but you cannot imagine my surprise.
When you wrote of your wish to open an account with us, I
simply assumed . . . that is, you mentioned in your letter the
successful management of a boardinghouse and your wish to
deposit monthly receipts, and I thought . . ."

"Yes, I have the receipts right here." Elly had slipped off

her coat, and now removed the brown packet from her reticule. She handed it over to him, saying, "There is one
hundred and sixteen dollars here with which to begin our
account. That is enough, isn't it?"

"Oh, yes, certainly."

"I wish my name and that of my aunt, Adelaide Coombs,
to be listed jointly on the records." The thought of Aunt
Addie's dismay when she was informed that the precious
boardinghouse receipts were now deposited in a bank almost
caused her to falter. And that was only a small matter compared to what she intended to do. For a moment, she wanted
to snatch back the envelope and leave the bank without
another word, but then she reminded herself that it would all
be worthwhile if her plans came to fruition. It was the thought
of her goal that enabled her to continue. "There is one other
thing, Mr. Ross," she said as he opened a ledger before him
and took up his pen. "I also wish to secure a loan."

Edward Ross froze. He set the pen down with a soft click
on the desk. "A loan?" he asked incredulously. The benevo-
lent expression on his face had vanished. "I'm afraid that is
quite impossible, Miss Forrest."

Elly smoothed her wool skirt with a hand that shook ever
so slightly. "I require only a very small loan, Mr. Ross."
Steady, steady, she warned herself. *Don't let him see your
fear.* "Five hundred dollars will be sufficient."

"It is out of the question."

Elly's lips were dry. "May I ask why?" she said in a calm
voice that cost her much to maintain.

"The Hamilton Bank does not extend loans to women.
Certainly not to young women, and certainly not to a young
woman with neither husband nor father to co-sign her note. I
can only assume," he said, peering dryly at her through his
spectacles, "that you have no such male protector, or he
would certainly have taken on this endeavor himself."

"That's true, Mr. Ross, but I assure you I can handle the
responsibility of this loan." She began to speak quickly,
quietly, desperate to persuade him. She could not proceed any
further with her plans without sufficient funds to back them.
"It is true, I am not quite nineteen years old. To some that is
a tender age, but I have been caring for my family for some
time now. I am accustomed to responsibility. There is the
matter of my aunt's boardinghouse," she said suddenly, her

eyes brightening. "I have managed it for the past year and a half, and it is doing splendidly. Our rooms are all occupied, and it is clean and well run. Mr. Ross, let me explain what I wish to do with the money from the loan." She leaned forward, aware that the bank officer was listening, though there was no sign of encouragement or softening on his face. "It is a business loan! I intend to open a tearoom in my aunt's boardinghouse. I am certain it will be profitable. If my calculations are correct, the loan ought to be repaid in six months' time. I have some figures with me, if you'd care to see them, which will show you how everything shall work. Everything has been meticulously researched, and I'm sure you'll find . . ."

But he refused to accept the paper on which she had so carefully printed the figures it had taken her weeks to calculate and arrange. "I am sorry, Miss Forrest. It is not the policy of this bank to enter into business transactions with females," he said curtly. "I cannot and shall not grant you a loan."

"Even with the boardinghouse offered as collateral?" she countered in desperation.

He shook his head.

Elly's shoulders sagged with defeat beneath her frilly white shirtwaist. Not to be given a chance, not even a chance to make a success of herself, all because she was a woman. She fought the urge to scatter the contents of Edward Ross's carefully arranged desk on the floor with a sweep of her arm. No, that would only confirm his prejudice against her, his belief, shared by all men, that women were too weak and emotional to bear the burdens of business and finance, even, some still thought, to endure the rigors of education. She perched like a crushed sparrow on her chair, her fingers clenching the string of her reticule. Smug and superior and aloof, he was watching her. She ached with frustration, but she refused to give any outward sign.

"Will there be anything else, Miss Forrest?" A thin smile, before he took up the pen to prepare her account. "This will only take a few moments."

"Thank you, Mr. Ross, but I do not wish to deposit my money in your bank, after all." Elly came to her feet. She plucked the brown packet from his desk. Though her voice and movements were controlled, there was no mistaking her anger. "The bank that will grant me a loan is the one that shall receive my business," she informed him.

"No bank in the city will do that, I'm afraid." They were regretful words, but he didn't sound regretful at all—only amused by her ignorance and foolish indignation. A cold, disapproving smile twisted the corners of his undertaker's lips. "Good day, Miss Forrest," he finished with a shrug as she stuffed the packet in her reticule and reached for her coat.

She felt his gaze follow her as she marched through the green and brown lobby. The prim, arrogant, self-satisfied man. Hatred burned within her, hatred for all the men who controlled and crushed women's lives. She didn't even feel the blast of frigid air that struck her as she emerged onto State Street and headed toward the nearest horsecar. Her mind was whirling with a fury and helplessness born of frustration. All of her hopes had been dashed by one man's narrow-mindedness, for she knew that all the other banks and bankers felt as he did: that women were not to be entrusted with money; that women could not manage business matters on their own. Her heart had dropped into her stomach by the time she boarded the car, which plunged off through the snow, nearly colliding with a phaeton.

It had started to hail. Light, swift stones of ice hurtled down from the lead-gray sky, stinging the horses and pedestrians who packed the streets and sidewalks. The car was crowded and Elly was unable to find a seat, so she stood gripping one of the leather straps that hung from the ceiling of the car, swaying and bumping the other bundled-up passengers as the vehicle jostled its way through the teeming business center.

Bitter disappointment filled her heart. Her vision of the planned tearoom swam before her eyes, misting and fading at the edges as the dream dissolved. She had thought it all out so carefully. The small carved tables placed about the parlor, splendid with white linen and pretty floral-patterned china. The big oak table in the dining room, grandly set for large parties, such as birthday celebrations or ladies' club meetings. The doors opening at two o'clock to small groups of genteel patrons seeking a light repast of tea or coffee, iced cakes, and tiny sandwiches. New satin draperies in the parlor, pretty gilt chairs, and a cook's assistant to help Mama in the kitchen. And Elly and Caroline serving, with Aunt Adelaide welcoming the patrons and showing them to their tables. All of it, all of it, would have been lovely and exciting and hugely successful, she was certain! Now, without the bank's loan, it would take months, maybe years, for this dream to come to pass. Through her frustration, Elly suddenly became aware that the neighborhood through which she was passing was totally unfamiliar. The buildings were tall, fronted by garish signs. Taverns, livery stables, and warehouses fled by. She leaned forward and peered out the window, past the cloaked heads of the passengers seated near her. A quick calculation brought her to the realization that she was in the wrong part of town, with each passing block traveling farther from the boardinghouse. She moved forward, chagrined, and stepped down from the car at the next corner, peering around uncertainly.

Though it was only midafternoon, the gray sky seemed to have darkened and the wind to have picked up. A dismal duskiness had fallen over the streets and buildings, even over the light pelting snow that had replaced the hail and now fell briskly over the planked sidewalk and the unlit lampposts. A lone wagon chugged down the center of the street. From somewhere nearby came the bellow of a drunk, and then a woman's high, jeering laughter. Three dogs, running low in a pack, rounded a corner and dodged behind a freight office shed.

Elly felt a steely chill knife down her spine. It was due not to the bitter cold of the air but to the unfamiliar and seedy neighborhood in which she found herself. Fool that she was, she had wandered into one of those sections of Chicago she had heard about from her aunt but never visited. In such vice districts, like Hairtrigger Block, between State and Dearborn, slum shacks and taverns, brothels and gambling dens flourished, and the gamblers who had come up the Mississippi with the outbreak of the Civil War, and settled like hordes of locusts in the northern city made rich by war, were kings of wealth, their influence spreading even to City Hall. Sometimes their corrupt domains were to be found only a few short blocks from the wealthiest mansions; often their power extended over entire areas, encompassing massive crime and violence. And Randolph Street, she remembered, reading the sign on the corner ahead of her in dismay, was notorious as a hotbed of gambling houses and bordellos. She had to get out of here—and quickly. Clutching her reticule, with the precious boardinghouse profits wrapped in their brown paper packet inside, she scanned the street in both directions, praying for a streetcar heading south. With the whirling snow, she could not see far, and no such car appeared. She started to walk, holding her reticule close against her coat.

A passing vegetable wagon skidded past, careening on the slippery street and splashing her with wet snow. She kept walking, remembering belatedly that she had promised to buy vegetables for tonight's soup. At this rate, she thought in rueful dismay, she would be fortunate to arrive home in time for dessert.

Everything was going wrong, and all because she had allowed herself to be distracted by Edward Ross's refusal. In silence she berated herself for her carelessness. Head bent against a sudden furious gust of wind, shoulders hunched beneath her coat, she had no warning of what happened next. A trio of drunks emerged suddenly from a brightly lighted brick saloon and tumbled down a flight of steps directly into her. The impact knocked her to the ground and sent her reticule flying into the snow. She lay still a moment on the pavement, stunned and breathless.

"Lookee here. Lookee what you clumsy oafs did to this pretty lady," one of the drunks wheezed, crawling over to peer into her face. His reeking breath and close proximity revived her, and she hastened to her feet, but not before his companion, a wizened fellow in a gray wool jacket and yellow cap, grabbed her reticule.

"Here, pretty lady, you dropped this." He held it out before her with a snort of laughter. "Maybe you'll give me a reward if I hand it back to you, eh?"

Elly snatched it from his grasp. He blinked bloodshot eyes in surprise. "Aw, that wasn't polite," he whined.

She ignored him and started to hurry past, but the third man, an emaciated fellow with a red muffler and greasy hair that smelled almost as bad as the gin on his breath, lurched into her path. The other two joined him, deliberately blocking the street. The second drunk chortled and nudged his companions.

"Wait a minute, lady. We jist wanna 'pologize proper, that's all. Why don't you let us buy you a little drink?"

"Please get out of my way."

"We're jist lookin' for some fun. We'll even pay. We've got money from a dice game. You ever play dice, little lady? It's a dandy game."

"We'll teach ya—come on," the man in the red muffler coaxed.

Elly turned aside and started to cross the street, but he lunged out and grabbed the collar of her coat, hauling her backward, dragging her up against the side of the building, as terror pounded in her heart.

"Maybe you think we don't have money to pay you." His voice was jeering now. Spittle dribbled from the corners of his mouth. "You're wrong, pretty lady." She heard the jingling of coins in a pocket. Her breath came in short, hard puffs before her as she tried unsuccessfully to wrest her arm free of his grasp. "We'll make it well worth your while. Nothin' warms a man up, y'know, like liquor and a little tumble with—"

All of a sudden, the man before her went flying into the street. One moment he had stood there pawing her arm and holding her against the wall, the next he lay huddled in a drift of dirty snow. The other two followed him with a thrashing of bodies and a babble of drunken grunts. In their place, beside her, stood a dark-haired young man so tall and handsome she thought she must be dreaming.

"Never let it be said that an Irishman could ignore a lady in need of assistance," he said with a smile that would have melted a snowball. He ducked his head toward her in concern. "Are you all right, lass?"

"Yes. Thank you. I was . . . just frightened."

"Of that drunken scum? No need to be. My friend, as you can see, has them well in hand."

Beyond his shoulder, she saw another tall young man in a tweed coat and derby administer a hard right fist to Red Muffler's jaw. The drunk teetered down again in the snow. Yelping and cursing, he and his companions began crawling away.

"Those ruffians won't be bothering you again, lass. Now come away, if you please. This is no neighborhood for a young lady alone. We'll see you home."

By the time they reached the streetcar, Elly's head was whirling with the image of his fire-blue eyes and square, solid jaw. His soft brogue caressed her ears, and she could barely spare a glance for his fair-haired giant of a companion.

"We've only just arrived in the city today. We wandered into that district by mistake, just as you did. What a place. Why, there are saloons up and down each block. And gambling dens. The Grayson Hotel, where we're staying, isn't far from there, but the neighborhood is far better. Who would have thought we'd end up in such a rotten corner of town when all we were looking for was a decent restaurant, not too expensive, where we could get dinner? Ah, but then we wouldn't have met you, and that was fate, now, wasn't it?"

The horsecar rumbled along, the gas lamps leaped to life one by one in the darkening sky, and Elly sat mesmerized, listening to his deep, richly timbered voice. That voice was like molasses, smooth and sweet and melodic, alive with laughter and warmth. She lost herself in it, and in his handsome, exuberant face.

By the time they reached the boardinghouse, twilight had fallen, the snow had stopped, and she vaguely remembered that she had forgotten all about Aunt Adelaide's shopping list. But she didn't much care, and in the end, it didn't matter. Mama and Aunt Adelaide had managed without the vegetables. They had roasted lamb meat and boiled some rice and prepared a sweet bread pudding for the boarders' dinner. Mama was standing on the front porch, peering worriedly up the street when they came into view.

When she heard the story of the drunks, Bess trembled and embraced her daughter.

"You gentlemen must stay to dinner," she insisted, showing them into the house with her most gracious smile. "By the way, Elly, what are the names of your young men?"

Bess took their coats, while the smells of roasted meat and fresh-baked bread floated down the hall from the kitchen, adding their own tantalizing welcome to the visitors.

"This is Boone Walker, Mama," Elly replied, indicating the fair-haired man with a graceful incline of her head. She turned eagerly toward the Irishman, unaware of how her oval face lit as he met her smile. "And this is Connor Maguire."

Connor Maguire. Connor Maguire. Connor Maguire. The name sang upon her lips all through dinner and the evening beyond, like a poem written on the night. She had been rejected by Edward Ross and the Hamilton Bank today, stranded

in a seedy part of town, and accosted by drunks. She had
been cold and lost and frightened. But none of it mattered.
She had been rescued from it all by a man as bold and
exciting and kind as he was handsome. A man she thought
about for many hours in her bed that night, a man named
Connor Maguire.

🌿 Eleven

"ELLY, LOOK AT me! Here I come!"

Timothy shouted in delight as the brand-new sled with the
painted runners zigzagged down the snow-frosted hill and
came to rest with a whoosh of flurries at the foot of the slope.

"It's grand—simply grand!" He scrambled off, his face
flushed with excitement. All about him in the little park, boys
and girls skated and shrieked and tossed snowballs at one
another. Timothy ran up to Connor. "Thanks for buying it for
me, Mr. Maguire. Do you want a ride, Caro? But then I want
another turn. Unless you want a chance, Elly . . ." His voice
trailed off, and then he gave a short laugh. "Nah!" Beneath
the thick blue cap that completely hid his fair hair, his eyes
sparkled with boyish scorn. "You're too busy holding hands
with your beau."

"Now, lad, that's no way to talk to your sister," Connor
admonished. "Let's have that rope and let the girls have
some fun. Elly?"

"You'll never get me on that thing, Connor Maguire, so
don't even ask." She laughed up at him, feeling ridiculously
giddy and coquettish. "But Caroline would enjoy it, I'm
sure." She turned to her sister who was sitting immobile on
the park bench. "Remember how you loved that old wooden
sled Papa made for us the year the Miller farm burned down?

You used to plead with him to take you sledding Sunday afternoons when all he wanted was to sit by the fire with a mug of Mama's apple cider and a book in his hand.''

"Elly . . .''

"Go ahead. Connor will help you, and Boone and I will watch.''

"I don't want to, Elly.''

"But Caro . . .''

"I don't want to!''

Elly sighed. Connor put his hand on her arm. He spoke in a low tone. "There, now, we can't force the lass. Maybe when she sees all the fun you're having, she'll change her mind. Now, come along.''

"But I told you—''

He grinned. "Never mind that. Come along, I say.''

Before Elly realized it, Connor was dragging her, laughing and protesting, up the hill. Her face was flushed with cold and excitement. Her cloud of sable hair fluttered becomingly about her blooming cheeks as she allowed him to seat her securely in the center of the sled. Quickly, she arranged her gray plaid skirt about her ankles and waved to Boone, Timothy, and Caroline below.

Boone, watching intently from his post at the bottom of the hill, returned Elly's wave, then glanced at Caroline, who was huddled on the far end of the bench. In her red jacket and peplum skirt, with the dainty little red and black cap tied beneath her chin, the girl looked like a china doll, complete with rosy cheeks and brilliant eyes. The one thing lacking was a smile; no painted doll wore such a downcast mouth.

"Cold?'' Boone asked. She shook her head. "It's safe, you know. I'll take you up if you'd like.''

"No,'' she mumbled. Fear had darted into her round blue eyes. She quickly averted them, whispering, "No, thank you.''

Boone leaned against the bench. He didn't understand her desire to be left alone, a pretty young girl like that, but he respected it. A solitary, withdrawn existence had been his way of life for many years after leaving Kentucky. He had been forced to be ever careful, ever wary, lest someone uncover what he'd done that night in the farmhouse on the fringes of Hickoryville. He had built invisible walls around himself since then, and he allowed no one to breach them.

Until recently, only Connor Maguire had done so. Now Louis Whitcomb was battering away, splintering down some of the isolation that had become so much a part of his life. And strangely enough, the bond he'd shared with Connor, so similar to what he'd known with his brothers before leaving home, seemed to be undergoing a subtle change of late, a weakening, perhaps a fraying? He couldn't put his finger on it, for it was as vague and indefinable as the mist that rose over Chicago Harbor in early morning, but it was there nonetheless. The reasons for it were not completely clear, but as he watched Connor bend to help Elly Forrest from the sled, his dark head close to hers, there was a tightening in Boone's chest.

He watched through narrowed eyes as Elly and Connor strolled about the gay little park. The cold, bright day might have been a painting in a storybook: the gleaming velvet snow, the jewel-blue sky, the running, skating boys and girls in their brightly colored coats and mittens. Snowmen and sleds, carriages and jingling harnesses, shouts and joyous laughter. Boone saw and heard it all only as a backdrop to the object of his attention. He couldn't tear his gaze from Elly Forrest.

Even in her shabby blue coat and plain cap, she was beautiful. There was grace in the brisk way she walked, in the tilt of her head, in the slope of her shoulders. Black silk hair streamed out from beneath her cap, and he longed to touch it, to feel the soft, shiny threads in his hands, against his cheek. He was shocked by his own thoughts, though, shocked and angry with himself. She was Connor's girl. She adored Connor. And Connor . . . well, Connor had been pursuing her shamelessly for the past two weeks. To Boone's amazement, his cavalier friend had given every appearance of being genuinely smitten.

From clear across the park, he heard Elly's sudden, husky laughter. He saw her face, upturned toward Connor, glowing and lovely in the day's pure crystal light. He wondered for the thousandth time what would have happened that first night they'd met if *he* had been the one to reach her first, to hurl that damned, mauling drunkard into the street.

It was ironic. Connor had been so excited about having won thirty dollars at faro that night that he hadn't even noticed the scene at the end of the street. It was Boone who had pointed out the young woman cornered by drunks, Boone who had suggested she might need help. Connor had barely listened. But when they'd reached the girl and seen her pinned against the wall by that hooligan, somehow Connor had sprung forward an instant before Boone, flinging the drunk aside. And while Connor had remained to bask in the glory of her gratitude, Boone had dealt with the other two, receiving in return for his efforts a brief, polite smile but none of the adoration she had shown for Con. Oh, hell, he decided, springing to his feet and stuffing his hands into the pockets of his heavy tweed coat. What had he expected? It was no good feeling sorry for himself. It was always this way where Con and women were concerned. But this time, just this one time, he wished it were different.

"What do you say we head back to the house for some hot chocolate?" Connor called as he and Elly approached. He pointed at Timothy, running with the sled up the slope. "I think that young devil is getting the sniffles. We'd best get him inside."

They were greeted at the boardinghouse by the aromas of cinnamon and spice. Gingerbread cookies. Boone felt a stabbing of pain as he remembered his mother's farmhouse kitchen fragrant with that same delicious smell. Ma had won a prize once for her gingerbread cookies. She'd been so proud. And Clay had whooped like an Indian. And Tom, Tom had . . .

Angrily, he stopped the flow of memories. There was no going back, no point in thinking about home or family. That was all done with. He glanced around at the Forrest family and the boarders wandering through the house, at Connor, joking with everyone, and Elly casting breathless, happy glances at the tall Irishman who was the center of attention. *I don't belong here either*, Boone told himself silently. *Not in Kentucky, and not here with Elly Forrest*. But he stayed, watching the girl in the plaid dress move nimbly and efficiently about the kitchen.

Elly hummed softly to herself as she rinsed and dried the plates and cups a short time later. Connor Maguire and his boldly handsome face filled every corner of her mind.

She had never known life could be so exciting, had never dreamed such strange and delicious feelings lay dormant inside her. It was Connor who had awakened her as if from a dull gray dream, Connor who had brought the whole world vibrantly alive.

The house seemed warmer, brighter when he was here. The very air seemed to crackle and snap with vitality. She had watched him eating gingerbread cookies in the kitchen, drinking cocoa, tousling Timothy's hair, and punching Boone Walker in the arm. All the while she was filled with wonder. It was incredible to her that this man was courting her, had been courting her assiduously for the past two weeks. A man like Connor could have any woman, and she failed to see what drew him to her. Her neck was too long, she knew; her face too plain. Even her body was tall and gangly, or at least, it had been. Not long ago, Aunt Adelaide had remarked that she was reminded more and more of Bess when she looked at Elly, that Elly carried herself with a newfound grace reminiscent of her mother's dignified carriage. Elly had paid scant attention. But now she wondered if it was that which had attracted Connor's notice. Whatever it was, she thought, as she wiped her dripping hands on a towel, she prayed it would continue. She couldn't bear it if his attentions came to an end.

With one last satisfied glance around the spotless kitchen, she hurried into the hall. Caroline had gone to her room with a headache a few minutes earlier, and Timothy was upstairs arguing with Mama about that ridiculously boisterous stray dog he had adopted against her wishes. If only Boone Walker would leave, she and Connor could have a few precious moments in the parlor alone.

"Andrew Carnegie is nearly ready to roll the first rail from his steel plant on the Monongahela. And the Hudson plant is being built at a good clip, too," Connor was saying as she approached. He sounded angry. "Boone, if old man Whitcomb keeps dragging his feet, that steel plant we want to build won't even make it to the start of this race!"

"I know how you feel, Con, but Whitcomb is cautious."

"Too damn cautious!"

"He wants to be sure of the country's financial recovery before jumping into a steel enterprise, that's all. I think he's almost ready to make the move. He sent us here, didn't he, to explore those freight and farm machinery contracts?" Boone Walker, as usual, spoke in his quiet, steady tones.

"Well, why shouldn't he? The foundry is showing a profit, even with this stupid financial crisis going on. He'd be a

complete fool not to—'' Connor broke off, spotting Elly just
inside the parlor door. His face, tense with frustration, softened, and he gave a chuckle. ''How long have you been
there, lass? Aren't you bored listening to all this man's talk?''

''It reminds me of my home when Papa was alive,'' she
said, moving forward into the room. ''He was always arguing
or debating with whoever would listen. Mama grew sick of it,
but I used to love asking him questions and hearing him go on
and on. Papa was very eloquent.''

She sat down beside Connor on the medallion-backed maroon sofa. Behind her, heavy velour drapes of the same color
fell in thick folds across the double-hung sash windows.
''Tell me about this steel plant you're so anxious to build,''
she urged. ''Isn't that a tremendously expensive undertaking?''

''Not for Louis Whitcomb,'' Connor muttered. He threw
an impatient glance at Boone, who was standing before the
mantel. ''Boone thinks I'm in too much of a hurry. He's as
cautious as Whitcomb. But I can't help dreaming, Elly, and
wanting to make my dreams come true as quickly as possible.''

''But the foundry—surely that keeps you as busy as you
can be?''

''We started that foundry, Boone and me, but now others
can take over the running of it. We have some good men
down there. As for me, I'm ready to tackle something even
bigger.'' Connor leaned toward her eagerly, talking in the
swift, excited way that was characteristic of his fiery charm.
''Actually, the whole steel operation was Boone's idea from
way back. He convinced me of the merits of Bessemer steel.''

At Elly's blank look, he explained. ''The Bessemer process
is a cheaper, easier way of making steel. If we build a
Bessemer plant, we can produce steel that's more affordable
for locomotives, railroad tracks, bridges, farm machinery,
everything.'' His enthusiasm shone in his eyes, but it changed
swiftly to dark frustration as he cast another glance at Boone.
''But if we don't hurry up and start manufacturing it,'' Connor declared, ''everyone else in Pittsburgh will snap up all the
contracts and we'll be left out in the cold.''

''We're moving forward step by step, Connor.'' Unconsciously illustrating the point, Boone strode forward and put
his hands on the back of Aunt Adelaide's brocade wing chair.
''Lining up these freight contracts, getting estimates on

construction—all this takes time, you know that. To rush
things would—''

"Would make us rich men, no doubt. We wouldn't want
that to happen, saints forbid!''

Boone grinned, his keen gray eyes lighting. "Patience was
never Con's strong suit,'' he explained to Elly.

"But I do know when's the time to play my cards, lad!
And the time is now.''

Elly decided to change the subject before they could continue the argument. "Mama wishes you both to stay to dinner. You will, won't you?''

"Nothing could keep me away.'' Connor stretched an arm
across the back of the sofa. "Not when the prettiest girl in the
Midwest is going to be sitting across the table from me.''

The easy color stole into Elly's cheeks, turning them a
vivid pink. She was unused to such outrageous compliments,
or to his engaging, teasing ways. With an effort, she tore her
gaze from his dancing blue eyes and looked at Boone. "You
will stay, too, won't you?''

He hesitated, thinking of the dimly lit, solitary room awaiting him at the Grayson Hotel and then of the cheerful warmth
and bustle of this house. Even this parlor, despite the slightly
frayed maroon draperies and the faded slipcovers on the two
Queen Anne chairs, was bright and polished and alive, with
its bric-a-brac, its gilded mirrors, its darkly polished wood-
work. Then, catching the glance being exchanged between
Elly and Connor, his mouth suddenly tightened. The two
might have been alone here for all the notice they gave him.

"I'd best be going. I've got work to do before tomorrow.''

Yet he lingered at the door, and his mind raced as he tried
to think of something amusing to say.

She was enchanting in the lamplight, a slim, elegant figure
with luminous eyes, a firm, dainty nose, and a mouth that
was unconsciously sensuous and inviting, for all its innocence. Beneath the flickering gas jets of the hall chandelier,
her creamy skin had a lustrous glow, and her hair, tied with a
wide green ribbon, glistened black as coal. He wanted to
reach out and pull her into his arms, to feel her soft, lithe
body close against his. Instead he said, "Good night, Elly,''
and satisfied himself with watching the way her face lit up
when she smiled.

"Good night, Boone.''

Elly stood in the doorway and watched him leave. A cloak of darkness had fallen over the streets. The sky was murky with gray, scuttling snow-clouds. With his collar turned up against the quickening wind, Boone Walker strode off, and for a moment, Elly felt sorry for him. He looked forlorn, somehow. Perhaps he had been more concerned by Connor's statements about the steel plant than he had let on. Or perhaps he wished for a young woman of his own to share the cold winter's evening with, she mused. One could never be sure with Boone. Though he was Connor's good friend, she didn't yet know him well. He wasn't a man who gave away much of what he was thinking.

Despite his gigantic, imposing presence, he spoke little, staying for the most part in the background. He was reserved and quiet, she had noticed, his thick sandy hair and gray eyes a contrast to Connor's dark and vibrant good looks. Yet she had seen on more than one occasion that Boone was kind, serious, and hardworking, all qualities Elly respected. Nevertheless, they were hardly exciting. Connor, on the other hand, exuded an aura of boldness, a sweeping, dynamic energy that made her heart spin every time he was near. Now, remembering that he waited for her in the parlor, she promptly forgot all about Boone Walker. She shut the door and, with her pulse racing, hurried across the hall.

"See that?" Connor stood at the window, the draperies parted to reveal the glistening white street. A handsome carriage drawn by two stunning chestnuts flashed by in the dusk. For one dazzling moment, the streetlights illuminated the carved panels of the doors, the glittering silver trimmings, the white ribbons wound in the manes of the sleek and spirited horses, before they streaked by and were gone. "One day, Elly, I'm going to have a carriage like that. And a fine pair to pull it. But they'll be thoroughbreds, black thoroughbreds, the most beautiful thoroughbreds in the world."

"I don't suppose you'll take a poor working girl for a ride in such a fancy rig," she teased softly, coming into the room.

Connor let the draperies fall back into place. He turned to face her. "Oh, I might, I just might." He smiled into her eyes, and a thrill like bright blue fire burned in her chest. He drew her over to the sofa and sat down next to her.

"I have to leave Chicago soon."

"When?" Elly felt the world dropping away from her.

"On Thursday."

"Oh. Oh, I see."

Her voice sounded high and weak. The boardinghouse had grown strangely quiet. Or maybe it was just that the pounding of her heart drowned out the other sounds.

"You knew all along this was only a short business trip that brought us here." Connor's blue eyes were fastened on her, and for once, he was serious. No merry lilt softened his voice, and his mouth was straight and firm. "Boone and I must get back to Pittsburgh and the foundry."

"Yes, I understand." Why was her mouth so dry? She could barely speak.

From far away, a freight train whistled. Its mournful wail echoed the death knell in her heart. Elly tried to pull away from him, to avert her head so that he couldn't see the pain she knew must show in her face, but Connor grasped both her hands in one of his and, with the other, tilted her chin up so that she was forced to look into his eyes.

"Will you miss me, Elly?"

"Yes, of course I will," she said woodenly, trying with all her will to hold back the threatening tears. It would never do to let him see how devastated she was. Young women simply didn't cry in the presence of young men bidding them farewell. She had to preserve something of pride, of dignity, or she couldn't bear to live with herself.

"I . . . enjoyed the time we spent together. I'll always think of it." She tried to sound cheerful.

"So did I. As a matter of fact . . ." He broke off and took a deep breath. He almost couldn't believe what he was about to do. But then, who would have believed two weeks ago that he would meet a girl like Elly?

It had started out as an ordinary flirtation. She was a nice young woman, of a decent, hardworking family, and she had an aura of elegance that appealed to him. From the way she moved and spoke to the unusual beauty of her dark hair and white skin, she seemed to Connor the embodiment of something finer than himself. He had thought to amuse himself with her while he and Boone were in town, but without his knowledge, his intentions had undergone a change during the course of their time together. He had been surprised by her intelligence: she was much more clever, straightforward, and enterprising than any girl he had known before. She was warm, caring, and devoted to her family, managing them and the boardinghouse with a maturity that went beyond her eighteen years. He'd been bitten, Connor had realized as he looked forward more and more to his time with her. Bitten by the snake of love. The parlor fire sent out its waves of warmth as they sat together on the sofa, and suddenly he blurted out what he'd been intending to say.

"Elly, the truth of the matter is, I want to marry you. I love you, lass, with all my heart, and I want us to spend the rest of our days together. There, it's done."

He squeezed her hands tight, studying her astonished face. He didn't doubt she'd accept him, but he wanted to savor her delight. "Will you do me the grand honor of becoming my wife?" he finished, and kissed each of her hands in turn.

His wife, Elly thought. Connor's wife, to live with him always, sleep with him, have children with him. Her joy was a tangible thing, leaping from her blood to his, igniting them both with a sudden roaring fire. "Connor, I thought you were telling me good-bye!"

"No, darlin', that's the furthest thing from my mind," he vowed. He took her in his arms, holding her tightly, kissing the tip of her nose. "Elly, lass, I never thought such a thing would happen to me, and not this way. It's only been two weeks, but now I don't want to live without you." Beneath the shock of black hair, his eyes danced with excitement. "Is it settled then? We are betrothed?"

"Yes, yes. We're betrothed! Connor, I'm so happy!"

"I must speak with your mum, of course, but . . . a kiss, then, Elly, to seal the bargain. Ah, Elly, my darlin', my sweet, bonny love."

Elly was shocked by the intensity of the kiss. He had never kissed her before—no one had ever kissed her before, except Billy Moffett, and that had been nothing like this. A thread of delicious electricity jolted through her body as his warm, strong mouth moved over hers. He held her close, urged her lips apart. There was fire in every place his hands and body touched. It was wonderful, thrilling. He tasted of gingerbread and cider and spice. She felt the powerful muscles of his chest and arms as he held her close against his tall frame, kissing her softly, yearningly, with ever increasing hunger. Again and again, endlessly, he kissed her, until she felt the world spinning and dropping away. It was shocking and wicked, she thought dazedly, but she didn't care. She didn't want him ever to stop. She clung to him, opening her lips and her heart to him. She felt incredibly warm, incredibly wanted.

"I'm going to make you so happy," he whispered, his mouth against hers. "The happiest woman in the world."

Elly could barely speak. "You've already done that."

"I'm going to take care of you. And your family, too."

How wonderful that sounded. No longer would she have to worry so about keeping everyone safe, sheltered, and fed. A weight of iron slipped from her shoulders. She felt light, free. Always at the back of her mind had lurked the fear that men like Silas Emmett could take everything away again if she wasn't constantly vigilant. But with Connor . . . She leaned back in his arms and smiled at this tall, broad-shouldered Irishman with his curling black hair and laughing eyes. Connor's raw strength, his confidence, his bold, lighthearted vitality blunted every needle of fear.

"I can't wait to tell Mama. She'll be so pleased. She thinks you're a fine young man. She says you're going to make something of yourself."

He chuckled. "So I am." He was tempted for a moment to tell her the idea he was considering, a plan that might earn him riches far quicker than any iron foundry, but then thought better of it. He'd wait until he'd made up his mind.

As Elly leaned against him, thinking of her family's reaction to their announcement, a horrible thought struck her. "Connor, will I . . . will we . . .?" She could barely speak the words, so affected was she by their implications. "Will we have to live in Pittsburgh?"

He hesitated. "Well, that's where the foundry is, darlin'."

"But I can't." Her mouth went dry. Joy turned to dismay. "My family is here, Connor." She was pleading. "They need me."

"Well, if it comes to that, they could live with us in Pennsylvania. I know how dear they are to you, Elly."

"No! They can never go back there . . . I can never go back there!"

"And why not?" he demanded in surprise. Elly hadn't provided much detail about her family's past. She had said only that her father had died working in a rug factory in some little town in Pennsylvania, that they had struggled along without him for a while, and that a little less than two years ago they had left to start over in Chicago. "Too many memories of your da and the hard times you had after he died?" Connor asked in a more sympathetic tone, his arm tightening around her shoulders.

"Yes . . . too many painful memories." Maybe she should tell him about Emmettville, Elly thought frantically. If Connor was going to be her husband, she ought to tell him why she couldn't go within a hundred miles of Emmettville and why she would never dream of taking Caroline back there. "You don't understand, Connor . . ."

"A wife follows her husband, darlin'," he interrupted. His tone was still gentle, but there was a firmness now in his handsome face. "Those sad memories will all fade away when we're together in the fine house I'm intending to build for you. You'll see. But . . ." Sensing her distress, he decided to give her a hint of the alternative. "There *is* a possibility we might not settle in Pittsburgh."

She jumped at this like a starving bird to a scrap of bread. "Why, Connor? How would that be? If the foundry is there and you and Boone are partners in it, I don't see how . . ."

"Hush, lass." Chuckling, he brought his lips down on hers again, effectively silencing her questions. "You're not to worry," he ordered a moment later. "I'll let you know the lot of it in good time. But you shouldn't fret about such things. All you need to know is that wherever we are, I'll take care of you."

Not to fret? Impossible. Everything depended on his decision. With a tightness in her chest, Elly realized she might not be able to marry Connor—not if that meant deserting her family and moving to Pittsburgh, which was dangerously close to Emmettville. Her head started to throb and, with it, her wrist, the one Jason Emmett had broken when he twisted the gun from her grasp. It had not been set properly, and she still used it with care and a small degree of accompanying pain. Now it ached as if to remind her of what she had suffered at Jason's hands. And that was only a tiny fragment of what Caroline had endured, she reminded herself with a shudder. Even Connor's arms enfolding her protectively against his chest couldn't banish the churning fear within her.

When a soft knock sounded on the open door, she started. Caroline poked her head into the room. "Mama needs you in the kitchen, Elly," she said diffidently. She ducked her head in embarrassment at finding them so close together on the sofa, holding hands before the blazing fire. Without even waiting for an answer, she hurried back the way she had come.

"Shall we tell your mum at dinner?" Connor's voice was full of enthusiasm.

Elly tried to shake off her anxiety, to match his euphoric mood, wishing she could recapture the joy of a few moments ago. "I'd rather wait a bit, if that's all right with you." She thought of her promise to Aunt Adelaide, and of Timothy and Caroline and Mama, who needed her so. "Let's enjoy the secret ourselves until we know more about . . . our plans."

He looked disappointed, but then dropped a quick kiss on the top of her head. "Sure, darlin'. Why not? I'll have to go to Pittsburgh with Boone on Thursday, but soon enough I'll be back for you, and we'll make plans. You'll be Mrs. Connor Maguire in less time than it takes a leprechaun to wink."

Elly nodded and smiled, but her heart was heavy. She could only pray that Connor would find a way to stay in Chicago. If not . . . She couldn't bear to think of that possibility. She couldn't bear to think that she might have to choose between what was best for her family, and becoming Mrs. Connor Maguire.

Dinner was a long, difficult ordeal. She ought to have been happy, filled with wondrous delight at the prospect of marrying this fine, handsome man whom she loved, but all she could think of was Emmettville, a few short miles from Pittsburgh's hub. She didn't taste the savory stew Mama had prepared or the fresh, crusty bread or the vegetable pie Aunt Adelaide offered her. She watched her sister's blond head across the table, looked into Caroline's bleak face and weary blue eyes, and knew what her answer must be.

Connor whistled as he rode the streetcar later that evening. Everything was falling into place. Things had gone just as he had hoped they would with Elly, and now his potential deal with Sean Fitzgerald lay before him. It was sounding better and better.

Instead of returning to the hotel, he went to Randolph Street. It was here he had first met the girl he was to marry, but his visit was not a sentimental one. He sauntered along the slush-covered pavement with the assurance of one who was traveling through familiar territory. Though it was Sunday night and most of the saloons and gambling halls were dark, he knew Fitz would have a card game going in the back room of his place. He was right.

"Well, if it isn't Maguire. Come to give us a chance at winning our money back, eh, lad?" The plump, barrel-chested Dubliner glanced up from the poker game with a welcoming grin. Sean Fitzgerald had a mass of freckles on his jowly face, a wide, loose mouth, and an easy smile. His hair was carrot-colored. In his plaid vest, frock coat, and white linen shirt with the sleeves rolled up to his elbows, he looked like exactly what he was: a good-natured saloonkeeper with a love of fast horses and easy women. He watched Connor saunter across the square, dimly lit room filled with benches and tables and mugs of whiskey and beer. His eyes were speculative, narrowed. For all his jolly, nonchalant air, Sean Fitzgerald's shrewd ice-green eyes missed nothing.

"I came to talk, Fitzgerald," Connor answered with his ready laugh. "I've already given you plenty of chances at my money." He straddled a chair with sinewy grace and watched the card play with interest. "I'm feeling far too lucky to lose at anything these days," he remarked, and pulled a cigar from the pocket of his coat.

"That so? Then we'd better talk. A man can't afford to waste any little bit of his luck." When the hand was over, Fitzgerald pushed his chair back. "Deal me out, lads. I'm buying Mr. Maguire here a drink."

"A toast is in order," Connor told him as they left the back room and went to the darkened main bar, where the Dubliner lit lamps and poured whiskey into glasses. They sat together at a small table. "I'm getting married to the finest girl in Chicago."

"Are you, lad? The one you told me about, that you met the first day you came into my place?"

"Yes, but don't ever mention that little fact to her, Fitz." Connor took a healthy sip of his whiskey, relishing its warmth going down into his belly, particularly after the cold of the February night. "She's a quality kind of girl, you see," he explained, as the other man raised his brows in surprise. "Very refined. I told her we just wandered into this part of town by chance that day—not that I had come to find a good saloon and a run of luck at faro. Women don't understand why men enjoy such pastimes." He shook his head and took a puff of the cigar. "Elly wouldn't, that's for sure."

"I know what you mean." Fitzgerald winked and chuckled. He licked a drop of whiskey from his lips. "Am I to meet her, then?"

"Sure and you will, if we're to be business partners. You're bound to meet her someday."

The ice-green eyes brightened. "Ah, then you've made your decision? The theater's a go? What'll you do, lad, sell off your share of that Pennsylvania foundry to buy in?"

Connor sighed. "Boone will call me every name in hell, but that's what I'm going to do, I think."

"You think?" Sean Fitzgerald frowned at him. He set his glass down on the table with a thud. "You'd better make up your mind soon, lad, or I'll have to find another partner. I can't wait much longer."

"I know, I know." Connor drained his glass and tilted the bottle over it again. "I've just about decided, only . . ."

"Only what? You said the old man in Pittsburgh moves too slow for you. You said you're fed up with all the delays. And you know what, lad? You're not cut out to make iron and steel for the rest of your days. You need excitement. You need to be surrounded by famous people, important people. Imagine, lad, what a grand thing it is to own and operate a theater. And such a theater as we will build together! Magnificent it will be! And everyone will come, the rich and the not so rich, for if it's one thing people love to see, it's an entertainment." Fitzgerald spoke swiftly, urgently, his face brimming with enthusiasm. He drummed his stubby fingers on the table. "Plays, burlesque, musical revues," he continued gleefully. "We'll make ourselves a tidy fortune. So decide, lad. Decide." He puffed his cheeks out in a challenging expression. "Are you going to be a foot soldier all your life for that stuffy old general in Pittsburgh and for your mate, the lieutenant, or will you become the co-owner and manager of the grandest theater Chicago has ever known?"

"You tempt me, Fitzgerald, you sorely tempt me," Connor mused. In his mind's eye, he saw himself attired in rich broadcloth and fine linen, staring out at a full house in the splendidly appointed theater. The crimson velvet upholstery of the boxes, the golden frescoed ceilings, and the shimmering crystal chandeliers would complement the finery of the theater's patrons, all the wealthy and important people of the city. It would be a far more attractive setting for him than the gritty warehouse offices he shared with Boone at the foundry, where smoke and fumes and clutter and the steady dull roar of iron-casting filled every moment and space. And it was true what Fitzgerald had said about Boone and Whitcomb. They were the commanders of the foundry's operation; despite the equal time he had spent proving himself with Boone, he was nothing but a foot soldier, especially in Whitcomb's eyes. From the very first, it was Boone whom Whitcomb had turned to with trust and respect, Boone whom he listened to when it came time for crucial decisions. And he was fed up with all of Louis Whitcomb's orders and demands and delays. Damn it, he *ought* to strike out on his own and show them both what bold initiative could yield.

Then there was Elly. Elly would be able to stay here with her family, and that would please her no end. They could live in the boardinghouse until the theater opened and the money started rolling in. Then he would build her as fine a mansion as any in this booming town.

Fitzgerald was studying his face. "So what's it to be, lad? Are we partners?"

Connor scraped back his chair. He thrust out his hand. "Aye." Pride and pleasure shone on his lean, flushed cheeks. His eyes were alight with keen excitement. "Partners."

🌿 Twelve

THE FIRST HINT of trouble came in early May, one month after Elly and Connor were married. Caroline appeared late one afternoon at the door to the bedroom Elly and Connor now shared. It was a large, frilly room with peach and white wallpaper and a settee covered with pale green silk over in the corner by the window. Bess had previously occupied this room alone, but after the wedding, she had moved into the yellow bedroom with Caroline. It was an arrangement that suited them both admirably, as close as they had always been. In fact, every aspect of life in the boardinghouse had improved in Elly's eyes since the wedding, for Connor had quickly become a member of the family and had proven helpful to everyone in many ways, seeing to small repairs, moving the heavy furniture during spring cleaning, even entertaining the boarders at dinner with his lively stories. Until the moment she saw Caroline in the doorway, pale and trembling, Elly had been in a state of euphoria. She'd been thinking of the pleasures she and her husband had shared the night before in the wide, creaky-springed bed. She'd been pondering dreamily how fortunate she had been to marry a man as handsome and exciting and tender as Connor Maguire.

"Elly, come quickly." Caroline's voice was a breathless, terrified whisper. "There's a man downstairs in the hall. He's asking—no, demanding—to see Connor."

"Did he give his name?" Elly asked in surprise. "Well, I'm certain there's nothing to be so upset about, Caro." She let the socks she was folding fall back into the laundry basket, a faraway smile still softening her lips. "I'm coming, so you needn't look so anxious."

"Elly, he's angry! Furious, in fact! What can he want?"

"We won't know until we ask him." Elly led the way to the stairs, her light muslin skirt of delicate pink rustling about her long legs. Despite Caroline's agitation, she was unconcerned. It took very little to unnerve Caroline. No doubt the man had something to do with the building of the theater and had mistakenly come to Connor's home instead of his office. She was too busy inhaling the fragrance of spring flowers blowing through the open windows of the boardinghouse to fret about the visitor.

Just last week she and Jeweline had taken down all the heavy winter draperies for cleaning and summer storage and had replaced them with the light summer curtains, which now stirred softly in the warm May air. Perhaps it was these light trimmings at the windows, or the sounds of children playing outside, or the fragrance of lilacs and tulips from the garden that gave the house its fresh, springtime aura. As she descended the stairs, the sunshine streaming in through the rectangular windows flanking the door bathed the hall with a pale amber glow, touching the rosewood table, the oaken floor, the vase of red and white tulips with shimmering opalescent light. A sense of well-being enveloped her as warm and comforting as the golden day. Thus it was even a greater shock when she confronted the black-haired beetle of a man who burst from the parlor at the sound of her footsteps and glared at her from beneath dark, scowling brows.

"Where is he? Tell me where to find Connor Maguire!" he boomed.

Harsh words spoken in an even harsher voice. Elly stopped short in dismay. The stout man before her was of medium height, with a neck as big around as a jug and arms that were thickly muscled and covered with hair. His sunken eyes were the color of onyx in his ruddy, pitted face. A nasty scar running across the left side of his nose and ending at the down-turned corner of his mouth gave him a sinister appearance. From his worn, stained work clothes, with the sleeves of his striped flannel shirt rolled up to reveal powerful muscles, Elly guessed he was a meat packer or a dockworker or something of that sort. He reeked of onions, sweat, and tobacco, and a vague feeling of nausea came over her as he planted himself before her. How in the world, she wondered, did this man know Connor?

"I am Mrs. Maguire. Perhaps I can help you. Why do you wish to see my husband?" She spoke as calmly as she could, but her hard-won composure only seemed to infuriate him further.

"I'll tell you why, missus!" Black eyes gleamed malevolently at her. "Your scoundrel of a husband owes me one hundred and seventeen dollars! He lost it fair and square at poker in Sweeney's place last week, and I want it settled. I'm sick to death of waiting. I gotta get to Halsted Street fast for my shift at the slaughterhouse and I wanna be paid *now*."

"That's impossible, Connor couldn't possibly—" she began to protest, then broke off as his face contorted with surging rage. "I . . . I'm sorry, I don't doubt your word, but . . ." She cast frantically about in her mind for some explanation that would make sense of this situation. Connor had lost that much money in a poker game? Her heartbeat quickened painfully in her chest. There must be a mistake, a terrible mistake. Behind her, on the stairs, she could feel rather than hear Caroline's shrinking presence. "Are you certain my husband is the man you're looking for?" she asked with a wild flicker of hope. "Perhaps it is a different Connor Maguire."

He snorted in contempt. "Big, good-looking Irishman? More charm than card sense? That's him."

The man's voice was a bellow, ricocheting around the hall like a bouncing ball. All the while they had been talking, Elly had been stifling the urge to quiet him. As he finished speaking, the sounds she'd been dreading came to her ears. Beyond the laughter of the children in the street came creaking footsteps from above. Mrs. Joseph's worn, gray head peeked around the second-floor landing as she squinted down at the little scene in the hall. A moment later, Jeweline, tall and spare in her brown work dress, appeared at the kitchen door, her black hands coated with flour, her handsome, weathered face creased with alarm. Her questioning eyes met Elly's over Caroline's fair head. And Caroline . . . Caroline stood like a statue glued to the wall. *I ought to be selling tickets,* Elly thought, her only consolation being that at least Mama and Aunt Adelaide were out, visiting the O'Riley family down the street with a basket of food and jellies, for poor Mr. O'Riley had lost his trainman's job only last week. At least they had been spared this scene. She spoke hurriedly, before any other boarders could congregate: "Come into the parlor, Mr. . . .?"

"Grunder, Joe Grunder." He bit the words off with furious impatience.

Elly led the way into the parlor, sending her sister a quick, reassuring smile over her shoulder. Unfortunately, she didn't feel as confident as she tried to appear. As she closed the door, her fingers trembled for a moment on the polished wood. Her head was whirling. Connor owed money, gambling money, to this man, Joe Grunder? One hundred and seventeen dollars? It was a staggering amount. Enough to buy groceries for a month. Enough to replace the old cast-iron stove in the kitchen with a new gas-burning one. Enough to purchase a trunkful of new clothes for every member of the family. And where was Sweeney's place? she wondered. Her throat was dry as sand. When had Connor gone there?

"Just tell me where to find your husband, missus." Grunder shook a grimy finger at her. "That's all I ask. I'll likely break his weaselly arm for putting me to all this trouble, but I'll get my money and I won't be bothering you again."

"There's no need to find my husband," Elly said quickly. Fear for Connor darted into her eyes, widening them as she faced the meat packer in the warm, sunlit parlor. Her hands were cold, despite the molten sunshine pouring into the room. "I'll pay you what he owes."

She nearly ran from the room. Scarcely able to breathe for the tightness in her chest, she went to the desk in the sewing room across the hall and unlocked the center drawer. From this, she lifted the wooden box that contained the month's boardinghouse receipts. Tears burned her eyelids as she counted out the money with shaking fingers. She'd planned to buy Caroline a pair of ivory hair combs for her seventeenth birthday next month. And she'd been trying to set aside enough to begin the tearoom come autumn. Now the plain wooden box looked pitifully empty. They'd be fortunate to get by until the next payment for room and board came due.

"Here, here is your money, Mr. Grunder. Now please go and leave us alone." She thrust the green bills at him, unable to hide her agitation.

Despite his earlier statement about the need for haste, Grunder took his time counting out the money. Throughout the whole procedure, the scowl never left his face.

"Well, it's all here, I see," he conceded at last. "Took long enough to collect. So now you can give your husband a message for me, missus. Tell him to stay away from the poker table unless he's willin' to pay up when he loses. A man gets real angry havin' to wait." He regarded Elly from under his beetle brows. Her pale cheeks and blue-gray eyes filled with distress seemed to give him some perverse satisfaction. "Just to make sure he understands, I'll show you what I mean, missus." Slowly, deliberately, he gazed about the orderly room. Soft opalescent light fell on the blue and maroon threads of the throw rug at their feet, touched the whatnot in the corner and its shelves packed with books, carved animals, shells, and fans. It sent a sheer springtime glow over the fireplace mantel, with its brass clock and assorted vases filled with dried ferns. It illuminated the whole gleaming parlor for Joe Grunder's scrutiny, from the stuffed, faded maroon sofa to the slipcovered chairs. "Show you what I mean," Grunder repeated, and as Elly gasped, he stalked to the whatnot and snatched up her mother's prized collection of delicate seashells in one hairy fist. In the next instant, before Elly could move, he had smashed them down upon the hard oak floor. Elly's heart stopped as the tinkling of fragile shells seemed to explode in her ears. She gazed in mute dismay at the tiny jagged shards scattered on the floor. Then Grunder struck again, sweeping an arm along the entire upper shelf. A pair of porcelain kittens followed the shells, shattering on the floor amid a pile of carved doves and squirrels and Aunt Adelaide's antique silk fan.

"No!" Elly cried in horror as he next lunged for the mantel and lifted a Chinese vase painted in delicate pinks and greens. "No, don't you dare. Put that down," she half ordered, half pled. Darting forward, she reached for the vase.

He knocked her aside. The vase splintered against the marble hearth, exploding into a thousand painted pieces.

"Get out! Get out, I said! Haven't you done enough?" Elly lashed out at him from between clenched teeth. She was trembling all over. For a moment she was afraid he meant to turn his violence on her, so darkly did he stare at her. Then a thin smile spread across his face. He tipped his cap to her in a mocking salute.

"Now your husband won't be able to mistake my mean-

ing,'' he said. He dusted off his hands with a widening grin.
"Good day, Mrs. Maguire.''

Scarcely fifteen minutes later, Connor arrived home to find
Elly kneeling on the parlor floor, painstakingly gathering the
broken fragments of Bess's seashells into her hand. ''Why,
what's all this?'' he asked in amazement, the merriment of
his mood still apparent in his voice. Then he saw her face.
Tears streaked her cheeks. The lovely eyes—neither blue nor
gray, but a luminous, hypnotic combination of the two—were
red-rimmed and swollen. ''Elly, darlin'.'' He crouched beside her, appalled. ''What in the name of heaven happened?''

She stared at him. Only a short while ago, she thought,
everything had been wonderful. Connor had been wonderful.
Now she was looking at a stranger.

"Joe Grunder was here,'' she said dully, watching his
face. It told her all she needed to know about the truth of
Grunder's words. Connor looked as though she had punched
him in the gut. She indicated the debris on the floor with a
tiny wave of her hand. ''He wanted to leave you a message.''

That night she readied herself for bed with the tired, weary
movements of someone mired in grief. And she was grieving,
grieving for the lighthearted joy and contentment she had
known only this afternoon. She wondered, as she slipped her
white cotton nightgown over her head and pushed her slim
arms through the short, puffed sleeves, if she would ever
again know that same blind trust, that delicious, soothing
serenity, which since her marriage had seemed as natural as
waking in the morning, as pleasurable as going to bed at
night.

She went to the pier glass above the doily-covered bureau
and, taking up her hairbrush, began to brush the long black
curls with listless strokes. Her hair fell about her narrow
shoulders like a velvet mantle. She looked like a specter, Elly
thought, meeting her own gaze in the mirror. Glazed eyes,
huge in her oval face, stared back at her, lifeless and dull.
Her skin was as gray as frost; her lips looked paler than the
lace at her throat. Only last night Connor had twined his
hands in her hair and inhaled its scent, and told her how
beautiful she was, how much he loved her, needed her. Only
last night he had lain with her in their bed and quenched her
inner thirst with his own passion and intoxicating desire. Now
he was downstairs in the kitchen alone, tippling a bottle of

Aunt Adelaide's brandy. And she stood here, empty, drained, yet quaking deep inside, beneath the deathly stillness that had overtaken her since Connor had come home. She was frightened, terrified. And there was no one to ease her fear.

Connor had apologized; he had explained. He had sworn he'd never gamble ten cents again. Yet her faith in him had been shaken to the core. That such a man as Joe Grunder could invade their home, destroy her mother's and her aunt's treasured possessions, threaten the very stronghold Elly had built around her family in the past year and a half filled her with panic. She had thought she was safe, that they were all safe, especially since Connor had come into her life. What could happen with Connor there to protect them, strong, dashing Connor with his blazing smile and hearty laugh, his gaiety and warmth and charm? But she had been deceived, or maybe she had deceived herself. Connor had brought Joe Grunder into this house, Connor had gambled and lost an alarming sum of money, Connor had shattered her peace, her faith, and her trust.

She put down the brush and moved slowly about the room, readying herself for bed with a heavy heart. Slipping beneath the sheet in the darkened room, she stared at the ceiling flickering with its faint pattern of light from the stars outside the open window. The May night was warm and fragrant with the scents of new flowers and damp earth drifting in from the garden. All was silent, except for a sudden unexpected gust of wind that blew into the peach and white room, fluttering the curtains and the edges of the dust ruffle around the big creaky bed. For no reason at all, her mind suddenly turned to Boone Walker.

Misgiving crept over her now because Connor had severed his partnership with Boone. She wasn't certain exactly why. In March, when Connor had told her of his decision to sell Boone his share of the iron foundry and the land on the Monongahela River, she had been relieved. Vastly relieved. There would be no need to make a decision between her family and the man she loved, no need even to contemplate returning to Pennsylvania. Though she had felt bad that Connor would no longer be partners with the man who was his closest friend, and had later wondered if it wasn't foundry business but anger over the dissolving of the partnership that had kept Boone from attending their wedding, these qualms had quickly faded from her mind. It had been obvious that the theater enterprise excited Connor; he was tremendously enthusiastic about it. And though she had not been thoroughly taken with Sean Fitzgerald the afternoon Connor had taken her to the theater site and introduced her to his new partner, she had known no reason not to trust him as Connor did. Yet as she lay in her bed, watching the circular beams of starlight on the ceiling, she thought how much safer and more secure she would feel tonight if Connor were still involved with Boone, if she knew that Boone, with his quiet voice and steady manner, was there to provide a solid influence on Connor. Elly turned on her side, propping her head up on one arm as she gazed at the gently waving curtains, amber in the starlight. Until today, she hadn't thought of Connor as needing a steadying influence. But Joe Grunder's revelation had changed all that.

The bedroom door creaked open. She lay still as she heard Connor's boots on the floor, then heard the door close with a tiny click. Suddenly, he was at her side, kneeling beside the bed and groping for her hands.

"You're not still angry with me, are you, Elly? I swear, lass, it'll never happen again." There was brandy on his breath, and some of it had spilled on his shirtfront, staining it crimson. His voice was blurred with liquor, but heartbreakingly sincere in its contrition. "S . . . sorry about your mum's things and your aunt's vase. I'll replace them, sure and I will. And no more gambling. And the money you gave Grunder—I told you I'd replace it tomorrow and I will. I've got piles of money stored in the safe in Sean's office, darlin'. Piles of it. That debt to Grunder is nothing, Elly. It wasn't worth even one of your tears, but I understand . . ." He hurried on as she drew breath to speak, as if he was afraid that she would reject him if he didn't plead his case swiftly and in its entirety. "I understand how you felt when that filthy bastard came here and told you about the poker game and bullied you and broke those things. I could kill him for that, lass, I swear I could! But you'll never see Grunder again, and I'll never make another wager again, and . . . oh, Elly, darlin', I need you to forgive me."

Tears smarted in her eyes as she gazed at Connor's dark head, bowed in shame, then let her glance travel down to the strong, callused hands, with their light tracing of hair, which gripped hers so desperately. Still kneeling beside her, unable to meet her gaze, Connor looked like a sad, shame-filled boy, a boy in a man's body, miserable and alone. No longer was he the brash, confident young man she had married in the downstairs parlor. Nor was he the spendthrift, the deceiving gambler whom she had confronted in devastation before, the villain who had made her home and her family vulnerable to strangers. He was like a small boy now, pathetic in his vulnerability, touching in his shame. She slipped a hand free and reached out, stroking his smooth, thick curls with a soothing motion. He lifted his head, hope and love and sorrow shining in his beautiful sapphire eyes.

"I love you, Elly," he whispered. "I need you so."

"I love you, too, Connor." She took a deep, quivering breath. "I just want . . . I *need* . . . to feel safe." She wanted so badly to regain the trust they had known before, to feel safe and protected once again. She wanted to believe him, to heal the hurts of this day.

Connor shifted his tall frame to sit beside her on the bed. He gathered her into his arms. He smelled of brandy and smoke. He felt like sinewy muscle and rock. "You are safe, darlin'," he said huskily. "I promise you, you'll always be safe."

She nestled there, joy flooding through her, and with it warmth and forgiveness and the now familiar desire. Beneath the thin nightgown, Elly's heart began to pound. Her breasts swelled, and her nipples hardened into tiny arrows pressed against Connor's broad chest. The ache of passion rose within her, and as it did, the doubts and the emptiness faded like a gray drizzle on a sun-dappled day.

One mistake, she told herself. He had made one mistake. Surely everyone on earth was entitled to one mistake.

The dark, scented night settled over them as they drew together in the bed and let the crests of their passion carry them on a journey far, far away.

The next few months brought rain, warmer temperatures, and then an abundance of summer sunshine. The evenings were warm and alive with the squeaking of porch swings, the sounds of young people playing croquet in countless neighborhood backyards, the yapping of dogs, and the whistling of distant trains. The Forrest family and their boarders sat on the

porch swing or on the steps until it was time for bed, or, like
General Willis and Timothy, they lingered in the parlor playing
checkers before the open window or talking about other sum-
mers, other nights, when the sky was a sea of purple velvet
and the stars glittered like bright pearls and the sweet damp
air of summer caressed the skin with the softness of a mother's touch.

More and more frequently, Connor was absent from these
pleasant, lazy evenings. Sometimes he claimed business kept
him away from home until late, and sometimes, with the odor
of beer or whiskey heavy on his breath, he came whistling in
from Jack's tavern, where, he told Elly, he'd had a few with
the boys. After a while, she began to grow used to his habits.
There was no repetition of the Joe Grunder incident, and she
had no way of knowing whether he gambled on these late
nights or not. She missed him, though, and loneliness often
washed over her in the midst of the surrounding chatter and
laughter. When she spoke to him about it and mentioned
tentatively that she'd like him to spend more nights at home,
he shook his head.

"But, darlin', the Gem will be opening soon. September
tenth is around the corner. Sean and I have much still to do."

"You'll be with Sean, then, tonight?" she asked. He had
already told her not to expect him at dinner.

"Aye, working. Though we might go downstairs, after the
meeting's over and the ledgers are put away, and lift a glass
with the lads at Sean's place. A man's entitled to a shot of
whiskey now and then after a long day, isn't he, lass?"

But as the summer days fled and the opening night for the
theater approached, Connor came home later and later and
was more frequently drunk. Elly tried not to comment, for he
was becoming more belligerent toward what he called her
interference and once had shouted at her to keep her puritani-
cal opinions to herself.

At last the opening night arrived. Even Timothy was to be
allowed to attend the momentous event. Dressed in her new
blue satin gown with a train edged in white silk roses and a
stiffly elegant French lace underskirt to match, Elly felt like a
child dressing up in her mother's clothes. She had never worn
anything so splendid; even her wedding gown had been a
simple beige lace dress. The blue satin was a gift from
Connor, who had brought it home one afternoon and swept it

from its box with a flourish. "We can't have Sean's lady friend outshining my wife," he had stated, eyeing her with satisfaction when she modeled the gown for his approval. The next day he had added a sapphire necklace and sapphire and pearl eardrops to the ensemble.

Turning her head before the mirror to admire the winking jewels, Elly fought back a sudden wave of nausea. This had been going on for several days now. She was certain of the reason, and the knowledge filled her with a greater joy than any theater premiere ever could. When the play was over and she and Connor had returned home, she planned to serve him a glass of champagne in their bed and then tell him the wondrous news.

At the theater, Elly gazed about in wonder. Connor and Sean had indeed done a magnificent job. With its thick Chinese-patterned carpet, tall marble walls, and huge domed ceiling carved in gold and inlaid with rubies and pearls, the Gem Theater was a sumptuous palace eliciting gasps of admiration from the mass of patrons streaming through the doors. Velvet curtains of a rich, vibrant crimson veiled the stage; the theater seats were upholstered in elegant gold satin; and from high above, a trio of gas chandeliers, each composed of a thousand crystal prisms, winked and glittered over the house, which was packed with finely dressed patrons. The evening's production of *Romeo and Juliet,* always popular with American audiences, was to star Hetta Strom and Richard Butler, two of the most acclaimed actors in current touring companies. They had drawn an eager crowd of gentlemen in silk top hats and tailcoats and ladies in gaily colored and sumptuously trained gowns.

"It's like a storybook," Caroline breathed as she stared in wonder about the lavishly appointed theater and, closer at hand, at the velvet-upholstered private box in which the family was seated. For once, her lovely face was animated and flushed with color; she looked like a radiant sunflower in her yellow gown festooned with green ribbons, which Mama had copied from an illustration in *Godey's Lady's Book.* "Elly, might we go backstage and ask Hetta Strom for her autograph? Please?"

Elly was about to suggest that they wait until after the performance, but Caroline's eager expression dissuaded her. Her sister found joy in so few things that Elly couldn't bear

not to indulge her when the opportunity arose. With Timothy
in tow, they slipped past Bess and Aunt Adelaide and picked
their way through the bustling throng.

Connor greeted them backstage and directed them to Hetta
Strom's dressing room. Elly lingered behind to exchange
pleasantries with Sean Fitzgerald and his companion, a full-
breasted, sultry young woman with beautiful tawny eyes and
hair the color of honey. Her name was Mary O'Rourke.

"A grand place, isn't it, Mrs. Maguire?" Fitzgerald said
expansively, looking like a smug, plump alleycat in his striped
waistcoat and trousers. The green eyes flickered apprecia-
tively over Elly's slender figure clad in the billowing blue
satin. They lingered for an inordinate amount of time, Elly
thought, on her décolletage. "And you're looking splendid,
lass. That's a lovely dress." He chuckled suddenly and winked
at Connor. "You've good taste in jewels, my lad." He was
eyeing her necklace and the gems at her ears. "Now I see
where Sleek Sally's winnings went!"

Connor stiffened.

"Sleek Sally?" Elly had gone deathly still.

In his excitement at the opening of the theater, Fitzgerald
didn't notice the blanching of Connor's lean, brown face. His
gaze was roving shrewdly about, watching the stagehands
moving scenery into position, the actors in their costumes
pacing back and forth, reciting their lines. "Yes, the filly
won handsomely a few weeks ago," he went on recklessly.
Elly suspected he had already imbibed more than one glass of
celebratory champagne. "Connor and I cleaned up in a mighty
fine way." With a jerk of his thumb, he indicated the ruby
necklace sparkling from Mary's throat. It was the identical
shade of her shimmering satin and taffeta dress. "That's
where my lass here got this little bauble. A victory gift, you
might say, after the filly's triumph. I always buy her a little
something when a big wager comes through."

A big wager. Elly felt as though her breath had died within
her. And if the horse had lost? How many other horses, other
races, had been lost? How many poker hands and how many
other games of chance had been lost—or might be lost tomorrow? The sapphire necklace seemed to tighten about her
throat.

Connor put a hand on her arm. "Here come Caroline and
Timothy," he exclaimed, his rich Irish brogue sounding hol-

low to her ears. "You'd best return to your seats." He
attempted a bright, jovial smile, all the while studying her,
trying to judge her reaction to Fitzgerald's words. "The
curtain will be going up soon."

She made no answer.

"I can explain it all later, darlin,' " Connor whispered in
her ear as she turned away.

She couldn't bring herself to reply, nor did she hear a word
her brother and sister said as they returned to the box.

"I'm so proud of Connor," Bess whispered as Elly took
her seat beside her. Elly stifled an hysterical desire to laugh.
She glanced sideways at her mother, then looked away, fearful Mama would see how shaken she was. But no, her mother
was too caught up in the festiveness of the moment. Bess's
elegant face wore some of its former regal luster in these
plush surroundings. "He's quite an enterprising young man,
and he's going to be very successful," she assured her daughter. With a sigh, she continued. "Samuel was a fine man,
Elly, but the truth of the matter is, he was more concerned
with principles and lofty ideals than with getting ahead." Her
blue-gray eyes, so like Elly's, misted over for a moment as
she looked back regretfully in time. Then she gave her shoulders a tiny shake. "Connor Maguire has proper ambition,"
she said firmly. "He'll be a solid provider for you. Thank
heaven you'll never have to worry and scratch out a living, as
I did. You and your children will be cared for and safe."

Safe. Again Elly controlled a wild impulse to laugh. As the
lights dimmed and the audience settled expectantly in their
seats, her hands slid protectively across her belly where, deep
within, the tiny helpless being nestled in its innocence. Safe?
The stage curtain went up, thunderous applause ensued, and
the actors began to speak. What she saw, though, was not the
characters of a Shakespearean drama or a brilliantly lit and
decorated stage. She saw in her imagination Joe Grunder's
face. It was grinning malevolently, opening its mouth. Words
gushed out—harsh, mocking words.

*Safe? You'll never be safe. Your husband's a gambler.
You'll never be safe. You'll never be safe. You'll never be
safe. . . .*

She sat like a statue, blind and ill, until the final curtain
fell.

❦ Thirteen

Pittsburgh, 1877

"NEVER THOUGHT THE day would come when I'd say this to any man, Walker, but it has. You work too damned hard. Much too damned hard." Louis Whitcomb rapped his ivory-handled walking stick on Boone's desk. "When was the last time you slept?"

"Can't remember," Boone groaned. He ran a hand through his unruly thatch of sandy hair and sat back in his chair. Every muscle in his body ached. His brain felt foggy. He couldn't remember when he'd last eaten, either, he realized in surprise. It seemed he'd been living on coffee for days. The sight of the cup of black liquid on his desk, long ago gone cold, made him shudder in revulsion. The cup crowned a pile of papers, and more papers buried the rest of the desktop. Outside the window, pale April sunlight slanted down on the rows of warehouses and buildings that composed the Whitcomb and Walker Steel Company.

"Go home," Whitcomb ordered. From beneath his reddish brows, foxlike eyes regarded the exhausted man before him. "You're no use to me like this. Go home and get some sleep."

"I'm expecting a telegram any moment now on the Spring Creek coal mine deal. When that's wrapped up—"

"Murphy can handle it," Louis barked. "By George, man, you've already locked up the shipping deal with Anderson this week. You can rest on your laurels a bit. Damnation, one would think we couldn't run this company without you working eighteen hours a day." He snorted and plopped himself down in a cane-backed chair. "Let the damned labor unions chew on that one—they're so worried about passing an eight-

hour day, they ought to see the slave hours the vice president
of this company keeps.''

"At least I'm well compensated," Boone drawled and
glanced down at his finely made broadcloth suit and buffed
leather shoes. His clothes, the fine gold watch tucked inside
his vest pocket, and this richly paneled corner office on the
third floor of the warehouse were a far cry from what he'd
had during his days in the Mason Iron Works. Beneath its
mound of papers, his desk was solid mahogany, carved with
scrolls and tiny lions' heads. Thick brown carpeting cushioned the sounds that came from far below of men moving,
storing, and packing huge ingots of steel. The long rectangular windows were covered with handsome draperies of dark
tan damask; the walls boasted a varied collection of maps,
lithographs, and oil paintings, Boone's favorite being a brass-
framed scene of the Monongahela River in autumn, with the
surrounding trees and foliage gowned in subdued shades of
amber, brown, and gold. The men who worked for his company called him Mr. Walker and jumped when he glanced
their way. Yes, he thought with an odd lack of satisfaction, in
terms of material comforts, he was very well compensated.
He'd come a long way.

"You win, Louis. If I don't get some sleep, I might
underbid badly on that new warehouse we're trying to buy. I
had planned to study the figures tonight . . ."

"That's Ted Ross's job. You come to my dinner party
tonight."

Boone stretched weary muscles, extending his arms over
his head. He threw Louis an amused glance. "I thought you
wanted me to get some sleep."

"*Now,* you jackass. Get some sleep now, and then come to
dinner. Victoria planned this thing at the last minute, unusual
for her." He grimaced. "But she made a point of telling me
how miserable my evening will be if I don't persuade you to
come."

"That anxious, eh? She must have quite a specimen for me
to meet tonight."

Louis guffawed. He came to his feet and shot Boone a
shrewd glance. "Can't say. But you know Victoria; she never
gives up."

Boone sighed and pushed back his own deep leather chair.
"If she were a man possessing that kind of determination,

she'd be running the country by now," he remarked, and there was fondness as well as a kind of rueful respect in the words. For the past year, Victoria Whitcomb had been trying to marry him off to every pretty, unattached socialite in Pittsburgh. Having overcome her aversion to his southern drawl, she had discovered that the strapping young man with the cool gray eyes who worked so indefatigably beside her husband, and who possessed, as Louis had commented admiringly many times, a "truly brilliant business sense," also had excellent, quiet manners, a kind heart, and an easy smile. He had won her approval and her respect, and as time had passed and he had worked many more late hours with Louis in the Whitcomb library, he had even begun to earn from her the kind of warm, motherly affection she had felt for her lost son. Her goal was to see him happily married, settled down in a fine home with a properly attentive and supportive wife. In these past few months, her determined efforts had grown to be the bane of Boone's hardworking existence.

"Tell her I'll come," he said and took one last glance around the brass and leather office, grimacing at the sight of the papers and inkwells and metal-nibbed pens that cluttered his desk. He followed Whitcomb to the door with something like relief. Louis was right. A few hours of sleep would refresh him, and a good meal wouldn't hurt, either. After humoring Victoria at the dinner party, he could return to his office and, without interruption, spend the rest of the night studying the warehouse figures Ted Ross had prepared.

Striding through the warehouse yard toward the stable where his carriage waited, Boone surveyed the workers and edifices of the iron foundry and adjoining steel plant with satisfaction. Plush surroundings and expensive furniture might not fill him with elation, but the expanse of gray and red brick buildings, the great, smoke-spouting furnaces, the yards crammed with wagons and crates and men and machinery, sent pride surging through his veins. He had built all this. With Whitcomb's help and a hefty amount of patience, added to a string of successfully implemented ideas, he had seen his iron foundry expand into one of the most ambitious steel operations in the region. Steel! It was earning him and the other investors a fortune, but only because they had waited out the panic of 1873 and acted on Boone's suggestion that they broaden their holdings, so that Whitcomb and Walker would control the costs and shipment schedules of various operations necessary to the production of their steel.

Boone's key plan, and the one that had taken the longest to persuade the ever-cautious Louis Whitcomb to adopt, had involved purchases on a gradually increasing scale. First there had been the land in the Lake Superior iron ore district, then a Connellsville coal mine, then limestone quarries, docks, and warehouses. They could control every aspect of their steel business, Boone had argued, if they could buy interests in the raw materials they needed to manufacture steel and if they could also own the means of transporting them. Such an undertaking required a fortune, it was true, but Louis Whitcomb already possessed that fortune. He stood to make an even greater one, Boone had reasoned, if the plans came to successful fruition. The logic of it, and the strength of Boone's determination and unceasing dedication to his work, had convinced Whitcomb to follow Boone's recommendations. And already, though they had only a few such enterprises under their control thus far, the plan was paying off. In the companies they owned, they had total control of prices and wages and schedules. Everything revolved around their steel. And they were manufacturing it at a furious pace. Costs were low, profit margins high. Thanks to the Bessemer converter, steel was now affordable for products previously made from wrought iron. The potential market was immense: locomotives, railroad tracks, bridges, farm machinery. And four years ago, in 1873, an Illinois farmer named Joseph F. Glidden had invented barbed wire, which had potentially widespread use in fencing the developing western prairie.

Steel. Better than gold, Boone thought as he ordered his coachman to take him home. He climbed into the carriage, settled back in the upholstered seat, and gazed out at the hazy spring day. The Monongahela glittered like a silver bracelet in the sun, the leafy trees seemed to stretch their branches toward the mild blue skies, and riotous wildflowers blossomed on the banks of the river and on the emerald hills, but Boone noticed only the dock teeming with barges, the billowing black smoke clouds in the sky, which signaled never-ceasing production, and the rows of finishing mills and warehouses grouped together in well-laid-out clusters, like a garden, he thought, that has been carefully planted.

He awoke in his hotel room several hours later with a

gnawing hunger. After washing himself and stuffing his arms into a stiffly pressed shirt, he realized that his brain had cleared. He was rational enough to dread what Victoria had planned for him. Another evening wasted being polite to one of her "special young ladies." Another few hours of being questioned and petted by the fluttering mothers of these all-too-eligible females. Boone had learned months ago that these were either empty-headed young beauties or scheming, desperate women on the verge of spinsterhood. Either way, he wasn't interested.

He wandered into the sitting room of his suite. Nearly a year ago, at Louis Whitcomb's urging, he had moved out of Mrs. Shepherd's boardinghouse and into the Allegheny Hotel. It was more fitting of his new status with Whitcomb and Walker Steel, Louis had proclaimed, stroking his mustache and nodding in his peremptory way. Though Boone was usually too immersed in paperwork to take much note of his surroundings, he did appreciate the comfort of the place. With its overstuffed brocade sofas and black marble hearth, its Louis XV desk and tall windows, its separate bedroom appointed in masculine brown leathers, onyx, and brass, he had plenty of space in which to work, and pleasant surroundings in which to entertain an occasional business guest. The hotel sent up brandy, Boone provided the fire and the paperwork, and more than one important deal had been concluded with a handshake and a mutual puffing of aromatic cigars. At the moment, though, it was not a cigar Boone sought, or even a before-dinner drink. It was a document detailing a farm machinery contract that W-and-W sought to gain. He had been perusing it a few nights ago and had forgotten to take it back to the office. He shuffled through a stack of papers almost as high as those at the plant, swearing vehemently when the one he sought was nowhere to be found. Finally, he opened the desk and discovered it beneath a list of foundry operating expenses he'd made up his mind to curtail. As he drew out the document, another paper fluttered from between the pages in his hand. He stooped to pick it up and happened to glance at the writing on it. Instant recognition brought a jolt of memory. It was a letter—the last letter he had received from Connor Maguire.

Boone ran his thumb over the stationery. He had no need to read the letter again. Though he had received it nearly a year ago, he still remembered every word. Connor had boasted of how well his theater was doing, of the fine carriage he had bought to carry Elly and their baby about town in style, of the dusky black curls and sapphire eyes of little Cassandra, whose first birthday would be celebrated on the twenty-second of May. "Elly sends her regards," Connor had written, words that had brought a painful constriction to Boone's chest. Her regards. It was like a morsel fed to a starving man. He longed for her love, her heart, flesh, and soul, but those belonged to Connor. He received only her regards.

His fist crushed the paper, something he should have done a year ago, he thought savagely, instead of keeping it in this drawer like some kind of pathetic memento. It had been years now since he'd seen Elly or Connor; he hadn't returned to Chicago since that long-ago February when Connor had told him of his decision to marry Elly, to sell his share of the foundry, and to build instead a theater with that faro-dealing saloonkeeper. Boone hadn't even gone to their wedding, though Connor had asked him to be his best man. He'd made an excuse of too much work required at the foundry, but it had really been his jealousy of Connor that had kept him away. It would have been far too painful to see Elly in her bridal gown, with veil and flowers, and her sweet, luminous smile, knowing that she was giving herself forever to Connor, that all chance of Boone ever holding her in his arms, drinking in her kisses, sliding his fingers through her silken blue-black hair, was gone.

With an oath, he hurled the letter into a wicker basket under the desk and hurried back to his bedroom to finish dressing. The suite suddenly felt stuffy and depressing; he was in a hurry to get out into the balmy night air, to run and hide amid the chattering assembly he'd find in Victoria's dining parlor.

But there was no escape from the memories the letter had conjured up. In his carriage, clattering toward Penn Avenue, he was besieged by thoughts of Elly Forrest—no, he corrected himself angrily—Elly *Maguire*. Lulled by the mild April night, by the starlit darkness, his mind was filled with her image. So long it had been since he'd seen her, and for such a brief time, yet she was embedded in his memory, like a beautiful portrait which, once seen, haunted and lingered in the deepest regions of the heart. Leaning back against the seat of the carriage, he closed his eyes, seeing her rich dark hair framing that delicate, yet oddly determined oval face. He saw her eyes, large and lovely in their brilliance, the color of a storm-tossed ocean. He saw her lips, full and inviting and soft with innocence. The memory of her slender, high-breasted figure, her low, husky laugh, the briskly graceful sway of her hips when she walked—all these brought him pain and a powerful yearning. He tried to ignore the pain, to remind himself that she was a married woman now, the mother of a child. Yet the feelings aroused by this particular black-haired, dignified girl would not die down; they hurt and rubbed against him like a continuing wound on an old, unhealed sore.

Boone had learned long ago to stifle his emotions. Feelings, he knew, only brought pain and trouble. When Tom and Henry had enlisted in opposing armies during the war, Boone had seen the grief that had torn his mother apart. He had suffered a good measure of it himself, and so had Clay. *Never again*, he had vowed, hearing his ma's sobs on the night they'd learned that Tom had died at Vicksburg, and again when news of Henry's death had come. Never again would he lay himself bare to the kind of pain that loving someone brought. What you loved you could lose. What you felt inside could be used against you, as his stepfather, Ezra Wells, had done so many times, with his teasing and tormenting, his threats, and his jeers. Feelings got trampled on, so better to squash them yourself before someone else had the chance. Yet, when he had come home that night in 1866 from the tobacco fields and seen Ezra Wells beating his mother senseless, with little Rose, no more than five years old, cowering silent under the rocking chair, the emotions he had thought he'd learned to control had raged like demons within him. Wild with fury he'd torn into his stepfather like a crazed boar. Ezra had pounded the not-yet-grown boy mercilessly, but Boone's rage had kept him alive and fighting, kicking, gouging. In the midst of the whirlwind of bodies, grunts, yells, of his mother's screams and Rose's wailing, Boone had grabbed the rifle. He'd meant to hit Ezra with it, but somehow, in the jostling and diving and brutal confusion, it had gone off, and Ezra had fallen like a dropped mountain cat. There was blood everywhere, a gaping wound in Ezra's chest. His mother's screams reverberated in his ears, and he was stricken with the realization that he had killed a man, robbed him of life forever and ever.

Boone had fled, fearful of his mother's wrath and of the hangman's noose and of his own savage deed. He'd never gone back. But that hadn't stopped him thinking of them, of Ma, of Rose, of Clay. What had happened to them? Did they hate him for what he'd done? Did they ever miss him as he—Lord help him—missed them?

All these thoughts because of Elly Maguire, Boone mused, as the carriage turned up the Whitcombs' long, winding drive, ablaze with starlight and lamplight and the reflections from the brightly lighted windows of the house. He resolved to erase her from his mind. Thinking of the past, of loved ones lost and loved ones he had never even had, brought pain and, ultimately, sorrow. A woman and a family were the last thing he needed, especially now, Boone reasoned. He ought to be grateful to Connor for having saved him from a morass of feelings that could only drag him down. Hard work, planning, and single-minded effort, with no distractions, were the things that could help him achieve his goals. Real pleasure came with power, Boone told himself, with building something of strength and permanence. He alighted from the carriage, issued orders to his coachman, and strode toward the house.

"Good evening, Mr. Walker," Humphreys greeted him with a deferential duck of the head as Boone's long legs carried him through the high-ceilinged hall. Boone's dark mood dissolved in a flash of amusement. Once the man had tried to bar him from this house. Now he merely accepted Boone's hat and cane with a tight little smile and watched him cross the blue marble floor into the front parlor.

This splendid room was ablaze with light and laughter. Victoria had the house filled with flowers; delicate violets and orchids overflowed from every silver bowl and Chinese vase in sight. Together with the elegant blues and creams of the furnishings, the Aubusson carpet, and the velvet draperies, they created a backdrop of harmonious elegance for the silk-clad ladies and gentlemen who mingled before the crackling fire.

Boone recognized quite a few people, among them a man who met his look across the room and deliberately turned away. He smiled grimly to himself. Jason Emmett had never liked him, not from the first time they had met when Boone had beaten him at billiards right here in this house.

"Beginner's luck," he had sneered, causing Connor to step forward as well and challenge him on the spot. Neither Boone nor Connor had ever played the game before, but they had both emerged victorious. That hadn't sat well with Jason, especially when Silas Emmett had snorted in derision at his son's lack of ability and even Louis had had to struggle to keep the chuckle from his lips.

Jason had been a part of the original foundry partnership because he was Louis's nephew and his father had wanted him to begin participating in the family's business affairs, but the younger Emmett and Boone and Connor had never gotten along. Perhaps it was because Jason had made it clear he was unhappy being associated with men who had actually worked in an iron mill, or perhaps it was his arrogant way of dealing with people, or his tardiness in arriving at every meeting called pertaining to the foundry. Boone found him a conceited jackass. When it had come time to assemble a group of investors for the steel works, Boone had managed to keep the Emmetts' participation minimal. They owned a small percentage of the company, but had little say in management or purchasing decisions, which was just as well, especially since Silas had died early last year and left his son in charge of the family's fortune. Everything Boone had seen and heard convinced him that Jason possessed his father's voracious appetite for wealth and power but lacked the willingness to work hard in order to achieve and maintain them. Louis had told him his nephew was to be married over the summer and that it was to be hoped his wife would have a stabilizing influence on him. As Boone observed the petite, pert-nosed blonde whose hand rested on Jason's arm, he felt a flicker of doubt. She looked as if she'd only be concerned with diamonds and servants and balls, not with inspiring a lazy husband. At least, he thought with a shrug, regarding the pair through narrowed eyes, they wouldn't have a speck of influence on his life through W-and-W. If they ran their Emmettville concerns into the ground, it was no matter to him.

"Why, if it isn't Boone Walker, the very man I've been wishing to find," Victoria's light, even voice sounded behind him, and he turned to smile down into her sky-blue eyes.

"Good evening, Victoria." From the corner of his eye, he

could see beside his hostess a narrow shoulder of lavender
satin, a sleeve trimmed with violet ribbon, a long and glossy
chestnut curl dangling over a well-formed bosom. He braced
himself for the introduction to follow. Hell, how he hated
these little rituals. He felt like some big damned fool, trying
to make polite conversation with women he scarcely knew,
trying to appear as if he didn't understand the embarrassing
little game of speculation and evaluation being played. He
never had gotten over his awkwardness around women, though
he'd learned to cover it a little. Still, the stream of introduc-
tions and coy observations by all concerned were as harrowing for him as a round of bayonet fighting on the battlefield
would have been for most men. If he weren't so fond of
Victoria, he wouldn't have subjected himself to it at all.

"You're as ravishing as ever tonight," he said gamely, and
earned for his efforts a beatific smile.

"Why, thank you, my dear." She laid an arm across the
shoulders of the young woman beside her, drawing her into
the conversation and permitting Boone's gaze to shift accord-
ingly. He found himself staring into a pair of cool hazel eyes,
set within a small, adorable face. The girl before him was
slim and fetching, with curling brown hair, a straight, aristocratic nose, and a small, prettily curved mouth. Her gown of
lavender satin revealed a most alluringly feminine figure. He
was pleasantly surprised. While he took her measure, she
quite boldly did the same, taking in at a glance his correct
black tailcoat and white silk gloves, the breadth of his powerful shoulders, the golden gleam of his carefully brushed hair.
A faint smile touched her lips as Victoria tripped blithely on.
"We shall be going in to dinner soon, but I simply must
introduce you to this charming young woman. Isn't she lovely?
Lady Penelope Stanton, may I present Mr. Boone Walker."
She paused, beaming. "Boone, Lady Penelope is an English-
woman, the daughter of the earl of Waterbury. She is visiting
the Beckworths through the summer. Boone is the young man
I told you about, my dear. Louis's business partner in that
marvelous new steel plant on the river." She snapped her fan
shut with a graceful flourish. "Oh, dear, I believe Louis is
hunting for me. I just know you two will get along delight-
fully. Won't you please excuse me?"

With these words, she slipped away into the sea of guests,
leaving the pair alone. Boone, startled by this unexpected

maneuver and not yet having mastered the art of small talk to a girl he had only just met, searched his mind frantically for something witty or interesting to say. To his relief, Lady Penelope spoke first.

"Isn't it horrid the way married ladies treat a man who happens not to possess a wife?" Her British accent added a slight crispness to a voice that was softly refined. "I've seen it countless times, and think it perfectly outrageous. Of course," she continued with a slow smile, "no more outrageous than the way they behave toward girls who do not possess a husband. What in the world do you suppose we ought to do?"

Boone was so stunned by this forthright speech that he almost choked. "D-do?" he stammered.

She gave her head a tiny shake. It made her hair wisp slightly about her dainty ears. "Please, Mr. Walker, do not feel you need to keep me company for appearance's sake. I am visiting friends here, as Mrs. Whitcomb told you, and I see dear Alicia Beckworth just over there. You may amble off and be well rid of me, and I shan't be in the least offended."

"Rid of you . . . ma'am?" Boone controlled an impulse to tug at his collar, which suddenly seemed several sizes too small. "I . . . I don't want to be rid of you," he protested.

This gallant speech was rewarded with a dazzling smile slanted up at him from beneath a curtain of brown lashes.

"Then I suppose you'd best escort me into dinner," Lady Penelope murmured. Hazel eyes glimmered into his startled gray ones. "Oh, do not fear, Mr. Walker, I promise not to bore you with insipid smiles or rattling, inconsequential talk. I am outrageous, haven't you heard? No, of course you haven't," she rushed on, with another one of those slanting smiles. "I haven't been in America long enough to shock the colonists yet. But any day now—pray, any moment, perhaps— you will hear tales of the daring Lady Penelope Stanton."

"I never believe gossip," Boone said cautiously, uncertain how to react to this unusual girl. He had never met anyone like her before. Her direct speech reminded him somewhat of Elly, but Penelope combined it with a cool, breezy self-assurance that was distinctly her own. From across the room he saw Louis Whitcomb watching them intently through his monocle, as if looking for a sign of his wife's success or failure in arranging this match. There was no sign of Victoria.

Suddenly, Boone laughed. He laughed so loud and so hard that several other guests turned to stare at him. Louis dropped his monocle; lady Penelope raised her delicately arched brows.

"Sorry, but . . . Victoria's never introduced me to anyone . . . daring before." He grinned. "I have to admit it's a welcome change. I hope she doesn't faint when she sees I'm actually enjoying myself."

"I hope she does," the irrepressible young woman replied. "It would add a bit of the spectacular to the evening. Not," she added, placing her lavender-gloved hand on his arm as they joined the procession strolling toward the dining room, "that meeting you hasn't been spectacular in itself. I must say, if you had only seen the creature Alicia Beckworth thrust upon me the other night at that Chorale Society Ball, you would understand why I am positively *thrilled* to be going into dinner with *you*. But never mind, Mr. Walker. Let's ignore all the stares and whispers. I always do so, at any rate. Tell me about you."

On the way back to the hotel that evening, Boone had time to remember her trim figure gowned in lavender satin, her trilling, infectious laugh, and her willingness to say exactly what she thought about every topic imaginable. He found her charming. Her airy boldness made him laugh, and when he laughed, he forgot to be shy and awkward. The next day he sent his coachman to the Beckworth house with a written request that the Beckworths and their friend, Lady Penelope, be his guests at the opera the following week.

Victoria Whitcomb, elated at her success, finally, in introducing Boone to a woman who caught his fancy, planned a Sunday outing for a select group in Allegheny's beautiful park on the Commons, arranging for Boone and Penelope to ride in the same carriage. And Alicia Beckworth, not to be outdone, gave a ball in her young guest's honor, at which Boone was invited to be Penelope's escort. After that, it became usual for the members of Pittsburgh society to see Boone Walker squiring Lady Penelope about town, to concerts and dinner parties and plays. They were spotted driving in the park, playing croquet on the Beckworths' manicured lawns, sailing with a party of friends on the Allegheny River beneath a pearly summer moon.

One day in early August when broiling temperatures made it almost impossible to concentrate on work, and Boone toiled at his desk in his shirtsleeves, Louis Whitcomb sauntered into his office with his usual clipped step and brusque manner. It always amazed Boone that, no matter what the temperature, Whitcomb looked neat and tidy, with his curling brown hair and sideburns, his fine clothes and spotless boots. Today it amazed Boone to see Whitcomb at all. For the past month, the Whitcombs, the Beckworths, and their set of friends and acquaintances had been in Newport, basking in the breezy luxury of what they called their "summer cottages." From all Boone had heard, these places were anything but the tiny dwellings connoted by those words. The Beckworth place was a twenty-room mansion constructed of Italian marble; the Whitcomb home, called Somerset, was all of slate and boasted three floors of tiled, tapestried, and carpeted rooms, a sunken garden, extensive stables, and an army of servants. Boone was to be their guest at the end of the week for a ten-day visit, during which time he could spend every day with Penelope, for the Beckworth place was only a mile down the road.

"Don't tell me—you've come back because of the strike. There was no need, Louis; our men are all under control." Boone was referring to the Pennsylvania Railroad workers' strike, which had resulted in riots late last month. He'd been in constant telegraph contact with Whitcomb when the situation had been at its most tense. For a while it had seemed that every worker in the city would join in the riots and looting that had followed the initial strike and the routing of the state militia. Sixteen hundred railroad cars and one hundred twenty-six locomotives had been destroyed.

"Who'd have thought such a thing could happen?" Whitcomb rumbled, shaking his head in amazement. He closed the office door and settled into a chair. "Couldn't believe what I was reading. Destroyed the Union Depot, the grain elevator, all those buildings. And the railroad cars. Damned unions—they're nothing but trouble."

"The railroad workers had a right to be upset, Louis," Boone countered. He put down his pen. "The Pennsylvania reduced all the crews' wages by ten percent and started running all freight trains between here and Derry as double-headers. That meant each single crew had to run two trains and two engines—pretty dangerous and grueling work."

"Other railroads have taken similar measures," Whitcomb started to argue, but Boone interrupted him.

"That's what Thomas Scott said. Now, I know he didn't get to be president of the Pennsylvania for nothing, but he should've seen that the climate's not right for such actions. Union sentiment is strong now, or at least it was until this particular strike turned so violent. I think things will cool off for a while." He leaned back in his chair, his expression grim. "Twenty people were killed, you know, most of them innocent bystanders caught in the crossfire when the militia tried to clear the tracks at the Twenty-Eighth Street crossing. Ted Ross's brother was one of them. His nephew was wounded."

Louis scowled. "Nasty business. I'm glad Victoria was away from the city when all this was going on. I would have come back sooner, Boone, but I knew you could handle things here."

"Our men are relatively satisfied. You know I believe in fair wages for a day's work, and the eight-hour day has been my policy all along." He met Whitcomb's glance directly. "From my own days of working on the floor of the mill, I can tell you that a twelve- or even a ten-hour shift does far more harm than good for the overall profits of a company. It's too much. The men get tired out and never have a chance to recover. Then they get resentful and angry. That attitude doesn't do a company any good."

"Well, I can't say that I've always agreed with you about that, but I must admit, morale and energy are high around here, and we're not constantly threatened by strikes, like some companies," Whitcomb conceded. He sat up straighter in his chair. "I just hope this Amalgamated Association of Iron, Steel, and Tin Workers doesn't get too big for its britches and start making all kinds of unreasonable demands."

"We'll deal with that if and when it happens" was Boone's steady response. "Now tell me, if you knew I had things in hand here, what did bring you back to town?"

"Got to talk to you, boy," Louis replied after a moment's hesitation. He fidgeted with his mustache in the familiar gesture that was his habit. "Don't like it, but it's got to be done. I like you, Boone; you know that. Victoria and I are both fond of you. That's why we feel it's our duty to give you a warning."

Mystified, Boone raised his brows. "About what?"

"Lady Penelope Stanton."

Boone grinned. It was exceedingly warm in the room, breezeless and humid, and he wiped an arm across his perspiring forehead before asking good-naturedly, "What are you babbling about, Louis? You introduced me to her."

"Yes, Victoria took it upon herself . . . Well, who was to know, after all?" Whitcomb looked down at his hands and frowned. "We've only just learned some things—how much do you know about the girl?"

"Everything I need to know." Boone's mouth began to grow taut, and his eyes narrowed to smoke-colored slits. "What the hell is this all about, Louis?"

Whitcomb cleared his throat. "Well, as you know, she is a distant cousin of some sort to Arthur Beckworth. Now, Victoria and I were aware, as you are, that she had come over for a lengthy visit. To get a look at America, meet her American relations, that sort of thing, but that's not the whole of it." He sighed and took a handkerchief from his coat pocket. He began to pat nervously at his temples. "Damn it, boy, this isn't easy."

"Just say it, Louis, and be done," Boone ordered.

"You do know, Boone, that the girl's father is an earl? An old, very fine family, they say."

"You and Victoria have mentioned it several dozen times."

"The point is, what Victoria and I didn't know, and what Arthur Beckworth never mentioned—though I can't say I wouldn't have done the same in his shoes—is that the girl's as poor as a dormouse." Suddenly, he clenched the handkerchief in his hand and banged both fists on the mahogany desk. "Her blasted father squandered away every last cent, and his estates over there in England are mortgaged to the hilt! Son, that girl came here hunting for a rich husband . . . and I hate to say this, Boone, my boy, but Victoria and I believe you're her quarry."

Boone burst out laughing. The tension, the anger, had gone from his face. "Is that all? Damn it, Louis, I thought you were going to tell me something awful about poor Penelope. And I was damned close to throwing you out of this office. What the hell do I care if she's not wealthy? It hasn't been all that long since I was poor as a dormouse as well! Heaven help us, there's no crime in lacking money—at least not yet, there isn't.''

''You don't understand, Boone.'' Whitcomb in his agitation leaped to his feet. His voice rose. ''She's not just poor. She's *penniless*—or damned near it. Lady Penelope Stanton is a fortune hunter, plain and simple. She needs a bundle of money to bail out her father's lands—and to save herself from the humiliation of visiting the old coot in debtor's prison!''

''So?''

Whitcomb looked as though he was about to explode. ''Do you mean to tell me you don't mind being taken for a fool? Why, that girl is bamboozling you. None of her own countrymen will have her, for they all know the situation, so she's come over here to try to—''

''That's enough, Louis.''

Boone spoke very quietly, but there was deep anger in the set of his jaw, in the low rolling drawl of his voice.

Startled, Whitcomb drew breath and stared at him. ''You think I've overstepped my bounds,'' he began, but Boone cut him off in midsentence.

''I told Penelope once that I don't listen to gossip, and it was the truth,'' he said coldly. ''You've said enough. I have to get back to work.''

''But . . .''

Boone stood up, towering over the other man, his anger and voice restrained, except for the steely glint in his eyes. ''Go away, Louis. Go back to Newport. I'll see you up there at the end of the week.''

When Whitcomb had stamped out, shaking his head and rapping his walking stick on the floor in a manner that left no doubt of his frustration, Boone steepled his fingers atop his desk. He stared across the room at the painting of the Monongahela without really seeing it. Deep thoughtfulness came over him as late-afternoon sun poured into the office, splashing pools of light on the center of the brown carpet, shimmering gold on the oak-paneled walls.

He hadn't known of Penelope's situation, but what he had told Whitcomb regarding it was the truth. It didn't matter to him. If she was in search of a rich husband, well, why not? Pittsburgh was full of fortune hunters; so were New York and Chicago and St. Louis and all the other big cities where men accumulated vast quantities of wealth and women were relegated to the role of wearing, buying, and signifying the symbols of that wealth. There was no crime in poverty, Boone reflected wryly. And no crime in trying your damnedest to escape from it.

It would be different, he thought, if Penelope didn't care for him, if she was interested in him merely because of the money he'd made through Whitcomb and Walker Steel. Boone didn't think that was the case. Certainly, the wealth he had accumulated in a relatively short period of time, and the greater wealth anticipated in the future, might have made him eligible in her eyes, just as a pleasing smile and a buxom figure might make a woman eligible in a man's estimation. But it was not all there was between them. The warm feelings, the laughter, and the spark of sexuality that flared whenever they were together were genuine and strong. If desperation lurked beneath the surface of Penelope's outrageous manner, he was sorry for it, for she possessed a great quantity of feminine charm, and Boone had no wish to see any woman, particularly one so brave and gay, suffer for a man's mistakes. The old earl was a fool to have lost his fortune; but his daughter was only the victim of an unkind fate.

Yet, as Boone sat in the sweltering confines of his office staring out the open window at the flower-dotted hills beyond, he thought of another girl, one with black silken hair and eyes that could wring at his heart. He still loved Elly, but she was lost to him. She and Connor were happy and well, wrapped up in their own warm little family, with their own child and their own blissful lives. And if he could never have Elly, he thought, a shadow of resentment crossing his features, why shouldn't he have another woman, one who had both a need and a desire and a wish for his love?

He didn't doubt that Penelope would accept him if he were to offer marriage. She had made comments that left no doubt. And if he couldn't give her his total, unbounded love, his complete, single-minded devotion, Boone thought, his gaze fixed on the blazing dome of azure sky that hung over the Pennsylvania hillside, he could at least give her companionship, protection, admiration—and access to his fortune. It would be a compensation, he thought, that would not distress her. Somehow he didn't think Penelope expected him to lay down his heart for her, only to care about her, protect her, appreciate her as an alluring and desirable woman. That he certainly did. In all these respects, he could accommodate her. *Accommodate*. Yes, he decided, with a small, curling smile. That was a good word to describe their pairing. He and Penelope could quite admirably accommodate each other.

His thoughts were interrupted by his clerk, Evan Murphy, who stuck his head around the door.

"Someone here to see you, Mr. Walker. Says you know him. He's looking for a job."

"Send him in," Boone replied abstractedly, turning from the window. He was still thinking of Penelope, pondering the prospect of marriage to her, when a stoop-shouldered red-headed man ambled in through his door. Boone glanced at him and froze. His entire body instantly stiffened, and the dreadful beat of his heart pounded like a deafening surf in his ears.

"I'll be damned," he muttered through dry lips as he stared in disbelief at the visitor. His past and all his ugly memories of Hickoryville rushed at him with the ferocity of an oncoming locomotive. "Caleb Dunne," he managed to say in a passable imitation of his usual calm way. "What the hell are you doing here?"

🌿 Fourteen

CALEB'S FRECKLED FACE split into a grin. His drooping mouth revealed yellow, broken teeth. "I need a job, Boone, need one real bad. Mind if I come into yer office, or is this Hickoryville boy too dirty and low for such a fancy place?"

Beneath the humble words, there was malice and jealousy. Boone could sense it in the way Caleb ran his tongue around the corners of his lips, in the way his slitted eyes darted about the richly paneled office. Wariness gripped him. He was not physically afraid of Caleb Dunne; that would be impossible. Caleb, who as a boy had seemed a giant bully, was now a good five inches shorter than Boone, and his rawboned body had neither the strength nor the muscle that Boone's possessed in such abundance. Boone was taller, broader, his flesh packed solid with rock-hard muscle formed by years of backbreaking work. Yet, deep within, apprehension flickered as he met the snickering gaze of the other man.

Boone controlled his uneasiness. He kept his features impassive. Only the faintest glint in his piercing eyes showed his guardedness. He walked forward and shook Caleb's hand. "Good to see you, Caleb. I'm amazed, though. Come in, sit down, and tell me how you found me."

"Wal, now, don't mind if I do."

A long, cool shadow fell across the room as both men took seats. Clouds scuttling across the sky had hidden the molten August sun. Suddenly, the air smelled of rain, and a damp breeze swept across the sultry air, rustling Boone's papers.

"Got to Pittsburgh last week," Caleb said, slouching back in the chair. In his faded jersey and patched trousers, with the old railway cap in his hand, he reminded Boone of a scrounging dog he'd once seen in a back-street alley. "Jest missed all the excitement with that there railwaymen's strike. Bet it was purty wild. Anyways, I got to town and what the hell do you think happened? I saw your name in the newspaper, big as you please. Boone Walker! You coulda knocked me down with a feather, boy." He chortled suddenly. "Guess all thet schoolin' my ma pushed on me back home came in handy after all, else I never would have been able to read your name, or all 'bout that ex-panded wharf you're buildin' on the river. Boone Walker, of Whitcomb and Walker Steel, it said. And I thought to myself, that can't be old Boone from Hickoryville. Naw, couldn't be him. But jest on the off-chance of it, I figgered I'd find out for myself." He scratched his nose with a grimy fingernail and studied Boone again. Greasy red hair straggled forward over his eyes. "You've done real fine fer yourself, boy. Yessir, real fine. I reckon the folks in Hickoryville would be mighty proud."

"What can I do for you, Caleb? You say you need a job? Ever worked in a steel mill before?"

"Nope."

"How about an iron foundry?"

"Nope."

Boone's lips curled in a faint smile. "Well, I suppose we could find you something."

"That's real kindly of you, Boone. 'Specially since you and me, we practically grew up together. Till you disappeared all of a sudden, that is."

Here it comes, Boone thought, bracing himself in his chair. For a moment, he saw himself staring down the barrel of Sheriff Tubbs's shotgun, the lawman's dogs yapping at his heels. He reminded himself that Ezra's death had been eleven long years ago, that he was no longer the ignorant, terrified boy he had been then. But murder was murder. If Caleb sent back word of where he was, would they still come after him? He saw his mother's face, older now and haggard, peering at him as he sat behind iron jail bars. The image was like a knife twisting in his heart. Would Ma even come to visit him? She had forbidden him even to fistfight with his brothers, then had seen him kill her husband. He'd doubted all these years that she could ever feel anything for him again except anger and shame.

"Yep, I always wondered why you took off like that so sudden." Caleb was regarding him curiously. "Heard tell it damned near broke yer ma's heart. No one could figger why you did it."

Boone had gone very still, his gaze riveted on Caleb. "I thought it was pretty plain at the time why I left," he said heavily, still watching, watching the other man's face. He hated the fact that, even after all these years, talking about home could still evoke such powerful emotions in him. Fear, shame—and loss. Gut-wrenching, agonizing loss. It was a struggle merely to contain the feelings exploding inside him, yet somehow he managed to keep his features impassive, to control the pain that threatened to consume him.

Caleb shook his head. Bafflement was written across his large, homely features. "Plain? It didn't make a lick of sense, boy. After Clay and Ezra had that there accident, yer ma had enough trouble on her hands. And then, when Ezra run off with the little girl—"

"*What are you talking about?*" Boone was on his feet, gaping at Caleb with the expression of someone hit by a lightning bolt. Accident . . . Clay and Ezra? His mind clicked along at a rapid-fire pace, trying to make sense of Caleb's words. "Are you saying Ezra ran off with Rose after I left? You mean . . ." He wet his lips as Caleb had done, trying to speak, trying to make sense of the chaos spinning through his brain. "You mean Ezra *lived?*"

"Sure as shootin', boy. Clay only nicked him when that shotgun went off. Hit some muscle and bone, and the old man lost a lot of blood, I heard tell, but the shot clear missed his heart. Plumb lucky, I say. Old Clay sure learned a lesson in how to clean his gun without firin' it at someone." He chuckled, then became aware of Boone's deathly pale face. Caleb pushed himself to his feet. "What's the matter with you?" He came around the desk toward Boone. A shrewd, appraising glance narrowed his eyes. "Don't tell me you thought your brother killed Ezra that day. Thet why you left?" He gave a loud guffaw. "Thought you had more gumption and sense than that."

Boone staggered past him to the window. He gazed unseeing at the craggy hills in the distance, their misty lavender beauty marred by the black smoke rising from the mills below. An unexpected rain had begun to fall, banishing the sun, turning the sky to the color of dust.

Ezra had lived. He couldn't believe it. *Ezra had lived.*

The nightmare he had run from for so long was nothing but a phantom. A damned phantom. He had fled a phantom for eleven years of his life.

"Ma." His voice broke. "My ma—how is she?" he croaked from the window.

Caleb shrugged. "She was doin' poorly back a year ago when I left. I ain't been back or heard anythin' from home since."

Boone wrenched away from the window. "Tell Evan Murphy to put you in the warehouse," he shot over his shoulder as he headed for the door. "You can start tomorrow. Tell him I'll be back in a couple of days."

"But . . . Boone." Caleb stared after him in astonishment. "Boone Walker! Tarnation, boy, where in hell are you goin'?"

There was no answer. Boone was already gone.

Sunset wisped across a purple sky as Boone paused before the mangled elm. Eleven years had passed since he had crossed this spot. Eleven hard and lonely years. Yet how sweetly, achingly familiar it all seemed. The moist black earth, gray gravel, and dry dust, the blue-green hills sloping gently against a soft-hued horizon, were images he had carried with him from childhood. Kentucky. *My Old Kentucky Home*.

The sharp odor of tobacco from the surrounding fields filled his nostrils as he moved on, up the path that led to the farmhouse. As he approached, a jumble of emotions crashed inside his chest. Fear, joy, a welling up of memories so intense they brought tears to his eyes. Any moment now, any moment he would see Ma. And Clay.

His throat was dry as he drew near the house.

Gray and weathered, it looked the same. The fence needed painting, he noticed. Chickens squawked in the yard. There was an ancient-looking sparrow's nest in the hemlock tree beside the well.

Boone's footsteps were the only sound in the fading day. Above the weather vane on the shingled roof, ribbons of deep rose and violet made colored curlicues in the sky.

Then the farmhouse door opened. A young woman stepped out. She wore an old gingham dress that was too snug on her belly, full with child. A straw-haired toddler clung to her knees, crying pitifully.

Boone stopped, stared at the woman. "Clay," she called in a scared, high-pitched voice. "Come out here quick!"

When his brother pushed through the door and peered at him in the road, Boone could only stare in shock at the tall, gaunt figure. In faded dungarees and a patched shirt, Clay looked old, old and beaten. His once-broad shoulders sagged, his eyes squinted in the fading light of day, and his hair, which had once been pale gold, now looked a dirty gray as it curled around his ears and beneath his frayed collar. He held a rifle in his hands as he came to stand beside the woman and the little girl on the porch.

"Who's there?" His voice, harsh with suspicion, lashed the air.

Suddenly Boone became aware of the sweat running down his neck, soaking his shirtfront. He felt the hard, painful thumping of his heart. What was he going to say to Clay? How could he explain these lost years?

"Who's there? What do you want?" Clay rasped.

Boone walked forward with slow footsteps until he reached

the bottom step leading up to the porch. "Not a very kindly welcome for a weary traveler, Clay," he said softly.

As he watched, recognition and stunned disbelief washed over his brother's features.

"Boone!"

He shoved the rifle into the girl's hands and started down the steps, but an instant later, he froze. The joy that had been there for a brief flashing moment faded from his face, replaced by a wary coldness that clamped down upon his grim features. With a jerk, he stepped back onto the porch.

"What're you doin' here?" The next words were a snarl. "Come to see Ma?"

"And you." Boone, who had been ready to hurl himself into his brother's arms, felt a stab of pain at this hostile reception. But what had he expected? A royal welcome for having stayed away all these years? "Clay, we have to talk." He put a foot on the step. "I've got a lot of explaining to do. Caleb just told me— "

"Caleb Dunne?"

"Yes. Clay, it's a long story. Can't I come in and see Ma and tell you both all about it? Seems to me we have a lot of catching up to do."

"No."

Boone stiffened. The sun had disappeared in a haze of rosy gold, and now streaks of charcoal dusted the sky. "Why not?" he asked slowly.

Beside Clay, the pregnant girl made a small movement. The child leaning against her legs watched the stranger in mute fascination. She sensed the tension in the air, sniffled in fright, and began to cry.

"No, you can't see Ma." Clay's short-lashed blue eyes seemed to pierce right through Boone. His brother's gaze flicked over his rumpled city clothes, noted his bowler hat and knotted tie, his dust-speckled leather boots. Something in Clay's face twisted and hardened. "Seems like you came a long way. Too bad it was all for nothing. You can't see Ma," he repeated. "Not unless you go 'round back to the graveyard." Clay's mouth was an iron line in a face of stone. "But I don't reckon that's what you had in mind."

It was all Boone could do to keep from staggering backward. He clutched the porch rail, clinging to it. All the air seemed to have rushed out of his lungs.

"Ma's dead?" Just saying the words brought the sting of tears to his eyes. He shook his head, dazed, filled with a surging despair. "Then I'm too late."

"Six months too late," Clay shot at him. He spit on the ground an inch from Boone's foot. "Come on, Lula Mae, back in the house. Hetta, you hush or you'll catch the back of my hand. Sun's gone down and it's time for supper. Let's eat."

He took the gun back from the girl and started herding her and the child into the house.

"Clay, no. It's Boone!" The girl shrank back and pleaded with him, her voice shaking with emotion. Boone recognized her now; it was Lula Mae Dobbson, the blacksmith's daughter. She'd been ten years old when he left, a lank-haired tomboy, with huge eyes and a slingshot always in her hand, who'd been sweet on Clay from the moment she first saw him. Now she grabbed Clay's arm and shook it. "You can't just turn him away like this. Invite him in to supper, Clay. Please . . ."

"No!" He spun toward her furiously. "He stayed away this long, he can just stay away forever, far's I'm concerned! And I don't want to hear another word about it!"

Boone sprinted up the steps and laid a hand on his brother's arm. "Clay . . ."

With an oath, Clay knocked his arm aside. The little girl started to wail, and Lula Mae hastily picked her up. With one glance at Clay's face, she rushed with the child into the house. The door banged behind her. Boone and Clay faced each other on the porch.

A board creaked under Boone's foot. He shifted his weight as grief rocked him. It wasn't only his mother's death that filled him with an unspeakable pain—it was Clay. Clay was like a stranger, a bitter, angry stranger. The brother who had worked beside him in the barn and in the fields, who had protected him from bullies at school and from Ezra at home, who had taught him how to whistle and how to play checkers by the light of the stars, now faced him like an enemy.

"Clay, listen to me. I was scared to come back. I thought Sheriff Tubbs would arrest me for murder. I thought Ma hated me for shooting Ezra. I was ashamed and scared."

"For eleven years?" Clay sneered.

Boone fell silent. Inky darkness slithered over the land,

hiding Clay's face, but his rage and contempt were clear in his voice. Boone forced himself to go on speaking despite the desolation in his soul. "Yes. I was scared for eleven years. I couldn't face Ma. You were there. You heard what she said."

For a moment the brothers were silent, carried back together to that distant night when Clay had come bounding up the path to his home after hearing a shotgun report that had echoed, ominous as cannon fire, through the silent fields. He had found thirteen-year-old Boone with the shotgun in his hands, Ezra a bloody heap on the floor, Ma kneeling over him, her own bruised face lifted to her son.

"Murderer!" she had hissed in shock and horror. *"You've killed him!"*

And she had wept over Ezra's unmoving form.

"You damned fool." Clay's voice cut through Boone's dark reverie. "She wasn't grieving for Ezra, she was grieving for you! She was scared to death you'd hang for his murder. She was praying harder than hell that he would live so *you* wouldn't have his soul on your hands. Well, he did live, Boone. And me and Ma cooked up a story that left you without any blame at all. You know why? 'Cause we loved you, that's why. We thought you'd hide out in the hills for a while and then sneak back to see us and we could tell you that you were safe. But you never came back. You never even sent us one single filthy letter."

"I sent money—" Boone began, and then stopped short at Clay's contemptuous bark of laughter. Shame inched through him.

"Money? Yep, you sent money. Do you think Ma cared a whit for money? She wanted you, Boone, but there was never so much as a word of how you were doing or where in hell we could find you. She died calling your damned low-lizard name!"

Clay's fist shot through the darkness then, catching Boone unaware. It hit him in the jaw and set him reeling against the porch railing. White-hot pain slammed through his face. He held the railing and shook his head, trying to clear the blinking lights from his eyes.

"Clay . . ." he called hoarsely, but heard only the bang of the farmhouse door.

Boone sank down on the porch steps and threw back his

head. It was hot outside, but he felt cold, icy cold. And sick. His shoulders heaved with silent sobs for all the years lost, all the precious moments wasted. Better he shouldn't have come back at all than to have everything end like this.

He didn't know how long it was before he pushed himself to his feet and made his way to the family plot several hundred yards behind the house. Jeb's and Hannah's gravestones stood side by side in the plucked and tended grass. A circle of flowers surrounded them. Boone stared down at the site, illuminated by a sliver of moon.

"I'm sorry, Ma," he whispered into the thick, hot summer air. The scent of the flowers drifted on the rising wind. Boone squeezed his eyes shut to hold back the flood of tears. In that moment he remembered the wispy, dry feel of his mother's hair. He remembered her eyes set deep within her lined and tired face, he remembered the freshly laundered smell of her faded dresses. He almost heard her brusque voice giving orders, almost felt the gentle touch of her hands. He remembered homemade suppers, darned socks, a crooning melody when he was sick, and the quick, infrequent peck of her lips against his cheek when the soft mood came on her and no one else was around. And an emptiness filled him like none he had ever known before.

"Ma never did like fightin' between us young'uns." Clay spoke from the darkness directly behind him. "I reckon she's none too pleased with me right now."

"Forget it." Boone turned slowly. "I guess I had it coming."

"Boone." There was an urgency in Clay's voice as Boone started to move past him. Boone waited. In the darkness, he tried to read his brother's face.

"Supper's waitin'. Lula Mae set an extra place."

"Not necessary, Clay. I was just about to leave."

Clay grimaced. Time and worry had marked his young face with lines and left permanent tired smudges beneath his blue eyes. Boone couldn't look at him without feeling a wave of loss for the stout and handsome brother he had loved and looked up to years ago. "There's no place to go till tomorrow," Clay said. "You might as well stay the night."

"I don't stay where I'm not wanted."

Silence. Then, "Who says you're not wanted?" came the gruff reply. With these words, he turned and started back to the house.

So there was still a chance, Boone thought, watching Clay's retreating figure, though not much of one, considering all that had passed between them. They were strangers now, no longer brothers linked by childhood bonds. But at least Clay was willing to try bridging that painful gap. Maybe there was a place, a middle ground where they could find some kind of peace with each other after all that had happened.

Boone cast one final glance at the headstones, then followed his brother through the thick August night.

They sat in silence in the parlor after supper. The familiar creaking of the house settled about Boone, painful in the memories it evoked. The house looked nearly the same as it had when he had left it eleven years ago—the same kerosene lamp on the three-legged table, the same faded chintz curtains at the window, the same orange and green rag rug on the thin-planked floor. Only the horsehair sofa was new, that and the embroidered seat cushions on the hickory chairs. Clay smoked a cob pipe and stared into the empty hearth while Boone smiled at his brother's child, who inched across the floor to cautiously show him her corn-husk doll.

"That's mighty pretty," he said, receiving a glorious smile in return. Hetta had Clay's bright blue eyes and her mother's straw-colored hair and freckles. Her little face and body were brown from the sun.

"How old are you?" Boone asked.

The little girl held up two pudgy fingers. The childish gesture reminded him sharply of Rose, the little sister he had not wanted born because she was Ezra's child. Yet Rose had enchanted her older brothers from the moment of her first howl. She had been small, thin, and pretty as a solemn little wren. Boone remembered her when she was Hetta's age, toddling about the house, under everyone's feet, a sweet and silent child for whom he had fashioned dolls just like this one and carved tiny birds and animals from wood.

Lula Mae, knitting on the sofa, glanced up and watched them together with glowing eyes. All through dinner she had seemed in awe of Boone, but now she encouraged the little girl to speak to her uncle. "Tell Uncle Boone your dolly's name," she urged.

Hetta suddenly grew tongue-tied. She twisted a finger through her hair.

"It's Hannah," Lula Mae told Boone, with a flickering

glance at Clay. "Poor Hetta, she misses her granny real bad."

"It's time that child went on up to bed," Clay said abruptly.

Lula Mae rose with difficulty from the sofa, one hand on her swollen belly. "Say good night to Pa and Uncle Boone, Hetta."

Boone was relieved to see the softening of Clay's features when he patted the child's head. He had begun to fear that Clay was devoid of feeling for is wife and daughter, so distant had he seemed all through the meal and the evening hours. "He ain't usually like this, I vow," Lula Mae had whispered to Boone when Clay had gone outside for a moment. "He's usually a kind, loving man. But he's hurtin' inside, Boone, hurtin' 'cause of you and your ma and poor little Rose and all. Seein' you brought it all back to him. Get him to tell you about Rose."

When Hetta shyly came to him and mumbled good night, Boone felt a lump rise in his throat. Looking at his tiny niece, not much younger than his sister had been the last time he'd been in this house, brought back a flood of tender memories that ripped at his heart. Carefully, he leaned over and kissed her on the cheek.

"I'm going to send you another dolly—from Pennsylvania," he told her, warmed by the widening of her wondering eyes. "A china doll with a real lace dress and a bow in her hair. She'll be a friend to you and Hannah. Will you like that?"

Hetta nodded, her small face shining. At a word from Lula Mae, she turned and scampered up the stairs.

"She doesn't need no present from you," Clay said from his chair. His face was turned toward the empty grate, and Boone could only see his hardened profile. "After you leave in the morning, you can forget about us, just like before."

"I never forgot about you, Clay." Boone rose and walked to the fireplace, positioning himself directly in his brother's sight. "This house and everyone in it haunted my dreams for years. I tried my damnedest not to think about it, but it was always there, at the edge of my mind—the loneliness, the wondering, the shame and worry for you all."

Clay was silent.

"Tell me about Rose," Boone ordered at last.

It was not a pleasant story to hear. After Ezra had recovered from his wound, Clay and Hannah had told him to leave. The boys had never known that Ezra beat their mother, for he did it only when they were away from home, and never did he strike her face, where they were sure to see the bruises. But it had been going on for years, she had told Clay following the shooting. It had started during the war years, when times had grown so hard. Ezra—unable to withstand the pressure of the failing farm, the two oldest boys away fighting, the unstated but palpable dislike of Boone and Clay—had taken out his anger and petty frustrations on Hannah. And she, fearful that his violence would be turned on her sons if she spoke up, had endured it. Until the day Boone had come home in the middle of one of Ezra's beatings and had exploded in an unstoppable rage. After that, and Boone's flight, Clay had circulated the story in town that he had shot Ezra accidentally while cleaning his gun. Ezra, grateful for Hannah's nursing, had reluctantly agreed to hide the truth. But when he was well and Clay had thrown him out, he had had his vicious revenge. He had sneaked back into the house that same night and taken Rose from her bed. In the morning, both had completely disappeared.

"It nearly killed Ma," Clay said in that flat, expressionless tone Boone guessed hid a wellspring of pain. "She cried for days, and you know, Boone, Ma never was one to cry. But her heart was broke. You know how she doted on that child. Lord, we all doted on her, sweet thing that she was." The corncob pipe sat forgotten in his hand. Clay was drifting back, back to the days after the little brown-haired girl had vanished from the farm.

Only the song of the crickets across the endless open fields broke the silence until he shook himself out of his reverie and spoke again. "Losin' her, especially after losin' you, well . . . it was almost more'n even Ma could bear."

Boone stared at the floor. In the rich golden glow of the kerosene lamp, the room was warm and cozy, but suddenly a chill overtook him. Too much sadness, too much suffering had gone on here. What had happened to the loving family he had known as a boy, when Jeb was alive and his brothers whistled at their chores? Ma . . . Ma had been happy then, quick and busy and sharp in her work, but always kind underneath, always ready to comfort if there was a need.

"You searched for Rose?" he asked quietly, lifting his head.

Clay nodded and shrugged. "For weeks. It was no use. That old varmint probably headed straight for the hills where he came from, and he knew every shack and cave and ledge there was in those parts. We could never find 'em there."

Boone hurt for all of them. He shuddered to think of his timid little sister at the mercy of Ezra Wells all these years. He grieved to know of his mother's pain. And it hurt him, too, to see the lines of sorrow and loss carved on his brother's brown and haggard face.

Suddenly he pushed away from the mantel and strode toward Clay. "Life hasn't been exactly sweet for the Walkers all these years, then, has it? But isn't that all the more reason why we should join together now? Clay, I . . . I've missed you, all of you! Lord knows, I wish to hell I could see Ma again and make things up to her, but I can't. I'll have to live with that. But you, you're still here, and you have a fine family." He ran a hand through his hair in frustration. "Lula Mae and Hetta and the new baby that's coming, they're my kin, too. Let me know them; let me be a brother to you again. Don't lock me out of your lives, Clay. I want to be a part of them. I want to get to know you again and help you."

Clay pushed himself to his feet. He was just a shade shorter than Boone, but still tall, and his eyes held a hard determination that was startlingly similar to his brother's. "We don't need or want your help. Jest because you're now a rich man in the steel business, able to hire the likes of Caleb Dunne, doesn't mean your kin'll take charity from you."

"That's not what I meant." Boone frowned. "You're deliberately twisting my words."

"You don't belong here anymore. You've made a new life for yourself. Look around. This isn't your home. It's not what you want. You're goin' back to your city and your fancy steel company, and we're stayin' here, where we're about as happy as we're ever goin' to be."

"Fine. But I'm still your brother, and if I want to send my niece a new doll, or a damned new blanket for that baby that's coming, I'm sure as hell going to."

Clay's features seemed to break apart. He edged away so that Boone couldn't see his face, and flung his words over his shoulder. "D . . . dammit, Boone, why in hell didn't you stay where you were? We were gettin' on fine till you showed up. Now what the hell am I supposed to do?''

Boone's strong hand on his arm spun Clay around. ''Be my brother again, Clay.'' He grasped Clay's shoulders and met his tortured gaze. Suddenly he clasped the other man against him and held him tight. ''That's all. Just be my brother.''

Clay began to sob. Boone felt the tears running down his own cheeks. After a moment, Clay broke away. ''I'm going up to Lula Mae.'' He wiped his patched sleeve across his eyes. ''Don't like to leave her alone long when she's this close to her time.'' He strode toward the stairs, his steps quick and hard. At the bottom step, he paused. ''You'll still be here in the mornin'?''

Boone nodded. ''I'm not going anywhere again without saying good-bye, Clay.''

He lay on the horsehair sofa with a homemade blanket folded up for a pillow and tried to sleep. But he kept thinking that Clay was right about one thing: he didn't belong here anymore. As tender and painful and vibrant as his memories of this home were, they were only memories. Echoes of the past. It was time to let the phantoms go.

Perhaps now, after confronting his past, he could move on and find the peace that had eluded him. Maybe, he reflected, as he stared up at the wood-beamed ceiling, he could even find a smattering of happiness.

His place now was in Pittsburgh and his future was on the banks of the Monongahela River. That much was clear. But it was more than his work that Boone was thinking of. For the first time in his life, he thought about starting a new family, his own family. Clay was here with Lula Mae and Hetta. Connor Maguire and Elly had their own little daughter. A powerful yearning came over him for a child of his own. Son or daughter, someone to love and care for, to protect from life's woes as best he could manage.

His thoughts centered on Penelope. In the darkness, he could see her cool and lovely face. He would offer her financial security and the benefits of fortune and all the respect and affection he felt for her in his heart. She could give him a child and a merry home; she could be a wife with high spirits and good cheer who would welcome him, warm him, make all his hard work worthwhile. When the mantel clock struck two, he closed his eyes at last, thinking of the ring he would buy for her, of the home they would build together, of the child she would bring into the world. *A family of my own*, Boone thought as sleep overtook him. *A new beginning, a chance to be happy, to belong once more*. He dreamed of Penelope, slim and mischievous, with her soft, dry English voice and caressing lips. The mother of his child.

In his sleep, Boone sighed and smiled.

❧ Fifteen

Chicago, 1877

"SEE DADDY NOW. I go see Daddy now." Two-year-old Cassandra Maguire decided with a firm nod of her little head. She dropped her doll on the floor and started toward the sewing room door. Caroline darted in front of her and scooped the little girl into her arms.

"Not yet, darling," she sighed. She pressed a kiss to Cassie's sweet-smelling cheek and then studied the child before her. Dusky ringlets framed a round pink face with tiny bow lips, a smidgen of a nose, and eyes so large and so brilliant a blue as to be startling. "Daddy's still asleep." She forced a smile, no easy task when she thought of Connor still passed out from his drinking binge of last night, sprawled across the upstairs bed and snoring so loudly that Mrs. Malloy had complained about hearing him all the way down the hall. "I'll take you up to see him later, I promise. But right now Daddy needs his rest."

Cassandra's sapphire eyes, so like Connor's, filled with tears. "Where's Mommy? I want Mommy!" she cried. Again, Caroline sighed, and hugged the little girl to her.

"Shh, darling, Mommy's busy. She has work to do right now. She's helping Grandma and Great-Aunt Addie serve the customers in the tearoom. Remember all the pretty ladies?

Well, when they're all finished with their tea and cakes, Mommy will come in and play with you. Here, let's pick up poor Daisy from the floor and give her a hug. Why don't we all have a pretend tea party right here? Come help me set the table, Cassie darling, and then you sit down beside Daisy. Oh, yes, we'll have a lovely party all our own.''

It was strange, Caroline thought, as she set imaginary dishes around the little table by the window in the sewing room, how children sensed the tensions going on around them. She wondered if Cassie had awakened in the night and heard some fragment of the argument between Elly and Connor the evening before, if the anger and animosity in their shouting voices hadn't somehow drifted upstairs from the parlor and touched her while she slept unaware on the cot in their room. Caroline had heard it. No words at first, just the angry voices. They had awakened her from her sleep, but then, she never slept very soundly anyway. Careful not to disturb Bess, who scarcely ever stirred once her head touched the pillow, she had tiptoed into the hall and stood there shivering, shivering and listening while a deep, sorrowful pity overtook her.

Such cruel things Connor had said to her sister. "It's all your fault," he had yelled in a voice so fierce with rage that Caroline had cowered against the wall as if she herself were under attack. "I invested in the damned theater because of you—so you could stay in Chicago with your damned family! I could have been in Pittsburgh right now—making a fortune in steel! But you wanted to stay here in this stinking town!"

Caroline hadn't been able to hear Elly's reply. Muffled words, something about debts and horses, and then she had caught the name of the Gem Theater. The theater, Caroline thought in disappointment. They'd all had such high hopes for the theater. If only it had all gone as Connor had planned. Instead, the Gem had been failing for well over a year. Too much competition, Connor complained. Too difficult to book the best companies, the best plays. Expenses were higher than they'd thought; profits never seemed to come up to par. Sean Fitzgerald was nearly ready to throw in the towel. So far, Connor had persuaded him to wait. If they could only find some fresh money, new investors, they could attract a really famous troupe, one that would make everyone forget about the gambler who'd been shot in the lobby last year and about the backstage fire that had ruined the dressing rooms and a half-dozen expensive sets. That's what Connor kept saying.

So many dreams that man had, Caroline thought to herself in dismay. But he drank and gambled too much to make any of them come true, and the luck of the Irish certainly wasn't with him. At least it hadn't been up until now.

The only lucky thing that ever happened to Connor Maguire, Mama had commented bitterly to Aunt Adelaide last week, was marrying Elly. And that, Bess now believed, was the worst thing that could have befallen her daughter.

Caroline had herself been the object of everyone's pity for so long that she understood how Elly must feel to know that everyone was aware of Connor's shortcomings. They were all disappointed in him and sorry for her. It was humiliating. But Caroline had noticed that Elly didn't shrink and cower into herself, as was her own way to deal with her pain. Somehow or other, Elly carried on with her head held high and her spine straight as a ramrod. Even with little Cassandra to care for, the boardinghouse and tearoom to run, and Mama and Aunt Adelaide constantly buzzing about Connor's late nights and drunken mornings, Elly continued to function as though she hadn't a doubt in the world that everything would turn out fine.

Caroline studied her red, chapped hands while Cassandra babbled animatedly to the little doll sitting beside her at the sewing room table. She envied Elly's strength, but knew she didn't possess it herself. Once in a while, on a summer evening, she had caught her mother and sister glancing at her as the sounds of laughter came from neighboring porches. She knew what they were thinking. The voices of young men and women, sitting together on a swing or playing croquet in someone's backyard, made them wonder if she didn't yearn for the gaiety of courtship and romance. She didn't. Threads of panic twisted inside her every time the milkman tipped his cap to her or one of the male boarders passed her in the hall. She couldn't help it. The very fact of their masculinity reminded her of what Jason and his friends had done to her in that dark and smothering glade. She hated the memories, hated the sick, shrinking feelings inside her, but she didn't know how to fight them, she didn't even know how to try. She still had nightmares, still woke up dripping in sweat. And every time she saw her sister working so hard to keep the tearoom and boardinghouse going, putting up with Connor's gambling and drunken tirades, she became more and more convinced that her only safety lay in staying away from all men, in scurrying about safe and unobtrusive within the house. Once, early in her marriage, Elly had suggested that Caroline get a job in a shop. Elly had even spoken to Madam Lucille, the milliner, about hiring her. But Caroline's tearful horror upon hearing this suggestion had resulted in a terrible scene, with her distress winning Bess's instant support and sympathy. The matter had been dropped. Elly had meant well; Caroline understood that. But her sister didn't understand that not everyone was as strong as she was, not all women could overcome the hideous things that happened to them.

"When can I see Daddy?" Cassandra whined, pulling at Caroline's sleeve.

"Soon, darling." Looking down at her niece, Caroline's heart broke for this innocent child, who must someday discover the truth about her father, about men, about the ugliness of the world.

Across the hall in the main parlor, Elly moved from table to table, checking on the comfort and satisfaction of her guests. Gowned in a polonaise of mauve taffeta with a purple satin underskirt, tight sleeves, and small jet buttons, she made an elegant and gracious hostess as she drifted through the bright and cheerful room refilling teacups from a silver pot, summoning Alice, the girl she had hired to help with the serving, to bring the tray of miniature sandwiches and cakes. Women of all ages and sizes reclined on the gilt chairs set about the little tables, sipping their tea from pink and gold china cups. The tearoom was a wonderful success. With the new satin draperies, the cheery fire, and the removal or rearrangement of the room's previous furnishings, the result was an inviting parlor able to accommodate twenty-four patrons quite comfortably for tea. Elly's feet were aching in her stiff, high-heeled shoes, but she kept smiling as Mrs. Henry Montgomery Addison summoned her across the room.

"My dear, the icing on these cakes is the finest in the city. So light and sweet—it is perfect!" Mrs. Addison, in her elaborate day gown of russet taffeta, received nods of agreement from her companions, dowagers of similar age, bearing, and obvious wealth. "You're to be commended. I have pa-

tronized this tearoom nearly every week for almost three
months, and never have I tasted a bite that was not exquisitely
delicious. Your cook ought to be working at Kinsley's or
Amberson's Palace, Mrs. Maguire.''

"Thank you, ma'am, but my cook is also my mother, and I
would hope she won't desert me," Elly replied with a smile.

Mrs. Addison raised her brows and then chuckled. "I
would hope not, indeed.''

"May I bring you ladies another tray of sandwiches? Or
perhaps you would care for more tea?''

"Why, yes, we should indeed.'' The wife of Chicago's
wealthiest lumber merchant nodded approvingly as she sipped
the last amber drops from her cup. "That would be lovely. I
believe we need some warm sustenance before venturing out
into that damp autumn air for the long drive to Prairie Avenue.''

Another hour passed before the last customer departed. No
sooner had the door closed than Elly slipped out of her shoes.

"You outdid yourself today, Mama," she said, carrying a
trayload of cups and saucers to the kitchen for washing. She
noticed a frown between Bess's brows, and it puzzled her.
Her mother generally enjoyed the bustle of preparing the tea
delicacies; it gave her pleasure to receive so many compliments for her culinary skills, and there was something
soothing and wonderful in preparing elegant little dishes like
those she had enjoyed in her privileged girlhood in Boston,
instead of the usual stews and sausages and soups she fixed
for the boardinghouse suppers. "What is it, Mama, what's
wrong?''

"Only a touch of the headache. I'll lie down with a cool
cloth on my head as soon as we're finished here.''

"Jeweline and Alice can handle the cleaning up. You go
upstairs now and rest. When you're ready, I'll bring you a
supper tray in bed.''

Bess wiped her hands on her apron and kissed Elly's
cheek. "That sounds lovely," she admitted. "I am feeling a
bit tired.''

Elly waited until her mother had climbed the steps to her
room before she went to reclaim her daughter. It had been
raining for three days now, but that hadn't stopped the steady
stream of patrons from filling the tearoom each afternoon.
Elly was both elated and exhausted. She was too thankful for
the excellent business she'd been doing to complain, but

weariness tugged at every inch of her body. Her feet hurt, her shoulders ached, even her cheeks throbbed from smiling continually at the daily guests. But she had taken in well over a hundred dollars today, and that was cause for celebration.

"Come here, my darling, and tell me what you and Aunt Caroline have been so busy with all afternoon!" She stooped and opened her arms to the little girl, who rushed headlong into them.

Beyond the window of the cozy parlor, with its cast-iron stove, chintz-covered sofa, and matching curtains bright with red cabbage roses on cream, autumn haze misted the streets and a flutter of falling leaves gathered in the puddles. A fine silver drizzle plinked continually at the glass.

"Mommy, we had a tea party! See Daisy? Daisy drinks tea! Mommy, is Daddy awake now? I want to see him."

Over Cassandra's head, Elly and Caroline exchanged glances. "Don't you want to play with me for a little while? I thought I'd tell you a story."

"I want to see Daddy." In her own way, Cassandra was already as stubborn and single-minded as her mother. Her tiny lower lip pushed outward in a pout.

Elly ran a hand through the girl's satiny curls. "All right then, darling," she said after a moment's hesitation. "Come along and we'll see."

"I'll lend them a hand in the kitchen," Caroline said quietly, and Elly nodded. Hand in hand with her daughter, she walked toward the stairs.

She dreaded facing Connor today. She wasn't sure what she would find or what kind of temper he might display before Cassie. They'd had a terrible argument the night before. He'd been drunk, of course, and probably wouldn't even remember half of what he'd said, but still, the angry words lingered between them like a wall of barbed wire. As she eased open the bedroom door and stepped inside, tension ran through her. The sight of him, still fast asleep across the unmade bed, caused sharp little knots to tighten in the pit of her stomach.

"Sleepyhead, wake up!" Before Elly could stop her, Cassandra yanked her hand free of Elly's and flew toward the bed. She was gurgling with laughter as, with difficulty but great determination, she managed to climb onto the mattress and crawl up on her father's bare hairy chest. "Wake up, Daddy, wake up and play with me!"

Connor groaned and put a hand to his eyes. "What the hell?" he muttered thickly. A grunt followed, as Cassandra pressed soft lips to his unshaven cheek.

"Ouch, scratchy," she complained when the dark stubble grazed her chin.

Connor opened his eyes and met his daughter's adoring gaze. He shifted his vision to Elly, silent at the foot of the bed. "Damn it, can't you see I'm in no condition to be drooled over and pinched? Get her out of here, Elly!"

Cassie, frightened by his tone, stared with slowly widening eyes. She stuck a chubby thumb in her mouth and began to suck noisily, as if to comfort herself.

"Get her out of here!" Connor roared, and swept the child from him with one brawny arm. Cassandra tumbled onto the blankets and began to wail. In a flash, Elly snatched her up.

"Daddy isn't feeling well today, darling," she said quickly, kissing the child's puffy red cheeks in an attempt to stem the flow of tears. "We'll come back tomorrow, and by then he'll be able to play with you. Come along now. Timothy should be home soon from Mr. Riccione's store. Let's see what he's brought you today."

Anger pumped through her as she took Cassie downstairs. It was awhile before the child grew distracted enough to forget her father's outburst. Elly entertained her, and Timothy showed her a shiny new whistle on a string, but when Elly later tucked her into bed, Cassie returned to the subject tearfully, clutching her small hands around her mother's neck.

"Mommy, I want Daddy. Why won't Daddy come?"

The big bed with its peach-colored counterpane was empty now. Rumpled sheets lay tossed on the floor.

"I don't know where Daddy is right now," Elly answered truthfully. She hugged her daughter, holding her tight. "Daddy loves you very much. He isn't mad at you."

"He yells at me."

"He doesn't mean to, darling. Sometimes Daddy doesn't feel so well. He gets tired and grouchy." She peered into the small, trusting face and forced herself to give a brilliant smile. "Tomorrow will be better, you'll see. Darling, I promise you, Daddy loves you very much. And Mommy does, too, more than the moon and the sun and the stars." She smoothed the baby-soft cheek with a gentle hand. "Now go to sleep and dream of angels. Dream of pretty silver wings and rainbows and a pot of gold. Isn't that what Daddy tells you to dream when he tucks you in? Yes, I thought so. Sleep well, darling."

Elly knelt to gather up the sheets from the floor before she left the room. Cassandra was already drifting off, her eyes closing, her soft little mouth drooping wide. Gently, Elly closed the door.

Down the hall, she could hear Mama and Caroline moving about in their room, talking in soft voices. Timothy had gone to bed in the little attic room he had made his own. Since taking a job after school every day at Mr. Riccione's dry goods store, he was tired out by the time supper was over. What with his chores at the boardinghouse, the rigors of school, and his duties at the store, he put in a grueling day. He rarely even had time to play chess anymore with General Willis.

"Elinore."

Aunt Adelaide was ponderously ascending the staircase as Elly moved toward the landing.

"Your husband is in the kitchen eating cheese and drinking brandy. He's in a fine mood, let me tell you."

"Was he rude to you? I'm sorry, Aunt Adelaide."

Her aunt shook her head as she reached the head of the stairs. "Who'd have thought he'd come to this? Certainly not me. You know I thought the world of him when he first came to this house. He and that Mr. Walker were such nice polite young men, up and coming in the world."

"What did Connor say?"

"He nearly snapped my head off when I started to wrap up the cheese and put it away. He told me he hadn't had a decent meal in this house for weeks. Imagine that! With him being drunk or absent 'most every night for dinner, then coming in and expecting there to be enough left over for him to feast on whenever he pleases." She clicked her tongue and said in a lowered tone, "I wanted to tell him that when he starts bringing in some bread money, he'll have a right to complain. Land sakes, Elinore, if you hadn't started that tearoom and managed it so well, we'd be starved by now, the lot of us! But don't worry, my dear, I didn't say a word. I just let him have his cheese, drank my warm milk, and I came up to bed. I think he's brooding over that letter he got today. The one from Mr. Walker.''

"I'll go to him," Elly sighed.

The kitchen was clean and warm and quiet when she slipped in from the hall. The stove effectively banished whatever damp autumn chill seeped across the back porch and under the crack of the door. A single kerosene lamp burned on the counter. Connor sat at the rectangular pine table, staring morosely at the letter in his hands. His eyes and nose were red, his hair tousled and greasy. He had donned a suit, but his shirtfront and jacket looked dull and wrinkled, and his trousers had a stain below one knee. To make matters worse, an unwashed smell emanated from his body. Elly fought back a wave of disgust.

How had they come to this? she wondered as she braced herself for the encounter. When she married Connor, she'd been happy as a nightingale, and now she was close to hating him. No, not hating him, not really. But she was as disillusioned with him as she was with herself. How could she have been so foolish and so blind? She had rushed into marriage with a handsome man, seeing only the beautiful smile, the lilting speech and merry ways. Sometimes, on days when he was sober and in an optimistic mood, she still saw these qualities, but now they were muted by the other side of Connor Maguire, the side that had emerged more fully as each month had passed and Connor's dreams had failed. Frustration had broken his gaiety and charm; gambling and a fondness for drink had eroded whatever stability and dedication to hard work he had once possessed. Elly hurt more for Cassandra than for herself. The child adored him. From the time she could crawl she had followed under his feet, fallen asleep on his shoulder, cooed and smiled just for him. On the days when he was sober, he spoiled her, but when liquor or a bad day at the racetrack weighed on him, he wanted nothing to do with her or with Elly, or with any member of the Forrest family.

"Boone's coming," he groaned when he found Elly watching him. He threw the letter down in disgust. "He'll be in town next week."

Elly didn't answer. She moved to the wooden counter and removed the day's loaf of bread from the box. With a knife, she began to slice it.

Connor followed her with his eyes, glaring. "I don't want him coming here to this house or finding out about that damned tearoom you're running."

She sliced sausage to go with the bread and put them on a plate. "Why not?" she asked, her hands shaking in anger. She was barely listening to this talk about Boone; Elly was still thinking of Cassandra and her questions.

"You know damned well why not! He'll think that I can't support my own wife and child! He'll think you've got to work so we can get by. I won't have it!"

But it's true, Elly thought grimly. *How are you going to hide the truth?*

"He wants to take us out to a restaurant for dinner," Connor said with a grimace. "Probably wants to show off, now that he's got money in his pocket to burn. Now that he's such a grand success in the steel business. Bah! Sure and he thinks he's a wonder for having made such a fortune. Do you know, Elly, how many tons of steel were produced in this country last year? It's no surprise the union leaders are going wild. Men like Boone are accumulating fortunes while the workers make barely enough to buy milk and potatoes!"

His jealousy was so blatant that Elly felt a shudder of revulsion. "I'm certain Boone is fair to the men who work for him," she replied as she set the plate of bread and sausage before him. The brandy glass was almost empty, she noted. The wedge of cheese was gone, too.

Connor grabbed her wrist. "Fair, you say? What makes you think so?" he demanded. "You barely know the man. And didn't you say your father worked like a dog to organize the workers? I don't see how you can defend Boone Walker."

"We have more important things to talk about than Boone, Connor. Aunt Adelaide told me you were hungry. Eat, and then we'll talk about Cassandra."

He ignored the food before him. "What about Cassandra?"

"Let me go, and I'll tell you," she said quietly.

Connor released her abruptly, staring in surprise at the red marks he'd caused on her wrist. He lifted his gaze to her drawn features, still fragile and beautiful despite the tiredness in her face. A tugging of various emotions played upon his countenance. "Ah, Elly, darlin', forgive me," he whispered suddenly. Misery clouded his beautiful eyes. For a moment he was the old Connor, the handsome, sweet, and earnest boy who had courted her three years ago. "I didn't mean to hurt you, lass. Or to snap at you! It's only because I'm so worried about things. It's the theater, Elly, that's the cause of all my problems. I'd such high hopes for it. Every night Sean and I go over the receipts and pray we'll be in the clear. And every night is another disappointment." He took her hand in his and brought it to his lips, pressing his mouth against her clenched fingers. "Ah, darlin', I only want a good life for you and our wee Cassandra." He laid his unshaven cheek against her hand, sighing. "I don't wish to hurt either of you."

"I know that, Connor." Elly pulled her hand free and sank down on a chair beside him. "But you hurt Cassie today, you know. You never should have shouted at her in such a frightening manner. She doesn't understand."

He rubbed his eyes. "Aye, it's true." He seemed to notice the food again suddenly. He reached out, took a piece of sausage in his fingers, and stuffed it into his mouth. "She's only a wee thing, and a lass at that. Now, if she were a laddie, she'd know that sometimes a man yells when he's in his cups and it doesn't mean anything. But she's a grand little thing, Elly, that's for sure, and I'm glad to have a daughter."

He swallowed the sausage and looked directly at Elly. "It won't happen again, darlin'. I swear to you."

How many times, Elly thought, had he sworn to her about one thing or another? No more gambling, he had promised. No more drinking, no more lies. She couldn't look at him. Instead she gazed down at her red, work-roughened hands, clasped on the table before her.

"It's no way for your daughter to live," she said, "never knowing when she'll see you, if you'll be drunk and shout at her, or if you'll dance a jig and make her laugh! We can't go on this way, Connor."

"You're right, lass, you're right. But there's good news." Connor's eyes shone with a new uncontained excitement. "I think my luck may be changin'." At the hard look that came over Elly's face, he rushed on quickly, "I know you hate the gamblin', lass, but this is one case where I know what I'm about. I got a tip about a certain trotter that's to run soon, and if I can come up with a proper sum of money—"

"Not a penny, Connor, not a single penny."

He flushed. As quickly as the contriteness had come upon him before, his mood changed again. "You needn't be speaking to me in that tone!'' He jumped up and began to pace about the kitchen, restless, filled with a mounting rage. ''I'm only thinking of you, trying to make things easier for you and for all of us! If I'd stayed with Boone in Pittsburgh, I'd be a rich man now, you know that? I could have bought you diamonds and pearls! But you wouldn't have it. You wanted to live here, near your aunt and your mother!'' He grabbed the glass on the table and gulped the last of the brandy, then wiped his arm across his mouth. ''I'd be part owner of that steel works right now—and the iron foundry—and maybe I'd be marrying an earl's daughter, too, bloody English bitch though she might be.''

Elly raised her brows in mystification. ''An earl's daughter?''

''That's who Boone is about to marry. He's to sail from Chicago Harbor for London when his business here is done.'' He picked up the letter and waved it in her face, scowling. Again he paced the kitchen with a frenzied restlessness. ''Well, I refuse to let Boone lord it over me. We're taking him to dinner, Elly, and I don't want to hear a word about it. And I want you looking like a queen—like a queen, do you understand me? Wear something magnificent, and don't say a word about the troubles with the theater or the damned tea-room you're running here or . . .''

''Or what?'' she demanded, with a slight, furious lift of her chin. ''Your drinking and gambling? Your debts? Is that what you want to hide from Boone?''

Connor spun away from her, his fists clenched. ''I'm going down to the Gem. Tonight's performance should be just about over by now.'' He yanked his umbrella from the corner behind the door. ''Lord knows, I can't bear to watch it again.''

''I'm certain if you stop in at Sean's place or Sweeney's on the way, you'll manage to get drunk enough so that you won't even notice the play,'' Elly said between clenched teeth.

Connor swung to face her, shaking with rage. ''If you'd only believe in me, my luck would change. It's your fault, Elly.'' He was shouting at her. ''It's all your fault. Remember that, and don't expect me home tonight to warm your bed!''

It had been so long since he'd laid with her sober that Elly could scarcely consider these words a threat. His lovemaking when he was drunk was rough and quick, a far cry from the tender and exciting union they had shared early in their marriage. "What does that mean?" she managed to ask in a peremptory tone as he flung open the kitchen door.

"It means I'll be back when I'm ready and not a moment before. Meanwhile, you'll have time to think about a wife's proper behavior if she hopes to keep her husband about." The door slammed behind him.

Elly didn't see him again for two days. When he returned, bearing an armful of roses for her and a new doll and Sunday bonnet for Cassandra, he acted as if nothing unpleasant had ever happened between them.

On the night they were to see Boone, Elly dressed carefully, but without any particular enthusiasm. She dreaded the deception Connor expected her to partake in, the pretense of prosperity and an easy life. This dinner tonight at Amberson's Palace, the new gown he had ordered for her from a dressmaker on State Street, and the carriage he'd hired for the evening all were horribly expensive. She was sick with worry just wondering how they would manage to pay for it all. Of course he had told her that the trotter he'd mentioned before had come through, and would again in a matter of days, but Elly could scarcely trust in such events. One roll of the dice, one turn of the card, and the small fortune Connor claimed to have won would vanish like a mist in morning sunshine.

"You look splendid, darlin'," Connor complimented her when she came down the stairs that night. In her new rose satin dress with the ivory petticoats and lace-edged train, she felt like a stranger, not the woman who ran the tearoom, worked her fingers raw in the boardinghouse, and cared for her daughter, but some magnificent impostor masquerading as Elly Maguire. Her sleek black hair was upswept, emphasizing the slender whiteness of her neck, her cheeks were the delicate pink of a camellia, and a pair of Aunt Adelaide's garnet earrings set in gold complemented her elegantly carved features. She looked royal, Connor remarked in the hired carriage, as the lights from the gas lamps cast a pale golden glow on the dark leather interior and on the woman beside him. He was as proud as a man could be to have her for his wife, he said, before reaching into his pocket and handing her a small box.

She gasped at the sight of the winking ruby necklace on its

bed of white velvet, nestled beside a matching pair of ruby earrings. But it was a gasp of dismay, not joy, that escaped her lips.

"Take off those garnets, lass," Connor instructed with a grin. "Only rubies will do you justice."

"Connor, no." She spoke in a low tone. "We can't afford—"

"Don't tell me what we can afford. I won't have you worrying about such things—especially not tonight. I promised you we'd be sitting pretty, Mrs. Maguire, and so we are. Now, put on those trinkets. We can't have Boone and the other patrons at Amberson's thinking my wife is deprived of the little niceties in life, can we, darlin'?"

As she dropped the garnets into her reticule, Elly wondered what he would think if he knew she had sold the sapphire necklace and earrings he had bought her in the past, when a winning streak had made him generous. She had done the same with a handsome emerald brooch. She had used the money from the sale of the jewels to establish her tearoom. It had been deceptive and perhaps ungrateful, but it had been the only way.

She fastened the necklace of small, brilliantly winking gems about her throat and secured the earrings as the carriage rattled along. Connor would be livid if he knew the truth, she reflected. The only way she had been able to deceive him all this time was by having the pieces reproduced in paste. Her deception had been necessary, though. She'd reached a point, shortly after Cassandra's birth, where she couldn't bear the uncertainty of her life any longer. When Connor was on a winning streak, he was extravagant in gifts he bought and lavish in spending his money, without thought or care for the future. He had even set up his mother and his brothers and sisters in a spacious new flat in New York, with three bedrooms and complete indoor plumbing. It was situated in a nice Irish neighborhood near a school and a church, and every month he received letters from his mother with effusive thanks and hints that one or the other sibling needed new shoes or a warm coat or a pair of mittens. All these requests were swiftly granted, as long as the winnings held out. Then, as soon as the tide turned and he was losing again, money became scarce, and whatever profits he might have brought home from the theater's earnings disappeared before he stepped through the front door. The letters from his mother went unanswered, and Elly came to realize that it was unwise for a woman to rely on anyone other than herself. The tearoom was the only way she had known of to produce a steady income beyond what the boardinghouse yielded. It had been her dream for a long time, a business all her own, which she controlled and which would feed her daughter, independent of Connor's streaks of fortune. In going ahead with it and making it a success, she had earned Connor's resentment and derision, but also the only measure of security she possessed.

"Grand, they look just grand." Connor squeezed her hand as he admired the jewels adorning her ears and throat. "I'll wager Boone's never bought anything finer for his future bride. Lady Penelope Stanton, that's her name. Sounds like upper crust, doesn't it?" He laughed shortly. "Fancy Boone Walker marrying the daughter of an earl! Well, never mind. I know all along it was you he fancied, and I came away with that little prize all to myself."

Elly had the beginnings of a headache, but this comment marshaled her full attention. "What on earth are you talking about?"

Connor flicked a speck of imaginary dust from the sleeve of his velvet-collared coat. Tonight he looked immaculate and devastatingly handsome. His black hair was brushed and glossy beneath his silk top hat, and there was a mirrorlike sheen to his evening-dress boots. "You mean you never guessed?" He shook his head. "Boone had his eye on you, lass, back in those days when we were courting. If I hadn't made it clear that he'd be trespassing, it's my opinion he'd have staked out a claim on you himself. Ah, but Boone's not the man to go after another fellow's woman, especially when he knows he can't win. So he sat back and accepted what couldn't be changed, but I always had a feeling that he fancied you for himself."

This idea struck Elly as ludicrous beyond words. She searched her memory for some incident, look, or gesture that would support Connor's statement, but could discover none. Boone Walker, she recalled, was simply a quiet and kindhearted man who had hovered in the background during her courtship with Connor. He had been Connor's friend, and thereby hers, but never, as she recalled, had he indicated that he had a *tendre* for her. Or perhaps, she thought, with a sudden startled realization, she had been too enamored of Connor to notice anyone or anything else. Those days, like brightly colored pennants, had passed by so quickly, so happily, that she hadn't paid much attention to the rest of the world. Connor had consumed all of her heart and her emotions.

"It's not possible," she murmured. "Surely I would have sensed such a thing."

Connor laughed again. "Didn't you ever wonder why he didn't come to our wedding? He was supposed to be my best man, you recall."

"He wrote that he had too much work to do. He couldn't get away from the foundry. And," Elly added, "I suspected he was hurt or angry over your decision to end the partnership."

"Aye, but I know Boone better than that. I saw how he behaved around you. Why, the poor fellow was even more tongue-tied than usual when you were about, poor bastard." But his voice had a triumphant, not a sympathetic, ring to it.

Elly sat very still. The edge of maliciousness beneath Connor's words repulsed her. She couldn't look at him. Even the handsomeness of his features couldn't hide the momentary ugliness. Boone had been, perhaps still was, his closest friend. This was no way for Connor to talk about him moments before they were to meet.

As the carriage lurched sharply rounding a corner, Connor's arm encircled Elly to keep her from being thrown. "But it doesn't matter now, darlin'. I've won you—you're mine. Boone might have a temporary advantage in the race for riches, but you are one prize that is mine forever more."

Her shoulders stiffened beneath his hands. His words had a chilling ring—like a parody of Edgar Allan Poe's words in "The Raven." "So I am nothing more to you than a prize in a contest? How gratifying."

"Now, Elly . . ."

She turned her head away, toward the thickening fog outside the carriage window. The throbbing intensified between her temples, but it was her heart that truly hurt. A feeling of great weariness washed over her.

Suddenly, beside her, Connor's voice rang out in excitement. "There's Potter Palmer's hotel—and Boone, waiting outside, just as we arranged!"

Connor reached over and opened the door as the carriage

clattered to a halt. "Remember now, lass," he said in an undertone, "not a word about the troubles with the Gem."

A moment later, Boone Walker swung his tall frame into the carriage.

❦ Sixteen

"WELL, DON'T YOU look devilish fine and prosperous!" Connor exclaimed with a welcoming smile as he and Boone shook hands, but his eyes had a hard glint in them, barely discernible in the dim light of the carriage. "So old man Whitcomb came through for you, after all. Who'd have thought it, my lad?"

The carriage pulled away from the Palmer House and headed up State Street. Boone grinned, and laid his ebony-handled umbrella on the seat beside him. "Hello, Connor."

In his single-breasted dress coat with gilt buttons and velvet collar, his silk gloves and top hat, he looked unexpectedly distinguished. Yet, beside Connor's dashing form, with his glittering jeweled tie pin, the carnation in his lapel, and his devastatingly handsome features, Boone seemed solemn, almost drab.

He looked older than he had the last time she had seen him, Elly thought, but then, three years had passed and a great deal had changed. Boone had risen from junior partner in an iron foundry to co-owner of one of the most vital steel works in the country, and some of the strain and effort that must have been involved in the process showed in tiny lines about his eyes and mouth. Yet for all that, Boone was the same. Brawny, clear-eyed, and smiling, he settled back in the carriage. His thick, sandy hair was neatly brushed beneath his top hat, and his rugged nose and jaw and firm mouth were all pleasantly attractive and familiar.

"It's been much too long, Connor."

Boone's pleasure in seeing his old friend shone in his face. Then his gaze shifted to Elly, taking in her upswept hair, the rich gown, the jewels. For a moment, his glance lingered. "And you are lovelier than ever, Elly," he said quietly, with a ghost of a smile.

The formality in his tone dispelled any notion she might have harbored that Connor's earlier comments were true. In fact, it made them appear even more absurd. If anything, Boone had always treated her with a reserve bordering on aloofness, and that was true tonight as well. It was not at all the way a man behaved when he was attracted to a woman.

"We're very glad to see you, Boone." She smiled, meeting his piercing gaze with warmth and sincerity. "Mama asked me to remember her to you."

When she smiled like that, Boone wanted to touch her so badly it hurt. She looked so beautiful. In that rose gown and with her hair so simply yet dramatically coiffed, there was a regal elegance about her that took his breath away. Yet the sensuality around her mouth and eyes, which he so well remembered, was still there, enhanced by her graceful carriage and slow, sweeping smile. He immediately averted his gaze and began to talk to Connor about the steel works, Connor's theater, the traffic, their days on the railroad, anything to keep his mind off Elly. Yet her perfume, light and delicate as a fresh plucked blossom, filled his nostrils, triggering a struggle within him. While the carriage maneuvered its way through the heavily congested Chicago streets and Connor regaled him with a stream of anecdotes and remembrances, a corner of Boone's mind kept summoning up Penelope's image, trying to hold it crisp and clear. They were to be married shortly. They would have a fine life together. But even though he could assemble the various parts of her features and anatomy and even, when he really tried, conjure up her voice, he couldn't keep them all together in his mind for more than a few seconds. Unsettled and frustrated, he struggled to maintain the iron calmness of expression for which he was known.

"The chef here is the best in the city," Connor informed him as they alighted from the carriage and passed beneath the blue velvet awning of Amberson's Palace. "Wait until you taste the filet of beef with mushrooms and the green turtle soup. And, Elly, my darlin', the desserts will astonish you. The grandest nougat cakes you've ever tasted—better than anything in New York or London or Paris."

Blue and white marble tiles graced the floor of the restaurant. It was a magnificent citadel of velvet and crystal, vibrant with flowers and the strains of violin music. Men in evening dress and women resplendent in beaded taffetas and satins dined on oyster patties and champagne at hundreds of candlelit tables. The Maguire party received immediate and courteous attention. Escorted to a plush white velvet banquette, tucked away from the sea of tables frothy with white linen, gold plate, and crystal, they were immediately served champagne by an impeccably clad waiter. He poured the sparkling golden liquid into the Waterford goblets with a flourish, bowed, and begged to be of service to them.

All through the meal, Boone concentrated on keeping his thoughts of Elly at bay, not an easy task when she was sitting so near. He was almost rude to her, confining most of his conversation to Connor, looking at her only when necessary. He talked at length about Penelope.

"She's wonderful—full of fun, vibrant, what Louis and Victoria call an animated beauty. We're to be married in London and then will tour Paris and Vienna on our honeymoon."

"Aye, and what does her father, the earl, think about his precious daughter marrying a reb farmboy?" Connor wanted to know, as he drained his glass and helped himself to the last of the champagne.

"I'm not a farmboy anymore, Con." He didn't add that the old earl was almost certainly so relieved to be rescued from his debts that he wouldn't have cared if his daughter married an aborigine. Penelope still hadn't confided in him about her father's woes, even when he had returned from Kentucky and asked her to marry him. She'd accepted him with eager pleasure, suggested he cable his formal request to the earl, and then had entered into wedding plans with zest, but neither she nor the earl had hinted of what monetary assistance was expected of him. Boone figured he'd learn all about those little details when he reached London.

"No, you're a steel tycoon, a titan of our times," Connor declared.

A flicker of amusement showed in the deep gray depths of Boone's eyes. If he heard the undercurrent of jealous derision in Connor's voice that made Elly wince, he gave no sign of it. "I never think of myself that way, Con, but I suppose when you come right down to it, that's true," he drawled.

He's changed, Elly thought. The old Boone would have flushed, belittled his accomplishments, dwelled on how far he still had to go. This man was at peace with himself; he didn't mind being baited. It occurred to her then that Boone Walker had always known what he intended to accomplish and that he had been quiet and steady and deliberate about it all along. He had set himself on a path and followed it, allowing nothing to get in his way.

Connor, by contrast, constantly found himself lost or waylaid. This knowledge made his bragging throughout the meal all the more difficult for Elly to take. Every false word about the success of the theater, the wonderful partnership with Sean Fitzgerald, the mansion he intended to build for Elly out of imported marble and limestone, made her flinch and only increased the tension throbbing inside her head.

As they ordered coffee and dessert, Elly wondered how many times Connor had dined in this place—and with whom. Several men of his acquaintance came by to greet him—business acquaintances, Connor explained—but they looked like professional gamblers to Elly. The waiter, an obsequious fellow with a disdainfully upturned nose and a long, pointed chin, seemed quite familiar with all of Connor's favorite wines and side dishes. Was this where he came when he was "working" late? Did he dine here with his precious gambling friends before spending an evening at the dives in the vice district?

She tried unsuccessfully to stanch the flow of questions. This was supposed to be an evening of special enjoyment, a treat. Their purpose was to entertain Boone. Yet she couldn't help worrying about the cost of such an elaborate meal and about the mounting pile of deceptions. To her discomfiture, Boone noticed her quietness when Connor excused himself to speak with a business acquaintance.

"Are you feeling all right, Elly?"

Despite the glow of candlelight, she was pale, and shadows of pain or tiredness flickered behind her eyes.

"I'm sorry. I have a slight headache." She put down her

fork, having only toyed with the nougat cakes and taken one bite of after-dinner cheese. Even the coffee in its demitasse held no appeal. "What a poor hostess you must think me!" She forced a smile.

"You're an enchanting hostess," he replied with such seriousness that her startled gaze flew to his face. "It seems to me that Connor is a very lucky man."

They talked about how quickly the autumn chill was descending, about Caroline and Timothy, and about the new invention used by so many businesses of late, the telephone. They talked about Cassandra, with Elly describing some of her daughter's more amusing antics. Still Connor did not return.

"I wish I'd had an opportunity to meet Cassandra this trip. But chances are, I'll be returning to Chicago soon."

"After your honeymoon, do you mean? You have further business to conduct here?"

He signaled the waiter to bring more coffee. "As a matter of fact, we're thinking about opening a branch office here. Chicago is a crucial shipping hub, and Walker and Whitcomb Steel already owns majority shares in several Illinois business interests. And of course, there are our contracts with the farm machinery companies. I may be coming in from time to time to make certain Joe Carson establishes a smooth operation here."

"Connor will certainly be glad to hear that," Elly murmured, but wondered what kind of fears and jealousies the knowledge would trigger. Connor would not want Boone to discover the true nature of their situation or the disappointing showing of the Gem. Uneasily, she glanced about the room. Where *was* Connor? He'd been gone for nearly an hour. The headache that had plagued her seemed to be getting worse. Suddenly, as a burst of violin music swelled through the room, dizziness washed over her. The brilliant candlelight and the myriad of colors in the room swam. Boone's kind, earnest features disappeared as she blinked and closed her eyes tight.

"Elly!" He leaned forward in alarm. "What is it? Are you sick?"

Influenza, she thought suddenly. Her mother had been ill with it the past week. Elly had thought she'd escaped it, but now she recognized it as the reason she'd been feeling so poorly from the start of the evening.

"Boone, I think I'd best go home," she managed to say as she leaned back against the velvet banquette, trying to steady herself, to ease the throbbing pain between her temples. She explained about the influenza that had afflicted her mother. "Do you suppose you could find Connor?"

"Of course." Instantly, Boone turned, his gaze sweeping the crowded restaurant. *Damn Con.* Where in hell had he disappeared to? "Will you be all right for a moment? I'm going to have a quick look around. It won't take me long to find him, and then we'll be on our way."

When she was alone, Elly passed a hand across her burning eyes. She had a high fever. No wonder she was dizzy. What an awful way to end an evening and Boone's visit, she thought. Tomorrow morning he would sail for London. She wished she could will this dizzy sensation and headache away, but every second she felt worse. All she wanted was to lay her head on her pillow and blot out all these lights and dazzling colors and the thrum of gaily chatting, laughing humanity swirling through the restaurant. If Boone could only find Connor quickly, she could get out of this place and go home, to quiet and darkness and peace.

Suddenly Boone was beside her, alone. She thought she saw a flash of anger in his face before he leaned down and spoke to her in a gentle way. "I couldn't find him, but I'm taking you home. Everything here is settled, and I've left word for Connor about what's happened."

The next thing she knew they were out in the cool September air and he was helping her into the carriage. Boone was very strong, she realized dimly as he effortlessly settled her in her seat. She had brushed against him as she'd moved past and had been aware of the hard-packed muscle beneath his suit. Connor had a tough, sinewy strength, an admirable physique, to be sure, but Boone Walker might have been hewn out of rock. She felt reassured by his strength, his decisiveness, his quiet, solid presence.

"It's all right," Boone told her across the swaying carriage. "You'll be home and comfortable before you know it."

Yet as moonlight flowed down on the graceful buildings they passed and on the other carriages bearing occupants along beneath the star-filled sky, the blinding throb in Elly's head increased unbearably. Where was Connor? she kept

wondering in the midst of her pain. He had left her like a
bowl of forgotten oatmeal. Humiliation vied with anger in the
turmoil of her heart. She was thankful that Boone was too
much of a gentleman to mention the subject again, but there
was no mistaking the fury in his face each time she forced her
eyes open in the rolling carriage and caught sight of him
unexpectedly, before he had time to wipe what he was feeling
toward Connor from his expression.

"You know how Connor is," she began once, spurred by
both embarrassment and loyalty into an attempt to explain.
She tried very hard to smile. "He has a way of getting so
engrossed in whatever he's talking about that he forgets everything else. He's so . . . intense sometimes. By now he is
probably searching for us, and the waiter will give him your
message."

Boone would gladly have choked Connor Maguire if he
could have gotten his hands on him at that moment, but he
forced himself to reply calmly. "Yes, I'm sure you're right.
Now, don't try to talk anymore, Elly. Just relax. A few more
blocks and you're home."

Despite his bracing words, his hands were clenched into
fists, and a very satisfying image of Connor's bruised and
battered face filled his mind. Where the hell had he disappeared to? he wondered for the thousandth time. And what
the hell kind of way was this to treat his wife?

"Connor Maguire, meet Big Dan Casey."

Connor shook hands with the enormous, broad-shouldered
man in the velveteen frock coat. What a stroke of luck,
running into Jed Turner here tonight. Turner had brought him
to this private upstairs dining room at Amberson's Palace and
kept him waiting awhile, but he was finally getting to meet
Big Dan. As one of the leading gambling bosses in Chicago,
with a wealth of City Hall connections, Casey could turn
things around for the Gem Theater, could open doors for
Connor that would make all the difference in the world.
Connor's stomach muscles bunched with excitement. He had
to make the most of this opportunity.

"Glad to meet you, Mr. Casey. My partner, Sean Fitzgerald, has told me if a man wants to get something done in this
town, you're the one to see."

"Right he is, Maguire. And Turner here has told me

something about you, too. I hear you fancy high-stakes poker as well as the trotters. Care to join me in a friendly game?''

Connor glanced quickly around the sumptuous private chamber, with its crimson carpet and draperies, its brass chandeliers and heavy furnishings inlaid with gold. This was going to be even better than he'd hoped, a chance to gamble and mingle socially with the big man. Boone would have to see to Elly, he thought quickly. He would send a note downstairs to let them know he had an important meeting, and couldn't rejoin them. He would smooth everything out with Elly tomorrow.

"A friendly game of poker sounds just grand, Mr. Casey," he said, flashing his easy, charming smile.

Then, as he opened his mouth to ask for writing materials, a paneled door from an interior room opened and a woman glided into the room. Connor could only stare. She was the most beautiful creature he had ever seen. She had emerald-green eyes and fiery red-gold hair, and she wore her low-cut gown of olive-green silk with the assurance of a woman who knew men coveted her. Her face was exquisite, pale but for the subtly painted cheeks, yet smoldering with sensuality. It was a bold, narrow face enhanced by glittering diamond eardrops. Her tall, magnificent figure, displayed to advantage by the décolletage of her gown, riveted every male gaze in the room. There were heavy gold bracelets on her wrists, and a red and gold pendant hung from the black velvet band at her throat. In her hair, piled high on her head, she wore a white feather aigrette and a cluster of poppies. She was sultry and provocative in every sense. As she crossed the room, a musky perfume drifted to his nostrils.

She smiled slowly as Connor, Dan Casey, Jed Turner, and a fourth man slid into comfortable leather chairs around a marble-topped table.

"Katrina will be serving us tonight," Dan Casey remarked. The smoke from his cigar wafted up toward the gilded ceiling. "Maguire, if you want a brandy, cigar, anything at all, just ask. Katrina will make you comfortable."

Connor was too busy staring at her to notice the exchange of satisfied smiles between Casey and Jed Turner. He forgot everything else as Casey broke open a pack of cards and the lovely Katrina leaned over his shoulder to nestle a brandy snifter in his palm. He smiled into her green cat-eyes. She smiled back. From that moment on, he was buoyant, afloat with dreams and a razor-edged excitement. His wife and Boone Walker might have been in a different world for all he knew or cared—a place far removed from this rich marvelous island of smoke and drink and cards and delicious, intoxicating perfume.

He didn't think about them again.

🌿 Seventeen

THEY WERE NEARLY home, thank heaven. The carriage rounded the corner by the park, which was carpeted with autumn leaves, and continued down Wabash Avenue. The street was deserted, the buildings dark. A soft wind fluttered the falling leaves in the cool silence of the night.

How comfortable she was with Boone, Elly thought as she lay back against the carriage seat. With innate consideration, he granted her silence, leaving her to her own thoughts. If he sensed her humiliation and anger at Connor's ill treatment, he gave no sign of it. Instead, in apparent deference to her indisposition, he sat across from her quietly, requiring her neither to speak nor to listen to needless chatter.

She couldn't have borne it if Boone had lambasted Connor's behavior. She'd have felt obligated to defend him. And she hadn't the strength or the heart to do that. It was a relief merely to sit in the darkness of the coach, to know that in a very few moments she would be able to collapse on her own bed.

Glancing at the profile of the man staring thoughtfully out of the carriage window, she noticed for the first time how fine and bright his sandy hair was beneath the silk top hat. His skin was a healthy bronze, his sharp gray eyes clear and piercing in the glow of the passing streetlights. He was an unusual man. So brawny that one expected him to be bold, overriding. Instead, he was quiet and reserved, yet there was an air of unmistakable purpose about him, something invincible in those keen gray eyes. It was odd that only tonight was she becoming fully aware of him, as if before now he had been only a shadowy figure sketched in the background of Connor's life. At this moment, traveling in the carriage while the fever burned and her head burst with pain, Boone was the most vivid and solid presence in her world, and the most reassuring one. Gratitude for him welled up within her.

Suddenly, as if sensing her gaze on him, he turned away from the window and met her glance. A quiver went through her. The gray eyes seemed to burn into her soul. Almost, she jumped. Something jarring, unsettling, yet strangely pleasant jolted through her blood. In sudden confusion, she dropped her gaze.

Why this sudden sensation—about Boone Walker? she wondered in alarm. Was it because he had rescued her tonight when Connor had abandoned her? Because she felt vulnerable and ill and he was so kind? Or was it just the fever playing tricks on her? Her face was flushed and hot, but her hands felt cold. Yes, yes, it was the fever, she realized with relief. Yet she avoided looking at Boone again, and relief rushed through her when the carriage swerved to a halt at the curb in front of the boardinghouse.

As she stepped out into the darkness, another wave of dizziness swept over her. With Boone's arm about her shoulders, guiding and supporting her, she managed to make it up the steps and into the hallway.

Mama had left the lamp burning in the parlor, and it sent a feeble glow into the gold-papered hall. In the faint yellow gleam she was forced to speak to Boone, to look into his face once more. Again that strange, sharp tingle shook her, filling her with confusion and dismay.

"I can't thank you enough . . ." she began, trying to sound calmer than she felt. These were distressing, inexplicable feelings, brought on, she was sure, by the influenza descending on her. She blinked and looked at him again. Yes, it was the same Boone, tall and broad and rugged, not exciting and handsome, as Connor was, but steady and calm. There was no reason at all for the absurd fluttering in her heart.

"Are you sure you're all right?" He looked so worried that the strange, trembling feelings inside her increased. "Let me help you upstairs. Or I can call to your mother," he offered, regarding her fever-flushed cheeks with a frown.

"Please, no," she managed to say, struggling to think clearly through the dizziness, the throbbing in her head, and her oddly jumbled emotions. She was intensely aware of his arms around her, supporting her. "There's no need to bother Mama. It's late, Boone. And I'll be fine. I'll rest on the sofa in the parlor until Connor gets home."

"At least let me see you settled." He took her arm and began to lead her across the hall. Elly remembered then the groups of chairs and tables in the transformed parlor—evidence of the tearoom.

"No, please, I'm fine," she cried. "I don't want to trouble you any further."

Boone stopped. He stared at her. "It's no trouble, Elly. In fact, I think I'd better stay with you until Connor gets home. I don't like the idea of leaving you like this."

"But—"

"Don't argue with me. You don't look in any condition to be left alone." His voice was rough with concern, but his arms held her with great gentleness. She stared at him, her eyes slowly widening. Something was happening between them. Something confusing . . . inexplicable . . . Elly felt a great bewilderment coming over her. It looked . . . it looked as if Boone wanted to kiss her . . . but no, that was impossible. Her mind was blurred with the fever.

A childish wail from upstairs shattered the quiet of the hall. A sob, piercing and terrified, that raised the hair on the nape of Elly's neck. She started and moved away from him. She half turned toward the steps. "That's Cassandra. She's having another nightmare," she murmured, almost to herself. Then she hurried on to address Boone in a low tone: "She's had quite a few lately. She gets so frightened. I'd better go to her."

"Of course."

The sound of Connor's child crying upstairs had drawn Boone up short. He decided that, for a moment, he must have gone mad.

He had heard about Cassandra, talked about her, yet she had been all the while not quite real to him. But that tiny

pathetic cry was real, reminding him of her existence, of the
bond that tied Elly and Connor together forever. For a few
moments in the carriage and later, the hall, he had nearly
forgotten all that. For an instant it had seemed to him that
something flickered in her face when she looked at him,
something he had only dreamed about, but now all her attention was focused on the little girl upstairs. Damn it to hell, he
told himself, inwardly furious at his own stupidity. He had
imagined the whole damn thing. How could it be otherwise?
Elly was ill, feverish. And she was probably worried half to
death about Connor.

She was peering upward, her shoulders tense, her face
strained with the effort of listening for her daughter. No other
cry had followed the first, at least, not yet. But that one wail
had drawn all of her concern and attention and had reminded
him of just how much an outsider he was here. Elly, Connor,
and Cassandra were a family. He wouldn't destroy that even
if he could. And of course he couldn't. That was impossible,
for whatever his faults, Elly no doubt still loved Connor very
much. This was their home, and that was their child sleeping
upstairs, and whatever had possessed Connor to abandon his
wife so disgracefully in Amberson's Palace was their problem
to resolve, not his.

It was none of his concern.

"I'll be going, then," he said at last, "if you're sure
you're all right. I have an early sailing tomorrow. By dawn,
I'll be under way, so this will have to be good-bye."

She wished him a fair voyage, a happy marriage, saying all
the things that were right and proper, but she did so hastily,
as another cry sounded from above. Boone took his leave.
The carriage stood waiting. And in the morning, he reminded
himself coldly, so would his ship. All the way back to the
Palmer House, he saw Elly's drawn face peering up the stairs
toward the sound of her daughter's voice. That sight had been
a vivid and much needed reminder to him of how firmly her
place was fixed with Connor Maguire and of how badly he
needed to get started on his own new life and family. And,
dammit, he would. When that ship set sail in the morning,
he'd make sure he left all thoughts of Connor's family firmly
behind him. The next time he set foot in Chicago, he'd be
married to Penelope and safe from making a damned fool of
himself in front of Elly Maguire.

Inside the boardinghouse, as the carriage clattered away into the night, Elly listened for another sound from Cassandra's room. There was none. Thankfully, she sank down on the steps, her head drooping onto her arms. Through a haze of fever and exhaustion, she told herself that she would rest just a moment before going up to Cassie. The child had probably fallen back asleep without fully wakening. Otherwise, surely there would have been more cries. She would rest a minute, no longer, just enough time to gather her strength for the long climb up the stairs. . . .

The crashing of the door awakened her. She started, roused from the murky cobwebs of slumber, dizziness making the hall rug spin before her eyes. Her body ached and her neck felt stiff, but whether this was due to the influenza or the cramped position in which she had been lying across the steps, she didn't know. All she knew was that Connor was staggering into the hallway, drunk and disheveled. From the corner of her mind, she heard the sewing room clock chime three insistent bells.

"Connor," she began, her voice a thick croak. She intended only to ask him to help her upstairs, but he never gave her the chance. Before she could say another word, Connor began to weep. He stumbled toward her, his damp, tobacco-stained shirt unbuttoned across his chest, his top hat askew, and his black hair a tangle of damp wild curls. "That bastard," he cried, wiping his sleeve across reddened eyes in a pathetic, childlike gesture. "That low, thieving bastard!"

In horror, Elly half rose from the steps. "What is it? What's happened? Where on earth have you been?"

"I've lost it, Elly," he gasped. "Lost it all. That bastard Casey cheated me out of it!" Sinking down beside her on the steps, he collapsed against her. His head was heavy on her breast. His tears soaked through the silk of her gown, staining it a deep crimson.

"What do you mean?" Alarm penetrated fever, pain, everything. She tried to push him off her, to see his face, but Connor was oblivious of her efforts, of her heated skin and pain-wracked muscles.

"I tried to stop, Elly," he wept, as though she hadn't spoken. "He kept forcing me to continue. He was challenging me, challenging me with his eyes, sneering at me, making those little remarks, as if he thought I wasn't man enough to

see the thing through. He kept raising the stakes. I couldn't
back down, darlin', couldn't stop, not with everyone watching me, even Kat— '' He broke off suddenly, as if some
semblance of sobriety was beginning to return. He straightened, and his glazed eyes focused on Elly, who was staring at
him in shock. "It's the theater, darlin'," he whispered on a
sob. He buried his face in his hands so that his words
emerged muffled and low from between his fingers. "I've
lost my share in the theater."

Elly couldn't move. She couldn't even speak. Her numb
mind struggled to take in the enormity of his words.

Connor hiccupped, belched, and gave a quivering sigh.
Then he threw himself down on the cold hall floor and began
to retch.

Dawn. Pink-yellow streaks in a dingy gray sky. A wren
chirping from the low branch of a tree. Another answering
with an excited call. They sounded anxious for the remnants
of darkness to fade, for the new day to begin. From the chintz
sofa in the sewing room, Connor groaned.

He stared blearily at the window, then rose and staggered
over to it, clutching the cabbage-rose draperies for support. In
despair, he leaned his head against the glass. "No, not yet,"
he muttered pleadingly, only half aware of what he said. He
wasn't ready yet, not for the day ahead or for thinking about
what he had done last night. He couldn't bear to face Elly so
soon. The weary silence with which she had cleaned up the
mess he'd made on the hallway floor had devastated him
more than angry words could have. She hadn't spoken a word
of reproach, not one word, but her disgust had been apparent
enough in her eyes. Oh, how she had stared at him, so
desolately and contemptuously all at the same time. Her face
had been oddly flushed before she had turned away to fetch
rags and a bucket. The rest of them, too, Connor thought,
would stare at him when they heard, their eyes cold and hard,
as if he was some kind of criminal or fool.

"It wasn't my fault," he whined into the draperies. "I was
cheated, tricked. It's all Casey's doing."

He lifted the brandy bottle in his hand and drained the last
drops down his liquor-thickened throat. "More," he gasped,
reeling toward the cabinet where a fresh bottle sat. "More."

Sitting down again with the bottle gripped tight in his hand, he wondered why he hadn't passed out yet, why he hadn't escaped this horrible turn of events with the blessed oblivion of brandy-induced stupor. Two bottles he'd finished since Elly had dragged herself up to bed. And still, here he sat on this gay chintz sofa, in this damned handsome house belonging to his wife's aunt, drinking himself sick to no avail.

"Sleep, I want sleep," he muttered, sinking back against the cushions. But he couldn't rest. He kept seeing a multitude of faces spinning before his glazed and burning eyes. Boone Walker, Bess, Sean Fitzgerald, Elly—all of them whirled like demons before him. Then Big Dan Casey, smiling in triumph, damn his soul. Casey was buying up every business he could on Randolph Street, making himself the undisputed king of the vice district. And now he had the Gem—fifty percent of it, at least. At the thought of Sean Fitzgerald's rage when he learned he'd been saddled with this new dangerous and powerful partner, Connor took another deep swig of the brandy. "It wasn't my fault!" he argued, to no one in particular.

Suddenly, as the dawn struggled to break through the last clinging threads of night, a deep, bone-stirring anger came on him. His fingers tightened murderously around the neck of the bottle.

None of this would have happened if he'd stayed in Pittsburgh with Boone. He'd be a rich man today if he'd stuck with the foundry. It was Sean Fitzgerald's fault, he realized wrathfully. Sean had talked him out of the foundry in the first place! And Elly—she'd kicked up such a fuss about leaving her precious family that he'd gone against his better judgment. " 'Tain't fair," Connor snarled, overtaken by a hot, surging fury at the injustice of his life. "All I ever wanted was to make her happy, and now they all blame me for everything that's gone wrong! Well, damn them all to hell, *it's not my fault!*"

He lurched to his feet and threw back his arm. Driven by a fierce and violent fury with the world, he sent the brandy bottle flying. Sweet satisfaction filled him at the resultant crash and splatter.

Suddenly, his bleary eyes widened. He stared and stared at the swirling flames where the kerosene lamp had been. The bottle must have struck the lamp, spilled the kerosene. A pool of brandy and kerosene had been ignited and was now flaming like the fires of hell.

"Fire!" Connor yelped, taking a step backward. His shoe caught on the claw foot of the sofa. He went down. "Fire," he screamed, as a horribly blazing orange wave rose over his head. He threw himself aside, knocking over a little table, tangling himself in the rug. In his panic and drunken stupor, he couldn't gain his feet.

"Fire!" He screamed again as the first searing flames overtook him. *"He . . . elp!"*

Red-hot flames shot up past the windows, blotting out the gentle light of dawn.

Through a haze of sleep, Elly smelled the smoke. It stung her nostrils, acrid and thick and choking. She struggled upright, blinking in the swirling darkness of her bedroom. The terrifying odors of burning wood and scorched fabric and flesh filled her lungs.

"Oh, my Lord, Cassandra!"

She was out of bed in a flash, despite the throbbing pain in her head. But an overwhelming dizziness sent her reeling back against the bedpost. "Cassandra!" she gasped, marshaling every ounce of her will to make her way across the room to the little girl's cot. Cassie cried out in fright as Elly snatched the child into her arms.

"Fire!" Elly screamed as she staggered with the girl into the hall. "Mama, Caroline, fire! Everybody, wake up!"

The boarders and the rest of the family were already awakening. Screams, running footsteps, and panic-filled sobs exploded in the night. As Elly rushed with Cassandra toward the head of the stairs, a dreadful brightness and thunderous crackling roared up from below. In her arms, Cassandra began to shriek.

Stark terror struck Elly as people crashed and collided in the smoke-thickened hall. The heat was searing. Like wild, blood-maddened bulls, everyone crowded desperately toward the stairs. The lower part of the house was aglow with flames, yet it was difficult to see and breathe for the smoke that streamed up through the house and out the popping windows. As Elly was swept along in the jumble of bodies, Cassandra clutched tight against her chest, a ball of exploding red and blue flames erupted across the lower hall, sending flying sparks and embers all the way to the front door.

"Hurry!" someone yelled. "It's almost to the door!" and

in the frenzied rush that followed, it was all she could do to hang on to Cassandra and keep her own feet.

"Mama? Connor? Timothy?"

Elly shouted at the top of her lungs as she stared frantically about for some sign of her family. Up ahead, she had a glimpse of Aunt Adelaide's plump shoulders and gray head almost at the door. But there was no sign of Caroline, Connor, Timothy, or Bess.

Suddenly, just as she reached the bottom of the steps, she saw her brother reach the head of the stairs above, helping old Mrs. Malloy with as much haste as he could. Then she had no more time to glance back, for she was carried along in the desperate rush for the door, holding the shrieking and terrified Cassandra tight in her arms.

Outside was a scene of bedlam. Screaming, weeping boarders milled about in horror, watching the smoke and flames pour out of the chimneys and windows. The fire brigade wagons arrived amid a clamor of bells, and the helmeted, canvas-coated firemen took charge with their hoses and ladders.

"It's all right, Cassandra. We're safe. Everything's going to be fine," Elly soothed, as she dropped down with the girl onto the dewy grass of a neighboring lawn. In the midst of the shouts, the heat, the stamping feet and mass confusion, Aunt Adelaide rushed up to her.

"Where's Caroline? And your mother? Good Lord, where are they?" Her voice rose to a hysterical shriek, engulfing Elly with terror, but even as she finished the words, she pointed. "Oh, thank heaven! There she is! Caroline!"

Caroline was being dragged from the house by a burly fireman. She was in her nightdress, kicking and crying. Elly pushed herself to her feet, told Aunt Adelaide to stay with Cassandra, and stumbled forward. Whether the blistering heat that seemed to scorch her flesh was a result of her fever or the heat cast off by the inferno inside the house, she didn't know. She only knew that she was living a nightmare, trapped in a scene straight from the depths of hell.

"Caroline, it's all right, you're safe," she called, rushing up to the wildly struggling girl. It was taking two fire fighters now to hold her still in the flamelit dawn.

"Mama! You've got to get Mama!" Caroline screamed, fighting anew against her protectors. Her eyes were mad with hysteria. "Let me go, I've got to get back to her. Let me go!"

Elly felt the blood draining from her face. Her hands, inside the burning skin, were icy cold. "Mama? Mama's still inside?"

As if to punctuate her words, the last of the upper windows suddenly exploded, gushing smoke and fire.

Caroline nodded, sobbing and helpless now in the firemen's arms. "I couldn't waken her! It must have been the laudanum—she had a headache tonight. Elly, I tried to drag her. I got her to the door. Then I went for help, but—"

One of the fire fighters, a young, spare man with a blond mustache, shook his head. His thin, boyish face was streaked with soot. "It's too late—too dangerous. There's no way to get anybody out now."

Elly turned toward the boardinghouse in a daze. Her skin had grown clammy. She was shivering, cold as death. In mute horror she watched the boardinghouse convulse with shooting flames.

"Mama," she whispered. For one agonizing second she had a vision of her mother trapped in that blistering orange conflagration. No, not Mama. Not Mama. Her knees buckled beneath her. Her fevered mind went blank, and she slipped into the blessed black oblivion of darkest night.

🌿 Eighteen

THE FAMILY MOVED into a dreary little two-bedroom flat in a tenement neighborhood known as the Rat's Tail. It was an area rife with sewage, mud, dilapidated wooden shacks, greasy factories, and the rats, both dead and alive, for which it was named. The building itself was squalid and cramped with

impoverished immigrant families, but its low rent was affordable to a trio of women left with practically nothing.

Elly and Cassandra shared a bed in one tiny cell of a room,
while Aunt Adelaide and Caroline set up cots along the
peeling, gray painted walls of the other. There was a potbellied stove in the kitchen, and an old horsehair sofa stood in
the living room, where Timothy made up his bed.

"It's fine, I like it," he said that first night when Elly
doubtfully watched him settle down with a thin, cheap blanket bought on credit at the secondhand store down the street.
"I'm perfectly comfortable."

Caroline, hearing the loudly creaking springs of the sofa in
the middle of the empty, low-ceilinged room, burst into tears.

"Caro, stop it. I'm fine!" Timothy said sharply, jumping
up from the bed.

His words had no effect on her.

"Why did all this have to happen?" Caroline waved an
arm helplessly around the ugly, cramped little flat. It was
cold throughout and dimly lit, with a stale, greasy smell that
no amount of scrubbing had been able to dissipate. "It's not
fair, it's just not fair! After everything else, I can't bear to be
so poor again! It's worse than Emmettville in the days after
Papa died. At least then we all had decent beds to our
name—Elly, I can't bear it! You have to do something!"

"I'm doing the best I can." Elly tried to hold back her
anger at Caroline's complaints. She knew that, deep down, it
was Mama's death that wounded her sister so, but Caroline
couldn't talk about that. Since they'd set foot in the apartment, she'd done nothing but weep and find fault.

"Caroline, I'm not a baby anymore," Timothy was saying.
His irritation showed in his face. "I don't need a cradle
swathed with blankets and pillows edged in lace. Plenty of
boys my age slept in trenches in the mud, covered with lice
and beetles and worms, all during the war. General Willis
told me all about it. After that, believe me, a horsehair sofa is
no hardship."

"But—"

"But nothing. Go to bed." Timothy slouched back onto
the sofa and pulled the blanket up to his chin, signaling his
withdrawal from all further discussion.

Caroline accepted the handkerchief Elly offered her and,
with only one more sniffle, allowed Aunt Adelaide to lead her

to her bed. The fire had aged Addie by several years. In it she had lost not only her sister-in-law but the house her husband had built for her forty years ago, a house that had been her shelter and her source of income for most of her life. Yet she had been stoic and uncomplaining, even when she'd first laid eyes on this dreadful little place, with its oilcloth floor coverings and torn, dust-laden curtains, and the tiny, grease-stained kitchen looking out on the fire escape of the next crumbling building. Elly sighed as she watched her aunt and sister pass through the door of their room, then turned back to Timothy. He sat up once more and ran his fingers through his hair.

"I'm sick of her crying all the time. And I'm tired of being treated like a baby. Elly, I'm fourteen. Do me a favor and let me do my share for once."

"You've always done your share." In spite of everything—her tiredness, Caroline's tears, their dingy surroundings, the chilly autumn air seeping between the frames and the sashes of the ill-fitting windows, and the wind beating furiously at the dirt-streaked panes—she smiled at him. "Your job at Mr. Riccione's store, your chores around the house—in addition to going to school—well, no one could ever accuse you of not taking on more than your share of the load, Timmy."

"Those days are over now, Elly. School, I mean. From now on, I'm a real working man."

His youthful determination tore at her heart. He was looking more like a man every day, what with the new broadness of his shoulders, his increased height, and the first pale shadows of stubble around his chin. At fourteen, Timothy bore an astonishing similarity to Bess—particularly about his almond-shaped blue eyes and in the patrician cast of his features—but he had the promise of his father's imposing build and large, strong hands.

"I hate for you to give up school," Elly said, sitting down on a rickety chair. It and the sofa were the only items of furniture left in the apartment by the previous tenant. "But I'm afraid it's going to be necessary for a time."

"I don't care about school," he assured her, but she knew that was a lie. Timothy had been an excellent student, and had shown promise in the study of history and in writing. He had always talked excitedly about one day going to college and even perhaps becoming a professor himself. Now when she reminded him of this, he dismissed it with a careless wave of his hand.

"That was before. I'm older now, and I know it's my duty to start taking charge of this family. I have to earn some real money so Caroline won't cry all the time simply from looking at this place." He glanced around the apartment. "Mama wouldn't like this place," he said in a sober tone. "She'd say it wasn't fit for her family."

Silence fell between them. Then Elly pushed herself out of the chair. "It'll have to do for a while. But I promise you that when we move again, it will be to someplace much better."

"Couldn't be much worse." Timothy grinned and plunked his head down on the sofa again.

That night in the bed she shared with Cassandra, Elly watched the shadows flit across the cracked and peeling ceiling. She was exhausted and could not have moved even if she'd wanted to, but her mind was wide awake. At moments like this, she couldn't help thinking of Connor.

It didn't matter that their marriage had deteriorated piti- ably, that his drunkenness had probably caused the boarding- house fire, or that he had failed at everything he'd touched since their marriage; a part of her grieved for him, for the lost knight with the handsome face and merry ways who was the father of her child. Cassandra hadn't been the same since the fire. Always perky and filled with cherubic laughter before, she now clung to Elly, crying piteously when she went away, screaming and screaming for Connor at various times of the day and night. She wouldn't set foot near the kitchen; the sight of a candle flame or steam from the stove drove her to hysteria. And Elly didn't know what to do, other than hold her and kiss her damp cheeks and try to explain, as she had to Timothy so many years ago, that her father wasn't coming back, not ever, that he simply couldn't.

As the days passed Elly was filled more and more with a new, hard determination. Timothy had been right; Mama wouldn't have approved of this place. As bleak and grimy as the apartment was, the neighborhood was worse, a slum pit of poverty and filth, the sounds of crying children filling the air all day long and for much of the night. No matter what she had to do, Elly decided, she would get her daughter out of here. Cassandra would not grow up hungry and ragged, a poor, despairing prisoner of a slum.

She had gone to see Sean Fitzgerald in the hope that Connor had left some money in the office safe, but Sean had shaken his head. "No, lassie, sad to say, not a cent. All he did was leave me with a new partner who'd as soon chop out my tongue as listen to what I've got to say. I've decided to sell my share of the Gem to Casey and let him do as he pleases." He had glanced around at the back room office above his bar and pursed his lips. "No offense to you, lassie, but throwing in with Connor Maguire was one of the biggest mistakes I ever made. The Gem flopped, and I lost my shirt on more than one gambling venture Connor talked me into. Me and Mary are tying the knot come Christmas, and starting over fresh, just the two of us and this place, like the old days."

He had gone on to express all the proper sympathies and then had rather quickly shown her the door. She supposed she couldn't blame him for his wish to be rid of her; Connor had left him in a horrid position with Casey and the Gem. Still, she had reflected upon leaving Sean's saloon, he was in no worse shape than she. She had five mouths to feed and precious little means to buy even a loaf of bread.

By the time the first snow drifted down over the tenement rooftops, Timothy had found work as a stockboy in Marshall Field's department store, and Aunt Adelaide had begun taking in laundry. But it was Caroline who surprised everyone. She had befriended a neighbor from the apartment above, a young Polish immigrant with three small children, whose husband had been killed in a knife fight on the docks. Marya was only nineteen, thin and pale, with stooped shoulders and tea-colored hair worn in thick braids. Speaking broken English, penniless, and grieving, she had been getting by on the small savings her husband had accumulated in a small, worn gunny-sack kept under the bed. Marya was an excellent seamstress, Caroline had learned, but she knew no one and hadn't the slightest idea how to begin earning a living. To everyone's amazement, Caroline had begun knocking on doors and stopping people on the stairways of all the surrounding buildings, telling them about Marya and her skill with a needle, and she had succeeded in stirring up enough business to keep the girl busily sewing for weeks. But that wasn't all. Caroline had arranged to care for Marya's children while the girl worked, in exchange for a small fee. That way, Marya could accomplish more, take in more work, and Caroline was compensated for her help in generating business and her tending of the children. It was a warmhearted partnership, and best of all, Caroline was immeasurably proud of the little pile of coins she plunked onto the kitchen counter at the end of the first week. It was the first independent money she had earned since leaving Emmettville.

At the same time, Elly began implementation of a plan so ambitious she dared not tell anyone else about it—yet. Aunt Adelaide, Caroline, even Timothy would think she was mad if they knew her ultimate goal. But on those cold winter mornings when she forced herself out of bed to dress hastily in thick woolen clothes, she reminded herself of words she had heard her father speak years before. "Dream of big things, of holding the stars in your palm," he had told her. "Never be satisfied, Elinore, with standing atop a rock, when you can climb a mountain."

In those well-remembered words, she found encouragement for what she was about to undertake. Throughout the long and frozen winter, she repeated them to herself often, like a litany of hope for the dream she meant to transform into reality.

She took a job, late in October, in the housekeeping department of the Devonshire Hotel. If not quite as opulent and imposing as Potter Palmer's establishment on State and Monroe, with its famed Garden of Eden barbershop which was paved with marble and imbedded with silver dollars, its twenty-five-foot rotunda, and its glittering array of dining rooms, the Devonshire was nevertheless one of Chicago's most beautiful and important hotels. Its marble floors and aristocratic English atmosphere and furnishings attracted a constant stream of wealthy and often famous guests. It was a particular favorite of visiting royalty. One wing of the hotel's second story was devoted to its business and operations offices, and it was there that Elly was hired to oversee a staff of fifty-five chambermaids. She reported directly to Ian Kirby, the corpulent, balding manager of hotel operations. Her salary was a more than respectable twelve dollars a week.

"How in the world did you ever manage to get such a fine position?" Caroline gasped joyously when she heard the news. Elly had just returned from her interview with Mr. Kirby and was showing the family her new uniform, a black wool skirt and a matching blouse with the words "Devonshire Hotel" embroidered in gold thread just below the shoulder.

"I think it was the note from Mrs. Addison."

"Who?"

"Mrs. Henry Montgomery Addison. She was one of my regular customers in the tearoom. I went to see her yesterday and asked her to write a note of recommendation for this job. After all, if I can run a tearoom well enough to win her praise, I can certainly manage a housekeeping staff."

"What did she say?" Timothy, sitting on the floor at her feet, eyed the uniform admiringly.

Elly's eyes sparkled. "Why, she agreed with me. She was most accommodating. And her letter apparently impressed Mr. Kirby no end."

"What a clever girl you are," Aunt Adelaide put in with a proud smile. She sat on the horsehair sofa with Cassie on her ample lap, fingering the skirt of the black uniform. "And are you certain you can handle this job, Elinore? Not that I doubt you, my dear, certainly I don't. But you've never been in charge of so *many* people before. I am certain it will be most demanding."

Elly's gaze drifted to Cassandra's bent head. The little girl was examining the black uniform carefully, her tiny fingers smoothing and crumpling the heavy wool. "I can handle it," Elly said quietly, but there was a hard line about her lips as she spoke, which left no doubt in her family's minds that she would.

During the next weeks, Elly struggled against physical exhaustion and mental despair. Many members of the housekeeping staff had never taken orders from such a young woman before; the previous supervisor had been an iron-fisted old battle-ax with more than twenty-five years of experience working in hotels. The chambermaids rebelled against the authority of the slender young woman put in charge of their duties, arguing about the schedules she made up, neglecting to follow the suggestions she made, and making sour faces when she addressed them. She quickly learned that friendly smiles and pleasant manners would not help her with these recalcitrants. They were challenging her authority, perhaps because she was young and pretty, perhaps because she was merely new, but whatever the reason, she could not afford to tolerate their disrespect. One fat, freckle-faced young

German girl named Gertie Schmidt had even taken to mimicking Elly's mannerisms and words behind her back. Elly had heard her doing so on the stairway, and the resultant laughter among the other chambermaids had caused the hot color to rush into her cheeks. She was tired out by the long hours and the constant pressure, and discouraged by her own failure to maintain order among her staff. That night she was tempted to resign. She was filled with doubts and nearly ready to give up the plan that was so dear to her heart. Then she looked over at her little daughter, asleep on the bed, black curls spread over the pillow. A tremendous yearning came over her, a yearning to protect Cassandra, to provide her with everything she could ever need for a happy life. She wouldn't do that by resigning. Only by succeeding. She steeled herself to go back to the Devonshire in the morning and to gird herself for battle.

When Gertie began to whine and argue about the week's schedule, as Elly had expected she would, Elly interrupted her.

"If you're not happy with the schedule, Gertie, I can certainly do something to help you." She paused, watching as the girl's face spread into a big, triumphant smirk.

"I am releasing you from your duties here. You can find another job, one more suited to your liking."

The smile faded from Gertie's face, to be replaced by an expression of outraged disbelief. "You can't dismiss me. Only Mr. Kirby can. You're bluffing. If you think you can scare me with threats, you're wrong."

Elly felt every pair of eyes in the room fix themselves on her. She rose gracefully from her chair, came around the desk, and walked straight up to the red-faced girl. "*Out*," she commanded with perfect, iron calm. She lifted her arm and pointed to the door. "Get out of here—*now!*"

Gertie took a step backward. "But—"

"You are dismissed!"

Stunned silence descended over the other chambermaids. Gertie's wide mouth drooped in dismay. Incredibly, her voice now held the hint of an entreaty. "Give me . . . give me one more chance, Mrs. Maguire. I . . . I'm sorry. I don't want to lose my job!"

For a brief moment, Elly debated whether she should stick to her decision or alter it in deference to the girl's apology.

She was not without compassion, yet she recalled all too clearly Gertie's frequent and outspoken jeers of the past days. Also, she was intensely aware of the other young women in their crisp uniforms and caps waiting for the results of the altercation. "You've already lost your job here, Gertie. Good day."

Elly turned on her heel and resumed her seat at the desk. "Sonia Wickstrom—there was a complaint about your service yesterday from the guest in room five-oh-three. In the future, see that you dust every mirror and lamp and table, and let there be *no* wrinkles in the bedcovers. I repeat, none at all. Is that clear?"

"Y-yes, ma'am."

In the wake of the shock reverberating through the room as Gertie Schmidt fled in tears, Sonia Wickstrom nodded in terror. *Good,* Elly thought with a new icy satisfaction. *Let them fear me if they must. I will take charge of them like a general in the field and turn them into the most efficient staff in the city. It is better that they fear me than think me weak.*

It was not for another month that she relaxed the strictness of her new attitude enough to smile at a few of the more industrious chambermaids and to compliment them on their work. Gradually, as more and more her days fell into a routine and she adjusted to the demands upon her and the young women under her supervision, she devised numerous ways to save them time in their cleaning chores, while expanding their duties in small ways much appreciated by the guests. On the day before Thanksgiving, Mr. Kirby called her into his office and told her what a fine job she was doing. If this continued, he said, she would receive a raise in her pay at the end of a year's time.

By the end of a year's time, Elly hoped to be doing something quite different, but she made no comment to Mr. Kirby about this. She merely thanked him for his kind words and wished him a pleasant holiday.

Thanksgiving that year began as a somewhat gloomy event. The family gathered around the scrubbed pine table, which they had moved from the kitchen to the living room for the occasion. All of the fine tableware and flatware and linen from the boardinghouse days had been lost in the fire. A plain cotton cloth was spread over the table, and a collection of simple plates and mugs was set upon it. Marya and her children joined them, as did old General Willis, who had taken a dingy room over a watchmaker's shop in the business district. They were all quiet as they waited for Elly to arrive home. Even Marya's children and Cassandra seemed caught up in the atmosphere of gloom. Though a turkey and a kettle of soup and a bread pudding filled the kitchen with delicious aromas, Caroline, Timothy, and Adelaide, busy with last-minute preparations, couldn't help thinking of past Thanksgivings, when Bess had prepared inimitable feasts, beaming with pleasure at their compliments, and when Connor had presided at the big oaken table, with his quick jokes and blarney, his vivid smiles and blazing personality infecting them all with a festive mood. The little flat seemed barer and dingier than ever, especially with the scudding gray snow clouds outside. And where was Elly? They couldn't begin the meal until she arrived home, and the children were getting restless. Suddenly, there was a rapping on the door, and Timothy dodged past the general and Marya to open it.

"Happy Thanksgiving," Elly sang out, as she sailed into the apartment. Her glowing smile was reminiscent of Bess, only hers was even more dazzling, more heartwarming to behold. In her arms, Timothy saw a brace of packages, and he hurried to relieve her of them.

"I've brought treats, delicacies," she called gaily, shedding her coat and whirling around like a ballerina to greet everyone.

"Did you bring me a present?" Cassandra chirped. She hurled herself at her mother's skirt and clung as if for dear life.

"I brought you chocolates!" Elly declared, giving her a hug. "And for you, too," she laughingly assured Marya's wide-eyed moppets. "And I have wine and flowers and pumpkin pie! Come, everyone, let us say grace and begin."

The room came alive with bouquets of violets and chrysanthemums, with excited talk and laughter. As they all took seats around the table and joined hands, Timothy was the one to speak.

"Recent times have not been easy—for any of us," he began falteringly. His gaze shifted from his aunt and sisters to the young widow and the old general, who was solemnly nodding. "We've lost loved ones, and we've lost our homes and possessions, and maybe, at times"—he glanced down at his hands and swallowed—"we've even lost our courage. But Elly has reminded us that we do have a lot to be thankful for. Tonight we're all here, alive and together." His boy's voice was solemn but held an undercurrent of pride. "We have shelter, we have food. We have hope for the future. Tonight, as we thank the Lord for our blessings, we would do well to thank Elly, too, because she's the one who makes us mindful of them. I . . . I guess that's all," he finished, flushing furiously as he beheld the tears shining in his elder sister's eyes.

Then Aunt Adelaide said formal grace, and the meal began, amid the flickering of the gas jets and the hiss of the stove, with the wind fluttering at the windowpane and the sound of children's eager laughter filling the suddenly snug and cozy room.

Each night when she returned from the Devonshire, Elly spent her evenings making notes. She wrote down quantities of linens and towels and soaps needed for certain numbers of guests; she wrote down names of suppliers and those whose goods she judged to be of the best quality. She wrote down all of the thoughts and observations that had occurred to her during the day about improvements or changes which might increase hotel efficiency or customer satisfaction, and also those guidelines that every fine hotel must adhere to and scrupulously follow. She gained a prodigious amount of information, not only from her own position in the housekeeping department, but by establishing friendships with the dining room chefs and the waiters, with the desk clerks and porters and bellmen. She listened and observed carefully every day, analyzing everything going on around her. And she learned.

Often she was exhausted at the end of the day, but she never let an evening go by without writing down her daily observations. The week after Thanksgiving, she was interrupted by Caroline, who poked her head into the kitchen, where Elly sat at the table with pen in hand, scribbling furiously on her pad.

"It's Mr. Fitzgerald at the door," Caroline whispered. "He says he must talk with you at once."

Sean Fitzgerald? Baffled, Elly set down her pen and followed her sister into the living room.

Connor's business partner was in the tenement hall, stamping the snow from his boots, when she appeared. She invited him in and offered to take his coat and bring some tea, but he refused. He perched on the edge of the horsehair sofa uneasily, twisting the brim of his hat in his hands. He had put on weight and looked uncomfortable all bundled up in his Ulster coat and leather gloves, but it wasn't merely his garments or the way he sat, or the nervous way he kept licking his lips. Something in the man's eyes told Elly what he had to say was important, and not an easy matter to broach.

She waited. Caroline had retired to allow them privacy, and Aunt Adelaide was already preparing for bed in her room. There was not a murmur from Cassandra, who was fast asleep, and Timothy was working overtime at the department store, doing the pre-Christmas inventory. Silence fell in the apartment, except for the squeaking of the sofa springs as Sean shifted and reshifted his hefty form.

"Might as well come out with it, Mrs. Maguire," he said at last. "I lied to you last time you came to see me. Connor did have some money in my safe when he died; at least it was there a few days after. A bet he had made the day before the fire came through—a certain trotter . . . well, no need to go into the details. Fact is, the money was there when you came to see me, and I . . . I didn't mention it. Thought Connor owed it to me, after saddling me with Casey and all." He pulled a money belt from his coat pocket and stared at it morosely, unable to meet Elly's stunned gaze.

"I didn't count on how I'd feel afterward. It was a bad thing to do, lassie, you being alone and havin' to take care of your wee daughter and all. These past nights I've hardly slept a wink, and Mary finally got me to tell her what was troubling me. Well, she fired up like only an Irish colleen can do, and she made me promise I'd come and make it right by you. Said she wouldn't marry me till I did." He peeled a packet of bills from the money belt and handed it to her, at last meeting her wide blue-gray eyes.

"There it is, lassie. Six thousand dollars."

"Six thousand dollars?" She was so rigid with shock that her lips could barely form the words.

"I hope it will make things easier for you and your wee lass." Sean flushed as he glanced around at the cramped, sparsely furnished apartment. He came heavily to his feet. His jowly cheeks were stained a bright shade of red, and for once his clever green eyes held no glint of calculation, only sorrow. "I'm ashamed of lying to you like that, Mrs. Maguire. 'Twas an evil thing. I hope you can forgive me someday," he muttered.

For a moment, Elly could only stare at the pile of hundred dollar bills in her hands. Then she became dimly aware that Sean was hurrying toward the door.

"It took courage to come here and tell me the truth, Mr. Fitzgerald," she said suddenly. She followed him across the room. "I thank you for it."

He stopped short and turned to face her, his cheeks reddening even more. "Don't thank me," he begged. "I can't bear it, lass." He flung open the door to the hall and hurried out. "Good luck to you, Mrs. Maguire," he called over his shoulder as he rushed toward the stairs.

For a long time, Elly could do nothing but stare at the money Sean had given her. Caroline tiptoed out to see what he had wanted and found her sitting in dazed silence holding a mound of bills. At the same moment, Timothy arrived home. Both of them shrieked wildly when Elly told them what had happened.

"Now we can fix up this dreadful place and buy some decent furniture and clothes," Caroline cried. "Your coat is nearly threadbare, Elly, and Timothy's is worse. Oh, just think of the lovely new one you can buy at Field's."

"No!" Elly said sharply. Timothy and Caroline stared at her.

"We're not going to spend a penny of this money. At least, not yet."

"Why not?" Timothy scratched his chin. "Have you got something better in mind?"

"Yes. I do." Her eyes gleamed at them, filled with a sudden, exultant excitement. "Oh, I didn't think I'd be able to begin the first step of my plan until at least the spring, but now I can put it into motion right away. So much the better." She seemed almost to be talking to herself, and with an irritated groan, Timothy told her to explain what she meant.

"We're going to put this money in the bank," she told him, leaning back against the sofa and folding her arms. "We're going to establish an account and a line of credit, adding to it as much as we possibly can from our various pays every week. And come, oh, say, April, we're going to open a

catering business. We shall prepare the food for those elegant
parties women like Mrs. Addison are always throwing. I can
call on all the ladies who used to patronize the tearoom; they
will beg me to cater their parties when I'm finished describing
our menus. And *then* we're going to scrimp and save and plan
and borrow until we have enough money to begin building the
enterprise that is our future," she informed them, speaking
with so much certainty and knowledgeable determination that
they listened in awe.

"And what . . . what might that be?" Timothy asked,
watching her with an expression half of wonder and half of
dread. The catering business alone sounded overly ambitious
to his fourteen-year-old ears.

"The Forrest Hotel," Elly replied calmly, glancing from
one to the other of them with a brisk smile. "The most
elegant, modern, and beautiful hotel in the city."

"Elly . . . are you mad?" Caroline whispered in a faint
voice.

Elly laughed and paced restlessly around the lamplit room.
"Even this dreary place is bearable, Caroline, if you think of
it as only temporary," she mused. "And it *is* temporary, I
promise you. You'll see."

❧ Nineteen

THE SITE WAS perfect, Elly decided. She stood in the blustery
April wind, filled with a rising excitement. Before her on
State Street, a little more than three blocks from the grandiose
Palmer House, an old three-story warehouse sat in crumbling
ruin beneath the blue spring sky. Its owner must have failed
in business, she thought. Maybe he didn't begin with enough
capital, or maybe he didn't plan for the proper contingencies,

or maybe he simply didn't work hard enough. She was well aware of all of those pitfalls. She was equally determined to avoid them.

Turning away from the site, she hurried across the heavily congested street and boarded a streetcar heading toward home. It was time to contact Mr. Whetherby again, time to begin the real work at last. While all around her passengers jostled and complained, intent upon their own discomfort and troubles, Elly's mind was full of the tasks she had to accomplish in the coming months.

"Did you see it? What did you think?" Timothy greeted her as she walked up the steps to the former Madison Street bakery, which was now the home of Forrest's Catering, and above which the family now lived.

Instead of answering him immediately, she approached the trim little man working frantically at the stove. He had a sleek black mustache and springy curls beneath his spotless chef's cap. As he worked, he was muttering commands right and left to the two harried cooks under his direction.

"Monsieur Jobert, is everything in order for the Williams's ball tonight? You have prepared the specially decorated nougat cake? I understand it is their daughter's favorite."

"*Oui*, only look, *madame*," he replied with a vigorous nod, indicating the lovely oval cake iced in delicate swirls to resemble rosebuds. "*Pardon, madame,* I must concentrate! Leave us, I beg of you. All will be ready in time. You have my word upon it."

With one final satisfied glance around the kitchen, which was completely up-to-date with the newest gas-burning stoves, iceboxes, and pantries, Elly headed for the stairs leading to the family's living quarters.

"Well?" Timothy demanded, following her like an overeager puppy. His voice had changed, it was deep and masculine these days, but he still retained the awkwardness and impish enthusiasm of a boy. "I asked the janitor a thousand questions," he continued rapidly as she walked through the big whitewashed kitchen to the flight of narrow steps behind the pantries. "The owner's name is Dennison. He's bankrupt and desperate to sell."

"We'll soon find out exactly how desperate," Elly replied. She turned on the landing and pulled him up the steps beside her, squeezing his hands. Excitement glowed in her face.

"Timothy, I'm sending for Whetherby. We're going to begin negotiations for the land."

His expression matched her joy. "You mean this is it? We're really going to begin?"

"Yes," Elly answered, slipping out of her coat and hanging it up in the closet near the parlor. "We're really going to begin."

More than a year had passed since the night when Sean Fitzgerald had turned over the money to her. During that time, Elly had so closely followed the plan she'd outlined for her brother and sister that they now had come to believe she would accomplish what she intended. The catering business, begun the previous May, was a success, and their clientele consisted of many of the most prominent names in the city.

Elly had searched for a month to find this bakery, which was large enough to accommodate the business she had in mind, had comfortable living quarters directly above, and an owner interested in selling. It had been well worth the effort she had expended to find it. In addition to its other attributes, Mr. Tambori's shop was situated in a respectable, if not wealthy, neighborhood. That was something Elly recognized as necessary not only for her business but also for her daughter. There would be no more slums for Cassandra. The filth and despair of the Rat's Tail neighborhood was behind them, permanently. Pleased with the neat and attractive street on which the shop was located, Elly had bought it for a fair price, remodeled it to her specifications, and moved her family into the cozy quarters above with the smooth efficiency that was so much a part of her nature. Then she had turned her attention to launching the catering operation. She had found it necessary to give up her job at the Devonshire, for she was working day and night on every detail of the new business, constantly aware that a mistake made in the beginning stages of an enterprise could doom it to failure. She had made certain no such thing happened to Forrest's Catering.

After hiring Claude Jobert, the Amberson Palace's renowned chef, who, she had learned from the chef at the Devonshire, was fed up with the Amberson's management and wanted a chance to do things his own way, everything had fallen into place. Jobert was more than worth the kingly sum Elly paid him every week to whip up impressive dishes like tenderloin steaks with truffles, olives, and tomato sauce; aspic of oysters;

roast leg of mutton; and charlotte russe. Each meal was unique, something Elly made vividly clear when she met with a prospective client. The hostesses of Chicago, intent upon competing with their wealthy social sisters in New York, strove diligently to outdo one another in the lavishness of their parties. Caterers and dancing masters and dressmakers were in great demand as the city, splendidly rebuilt since the great fire eight years ago, adopted the refinements and snobberies of the older, more established and more sophisticated cities. Monsieur Jobert had an extraordinary reputation, and his creations were in great demand by this newly elegant society. This, combined with Elly's natural managerial skills and business sense, and the contacts she had made with well-to-do matrons who had patronized her tearoom, resulted in the catering firm doing brisk business from the moment of its inception.

"Where is Cassie?" Elly inquired after peering into each of the three small but cozily appointed bedrooms in the flat to no avail. "And Caroline and Aunt Adelaide?"

Timothy sprawled on the blue velveteen sofa and picked up a leather-bound edition of Charles Dickens's *Great Expectations*, which he had purchased two days ago from Simon's Bookstore on Monroe Street. "Aunt Addie went out to buy a new spring hat, and Caroline took Cassie along with her on a visit to Marya. Funny, when we lived in the Rat's Tail, Caroline couldn't wait to get away from there, and now that we have, she keeps wanting to go back."

"I'm thankful she is finally venturing out on her own. Just think, after all these years, she is healing—at last. It's a blessing. We owe part of her incentive, I'm sure, to the fact that she misses Marya and the children. Still," she said, seating herself at the maple escritoire near the window, "I do wish she wouldn't take Cassie with her on these visits. I don't want her exposed overmuch to those dreadful surroundings. We've moved up in the world now, and we're going to go even higher quite soon. Cassie doesn't belong in the Rat's Tail anymore—not that she ever did," she added swiftly.

"Uh-huh." For a moment, Timothy was about to tease her that she was turning into a positive snob, but he refrained. He understood the real reason why Elly wanted Cassie out of their former neighborhood. There had been an ugly incident a few days before they'd moved out. Some of the children had

run up to Cassandra and pointed at her while she'd been out
on the stoop getting some air with Caroline.

"That's the one. Her daddy was a drunk and burned down
her house. I heard my ma say so."

"A no-good drunk," another had sneered. "And he killed
her gramma."

"Hush, children," Caroline had cried. "You don't know
what you're saying."

"Sure and we do!" The first little boy, a greasy-haired
youngster of about ten, wearing a torn cap and toeless shoes,
glared at Caroline defiantly. "Everyone knows her daddy was
a drunk!"

Cassie had begun to cry, and Caroline had picked her up in
great distress and carried her upstairs. For months afterward,
Cassie had grown distraught at the very mention of Connor's
name. And Elly, when she heard the report, was furious.
From that moment on, she couldn't leave the Rat's Tail
behind soon enough.

"Wretched little demons," she had muttered, her eyes
bright with contempt. "Most of their fathers are far worse
specimens than Connor ever was—even on his worst days.
Those wicked brats aren't fit to wipe Cassie's shoes."

"Now, now, children are cruel sometimes; they don't know
better," Aunt Adelaide had tried to soothe her, though she,
too, had been shaken by Caroline's trembling account.

"They ought to know better than to taunt a three-year-old
child!" Elly had snapped, shaken out of her customary calm,
and Aunt Adelaide had been forced to nod agreement. Since
then, Elly's determination to build a hotel that would enchant
Chicago had grown even more powerful. For the past eight
years she had struggled to find a way to protect her family
from men like Jason Emmett, from poverty, from grief and
pain. She was tantalizingly close now to being in a position to
encase them in a marble palace and keep them safe. When the
suites of the Forrest Hotel were filled with rich paying customers and the dining rooms and parlors overflowing with
guests, when Cassie and Caroline and Timothy lived in magnificent surroundings far from the sordid poverty of the Rat's
Tail, then she could breathe easily and know that they were
safe at last.

She set her lips together with renewed determination and
picked up a pen. "Dear Mr. Whetherby," she wrote, think-

ing that it was fortunate she had found a lawyer as ingenious and knowledgeable as William Whetherby. Sean Fitzgerald had recommended him to her when she had begun the catering business, and she was well pleased with his work. "I must meet with you as soon as possible regarding the purchase of a piece of property upon which I am going to begin a new enterprise. The property is located at . . ."

She paused, the pen in midair. Then she reached for the envelope she had just noticed on top of a pile of papers on the desk.

"A letter from Boone Walker?"

There was a sudden, inexplicable quickening of her heartbeat.

"It came today, I forgot to tell you." Timothy was deeply engrossed in his book and didn't even look up. Elly stared at the fine bold script in which Boone had written her name. Then she tore the seal and opened the letter.

It had been many months since she'd last heard from Boone. Immediately after the fire, she had sent a telegram to Louis Whitcomb at the Whitcomb and Walker Steel Company, informing him of Connor's death. She had known that there was no way to reach Boone at sea and had been unwilling to inform him upon his arrival in London. It would have been selfish to tell him the moment he docked, in the face of preparations for his marriage. Thinking of the way he had talked so fondly of Penelope, Elly was reluctant to spoil the happiness of his nuptials. After all, she had reasoned, there was nothing Boone could do. He might as well enjoy his wedding and honeymoon, instead of grieving for Connor, which would do no one any good at all. Instead, she had asked Louis Whitcomb to relay the news when he judged it best. Shortly thereafter, Boone had written to her, expressing his shock and sympathy at Connor's and Bess's deaths. He had requested her to let him be of help in some way, in any way. Elly had responded with gratitude, but hadn't taken him up on his offer. She hadn't even confided to him the circumstances in which they had been left. She didn't want anyone feeling sorry for her, and she didn't want anyone's help— even Boone's. Several years before, she had turned her life over to a man, counted on him to take care of her and keep her family safe, and all that had been for nothing. Never again would she make the mistake of relying on anyone other than herself.

Now, as she read Boone's letter, a puzzled expression crossed her features. Boone gave a brief account of his busy schedule, the purchase of some oil refineries in Illinois, and the successful branch office of Whitcomb and Walker that had been opened in Chicago. He expressed the hope that she and her family were well and reiterated his desire to be of service to them at any time.

Nowhere in the letter did he mention his wife.

In his first letter after Connor's death, Boone had mentioned Penelope, stating that she, too, sent her sympathy and regards. Since then, nothing. Elly wondered if he would bring her to Chicago the next time he came. But there was an odd tightness in her chest at the prospect of meeting Penelope Walker. Many times during the past year and a half she had thought of Boone and his aristocratic English bride. Sometimes she imagined them touring Europe on their honeymoon, or sailing back to America on a luxury steamship, standing arm in arm at the rail. Of late, she pictured Boone beside a sophisticated and beautiful brunette, as Boone had described Penelope to her long ago, entertaining guests in the ballroom of a grand home in Pittsburgh. With each imagining came a strange little flicker of . . . she wasn't sure of what. Not pain, exactly, or jealousy—that would be absurd. But . . . something. This reaction both disturbed and mystified her. She was certain that the odd feelings she had felt toward Boone that night in the carriage had been due to her fever and her upset state. Nothing more, certainly. And yet . . . there were nights when sleep wouldn't come, when she knelt at her bedroom window watching the stars, and at those moments her thoughts flickered to Boone Walker. For a brief moment, she would see his strong, pleasant face, his penetrating eyes and firm, sensual mouth, and sometimes she even heard his voice as he had spoken to her in the carriage: *Connor is a very lucky man.* When this happened, she would shake the image from her mind, chide herself for her fanciful musings, and return to bed, forcing herself to sleep. It was uncomfortable to feel this way, she decided now as she folded the letter and slipped it back inside the envelope. It was also absurd. Boone Walker was a friend, a concerned and dutiful friend, who was taking a kind interest in the welfare of Connor's wife and family. That was all. Biting her lip, Elly made up her mind to respond one more time, out of politeness, and then to put him from her thoughts once and for all. In her letters, she had mentioned the launching of a catering business, but nothing at all about the hotel. No one knew of those plans yet except Caroline and Timothy and Aunt Adelaide.

And now Mr. Whetherby would know, she thought, picking up her pen once more. She replied absently when Timothy exclaimed that he was late in going to the stable for the wagon and team that would convey Monsieur Jobert, his assistants, and their ample provisions to the Williams home for the ball. She was deep into her letter to Mr. Whetherby, giving him instructions and setting up an appointment with him in two days' time. Boone Walker, her life with Connor, and even, in a sense, the catering business were things of the past as far as Elly was concerned. Like an oarsman headed for the finish line, she bore down upon her goal with single-minded purpose. The only thing that mattered now was the future—the building, brick by brick, of the Forrest Hotel.

"Come in," a huge, homely girl in a gray wool dress called as Caroline hesitated outside the door of the glass-fronted shop. The door was partially open to allow the fresh spring breeze to enter the shop, and Caroline could see the girl gesturing for her to enter.

She hadn't intended to go in, only to stroll by with Cassandra and look at the place. Marya had told her about Roberta Dixon. She was curious. Now, it seemed, there was nothing to do but enter and meet the girl herself.

"Hello, may I help you? I'm Miss Dixon." The heavyset girl smiled from behind her desk.

"No, we don't need any help. This is my niece. I'm Caroline . . . Caroline Forrest. . . . We just—"

"Oh, Marya's friend! How good it is to meet you!" A smile as warm as all of July wreathed Miss Dixon's face. "Marya has told me so much about you, how you helped her after her first husband was killed, how your family was so kind to her! She is very, very fond of you, Miss Forrest! Even though Marya has remarried now and is being taken care of by her husband, she still comes in to help me fix up some of the clothes that are donated, the ones with missing buttons and small rips and such, and I certainly appreciate her aid! By the way, I couldn't help but notice that unlike many of the

immigrants in the neighborhood, her English is quite good.
She told me you were the one to teach her!''

"Why, y-yes." Caroline was somewhat overwhelmed by
Roberta Dixon's prolific chatter, but she was also pleased that
Miss Dixon knew so much about her. For a while, she had
felt miffed that Marya's conversation was sprinkled so liber-
ally with "Miss Dixons" all the time. Caroline had even
wondered if she was on the verge of losing her friend to the
wonderful young woman who had opened the secondhand
shop amid a cluster of dry goods stores, fruit markets, taverns, and a carriage works. She looked around the little shop
at the shelves filled with old, folded garments, the counters
lined with worn boots and shoes, blankets, linens, tableware.
There was an ancient rickety rocker near Roberta Dixon's
neat little desk and, on the floor nearby, a collection of
shabby dolls. Cassandra noticed these at the same instant
Caroline did.

"Oh, pretty!" she cried, letting go of her aunt's hand and
rushing forward to examine them. She knelt down and peered
into the scratched, painted faces.

"Be careful with them," Caroline admonished, while Roberta Dixon beckoned her forward, indicating the rocker.

"Won't you sit down, Miss Forrest? I was hoping you'd
come by one day. I particularly wanted to speak with you."

"Of course." Somehow, as she slipped into the rocker,
Caroline felt more at ease. Roberta Dixon had a way about
her, just as Marya had said. Though she was no beauty, with
her plump body and round cheeks, her small brown eyes
twinkled with friendliness and humor, and her mouth was a
perpetual merry smile. She wore her frizzed brown hair pulled
back in a chignon, which unfortunately revealed a thick,
flabby neck, but she showed no trace of embarrassment over
her excess weight or her plainness of feature. Roberta Dixon
was too busy for that. Caroline knew that in this secondhand
shop, which she had opened only recently, three short blocks
from the tenement building where the Forrests had temporarily lived, Roberta did her best to aid the most unfortunate
people of the neighborhood. In addition to providing a place
for people to buy and sell secondhand clothing and other
items, she kept a pot of soup simmering in the back and
offered some to any who needed it. She distributed oranges to

the neighborhood children and was trying, Marya had heard, to persuade a doctor to open a practice here in the neighborhood.

"What is it you wanted to speak to me about?" Caroline asked, with a trace less diffidence.

Roberta's smile broadened. "After hearing Marya speak of your goodness, your generosity, and your gentle way with people, I came to the conclusion that you would make an ideal assistant to me. I'd like to ask you—no, really to beg you—to join me here in the shop and help me accomplish more of what I intend to do."

Nothing could have come as a greater surprise to Caroline. To think that this competent, energetic young woman wanted *her* help in such a way filled her with astonishment—and pleasure. But then came the fear. "Do you mean you would like me to come down here to the shop every day and . . . and help you with the clothing . . . as a . . . a shopgirl?"

Roberta shook her head. "With everything, Miss Forrest. I have such wonderful plans! There are many ways we can help the people in this neighborhood. One of them is by teaching them to speak English. You did wonders for Marya, and many other immigrants could find better jobs and have easier lives if they could only speak English. And read! If they could only read!" She jumped up and began to pace around the immaculately swept floor, her arms waving with enthusiasm. "There is so much to do! These people live such cruel, desperate lives. Rats, filth, always in debt, always hungry. Here in this shop, I hope to do much more than provide an outlet for secondhand merchandise. I want to help people in whatever way I can. If that means giving them a bowl of soup or a friendly smile or a book or advice on how to rid their homes of roaches, I will do so! But only think how much we could accomplish if there were two of us together! And don't think I can't pay you, Miss Forrest, I can! I come from a fairly prosperous home, and when my dear father passed on, he left me with a most comfortable stipend, which will allow me to run my shop, aid the needy, pay *you,* and live out my days in modest comfort, if I'm careful. You see, I know I'm far too fat and homely for any man to wish to marry—none ever even courted me, you see—but that doesn't mean I shan't have a satisfying life."

Caroline gazed at her in awe and was met by a nonchalant shrug. "Perhaps I won't have children of my own," Roberta

Dixon went on, "or a husband to care for, but the satisfaction I get from helping those who need it is more than enough for me. You see, Miss Forrest, I believe we must do with life what we will, for otherwise, it shall run right past us as though we did not even exist, and then—poof—all our opportunity is gone. We shall be dead. Just like that." She snapped her fingers, then nodded, smoothing her gray wool dress across her plump hips. "Marya says you never married, never even agree to see any young men. Now, I won't ask why such a lovely young woman as yourself chooses to live as a spinster—I'm sure there's a reason—but if you want to do something worthwhile with your life, why not give my suggestion a try? I could certainly use your help and would dearly love to have it, I assure you!"

Caroline had stopped rocking. She could hear Cassandra whispering and giggling with the dolls on the floor, could feel the late afternoon sunlight on her face, could smell the aroma of potato soup from the back of the shop, mingled with the clean, scrubbed scent of the stout young woman watching her. Slowly, she shook her head.

"I should like to help you," Caroline heard herself saying in a small voice, "but it isn't possible." She searched her mind frantically for a reason. "My sister still needs me to assist sometimes with her catering shop, or to care for Cassandra."

"Come whenever you can," Roberta interrupted, then turned as the shop's door opened and a dark-haired, ragged woman rushed in with two urchins clinging to her skirt. The woman was crying, her face wet and mottled and red.

"What is it? Please be calm; I am going to help you," Roberta urged, for the woman was pleading in broken English laced with Hungarian, and was nearly hysterical. She kept wiping at her face with the corner of her grimy apron, pointing to the children and gasping words neither Caroline nor Roberta could understand.

The children peered at Cassandra and the dolls, but stayed by their mother's side as Roberta led her in and questioned her quietly. Caroline stood aside and urged her to sit in the rocker, smiling encouragingly at the children, a boy and a girl, both slightly older than Cassandra, dressed in tattered clothing. The woman obviously needed help, but her English was so poor that Caroline couldn't make out a word of it.

Roberta kept trying, though. Her patience impressed Caroline. She stood by helplessly, uncertain what to do. She knew one thing, though. She would be mad to commit herself to this shop, to Roberta Dixon's odd ideas, however compassionate they might be. It would mean coming down into the Rat's Tail every day, dealing with all sorts of people, facing all sorts of situations. Impossible. She wasn't brave or strong or determined like Roberta Dixon. And there was probably little she could do to help; she would only get in the way.

Then she happened to glance at the little boy, who had begun to sniffle while his mother's tearful lamentations continued. Caroline's gaze sharpened. She noticed what had escaped her first quick glance: there were bruises on the child's arm, visible through the gaping holes in his little sleeve.

"Miss Dixon," she said in alarm, kneeling as she spoke to look more closely at the child. Behind her, Roberta spoke quietly.

"Yes, I know. His mother has just told me. Their father beats the children. He beats the mother, too, sometimes. Last night he burned the girl's fingers on the stove, to punish her for being sick."

Caroline turned in horror to the silent, dirty-haired girl in the brown shapeless dress. Rags were wrapped tightly about the fingers of her right hand.

Caroline felt sick. She couldn't say anything, but her eyes brimmed with tears. Slowly, she came to her feet and faced Roberta.

"That is . . . monstrous!" she managed at last. "What can be done?"

"She's left him; that's a start," Roberta said, nodding toward the Hungarian woman with approval. "But she needs a place to stay, a place where he won't find her. I'm going to keep them here with me for a few days—I have living quarters above the shop—and then I'll have to find somewhere for them to go. Right now, though, they need food. And I must look at the girl's fingers. Her name is Gina, by the way."

Caroline looked at the child and saw in her frightened brown eyes the same lurking terror, the same anguish that she had seen in her own every time she glanced in a looking glass for the past six and a half years. To think that this child had suffered so, young as she was. She, too, had been cruelly abused—cruelly betrayed—by someone from whom she sought only love. In that instant, Jason Emmett's face flashed into her mind. Jason, as he had been so many times, handsome and teasing, superior, but, oh, so carelessly kind. Then she saw him again as he had looked on the night he raped her in the glade, his face cold, twisted with hate, ugly with a cruelty she couldn't comprehend. Yes, he had inflicted unspeakable pain upon her, even more cruel because she had thought he loved her, but then, so had this child's father inflicted a horrible agony upon *her*. And he, too, was supposed to love her.

Why? *Why?* Outrage, confusion, and a soul-wrenching sadness surged within her at the senselessness of it all. It was the first time she realized, truly realized, that she did not suffer alone, that there was a scope and depth of agony in the world incomprehensible to most people. With a bursting compassion that could only come from her own deep pain, Caroline reached out and enfolded the little girl in her arms.

"Why are you crying, Aunt Caroline?" Cassandra asked beside her. She sounded frightened, and Caroline quickly released Gina, brushed aside her own tears, and rose.

"It is time to go, Cassandra."

Obediently, Cassie replaced the dolls, lining them up in a row. Caroline turned to Roberta.

"I am taking Cassandra home, but I will return shortly with some blankets and food." She nodded toward the immigrant family. "I believe you ought to take them upstairs at once, don't you? The husband may come in search of them."

"Have no fears about that. I am taking them up right now." Roberta's smile was ecstatic beyond words. "This means you're going to help us, then? I thought for a moment there you were going to run!"

"So did I," Caroline muttered, her face grim. Then she smiled tremulously at Roberta and at the dark-haired, silent little girl. "I'll be back," she promised. "I'll do whatever I can, whatever you need me to do."

And with one final glance at the frantic Hungarian woman, looking so lost, so frightened in the cheerful little secondhand shop, Caroline went out. She no longer felt shaken by what she had seen and heard. Maybe Roberta Dixon's calm, competent manner was contagious. Or maybe, she thought, as she and Cassie walked quickly toward the streetcar in the fading day, which was cooler now, its springtime tang evaporating as night approached, maybe she was simply ready to do what had to be done. Those people were in trouble and needed help. How could she, who knew so much of pain and fear, refuse?

The answer was simple. She couldn't.

🌿 Twenty

"MY DEAR MRS. Maguire, this is not easy for me to say. As you know I have been one of your principal supporters. Why, no one in my circle is quite as fond of you as I am or more delighted that your catering shop has been such a success. But this time, much as I regret it, the answer is no. I cannot and will not help you. It is quite impossible."

In the lemon-yellow drawing room of Mrs. Henry Montgomery Addison, Elly sat with stiffly folded hands. Only the whiteness of her knuckles would have revealed to Mrs. Addison how tense she really felt, for her face was carefully schooled into an expression of calm, and her peach-colored walking suit, trimmed with a deep side-pleated flounce and cuffs and collar of ivory silk, hid the bunched muscles in her body. She appeared graceful and poised, even elegant, with the bonnet of Tuscan straw set upon her dark head and tied beneath her chin with ribbons of ivory satin. Yet as she sat there on the citrine velvet sofa, disappointment ran through her, sharp and strong. It was an effort to keep her shoulders from sagging with defeat.

"May I ask why you feel that way, ma'am?" she inquired in a steady tone. Within her reticule she had a list of ten of her best customers, all of whom she intended to approach as

possible investors in the hotel. Four had already turned her
down. Mrs. Addison was the fifth to refuse.

"It is simply an unthinkable notion, my dear." Mrs. Addison lifted her Limoges teacup to her lips, sipped, then set it
down in its dainty saucer. "My advice to you is to content
yourself with your catering shop. Why, it is in itself a grand
achievement for a woman. I certainly know of no other lady
who could operate such a business. It is to your credit that it
is so well run and so profitable, but I'm sure it is quite
demanding enough upon your resources. It would be folly to
attempt anything more—particularly something like a hotel!
Why, a hotel is a massive undertaking, and would be even for
a man!" She sighed, her haughty, lined face filled with
regret. "Now, I know the suffragists would have my head for
such a statement, but it is merely the truth, and I am giving
you good advice, my dear. If you are as intelligent as I
believe, you will put such nonsense out of your head. You
cannot possibly succeed, and all that will happen is that you
will exhaust yourself, throw away perfectly good money, and
in the end, become bitter with your failure." Kindliness
mingled with smug wisdom in her pale blue eyes. "And
besides that, even if I wished to help you—which in this case,
I do not—my husband would never hear of it. Mr. Addison
gives me a most generous allowance, of course, but if he
suspected for one moment that I was throwing it away on a
young woman's foolish attempts to prosper in business, he
would cut off my pin money in an instant." She patted a
delicately embroidered linen napkin to her lips and then waved
it in a dismissive gesture. "Now, then. With all this unpleasant business settled between us, my dear, would you care for
more tea?"

"No, thank you." Elly rose and extended a hand that was
clammy with despair. "You've been more than generous to
allow me so much time, Mrs. Addison, and I thank you. But
I must be on my way."

"Don't tell me you're going to continue this mad endeavor? Surely you don't intend to call elsewhere in an
attempt to find an investor?" Mrs. Addison demanded, her
gray faille gown rustling as she escorted Elly to the door of
the imposing Prairie Avenue mansion.

When Elly told her quietly that that was exactly what she
intended to do, the older woman clicked her tongue disap-

provingly. "Really. Why can't you accept what I've told you? No one, I repeat, *no one*, is going to even consider such a wild enterprise."

"I can only hope you are wrong, ma'am."

Bleakly, Elly turned away. She had encountered nothing but skepticism and rejection for the past two days, and her list of possible supporters was dwindling. Worst of all, Mrs. Addison's words had nearly exactly echoed those of the people she had already approached, leading her to believe that there was little chance the matrons she had yet to visit would hold differing views from those she had already seen. Yet, what choice did she have but to continue? Without a rich investor to back her, her plan could not possibly succeed. And yet, no matter how she stressed her former accomplishments, the tearoom and the catering business, no one thought it remotely possible that a woman could build and manage something as ambitious and complex as a grand hotel.

"Just a moment, Mrs. Maguire!"

To her astonishment, Mrs. Addison called out from her doorway. Elly, who had begun threading her way along the flagstone walk toward the street, turned in surprise, her up-turned bonnet shielding her eyes from the slanting May sun. "Come back here, if you please."

From the doorway of the three-story red sandstone mansion, Mrs. Montgomery regarded her from beneath her well-combed eyebrows. "Well, there is *one* person of my acquaintance who *might* be interested in your proposition," she said reluctantly. "She's somewhat eccentric, a widow. A free-thinker you know, belongs to several of those women's rights organizations and suffragist groups. Despite her oddities, I rather like her, even though she is not fully accepted in proper circles. If you'll wait a moment, I'll write down her name and her address. Her home isn't far from here."

A scant quarter of an hour later, Elly rang the bell of the huge white granite mansion sweeping along Drexel Boulevard. If she wasn't mistaken, this home was the largest of any she had seen in this opulent and prestigious neighborhood.

She presented her card, and a liveried butler showed her into an enormous drawing room furnished in shades of claret and royal blue. After informing her that he would see if madam was receiving visitors, he left her alone amid a profusion of roses in Oriental vases. Flowers were everywhere: on the blue marble mantel, the fruitwood side table, the lacquered sofa table, and the small round table before the blue velvet draperies. The room was bright and dramatic, with its Persian carpet and overstuffed burgundy sofas of elegant damask. The perfume of roses filled the air, almost stifling her with their rich scent. Elly's tension mounted as she realized that the woman for whom she was waiting might be her only hope. She closed her eyes, blotting out the heat of the warm room on this bright May day, the perfumed air, the dazzling, gaudy surroundings. She saw in her mind's eye Caroline weeping on their first night in the Rat's Tail flat, and Cassie's white, stricken face after the children's cruel taunting about Connor. Deep down, she knew that though she was dressed in a fashionable walking gown, and had a respectable business all her own, and was received with politeness and respect in the drawing rooms of Chicago's well-to-do ladies, if truth be told, she had not come so far from Emmettville, after all. Nearly seven years had passed since they'd left Pittsburgh on that clattering, dusty train, and still, poverty and cruelty nipped at their heels like a wild dog in endless pursuit. Safety! She had to bring them to safety, all of them—Cassie and Caroline, Timothy and Aunt Addie. She wanted to whisk them away from everything sad and painful and ugly, to protect them.

Well, she told herself, pressing her lips together with renewed determination, and so I will. In her imagination, she pictured the hotel she meant to build, a gleaming palace, an impenetrable marble sanctuary of such size and magnificence it could withstand any storm, any wind of ill fortune. Then the image wavered and vanished as a rough-edged New England voice broke into her thoughts.

"Elinore Maguire, is that your name?" A square-shouldered ox of a woman marched into the room. "I'm Olive Meeks. Just what is it that you want from me?"

Elly came hastily to her feet. Mrs. Meeks had a huge gray pompadour, a ruddy face, and a thick neck. She was in her late fifties, Elly judged, and from the piercing way she appraised Elly through tiny, flashing black eyes, she was nobody's fool. As Elly began to explain how she had come to be there, she couldn't help thinking that Mrs. Meeks looked very much like a fisherwoman. A fisherwoman in a bustled gown of striped purple and white silk whose flounces and furbelows did little to distract from the stoutness of her ample-bosomed figure. She discovered, not much later, that a fisherwoman was exactly what Olive Meeks was or, more accurately, had been. Her husband had begun his career with a single fishing boat on the coast of Maine. By the time he died of heart failure three years ago, Mrs. Meeks informed her over tea, he was the king of the steamships, owning a veritable fleet of prosperous merchant vessels.

"Which is why, I gather, you've come to me." She fixed Elly with a shrewd stare. "Winifred Addison told you he left me a damned fortune and that I might be daft enough to invest some of it in your hotel."

"No, of course not," Elly gasped, coloring at these forth-right words that were uncomfortably close to the truth. Then she caught the wickedly merry glimmer in Mrs. Meeks's eyes and laughed in spite of herself. "Well, something like that, but I assure you she spoke in the kindest of terms."

"Hmph." Olive Meeks swallowed a tea sandwich in one gulp. "Did she, now? Well, Winifred is not a bad sort, not like some of them hoity-toities who think the world is nothing but their own private croquet field and that they've got all the mallets! Well, enough of them. You can see I'm a plain-speaking woman, Mrs. Maguire. I'd appreciate it if you'd be the same with me. Tell me without a lot of fluff and flutter why I should invest a penny of my money in some foolish new hotel."

So Elly explained her ideas about the growing need for more hotels as Chicago continued to flourish, about her vision of a hotel every bit as elegant and beautiful as the city's finest, and about her already prosperous catering service, which would be expanded into a fashionable dining room on the top floor of the hotel. "And there will be a ballroom adjoining it and an enclosed terrace that will duplicate a garden setting, with ferns and palms and flowers, so that guests who wish to leave the dancing for a time may slip out, just as they might in a private home, to stroll through lush and fragrant grounds. Only it shall all be indoors—most romantic, elegant, and unusual."

"Hmph. It sounds mighty unusual." Olive Meeks gripped the handle of the ornate silver teapot in her large fist and poured herself more tea. "Interesting, Mrs. Maguire. Most interesting." She leaned back in her velvet-tufted Queen

Anne chair. "Do you have architect's plans for this hotel of yours? And record books from your catering business? I'd have to study every entry to know how your business has progressed."

Elly's pulse quickened as she reached into her leather valise. "I brought everything, ma'am. You're welcome to examine it all."

To her surprise, Mrs. Meeks went off to her study to peruse the books and papers and invited Elly to wait in the library. Elly was too nervous to read, but sat with a book in her lap for nearly two hours until the library door opened and her hostess stuck her head into the dark-paneled room.

"Come back to the parlor, Mrs. Maguire," she ordered, and led the way without waiting for Elly to join her.

Though Elly searched her face when they were seated in the rose-scented room once more, she found no indication of the other woman's decision. She waited in fretful silence, with her stomach aching from tension and her fingers stiff and cold in her lap.

"Well done," Mrs. Meeks said at last. She handed over the papers with a tight little smile. "You are thorough and you are prepared—and you have made a tidy profit with this catering business. I admire that. You see, I worked side by side with my husband for thirty-odd years, and I know what it takes to make a business work. I kept all John's books myself, and I still do, to this very day." She waved a hand in the air and gave a contemptuous snort. "Oh, I've got three sons who want to take over the business. They're clamoring at me all the time to let 'em take charge, but I'm not fool enough to allow it. John knew what he was doing when he left the whole fleet to me. Those boys of ours don't have sense enough to worm-bait a hook, much less run the company. But you do, Mrs. Maguire. Unless I miss my guess, you've got more sense in your right elbow than most men have in their inflated, pompous, arrogant heads."

"Does this mean that you're interested in my venture?" Elly felt her heartbeat quickening with hope.

"That all depends." Bright black eyes, like a raven's, watched Elly from that shrewd fisherwoman's face. "The world's a difficult place for a woman, always has been. I suppose Winifred mentioned my work with various women's suffrage organizations? Did she tell you Elizabeth Cady Stanton ate in this very house?''

When Elly shook her head, puzzled by this seemingly unrelated line of conversation, Olive Meeks went on in her booming, slightly nasal voice. ''Well, she did. And I'll tell you something else. I attended the very first women's rights convention in Seneca Falls, New York. That was in 1848. I've lectured here and there, and I've sponsored rallies all over the Midwest. My John, he knew every bit how strong I felt about the subject, and, Lord bless him, he supported me. He always told me the day would come when women would get the vote, and he reminded me of that when Wyoming did it in 'sixty-nine. I know in my heart it will happen all over this damned country someday, but it can't happen soon enough for me. Now, Mrs. Maguire, my point is this.''

She leaned forward in her chair and pointed a finger at Elly. ''I *enjoy* seeing a woman succeed, and I cheer and holler whenever I hear of it. And I'd be willing to help you with your hotel, mainly because I like you and I think you can do it. But I'm a sensible woman, Mrs. Maguire, and I also like having my considerable fortune. I don't want to throw away any part of it.''

''You won't be doing that, Mrs. Meeks. You'll reap even more money from your investment.''

''Well, that remains to be seen.'' She held up a hand for silence. ''Now, listen here. You've got a good head on your shoulders, and you know how to work hard and turn a profit. That's plain. But it takes gumption and drive to succeed on the kind of scale you're talking about.''

''I possess both of those qualities in abundance,'' Elly insisted.

''Maybe you do and maybe you don't. If you want my money, you'll have to prove it to me.'' She stomped over to a bud vase on the sofa table and plucked a rose from the crowded arrangement within. She sniffed its petals, inhaling deeply, then stuck the blossom back. Elly watched her with a dawning wariness.

''Prove it to you? How?''

Olive Meeks shot her a glance. ''Raise the first fifty thousand dollars on your own. I don't care how you do it, but prove to me that you can and I'll finance the remainder of the hotel. Simple as that.''

Simple as that? Elly could only stare at her for a moment. When she found her voice, she spoke firmly. "Mrs. Meeks, you might as well ask me to bring you the moon on a velvet cushion. I came to you precisely because I lack sufficient funds for the financing. You saw my ledgers from the bank regarding my catering business. If you asked me for five thousand dollars, yes, that I can certainly manage. But fifty thousand dollars . . . Surely you must know that the banks won't grant a woman a business loan."

A grim nod. "I do."

"Well, then. I've already told you of the reception my plan has received so far. If the other people I know echo Mrs. Addison's sentiments, they won't help me either." She lifted her hands in a graceful, imploring gesture. "You must realize that what you've asked me to do is quite impossible."

Mrs. Meeks yanked the tasseled bellpull beside her chair. "Well, then, Mrs. Maguire, our talk is over. I enjoyed it, though. Haven't had such stimulating company in a season of Sundays."

The butler appeared at the drawing room door.

"Harrison, show Mrs. Maguire out. And send that rabbit-faced Matilda up to help me dress for dinner. My dratted sons and their mealymouthed wives are due to arrive within the hour. Damnation."

"Mrs. Meeks—wait!" Panic ran through Elly like fire. She came to her feet in a smooth upward leap. "I . . . I'll try to raise the money. But it will take time . . ."

"Two weeks." The fisherwoman nodded at Elly's stunned look. "Raise it by June first, and you'll have yourself a mighty pretty deal."

Elly couldn't believe her ears. How could she possibly raise such a sum in so little time? For a moment she wondered if Olive Meeks was quite sane. But instantly she knew better. Mrs. John Meeks was simply a shrewd and tough woman who didn't intend to part with her money unless she was certain the person she entrusted it to was as shrewd, tough, and resourceful as she would be under the same circumstances.

"I'll have it in two weeks," she heard herself promise in a voice that sounded far more confident than she felt. Dimly, she was aware that she was holding out her hand, gripping the other woman's large, fleshy fingers. Like an automaton, she gathered up her reticule, ledgers, books, and papers and followed the butler to the door.

"June first," Mrs. Meeks called after her, as she passed through the ornately carved mansion doors. "Come see me at precisely two o'clock."

Two o'clock, Elly thought, walking dazedly along the street of stately South Side mansions. Two o'clock. June first. Fifty thousand dollars.

Why didn't she simply ask me to slay her a dragon? she wondered in despair.

But by the time the streetcar came to a halt two short blocks from home, an idea had already begun forming in her mind. It was amazingly simple, requiring only a small amount of audacity. With every step she took through the cool shadows of the late afternoon, her plan seemed more and more inspired.

Timothy. It all revolved around Timothy. And the bank, the Second State Bank, where her current account was held. It just might work. With Mr. Whetherby's help and a bit of luck and cunning . . .

The Forrest Hotel. Elly yearned to see it rising like a golden tower on State Street. She could almost see the velvet-and satin-clad guests strolling through the reading rooms and parlors, ascending the marble-tiled staircase, riding the plush-lined hydraulic elevators up to their rooms. She felt that she was close, tantalizingly close to achieving what she wanted. If that accomplishment required something less than complete honesty, well, then, so be it. The banking institutions of this city were the ones at fault for refusing to grant loans to women. If they wanted a man's signature on their precious legal documents, she would give them one—Timothy's. She would "sell" the catering business to him, and transfer ownership and all profits into his name; he would then offer the business as collateral to the Second State Bank. Mr. Timothy Forrest would secure a loan toward the purchase of warehouse property on State Street, and between her and Mr. Whetherby, they would contrive it so that no one need learn that the highly successful businessman with whom they were dealing was a gangly-legged boy not yet sixteen years old.

Brace yourself, Mrs. Meeks, Elly advised silently as she reached the steps of the catering shop and climbed them with revitalized energy. *I'm about to plunge a dagger deep into the*

*belly of that dragon. On June first I'll be ready to claim my
reward.*

The windows of the parlor were all flung wide, but it was
hot, stiflingly hot, with no breeze wafting in to stir the
curtains, no movement whatsoever of the moist, heavy air.
Elly paced back and forth across the floor, her customary
poise gone. Perspiration glistened at her temples and brow,
and her chignon was wilted and limp, with damp tendrils
curling around her forehead. She felt parched, but was too
miserable even to pause in her pacing long enough to pour
herself some lemonade from the nearby pitcher.

Timothy sat on the velveteen sofa, looking just as hot and
uncomfortable as she felt. He kept starting, glancing toward
the stairs, then slumping back against the cushions. "It'll be
all right, Elly. Whetherby will get here. He'll manage it all
on time."

"We're running *out* of time!" she snapped, whirling on
him. Then immediately she rubbed her eyes with her hands.
"Sorry, Timmy, I'm sorry." Her face pinched, she resumed
her pacing.

Timothy gulped down his lemonade. He slouched back
again, following Elly with his eyes. He'd never seen her so
frantic before. She kept moving, her gaze swinging again and
again toward the little mantel clock, which read a quarter past
twelve. If Whetherby didn't get here soon, Elly would explode. Or Timothy would. The tension was making his stomach hurt. Where in hell was Whetherby?

Cassandra's voice sounded from the street below. "Mama!"
she called toward the open window. "Hello, Mama! We're
back from our walk!"

Elly groaned, hoping she'd have the patience not to snap at
Cassandra as she had at Timothy just now. It was June first,
the day of her deadline with Olive Meeks, and Whetherby
was still at the bank seeking final approval for the loan. The
paperwork had been exhausting. It had proved a monumental
task to transfer everything over to Timothy's name so quickly,
to draw up all the contracts and agreements, and then to
submit the loan application to the Second State Bank for
approval, but Whetherby had worked feverishly at her bidding. For the past three days, he'd been pushing urgently for
the loan to go through, but so far . . .

Elly wondered if Olive Meeks would agree to an extension. Remembering that tough, uncompromising face and that nasal voice ordering her to raise the money by June first at two o'clock, she felt doubtful. Mrs. Meeks was not the type of woman to listen to excuses or have patience with delays. Once she made up her mind about something, she wouldn't be swayed. Elly moistened her parched lips. These past two weeks had strained her own energy and patience to the limit. There had been times when she had thought she'd never complete all the paperwork and legalities in time, that the bank could not be induced to expedite her loan application— Timothy's loan application, to be precise. Mr. Whetherby had done his best, but last night, here in the parlor over the bakery, he had looked grim. He would make every effort to secure the loan by today, but he couldn't promise anything. Bankers didn't like to be rushed. They were conservative, ponderous; they liked to study and reflect and evaluate in good time. But he would try. . . .

From below, Cassie called out again, and Elly, pressing a lace handkerchief to her brow, hurried toward the window.

Aunt Adelaide had seen how tense she was this morning as the minutes dragged past, and she had volunteered to take Cassie out for some air, in order to leave Elly free to fret in peace. But that had been over an hour ago, and there was still no word from Whetherby or the bank. Elly's nerves were stretched tighter than ever. She was about to scold Cassie, telling her not to shout while standing in the street, when she heard her aunt saying the same thing, but in a much calmer and more pleasant tone than she could have achieved.

She lifted a hand to them both, mustering a taut smile.

"Still no word?" Aunt Adelaide inquired when she saw Elly's drawn face at the window. She sighed as her niece shook her head.

"Oh, dear . . ."

Just then, a hack rattled forward through the throng of wagons and pushcarts and carriages in the street. It pulled up at the curb, and Mr. Whetherby alighted, his bald head shining brightly beneath the broiling June sun. Aunt Addie gave a cry of relief. Cassie sang out a chorus of greetings to the lawyer, who was already becoming a familiar member of the household. Elly went motionless. Behind her, she heard Timothy spring up and hurry to her side. She didn't spare him

a glance. The delicious cooking smells from below swirled
about her; so did sunlight, heat, and traffic noise from the
busy street below, but she heard, smelled, and felt none of it.
Her intense blue-gray gaze was fixed on the lawyer with
terrible anxiety, reflecting her mingled hope and fear.

He hurried toward the steps, greeting Aunt Adelaide and
Cassie cheerfully, then caught sight of Elly and Timothy at
the window. ''I've got it!'' he called jubilantly, waving his
business case in the air. ''It took some doing, Mrs. Maguire,
but I've got what you need right here!''

She sagged against Timothy, relief flooding through her
like a lovely, cooling breeze. As she embraced him, her arms
clasped around his neck, she sent up a fervent prayer of
thanksgiving. Life, color, sound, and scent all rushed back
with joyful clarity. From the street, she heard her aunt chattering excitedly to Cassandra and urging the girl to come
inside, she heard her daughter's silvery laughter and Mr.
Whetherby's tapping cane, and then she heard Timothy's
voice in her ear as he hugged her ecstatically.

''I knew he'd get it. What were you worried about, anyway?'' he teased.

She laughed and kissed his sweat-shiny cheek. All thirst,
anxiety, and the effects of heat had vanished abruptly with the
lawyer's triumphant words. She felt wonderful.

''What, indeed?'' she asked, her eyes glowing.

At precisely two o'clock she rang the doorbell of Olive
Meeks's white granite mansion. Harrison showed her into the
claret and royal blue drawing room, where Olive Meeks was
sipping tea.

''I can see by your face that you've got the money,'' Mrs.
Meeks observed, setting down her teacup and eyeing her
visitor shrewdly.

Hardly able to control her exuberance, Elly nodded. ''I
do.'' She produced the check from the Second State Bank
made out to Timothy Maguire and quickly explained how she
had secured the loan. ''I hope you are now convinced of my
competence and ingenuity, Mrs. Meeks,'' she added. ''I trust
you are prepared today to sign these partnership papers?''

''Partnership papers?'' Mrs. Meeks glared as Elly withdrew a sheaf of legal documents from a leather case.

''Yes.'' Elly smiled. She was the picture of beauty, composure, and self-assurance in her summer-fresh lilac muslin

gown and dainty plumed hat. "I took the liberty of having my lawyer, Mr. Whetherby, draw them up so that we need not waste any more time," she explained. "He will be stopping by shortly to answer any questions you might have after reading them over. I'm certain that, now that I've met your condition for investing in the hotel, you are as eager as I am to begin building it. Why not start immediately by formalizing our partnership today?"

Olive Meeks let loose a great bark of laughter. Admiration shone from her hard black eyes. "You're a businesswoman, all right," she said approvingly. "You think just like a man. It's my opinion that we're going to make a great deal of money together, Mrs. Maguire."

"You need have no doubt of that," Elly answered. She felt strong—stronger than she had ever felt in her life—as she shook Olive Meeks's offered hand.

🌿 Twenty-One

BOONE WALKER EMERGED from his hired hack onto State Street and gazed up at the elegant six-story hotel. A gust of sharp winter air nearly swept his hat off, but he grabbed it just in time. While the driver handed down his trunk to the waiting porter in dark green livery, he studied the gleaming white marble facade, the tiers of graceful bay windows overlooking the street, the carved marble pillars that marked the portals on either end of the building. A stream of magnificently dressed men and women paraded in and out of these doors, fur cloaks and capes and muffs protecting them from the December chill. An admiring smile lurked in his eyes.

She had done it, and spectacularly. Why and how she had undertaken such a tremendous venture he didn't know, but

Connor must have left her very well off indeed if she could afford to dabble in catering businesses and hotels the way other women dabbled in embroidery. It was quite a sight, the Forrest Hotel. It was already gaining considerable attention among Louis Whitcomb's Newport crowd, and even the New York papers had called it "one of the few civilized outposts in the savage jungle that is Chicago." In view of the biting contempt in which New Yorkers held the upstart city on the plains, this was high praise. One of the New York papers had even run an item on Mrs. Elinore Maguire, the lovely young Chicago widow who had become the new darling of the city's rich and elite.

"I'd like a suite, the largest one you have," Boone told the desk clerk, ignoring the man's bulging eyes when he signed his name to the register.

"Certainly, Mr. Walker," the clerk snapped to attention with nearly military precision, a salute to the nationwide importance of Whitcomb and Walker Steel and, Boone thought somewhat bitterly, to the notoriety his name had received in print of late.

"And may I say on behalf of the Forrest that we're delighted to have you with us, sir?" the clerk intoned.

"Where can I find Mrs. Maguire?"

The man blinked. "Is there a problem, sir?" he inquired anxiously, the perspiration beading on his pasty brow.

"No problem. She's an old friend. I'm eager to see her."

"Certainly, sir. Mrs. Maguire's office is located on the fourth floor. In the north wing, suite four-oh-two."

Boone nodded his thanks and proceeded through the lobby of glittering white and silver and rich forest green. He barely noticed the splendid surroundings, the numerous reading rooms and smoking rooms and parlors with their velvet-brocade armchairs and Aubusson carpets, the painted and frescoed ceiling from which hung hundreds of shimmering gaslit chandeliers, the damask wallpaper of silver upon which had been stitched the faint and graceful silhouettes of a thousand dainty trees. Vases of delicate flowers here and there warmed and brightened the various rooms, all of which appeared both beautiful and luxuriously comfortable. Boone was vaguely aware of all this, but the details were lost to him as he rode the plushly carpeted hydraulic elevator to his suite on the third floor. His mind was full of questions as to what he would find when he walked into Elly's office and saw her for the first time in four years.

He washed the travel dust from his face and changed his suit, then peered dubiously in the mirror. Despite the expensive, well-cut pearl-gray suit, the silk-lined derby, the snow-white crispness of his stand-up shirt collar, he felt more like a barefoot schoolboy from the hills than a man who owned a major share of one of the largest steel plants in the country, not to mention railroad stock, coke ovens, mines, and quarries and a dozen strategically located warehouses. The Kentucky boy who had made his fortune in Yankee territory, whose picture had been splashed in newspapers across the country, and who was now accepted into the highest social circles with open arms was about to do something he'd wanted to do for years, and he was scared. Damned scared. His legs trembled. His throat felt funny and tight. He cursed to himself in the quiet of his sweeping burgundy and gold suite. Then he swung away from the mirror, crossed the Axminster carpet in four quick strides, and headed for the stairs.

"I'd like to see Mrs. Maguire," he said curtly, to the wispy little man seated in the outer office of suite 402.

"Do you have an appointment, sir?"

"No."

"What is your name?"

Suddenly, nervousness and self-doubt erupted into a wild impatience. "Never mind, I'll introduce myself," he snapped, and before the secretary had blinked in surprise, Boone was through the door and striding into the inner office.

Elly spoke from her desk without looking up.

"Jennings, have the electric call buttons on the second floor been repaired yet? It is imperative that—"

"Sorry, it's not Jennings," Boone interrupted. He tried to look and sound calm as her head flew up and she stared at him with a stunned expression.

"Hello, Elly."

Silence. Utter silence. Boone searched for some hint of gladness in her astonished face.

She looked beautiful, so damned beautiful. Boone could scarcely breathe. She sat at a rosewood desk amid a sea of white carpet in a room as pink and white and delicate as the petals of a camellia. He was unprepared for the change in her.

To Boone, Elly had always been beautiful, ever since he'd first set eyes on her that snowy night on Randolph Street, with her dark hair and vibrant eyes, and her proud, graceful carriage. She had been eighteen then. Now, now she must be twenty-five—no, twenty-six—and her loveliness was more potent and intoxicating than he could have imagined. Though she was past her girlhood and the first blush of innocent youth, the intervening years had only deepened and intensified her beauty: it was exotic, dramatic, utterly captivating. In her gown of gray-blue faille and satin, trimmed in velvet of the identical shade, she was a vision of tall, slender perfection, her bearing elegant, her delicately chiseled features enchanting, her blue-gray eyes larger, brighter, more intelligent and sensitive than ever before.

"Boone!" she cried in astonished delight. Then she quickly rose from her chair and hurried around the desk to grasp his hands. "Oh, how *good* to see you. It has been so very long!"

He wanted to kiss those smiling, sensuously shaped lips, to clasp her in his arms, and at the same time, he despised his own foolishness. He reminded himself sharply that she didn't know anything of his feelings for her, that she never had, and that she had regarded him as a pleasant, rather distant friend for all these years. Even so, he kissed her hands, holding them tight in his own.

"You look as lovely as ever, Elly. Your success suits you."

"As does your own. I am forever reading about your accomplishments. Your letters never give the full details, since I know you don't care to boast, but the newspapers are full of information on the doings of the titan of iron and steel. Most impressive."

"You're the one who is impressive." He was still holding her hands, but she didn't appear eager to snatch them away. Boone felt a flicker of hope in his chest. "You've built yourself quite a palace. I never guessed you had yearnings to make your mark in the business world."

She smiled ruefully. "If that's what I've done, it's been a mere accident. My only real purpose has been to take care of myself and my family."

"But surely Connor left you well provided for. . . ."

She gently removed her hands from his, letting them fall to her sides. "It's been a long time since we've seen each other,

Boone. And there is a great deal about me—and about
Connor—that you don't know, things you never knew.'' She
shook her head. ''When I think of the last time I saw you, the
night the boardinghouse burned down . . .''

With the words, the memories returned in sudden, haunting
vividness. An image of the house consumed in flames flashed
into her mind, and she felt again the searing heat, smelled the
sickening odor of charred flesh. Pain shadowed her face.

''Don't Elly.'' Without thinking, he cupped her chin between his fingers. He couldn't bear to see her anguish as she
recalled the night that Connor and her mother had died. It was
almost equally unbearable for him. If he hadn't sailed at that
same time for London, these past four years might have been
so different. None of that hellish mess with Penelope would
have happened. ''Don't think about that night. I know what
it must have been like for you. I wish more than anything that
I hadn't left before finding out what had happened, that I
could have stayed and helped you through that time.''

''I managed.'' Elly stepped back from him, pulling herself
together. After all she had been through these past years—the
grueling work sixteen, sometimes eighteen hours a day, the
worries and pressures—it was hard to imagine falling apart in
front of a man who was practically a stranger. Yet she nearly
had as the memories of the fire rushed back. Seeing Boone
again had triggered them. The sight of him was a tremendous
shock. It made her feel quite strange to have him standing
here before her like this, looking so handsome and fit, so
confident and successful. She thought of the first time she
met him, when he had pummeled the drunks on Randolph
Street, a strapping young fellow in a tweed coat and derby
who was quick and handy with his fists . . .

And then her memory jumped ahead to that autumn night
of the fire, when he had stood in the lamplit hallway and for
one absurd moment, through the haze of her influenza, she
had thought he was going to kiss her.

It had all been so dreamlike, so absurd. . . .

''How long will you be in town?'' she asked, moving away
from him, back to the safety of her desk. She had almost
forgotten how tall he was. With his massive shoulders, he
seemed to fill her brightly lit office, and he looked somewhat
amusingly out of place in this feminine setting, amid the silk
settee and the gilt chairs and the French floral wallpaper.

"As long as it takes to complete my business," he answered cryptically. "Will you let me take you to dinner tonight? We have a lot to catch up on, Elly."

"Is your wife here with you?" She hadn't meant to blurt it out that way; it merely happened.

His face froze at her words. His tone was suddenly stiff, formal. "I'm here alone."

Into the silence that followed came Cassandra, bursting across the room like a shooting star. "Mama, Aunt Adelaide won't play checkers with me, and I *want* to play checkers. Please, please tell her she must! Or else you must play with me!" she said, her exquisite little face lighting up with the idea. After one curious glance, she ignored Boone and turned her gaze appealingly up to her mother with the full force of her six-year-old charm.

"Hush, Cassie. That is not a proper way to enter a room." Elly stroked one of her daughter's dusky curls, her tone mild despite the scolding words. "I would like you to meet this gentleman. His name is Mr. Walker and he was a friend of your father's . . . and mine. Boone, this is Cassandra."

Huge sapphire eyes, every bit as brilliant and magnetic as Connor's, lifted to Boone's face. Cassandra, in her ornately embroidered dress of pink taffeta with deep flounces just below her knees, and a wide white satin-ribbon belt tied in an enormous bow at the back, was a breathtaking vision, a miniature, feminine version of Connor's extraordinary good looks. She had Elly's elegant bone structure and thick, lustrous hair, but her eyes, vividly and magnificently blue and commanding, were pure Connor Maguire. Boone dropped to one knee and gravely took her hand.

"How do you do, Cassandra? What a very pretty girl you are!"

"How do you do?" She gave a graceful little curtsy, as Elly seemed to expect, then, after glancing at her mother for approval, rushed on, a kind of desperate urgency lurking in those beautiful eyes, "Did you really know my father?"

"I knew him very well." Boone smiled at her. "He was a fine man." As her face took on a glow of delight, he continued, "He was handsome and very brave and good at all sorts of games. He was liked by everyone he met." He paused as Elly's aunt came into the room, muttering abstractedly. "Good afternoon, Mrs. Coombs," he said, rising.

"Why, it's Boone Walker! For mercy's sake, this is a fine surprise. You must know we're forever reading about your accomplishments in the newspapers! How proud we are to have known you back when you were just getting your start in business. Many's the time I think—and I've told dear Elinore, too—that if only poor Connor had kept his share of that iron foundry, everything might have turned out differently—"

"Aunt Adelaide, please," Elly broke in, with a glance at Cassandra. The girl's eyes had darkened, and her angelic little lips were folded in a severe, straight line as she stared with cold, silent fury at her great-aunt.

"Oh, pardon me. I never should have—" Aunt Adelaide bit her lip, her plump, kindly old face a mass of wrinkled distress. She rattled on, trying to change the course of the conversation to her niece's accomplishments, of which she was so proud. "Well, now, Boone, it's certainly a pleasure to see you again, and I hope you can stay and visit a bit. As you can see, Elly's made quite a success of herself and we're all in her debt, for if she hadn't taken charge after Connor burned the house down around our ears—"

"Aunt Adelaide!"

"Oh, my! I didn't mean . . ."

But it was too late.

"I hate you! You tell lies about my father!"

Cassandra's face was bright red as she ran through the door into the adjoining salon, disappearing in a flash of pink taffeta and a patter of slippered feet.

"Elinore, I'm sorry—my foolish tongue." The old woman looked as though she was going to burst into tears.

Elly stared after Cassie in dismay. "It's all right. I'll go to her." She threw an apologetic glance at Boone. "I'm sorry you had to witness that. Please forgive Cassandra. She's a very sensitive, emotional child—quite easily hurt, especially where Connor is concerned." She moved toward the salon door, torn between concern for Cassie and a reluctance to end her reunion with Boone so abruptly. "I must go to her, but is it possible you can stay for a while? We could have tea."

"Why don't I call for you later and we can have dinner together?"

"That would be lovely."

"Six o'clock, then?"

"Yes, wonderful." She sent him a brief, luminous smile,

then slipped through the paneled door into the large salon beyond, which led to the family's private, specially designed suite of rooms.

"Don't feel bad." Boone walked to where Aunt Adelaide had slumped down on the white satin settee. "You meant no harm. It's obvious the child is high-strung. But Elly will soothe her and it will all be forgotten."

"I try to be patient, heaven knows I try." Adelaide fidgeted with the handkerchief she had pulled from the pocket of her gown. "But I never know what's going to set that little one off. She can be as charming as her father one moment—and you know for a fact he was charming—then, the very next instant, she's stubborn and obstinate and rude. She likes everything her own way. And Elinore lets her have it, more times than not! It's not good for the child!" Suddenly she gasped. "What must you think of me? I've gone on and on in this horrid fashion, all about my own dear relations."

Boone grinned. "I think you're a wise and caring woman, Mrs. Coombs, one who's had a difficult afternoon. Do you suppose you could do me a favor?"

"Certainly! Anything at all!" Adelaide peered up at him with increased liking and respect, thinking at once how handsome and fine and distinguished he looked, exactly like the steel millionaire he was, even though he was the same brawny, sandy-haired boy who had sat with such polite reserve at her table on Wabash Avenue years ago. "What would you like me to do?"

"See that Elly keeps our dinner engagement tonight. Don't let her change her mind at the last moment, or anything like that."

He looked so serious, so intent, and so hopeful that an exciting notion fluttered suddenly in Aunt Adelaide's mind. She nodded. "Sometimes she does do that. Cassie has a habit of clinging to her, of not wanting her to go away even for a few hours."

"From what I hear, Cassandra likes to play checkers."

"Ceaselessly." Adelaide giggled. "Very well. I'll divert her attention with the checkerboard and keep her content as a kitten. Elinore will be able to slip away without so much as a backward glance."

"Thank you."

When Boone returned to suite 402 at precisely six o'clock,

he wore a silk top hat, a black broadcloth evening suit, and carefully polished dress boots. In one hand was an ebony-handled walking stick inlaid with gold, and in the other, a bouquet of tissue-wrapped roses.

He had mentally rehearsed himself for the role of sauve suitor this evening, praying that his professional successes and the bitter years with Penelope had permanently banished his tongue-tied demeanor in the presence of women, but when Elly appeared to greet him in a beaded evening gown of turquoise lampas trimmed with turquoise satin and twilled ivory silk, with ivory gloves and a fur-trimmed cloak of ivory velvet over her arm, his breath caught in his throat.

"You look lovely," he managed at last, as she gazed at him from those misty blue-gray eyes, smiling with warmth across the bouquet he offered her.

"Thank you, Boone." Then, half turning, she said, "Of course you remember Caroline," and he had to force his glance away from her dark, upswept hair threaded with silken ribbons and jeweled combs, away from her delicately chiseled features with their alluring mingling of elegance, poise, and beauty, and focus instead on the petite young woman in a simple dress of dove gray India cashmere who came forward in a diffident but calm manner to greet him.

Caroline Forrest had greatly changed since the last time he'd seen her. Beyond the fact that she had matured from a pitiful, frightened girl into a softly pretty young woman with golden curls worn in a simple chignon, her eyes, her smile, her bearing and manner held an assurance that he had never glimpsed before. When he smiled at her and spoke to her, her glance did not slide away as it had used to do, and there was no furtive panic lurking in her eyes. She was still shy as she spoke to him, but in a pleasant way, far different from the disturbing, constant uneasiness he had once sensed in her, and as he shook her hand, he noticed that her skin was smooth and white, no longer rough and scrubbed sore as it used to be.

He commented on this to Elly as they left the hotel and entered the handsome, polished carriage he had hired for the duration of his stay here.

"Yes, Caroline has undergone quite a change in the past year or so. She is desperately busy helping immigrant families adjust to life in America. She works with a young woman

named Roberta Dixon.'' Staring out the window at the lacy
snowflakes drifting down onto the congested street, she spoke
with pride, tinged by a bit of frustration. ''They run a secondhand shop that doubles as a kind of shelter for unfortunate
people with nowhere else to go. Caroline teaches English to
new arrivals and collects blankets and clothing and food for
the needy. Their latest project includes bringing a doctor into
the area to set up a clinic. She is entirely consumed by the
plight of the needy.''

''Why do I detect a note of disapproval? Surely you haven't
forgotten what it's like for those who are poor and helpless?''

''Of course I haven't!'' A flush of crimson color swept up
Elly's throat and stained her cheeks. She regarded Boone with
simmering indignation. ''I give thousands of dollars to help
the needy. I have aided Caroline in many of her endeavors!
My father was a union man who fought for workers' rights,
and I have always—*always*—believed in that cause!'' She
took a deep, steadying breath and continued more calmly,
''What I don't approve of is her desire to actually move out
of the hotel and make her home above that wretched shop.
I've worked too long and too hard to see my sister consign
herself to a life, day in and day out, surrounded only by
poverty.''

''Is that what she wants to do? Live down there?''

Elly nodded. ''She says she feels like a hypocrite as she
leaves the shop and the terrible suffering in that neighborhood
each night to travel in my private coach to State Street and the
splendor of the hotel, to dine handsomely with all of us, to
sleep in such an elegant and comfortable bed, and then to
return in the morning to her work. She wants to immerse
herself in the grime and poverty of the people she is trying to
help, and there is no need for it, Boone! Living down there,
turning her back on the simplest pleasures of the life I fought
so hard to earn for her, and for what? It will not accomplish
any more for those unfortunate people, her staying there all
day, every day! It is pointless, obstinate, foolish and
ungrateful!''

''Don't you think that is for Caroline to decide?'' he asked
mildly.

He was right and she knew it. Yet it was not easy to
relinquish Caroline to a life from which Elly had struggled for
years to free her.

She sighed and clasped her hands together inside her otter-lined muff. As the buildings and vehicles of the city rushed by, she said quietly, "It is irksome beyond words that things rarely turn out the way we plan them."

"I couldn't agree more."

At his heavy tone, she shifted her gaze to stare at him in surprise. An expression of deep pain marked his face in the moonlit, snowy night. So he had his own private hell, did Boone Walker. It had never occurred to her that he would. So kind and straightforward a man as he was, it had always seemed that everything around him would take its tone from his own basic decency, his calm smile and steady ways. Now, as the carriage clattered through the city streets, harnesses jingling, a multitude of wheels grinding, hooves ringing on the cobblestones, and snow drifting down like a veil of clouds, she felt that she had been wrong. And she wondered, with an odd, unfathomable twisting inside her, if his pain had anything at all to do with his wife.

These past few years, she had managed to put aside her memories of that evening she had spent with him in the hours before the fire. Whatever emotions she had been on the brink of discovering that night could no longer matter, since he had married and begun a new life while she had been consumed by the necessity of rebuilding her own. They had moved irrevocably beyond that fleeting moment, and there was no journeying back. That was why it had been such a shock to see him today. He had appeared so suddenly, and he looked so startlingly, surprisingly handsome with his big, gentle grin and keen gray eyes and the aura of purposefulness with which he had come across the room to clasp her hands. As she sat with him in the carriage, she could no longer deny her attraction to Boone Walker. What had started four years ago on that night of disaster, and what she had held at bay for all this time, was back: it was a tangible, vibrant thing, this unacknowledged bond between them, this force that tugged so urgently now at her heart. She didn't know what to do, for looking at his face, she wanted to reach out and smooth away the pain, to caress him, and she had to keep her hands clenched tight inside the fur-lined muff to stop herself from so rash and revealing an action.

He has a wife, she reminded herself with a tiny indrawn breath. In that instant it occurred to her that this was an enormous mistake, riding with him in this carriage, sharing a dinner alone. It could only lead to her heartache.

"Boone, where are we going?" she asked abruptly, as she became aware that the business and social center of the city was behind them and they were traveling a lonely wooded road beyond the fringes of the metropolis.

"It's a surprise. . . . No, don't look that way, Elly." He laughed, leaning his shoulders back against the cushions. "I'm not abducting you. I'm simply taking you someplace I'll wager you haven't seen before."

"Where?"

"I told you, it's a surprise." He shook his head at her, and she sensed he was enjoying her bafflement. "You've been in charge of too many people for too long," he remarked, his eyes glinting in the faint silver moonlight that shone through the carriage window. "Maybe it's time someone took charge of you for a while."

"Is this how you 'take charge' of your wife?" she demanded without thinking, then noticed the bitter scowl that skittered across his features.

"I'm sorry, I don't know why I said that," she rushed on, mortified that she had caused him discomfort once again, though not really understanding why. His next words took her completely by surprise.

"I no longer have a wife," said Boone.

Snow whirled past the window, and the horses' gait quickened. From somewhere beyond the darkened woods came the hoot of an owl, followed from a great distance by the mournful whistle of an unseen train. She said nothing, but waited for him to go on.

🌿 Twenty-Two

"WE WERE DIVORCED last month." Boone's gaze appeared fixed upon the naked winter trees rolling by outside the carriage window. "In truth, our marriage only lasted a few months. In every real sense, it's been over for several years."

"I'm so sorry."

"Don't be." His lips tightened. "Marrying Penelope was the biggest mistake of my life—no, *one* of the biggest mistakes," he amended with a rueful laugh. "I've made more than my share."

"Haven't we all?" she murmured, thinking of Connor, of how she had rushed into marriage with him. She had looked to him for something he couldn't give her, expected him to be something he was not. And lived to regret her young, foolish fancy.

"If the truth be told, Elly, I married Penelope for the wrong reasons. You see, I couldn't have the woman I loved, but I wanted a wife and a family. So I settled on Penelope, who I thought was an ideal choice for that sort of arrangement. I couldn't have been more wrong."

Elly's blood had started to pulse in her temples when he spoke of not being able to have the woman he loved. Half-forgotten words of Connor's about Boone wanting *her* echoed in Elly's ears. Glances and words from that long-ago evening with Boone surfaced once again. She fastened her gaze on his strong, rugged face as he spoke, listening with almost breathless intensity.

"I didn't know Penelope nearly as well as I thought I did." Again that harsh, self-mocking laugh, so unlike the Boone she remembered. He had been hurt over these past years, she thought, hurt very badly. A sharp sadness pierced her.

"I hope you won't think me ungallant and overly bitter if I tell you that she was a lying, manipulative tramp. Penelope was never faithful to me, at least not after the first few months. She was grateful to me at first, in her fashion, for her father was drowning in debt when we married, and I was the one to fish him out. But her gratitude didn't last long, and it didn't preclude her wanting to live in New York at a time when I had to be in Pittsburgh or, more to the point, sleeping with the coachman or the groom or whatever visiting viscount happened to be in town during a particular week."

Elly went cold inside. She slipped a hand from the muff to touch his sleeve. "Boone, how awful. I'm so sorry," she whispered, anguished at the thought of his humiliation and pain. A haunted anger lingered on his face as he turned to her, but slowly, as she gazed at him, it faded, and he smiled with all the old gentleness she remembered.

"I'm surprised you didn't know already. I tried to keep it quiet, but the newspapers did manage to dig up some of the uglier details."

"I never read a word about anything like that."

"Well, none of it matters anymore. And I didn't mean to burden you with all this, Elly. Lord knows you've had enough troubles of your own. I only wanted you to know that my divorce is now official. I am no longer a married man."

She wondered with a sudden breathlessness why he felt this was so important for her to know. Before she could ask him, the coach drew into the snow-carpeted yard of an inn set near the edge of the road. A red and white painted sign reading "Rodgers Inn" stood out plainly against the pale gray shingles.

"It's charming," Elly murmured, as he helped her alight. "But I wish I'd known . . ." Her voice trailed off as she glanced down at her elaborately formal toilette, which seemed out of place in this rustic setting.

Boone grinned. "That would have spoiled the fun."

He guided her up the wide porch steps and into the hall.

"I heard about this place from a friend who owns a farm-machinery plant south of Chicago. It only *seems* that we're in the middle of the prairie, Elly. Actually, there's an Illinois Central depot not far from here, and Walker and Whitcomb owns a quarry nearby. Illinois is a good state for steel. As a matter of fact, I'm planning to take over the Chicago branch office so we can develop the full potential of this area. By the time I'm finished, we'll have a steel works out here equal to the Monongahela plant. Anyway, my friend told me the food here at the Rodgers Inn is grand and the atmosphere is completely relaxing and private. I thought you might like a change of pace from the bustle of the hotel and the Chicago social scene.''

Yes, Elly thought, enchanted by the large, low-ceilinged room through which the innkeeper led them, it was a delightful change of pace. She had expected to spend the evening in some opulent restaurant crowded with well-to-do Chicagoans. It was a pleasant and soothing surprise to find herself in this homey, shingled inn, with a fire crackling and snow drifting by the windows and the smell of fresh-baked bread and cinnamon-apple pies drifting in from the kitchen. Their table was situated near the open stone hearth. Only a few other tables were occupied, and this was by simply garbed travelers who, after staring for a few startled moments, swiftly lost interest in the lavishly attired newcomers.

Elly was touched by Boone's thoughtfulness. It was a perceptive man who understood and respected the strain under which she operated every day, consumed by the struggles to keep afloat in the business world. Perhaps he understood so well because he faced the same unceasing pressures and demands. Boone had given her a true respite from the tumult of the business world and the frantic pace of her city life. She felt a thousand miles from Chicago, from her worries about the upkeep of the hotel, about Caroline and Cassandra. She smiled at him as she lifted her glass of wine and took a sip.

''I can't imagine anything more delightful,'' she said softly, meeting his gaze.

Slowly. Go slowly, Boone warned himself, nearly undone by the warm, artless sensuality of her smile. It was an effort to keep from blurting out his feelings for her, like some kind of blithering schoolboy, making an ass out of himself, and ruining whatever chances of success with her he possessed. It was too bad, he thought over a dinner of wild duck in black currant sauce, that a woman's love couldn't be acquired as easily as a mine or a building. In business he never had any trouble going after what he wanted; in his personal life, he had squandered chances time and again. But now at last he had his divorce from Penelope, and Elly was free and appeared genuinely glad to be in his company—at least for tonight.

He reminded himself that in business, a steady, single-minded advance toward a goal, knocking obstacles aside one by one in a purposeful, deliberate way, usually achieved the best result. As they sipped their after-dinner coffee, he decided it was time to proceed.

"You and your aunt both said some things that puzzled me today." He watched the way Elly's eyes widened slightly over the rim of her cup.

"What sort of things?"

"About Connor."

"Oh." Elly set the cup carefully in her saucer and studied the leftover remnants of her apple pie. "What happened with Connor is a long and not very pleasant story."

The past was an obstacle, a murky barrier between them. Boone knew he had to conquer it in order to move ahead.

"I'd like to hear it," he insisted.

She didn't answer immediately.

It had been four years since Connor died. And even though their life together had not been a happy one toward the end, she still owed him something. Didn't she? Some loyalty, some respect? He had made it very clear on the eve of his death that he didn't want Boone to know of his failure or of their financial problems. Didn't she owe it to him to continue the charade, to leave Boone's memories of his friend intact, as Connor would have wished? Then something inside her rebelled. *No.* She owed it to herself to tell the truth, to let Boone know that she had not been left a wealthy woman who had, on a whim, decided to build a grand hotel, that she had worked all these years to keep her family sheltered, fed, and safe, and that the hotel was not a toy to her but her crowning achievement, her refuge, and her continual challenge. Never again would she relinquish her fate to a man's control, never would she slacken in her determination to keep the Forrest a brilliant success. It was hers. She had conceived it, built it, and invested her heart and soul in it. If ever there was to be anything more between her and Boone but friendship—and she was beginning to wish more and more that there would be—he must understand her dedication to the Forrest and her need to be in command of her own fate, to possess her own self-earned fortune. Only by knowing what had happened in the past could he comprehend how she must conduct her future.

So she told him. She was careful not to condemn Connor and not to paint a picture colored by bitterness. Connor had been a well-intentioned man, and she had loved him once, as he had loved her, though their marriage had not prospered. Elly had come to grips with her grief and resentment a long time ago; now she simply told Boone the plain, unvarnished truth: things had not gone well for Connor; his tendency toward drink and gambling had increased in proportion to his business problems and, in the end, had destroyed the happiness of their marriage and, indeed, Connor's very life.

"And yours," Boone muttered heavily when she was done. "I should have known. That night, when he left the table and didn't come back, I should have known."

"That would have been impossible. You had no way of guessing—he was adamant that you not suspect the Gem was failing," she asserted, shaking her head.

"To think that I sailed the next morning, leaving you in such a hellish mess!" He leaned back in his chair, his gray eyes dark with self-condemnation and regret. "Then I entangled myself with Penelope . . . and you never even let on in your letters that you were left without a penny. I could have helped you, Elly. You should have let me help you."

"Why should you have?"

He stared at her in sudden anger, almost ready to blurt out the truth: because he loved her; had always loved her, and wanted to keep her from harm, just as she wanted to keep her family from harm. But just in time, he stopped himself from so disastrously blunt an admission, saying instead, "Because Connor was my friend, and so were you. I care about you."

"Oh." Disappointment stung her, like tiny, stabbing darts. What had she expected? she asked herself angrily. A confession of love, of undying devotion? Boone was a friend, nothing more. Anything else she might have imagined or hoped for was sheer fancy on her part. Wasn't it?

Looking at him across the table, his sandy hair gleaming in the firelight, his strong, bronzed face watching her with that sharp, careful glance, she couldn't be sure. She suddenly remembered a poem her mother had liked to read aloud on the porch on summer nights when Elly was a girl and knew of no other place in the world but Emmettville. The words were those of Samuel Coleridge: "In many ways doth the full heart reveal The presence of the love it would conceal."

Boone had shown no sign of loving her. Caring about her, yes. Feeling concern for her well-being, yes. Even harboring affection for her, yes. But not love.

"There is no point in mourning over what is past," she said slowly, drawing a deep breath to steady herself. "Everything has turned out fine. My daughter is safe and need never fear being hungry and cold. My sister has found her own peace; she is happy and useful. And Timothy, you know, is working as a copyboy at the *Tribune*. I wanted him to resume his studies once the hotel was financed and under way, but he decided that he would rather be a reporter and began an apprenticeship at the newspaper. He always was inquisitive about everything, so in a way it was only natural for him to choose a profession where he has an excuse to poke his nose in anywhere he pleases." She laughed, trying to lighten the mood that had settled over the table.

"And what about you?" Boone inquired in that deceptively relaxed drawl of his. "Are you as happy as they?"

"Perfectly. Now that our futures are secure—at least as secure as anything can be in this world."

She had the impression he wanted her to say something more. When she didn't, he nodded and signaled to their waiter. Elly understood that both the meal and the discussion were over.

In the carriage as they traveled back toward the city, a silence fell between them. She was uncertain why. The night was crystal clear and lovely, with a canopy of new snow covering the tree branches and the winter landscape, and the air brisk and cool as icy spring water. Yet a grayness lay between them, caused by unspoken words and feelings both were wary to unleash.

Suddenly, as the horses drew the carriage over a series of ruts in the road, Elly was thrown forward and would have fallen had Boone not caught her. He eased her down on the seat beside him, his hands lingering at her waist.

She raised her head and looked at him. Her heart began to thud under the intensity of his stare, for his eyes pierced her in the darkness of the carriage, like relentless arrows, searching, searching . . .

For what was he searching, she wondered dimly? The answer came from somewhere deep within her—perhaps for a sign. A sign of love concealed. A sign of a full and yearning heart. A tingling thrill shot through her where his hands touched her waist. Beneath the turquoise lampas gown her skin seemed to ache for his touch. Slowly, while her heart trembled, she lifted her hand to his lean cheek and tenderly caressed his jaw.

She heard his swiftly indrawn breath, then felt the tightening of his hands at her waist. Almost roughly, he pulled her to him until she was held against him, their faces only inches apart.

"Elly," he breathed, and she was stunned by the pain and desire and longing in the single word. "I'm going to kiss you now, so if you have any objections, you'd better speak up."

"I have no objections," she whispered, and barely had the words left her mouth before he *was* kissing her, his lips warm and strong upon her own, his hands clamping her to him as though they were welded together. She felt herself drowning in that kiss, in the sheer joyful surge of love that rose up like a tide to engulf them.

"How I've loved you." Boone's voice was hoarse in her ear. "For years, Elly, for years I have loved you."

"I never knew. I thought you were only my friend—Connor's friend." She clung to him, her blue-gray eyes shining with tears. "Ever since that night when you brought me home from Amberson's Palace, I have felt something for you . . . something I could not—would not—let myself think about. But now . . . Oh, Boone. Oh, my love."

He was kissing her again, kissing her with great tenderness. She gave herself up to the exquisite happiness of being in his arms, of knowing she was loved, as the carriage rolled back toward the lights of the city and the snow drifted down like lacy bits of fluff.

In the faint glow of the lamp, Boone's burgundy and gold suite shone with a rich jeweled color that seemed to envelop them in a burnished warmth. Outside, the world was cold and white, but here, with Boone before her, so handsome and strong and vibrantly tender, she was in a world of their own making, a warm, seductive world complete with only the two of them. He stood before her in his evening clothes, his fair hair gleaming. As he gazed down at her, desire and concern mingling on his face, she wrapped her arms around his neck and gently pulled his head nearer. Softly, she kissed him on the lips to reassure him that she was exactly where she wanted to be.

"Elly, are you sure?" he asked a moment later, and she nodded, her blue-gray eyes smoldering with the desire that surged through her. She loved him; she wanted to be with him tonight. She felt no shyness, no false modesty. She had, after all, been married, and she knew well the pleasures of sexual intimacy, and yet, it all seemed new somehow—exciting in a deep and wild way, the thought of making love with Boone, this man who was so strong, so fine and caring and generous, who exuded an easy power, a sense of being in command of his own destiny. Her love for him was so strong, so sure, that she wanted to give herself to him fully and to know the intensity of his passion for her. She ached for him, and this time, when he pressed his warm and hungry mouth to hers, she responded so ardently that he tightened his grip on her waist and held her to him, their bodies fusing with a burst of passion as searing as flame.

"Oh, Elly, I love you so," he groaned, and his gray eyes glinted with a fierce, yet tender light that made her quiver beneath his gaze. His fingers began unfastening the pearl buttons of her beaded gown, all twenty-two of them, and all the while their kisses deepened and their hearts pounded as one. He undressed her completely, tossing aside at last her lace-edged chemise and silken stockings, until she was naked and lovely before him. Then, one by one, he removed the pins from her hair. The thick midnight curls tumbled down like a black velvet curtain across her shoulders and back and dangled provocatively over her rose-tipped breasts. She was trembling, her white body luminous and lush and perfect as he surveyed her.

"Lord, you're beautiful. So damned beautiful," he whispered.

Then he carried her to his bed.

Elly's heartbeat thudded wildly as his jacket and then his vest fell to the floor, and she slid her fingers between the buttons of his shirt. He was so splendid, so strong, with his broad, muscled chest and hard, flat belly, his powerful thighs and warm, knowing hands. When he, too, was naked, she pulled him down to her, reveling in the feel of him, in the burning touch of his lips against hers, his flesh against hers. She felt driven, caught up in an urgency that increased furiously by the moment.

"I love you, Boone. I need you so. Oh, Boone," she moaned as he kissed her breasts, the hollow of her throat, her face, the curve of her ear . . . and at last, again, her mouth, as he lowered himself over her and entered her feminine softness in a smooth, sure motion that made her clutch him to her with joy.

The night spun away as they merged together, joined in an ecstasy that built to a blinding crescendo and exploded at last in a waterfall of crystal light and color and sensation. It was so beautiful, so exquisitely a union of love and physical yearning, that it left them exhausted, yet filled with a transcendent happiness and a rare peace.

"I've waited a long time for this," Boone said at last, shifting so that he could gaze down at her as she lay entwined in his arms, her lovely, small-boned face still flushed and pink after their lovemaking.

"I hope it was worth the wait," she answered with the slow, sweepingly sensuous smile that never failed to make him catch his breath.

"You know the answer to that," he chuckled, and gathered her to him again. They held each other and loved each other until night fled the sky and dawn's pearly aura gleamed down upon the sleeping city, bathing it in a cool, pale glow.

Peace, thought Elly, as she drifted into sleep at last, her head on Boone's chest. The world was full of lovely, perfect peace. . .

The ballroom on the top floor of the Forrest Hotel glittered like a fairyland. Crystal chandeliers spun their golden light down on the gorgeously attired couples waltzing to the strains of Johann Strauss's "The Blue Danube." Four hundred guests dined and danced and toasted Elly and Boone on the occasion of their wedding. It was exactly two months since their dinner at the Rodgers Inn and the night they spent together in Boone's suite.

In her lace-trained ball gown of magnolia satin, with a spray of variegated roses on one shoulder and a garland of roses in her dark upswept hair, Elly whirled and whirled in Boone's arms. Her head was light, but not only with the champagne she had drunk. She was heady with happiness.

Olive Meeks approached the couple after the waltz had ended and warned her that too much happiness was a bad thing; it made one forgetful of the true, unpredictable nature of all life, but Elly only squeezed her arm affectionately and said she was very glad Olive had come. Sean Fitzgerald was there, and General Willis and Roberta Dixon, and Marya with her new husband; so were the Whitcombs from Pittsburgh and many members of Chicago's wealthiest and most important families, among them Mayor Carter Henry Harrison. Mayor Harrison, like Boone, was a native Kentuckian, and the two had taken an immediate liking to each other when they first met. Elly, glancing around the dazzling ballroom at the array of splendidly gowned women and dashingly attired men, was amazed to realize that she was acquainted with nearly all of these four hundred people. Some she had met at the hotel, and Boone had introduced her to the rest. It seemed not so long ago that she had arrived at the Illinois Central depot with her family in tow, a few suitcases filled with possessions, and a scrap of paper bearing Aunt Adelaide's Wabash Avenue address.

Clay and Lula Mae Walker, along with Hetta and their little son, Jeb, had also come to town for the wedding. It was the first time they had ventured beyond the boundaries of Kentucky, and Boone had told Elly privately that he considered it real proof of the reconciliation between him and his brother. At first overwhelmed by the roar and clamor of Chicago, with its massive buildings, traffic-snarled streets, its grain elevators, stockyards, factories, and railroads, Clay and his family had soon become fascinated by the number and variety of tall-masted ships, barges, and canal boats in the muddy black Chicago River and by the Exposition Building on Michigan Boulevard, where industrial shows, concerts, and conventions were held. Comfortably ensconced in a suite of rooms in the Forrest, setting forth on shopping expeditions to glittering department stores with Elly, and dining on exotic delicacies like oysters and champagne, Clay and his family had soon found themselves enjoying the novelty of the tumultuous city, and the wedding banquet was the culmination of all that had come before.

Of all of Elly's family, only Cassie was not altogether happy with the proceedings. She was jealous of her mother's love for Boone and inwardly fearful that this big, smiling man with the funny twang in his voice would replace her in Elly's affections. Yet she sulked and resisted when Adelaide, who had let her peek in on the festivities, told her that it was time for her to go to bed, and Elly had to promise to slip away and kiss her good night within the half-hour.

All in all, though, it was a splendid occasion. It was written up in all the country's major newspapers, for Boone Walker was one of the titans of the business world, and Elinore Maguire was a noteworthy woman in her own right. Their marriage stirred the public's fancy.

A few days after the wedding, in Denver, Colorado, a slight, grizzled man finished sweeping out the Hawkins Livery Stable and took himself off to the Gold Bar Saloon. He ordered a whiskey, drank it alone in a corner of the room, and called for another. His shrewd small eyes watched the men who were playing cards, the ones who stood at the bar, the ones who went upstairs with the tawdrily dressed girls who worked in and above the saloon. Then his gaze fell upon the newspaper some miner had left on the table beside him. He thumbed through it absently, sipping at his third drink. A boldface headline caught his eye: "Steel Tycoon Walker Weds Again." He lifted the paper close to his face and began to read, his gaze flying over the printed words until his vision blurred.

"Thet's him! Doggone it to hell, if thet ain't him!"

He smacked his fist on the table, spilling the glass of whiskey, but he didn't even notice. A mist of malicious pleasure descended over his tiny, squinting eyes, and he folded the paper into a neat square before tucking it under his arm.

"Ain't this jest somethin'," he muttered under his breath as he headed out of the saloon. "Wait'll I tell Rose. We're gonna git the chance to repay ol' Boone, after all."

He chuckled softly to himself as he stomped along the wooden boardwalk. "Boone, boy, don't you try to hide on me now. Ol' Ezra is comin'. Yes, sirree, boy. I'm a comin'."

🌿 Twenty-Three

IN A MOVE that had astonished his friends and associates, Potter Palmer in 1882 hired the architects Henry Ives Cobb and Charles S. Frost to build him a mansion on a most unlikely site—two miles north of the Chicago River, in an area of marshy wilderness and frog ponds. The millionaires of Chicago had been aghast. Until then, the South Side had been considered the grandest section of town, with Prairie and Michigan avenues reigning supreme among all the fashionable streets of the city. They were baffled and skeptical of Palmer's decision not only to move north but to invest in an entire section of land in such an unpromising vicinity. Yet with characteristic determination and confidence in his own instincts, Palmer had purchased a large portion of land from the city and had proceeded to fill its swamps with sand from the lake bottom. He confided to Boone his belief that this area would ultimately replace the South Side as the most splendid and sought-after real estate in the city. After hearing his friend's views, Boone had found himself in agreement. It was true, he had realized, that the Illinois Central railroad tracks passed too close to the South Side streets, and the noise and soot were ceaseless and annoying. He immediately saw the reason behind Palmer's actions and decided to follow his lead. Thus he became one of the first to purchase land in the new Lake Shore Drive development, commissioning architects and studying plans with keen-eyed enthusiasm.

The only problem was that it would take several years to complete the house as he wanted it, and Boone didn't wish to wait that long to move his family out of the hotel. Elly became pregnant only months after the wedding, and he was

determined that his child would be born in a home and not a
suite of rooms inside the Forrest Hotel.

So, in early summer of 1882, the Walkers moved into a
three-story brownstone on Prairie Avenue that Boone had
bought for the short term, intending to sell it when the Lake
Shore Drive mansion was completed. Elly thought he was
being ridiculously extravagant to invest in such a magnificent
house for such a short period of time, yet she could not really
argue with his motives. She, too, wanted her baby born in a
home. And the Forrest, as beautiful and luxurious as it was,
did not constitute a real home, a place of privacy and comfort
where they could all escape the pressures of the outside
world. It would be good for Cassandra, too, thought Elly, on
the first day in the new house, when she walked through the
domed oakwood entry hall with its elaborately carved wood-
work and stained-glass windows. She passed through a series
of spacious drawing rooms and parlors, then climbed the
stairs to the bedrooms and family sitting rooms. Cassandra
needed a house to surround her, with gardens to play in and
trees to sit under, and maybe even a dog to chase. Most of
all, she needed quiet family meals and evenings spent in the
parlor, reading and sewing and playing games. Unconsciously,
Elly wanted to repeat the pattern of her own childhood. Though
they had been poor, the Forrests had been a close-knit and happy
family. Now that she and Boone were together, they could give
Cassandra and the new baby the same kind of loving home
and happy memories, though on a far more luxurious scale.

The baby was born on the fifth of February after a brief and
not overly difficult labor. He was a big, healthy boy with a
bald pink head and clear, pale eyes, and they named him
Adam. Within a week, he had everyone around him thoroughly enthralled. Even Cassandra, who was showing a distinct reluctance to accept Boone as a substitute father, fell in
love with the tiny gurgling infant in the blue and yellow
nursery across the hall from her room.

One clear Saturday morning when Adam was three weeks
old, Cassandra was busy with her dollhouse and its miniature
furniture in the corner of her pink and white room, when she
heard voices in the hall. She went to the door and peered out,
just as Elly and a slight, frail-looking young woman in a gray
wool dress and apron reached the nursery door.

"Cassandra," Elly said with a smile, "this is Miss Rosalie Webb. She is to be Adam's new nurse. You must do everything you can to help her, darling."

She turned back to the brown-haired young woman. "Cassie knows better than any of us how to stop Adam from crying and what songs he likes sung to him as he falls asleep. She is a devoted sister." Elly then said to Cassie, "Why don't you come along with us to the nursery and help me to show Miss Webb about?"

Cassie studied Miss Webb with a critical eye as she followed her down the hall. Mousy, Cassandra decided, flipping one of her own glossy black curls over her shoulder. In her frilly lilac dress, with its satin overskirt and velvet sash, she felt herself far superior to the plain and freckled Miss Webb, with her small, pointed face and limpid brown eyes, and her knot of nondescript brown hair piled at the nape of her thin neck. Mrs. Woodward, Adam's old nurse, had been plump and cheerful, and far more interesting and pleasant, Cassandra decided. If only she hadn't been so badly hurt in that freight wagon accident last week. Mama said she would be unable to continue her duties. Cassandra knew she would miss her quick chatter and big, loud laugh. Mama had too hastily replaced her, Cassie decided with a sullen set to her lips. If Mama had only waited, certainly she could have done better than this dull creature.

Yet her expression changed the moment she saw her little brother in his crib. Adam was such a delight, so sweet and soft and fresh-smelling. She watched warily as Miss Webb reached down and picked the baby up, holding him carefully in her arms. Well, at least she seemed to know how to hold him—that was something to be thankful for!

"Miss Webb used to care for twins of a family in Colorado, until she came back here to live with her father. I'm sure if she can handle two babies, our little Adam should prove not too difficult for her," Elly remarked, giving her daughter's shoulders a squeeze.

Adam peered into Miss Webb's thin, pale face and made an expression that might have been a smile.

"He likes to be rocked," Cassandra offered, deciding it couldn't hurt to make a friendly overture. After all, Mama had already hired this nurse, and there was no hope of Mrs. Woodward coming back.

"Oh. Like this?" The new nurse spoke softly, almost mumbling. Cassie could barely hear her, but she thought there was something familiar in the girl's faint drawl.

"Are you from Kentucky, too?" Cassie demanded immediately. "Do you know my . . ." She paused, refusing to say "stepfather," for it contained the word "father," and she would not call Boone by that name, not ever. "My uncle Boone?" she finished, flushing as her mother's gaze came to rest upon her.

"No, of course Miss Webb doesn't know Uncle Boone," Mama answered, with a smile that implied Cassie was being silly. "She is from North Carolina, and I imagine her accent has remained with her from her childhood. But she has been living out west in Colorado for many years now, and I'm sure she'll be able to tell you and Adam some very interesting stories. But now," she finished briskly, stooping and gathering Cassie to her, "I must leave for the hotel. It's going to be a busy day. You mind Miss Webb and Aunt Adelaide, my darling, and I'll see you tonight at the dinner table." She kissed Cassie's cheek, straightened, and brushed a kiss on Adam's little head. "Miss Webb, should you have any questions or need any assistance, please consult with my aunt, Mrs. Coombs, or with Jeweline, who has been with my family for many years. They'll be glad to help you get used to our routine."

With a rustle of her velvet skirts, she was gone, and Cassie stared up at the silent young woman holding Adam in her arms.

"My mother is very beautiful, isn't she?" she said proudly. The new nurse bobbed her head.

"She's nice, too, the nicest mother in the world, and the smartest." Cassie hesitated a moment and then went on, "My father was the handsomest man in the world, too, before he died. He was much handsomer than Uncle Boone. Uncle Boone is not handsome. And he is not nice, either. You're lucky you're from North Carolina and don't know him."

To Cassie's delight, the girl looked frightened. "Is he really so bad?" she asked, with an anxious blink of her eyes.

Cassandra nodded vigorously, encouraged by the quaver in the nurse's voice and the sudden brightness in her gaze at the mention of Boone's name. Adam began to cry at that moment, though, and Miss Webb hastily carried him to the

yellow-cushioned rocker in the corner by the window, her
feet moving silently over the thick blue and yellow Brussels
carpet. Sitting down with the baby, she removed a bottle of
milk from the pocket of her apron and began to feed him
while Cassandra perched at her elbow and chattered with a
new sense of self-importance.

"Uncle Boone is *mean*." She spoke the words dramatically, with the full force of her almost-eight-year-old wisdom.
"He is horrid! He orders me about and looks at me in a way
that is meant to frighten me, but I am not frightened. I am
very brave, like my father," she told the nurse with a proud
smile. Then she pursed her lips. "I promise you, you won't
like him a bit. And you must be careful, because if you do
one tiny thing wrong where Adam is concerned, Uncle Boone
will shout at you and become so angry you will shake in your
boots. I don't think you're brave like me," she concluded
with a pitying note in her voice.

"No, no, I'm not," Miss Webb said breathlessly. Her
cheeks had grown even paler than usual while Cassie had
been talking. "But . . . I'll be sure to do everything right—
and to . . . to stay out of his way." Taking a deep breath, she
placed Adam against her shoulder and rubbed his back with
fingers that trembled. "I'm sorry you're so unhappy," she
said in her soft, slightly drawling voice. For a moment, her
gaze flitted about the charming nursery with its gay floral
wallpaper and toy clowns and trains, its bright wicker furniture and soft blue satin draperies. "This seems like such a
good place to live, but it can't be if your stepfather is so
cruel," she murmured. "And this poor little baby. Will Mr.
Walker be cruel to him, too?"

Cassie gazed down at Adam's soft, round face for a moment. "No, I don't think so. Adam is his true son, but I am
not really his daughter, so . . ." She shrugged and glanced
out the nursery window at the rows of fine homes, at the
bright clear winter sky, at the polished phaetons and landaus
rattling up and down the street. "But I don't know for
certain. Uncle Boone can be very stern. I *hope* he is not cruel
to Adam."

Suddenly she lost interest in the conversation and in the
new nurse. This afternoon she was to have a dancing lesson
and then a music lesson, and she wanted first to finish playing
with her dolls. She left the nursery with a quickly mumbled

good-day and returned to her own room, leaving the new nurse to rock little Adam in peace.

But the thin, brown-haired young woman was feeling far from peaceful. "Poor little girl," she whispered to herself over and over as the rhythmic movement of the chair lulled the baby in her arms into a state of drowsy contentment. "Pa is right. It will be a blessing to take her away from here, to take them both away." She stroked the infant's arm with a small, tender hand. "He is a monster," she told herself, fear knotting her stomach as she thought about Boone Walker. If he should discover her, recognize her . . . Terror burst through her at the thought. But no. She would be careful. It would only be a few days, until she had an opportunity, a chance to take both children away. Until then, she would stay out of his way and try not to arouse his interest or attention.

Pa would be very proud of her when this was over, she thought, especially since she'd been so fearful about doing it at all. He would be happy because of all the money they would collect from Boone and because at last they would be getting their revenge.

"How is the new nurse working out?" Boone addressed Elly as she lay in his arms, half dreaming.

Morning light shone through the amber draperies, bathing the room in a warm glow that mirrored Elly's mood. Still tingling and satisfied from Boone's lovemaking a brief half-hour ago, she murmured, "Fine, so far," and snuggled against his chest.

Boone chuckled. His fingers drifted through the satiny cloud of her hair. Her fresh, feminine scent filled his nostrils as she lay across him on their bed.

"What did you say her name was?"

"Miss Webb. Rosalie Webb."

"Too bad about Mrs. Woodward. Even Cassandra was fond of her."

"Yes, I know. But I'm sure Miss Webb will be a good replacement. Her references from the Healey family in Colorado were excellent." She smoothed her hand across Boone's broad chest, tugging lightly at the thick, sandy chest hairs.

"There is something else I need to talk to you about. Tomorrow night Caroline is bringing a guest to dinner. A young man."

Surprised, Boone lifted his head, staring at her. "That's good news. Who is he?"

"The young doctor Roberta persuaded to join Dr. Petersham in the Rat's Tail practice. Heaven knows, that neighborhood can use all the medical attention it can get. I'm glad this young man—his name is Gilbert Reeves, by the way—is venturing down there to help. He must be a very special person. This is the first time Caroline has shown an interest in a young man since . . ."

"Since she was raped," Boone finished for her gently.

"Yes, since then."

Boone had heard about the incident, though not all the details. He now knew enough to understand his sister-in-law's fearful behavior when he first met Elly. "Let's hope she's finally getting over it. It would be a good thing if she could start trusting a man, if she could let herself be loved."

"Yes," Elly sighed. A slight quiver ran through her. Her fingertips, her breasts, her whole body felt sensitive again to her husband's muscular form beneath her. She loved him so. Their bedroom was warm with the pool of winter sunlight spreading slowly across the gleaming oak floor, and the shadows cast by the rustling branches of the elm tree outside the window flickered in the early morning light. She felt an ache growing inside her. She wanted him again, wanted to lose herself in the warmth of his arms and the strength of his love. Slowly, she pressed a kiss to his chest and let her mouth rove upward until she reached his lips. "I wish she could know the kind of happiness we have found," she whispered, her breath catching in her throat as he gathered her to him, rolled over, and covered her body with his own. Then they were lost once more in a sea of pleasure, giving themselves up to the warm, crashing waves.

❧ Twenty-Four

"I HAVE A surprise planned for you today," Boone told Cassie at the breakfast table as Elly poured his coffee. "A winter adventure—an outing."

"What sort of an outing?" With great effort, she tried to hide her excitement.

Boone and Elly exchanged smiles. It was only the three of them at the table this morning. Aunt Adelaide was in bed with a cold and had taken a tray in her room, and Timothy had grabbed a hasty breakfast earlier and then gone off to attend church services with the family of his latest conquest, Miss Katharine Hall. In the past year, Timothy had suddenly erupted into quite a ladies' man: he was invited to so many card parties and balls that Elly wondered how he found the time to do his newspaper work. Yet he did manage, often staying up until two o'clock in the morning scribbling his stories, then appearing scrubbed, fresh, and energetic first thing in the morning with no apparent effort. He had a combination of good manners, natural charm, and an inquisitive, friendly nature, which, combined with his engaging good looks, proved irresistible to a great number of young women. Boone and Elly were accustomed to his frequent absences from their table, but often wondered to each other how long he could keep up his frantic and altogether whirlwind pace.

"A sleigh ride out into the country," Boone answered Cassie with a barely perceptible pause. "We'll have hot cocoa and sandwiches and cakes at a little inn I know, where they also happen to feature a puppet show. It's very lively and fun, I understand." He waited to see the sparkle enter her eyes; it did, but she managed to stifle it quickly, and glanced down at her heaping plate.

"Do you think you'd enjoy that?" Boone asked, as she nibbled a slice of toast with marmalade.

"I suppose so. Are you going, too?"

"Yes."

He controlled his disappointment at the crestfallen look on her face.

Elly said quickly, and with a touch of asperity in her voice, "Uncle Boone went to a great deal of trouble to plan this outing for us today, Cassie. I think it sounds wonderful."

"Is Adam coming?" Cassie asked hopefully.

"No, Aunt Adelaide will watch him, since this is Miss Webb's day off. Adam is too little to go on a sleigh ride. He'd much rather take a nap in his own snug bed."

"Very well. Then I guess it will be just the three of us," Cassie said, so resignedly that Boone had to laugh. Elly was looking upset at her daughter's failure to show proper appreciation, but he silently signaled her not to worry. He recognized that Cassie still had not accepted him fully; he knew it would take time. He was determined to be patient with her. He still remembered how he had resented Ezra as a boy and how he and Clay and Tom and Henry had refused to call Ezra "Pa." Now, looking back, he could see how the Walker boys' allegiance to their father must have chafed at Ezra like a burr under the saddle. But, he reflected, his gray eyes narrowing at the memories, it still was no excuse. No excuse for Ezra's drowning himself in Kentucky whiskey, for beating Ma, for letting himself become an ornery, vicious, resentful man.

Boone recalled himself to the present, his glance lingering a moment on his own beautiful and strong-willed stepdaughter. He hoped Cassie would accept him one day, maybe even come to love him. He wanted to love her and care for her as his own daughter. She was Elly's child, after all, and Connor's. Yet he recognized that he couldn't bribe her into feeling affection for him, nor could he force her to do so. Maybe as time passed she'd stop being so jealous of his relationship with Elly. Until then, Boone told himself—while Elly and Cassandra chattered about what to wear on the sleigh ride, and which mittens and muffs and hats to bring—until then, he had Adam. His son. Boone had never known it would feel so grand to have a son, a little person all his own whose future he could shape and mold, whose life would continue the line of Walker men.

He thought about Adam a great deal whenever he was conducting business in Chicago or Pittsburgh or New York, because he was sharply aware that every ton of steel sold, every railroad share purchased, every limestone quarry added to his company's ownership was another means of building not only his own future but that of his son as well. Though it seemed absurd, and Elly laughed at him when he did it, Boone sometimes held Adam, rocked him, and talked to him about the deals he was involved in or the people he had met or the latest production figures in the farm-machinery market. Even after the sleigh ride, which proved delightful and entertaining for everyone involved, he found himself so eager to see his son on his return that he bounded up the steps to the nursery two at a time and strode into Adam's room, forgetting to be quiet. His heavy footsteps roused the baby immediately from his nap.

"Look what you've done," Elly accused, hurrying into the room behind him as Adam started to cry. Aunt Adelaide, who had dozed off in the rocker with a handkerchief in her hand, jumped, too.

"No, let me take him," Boone said as Elly started to reach into the crib for the wailing boy.

Boone lifted his son in his strong arms and carried the baby into the cozy family parlor down the hall. While Elly curled up on the settee with a book, and Cassandra and Aunt Adelaide played checkers at the little table before the fire, he fed his son and gazed with fascinated pleasure into the baby's pale, bright little eyes.

My son, thought Boone, as deep contentment welled up within his chest. He'd waited a long time to find simple happiness like this—through all those years growing up alone, struggling, thinking himself a fugitive, through the years spent working, building the iron foundry, the steel works, throwing his whole body and soul into making himself a success. And then he'd been trapped in that sham of a marriage with Penelope—a nightmare. *Now*, Boone thought, marveling at the soft, trusting bundle in his arms, *now I have Elly, and our children, and a peace I only dreamed of.*

It was all a man could want.

*   *   *

"Did you see him?" Ezra demanded, eyeing her sharply. "Did you see Boone?"

They were in the rickety little hovel he had rented for their brief stay in Chicago. It was located in a weed-strewn yard behind a ramshackle roominghouse near the docks of the river, in a neighborhood of whores, pickpockets, and thieves. Rose Wells worked at the filthy stove, boiling coffee, slicing ham, and spreading the meat on thick slices of crusty day-old bread.

"No, Pa," she mumbled over her shoulder. "He wasn't there. I saw his wife and little girl, though."

"You be careful, now, when you do see him," he warned. He bit off a jagged and dirty fingernail, then spat it into a slime-filled cuspidor. "He jest might recognize you, even after all these years. You've a bit of your ma's look about you, but not much. If you're careful, it should be all right."

"Yes, Pa."

"Now, I been thinkin'," Ezra said slowly as Rose served him at the broken-legged table. "It don't make no sense to wait too long to do it." He stuffed the sandwich into his mouth, talking all the while. "What about tomorrow? Think you'll have the chance?"

"N-no. Not tomorrow." Rose bit her lip as she slipped into the chair opposite him. It was cold here in the shack. Cold and depressing. A far cry from the beauty, warmth, and spaciousness of the Walker house, she thought to herself. She stared at the food on her plate, but had no desire to eat it. Instead, she picked up the tin mug half full of bitter coffee. "Miss Cassandra has lessons all day and there is to be a dinner party tomorrow night. The cook said Mrs. Walker will be home early from the hotel to prepare for it, and everyone will be hurrying about." The coffee tasted awful on her tongue; she set it down. She was aware that Pa's tiny, squinting eyes were burning into her.

"What's the matter with you?" he rasped. "You're not going to start quivering and crying again, are you, girl?" He leaned toward her in such a threatening way that she instinctively recoiled in her chair, remembering the sting of his hand on her face when she had at first balked at his plan. The blow had knocked her across this very room. He had hit her a second time to make sure she understood his displeasure.

"Thet boy deserves to pay for what he did to us—both of us!" Pa said. She stared at him in silent fear, that gnarled little stick of a man with the hot glinting eyes and bony fists. Pa always got kind of funny when he began talking about Boone.

"Didn't he turn your ma against both of us and fix it so we had to leave? Didn't he try an' kill me? And he woulda done the same to you. Thet boy hated you from the day you was born. You know why? 'Cause he was jealous, Rose, plumb crazy jealous! On account of your ma lovin' you so much." Ezra pounded his fist on the table so violently that Rose jumped. "And 'cause you were *mine!*"

She stared at him fearfully, her brown eyes wide and uneasy beneath the intensity of his fury.

"I . . . I know, Pa."

"You had a hard life, girl. And so did I. I never would've ended up in thet Denver jail, and you wouldn't have had to work for all those different families to support yerself if it wasn't for Boone. He robbed you of your home and your mama—I'd think you'd be right anxious to pay him back."

She bit her lip, her eyes filling suddenly with tears. "I just don't want to scare the children. The baby's too little, of course, he won't know, but . . . Miss Cassandra. She won't understand why we're taking her away."

Ezra came around the table and grabbed her arms hard. His fingers dug into her flesh as he yanked her from the chair and shook her until her neck ached. "Girl, you jest do as I say. You fetch those brats to me Tuesday afternoon, you hear? They kin go back—after the ransom is paid."

"Y-yes, Pa." Rose began to whimper, and when he finally released her, she collapsed back in her chair.

When Rose Wells returned to the Walker house that night, there were voices and laughter coming from the second floor parlor down the hall from the nursery. Someone must have heard her footsteps, for Mrs. Walker came to the doorway, clad in a beautiful rose-colored velvet gown.

"Miss Webb," she called, "Adam is here with us. You may put away your cloak and then come and join us. I believe he is nearly ready for bed."

Rose's skin prickled. This was the moment she had been dreading. Boone was in that parlor; she would have to meet him.

Apprehension coursed through her as she entered the room. Her heart seemed to pound louder than the murmur of Cassandra's voice as the little girl read aloud from a children's book.

"Did you enjoy your day?" Mrs. Walker held the baby as she sat on the chintz sofa, firelight warming her beautiful features. Rose mumbled an answer, as the fair-haired, broad-shouldered man who shared the sofa came to his feet and smiled at her.

"Miss Webb, I'm Boone Walker. I haven't had a chance yet to welcome you into our household, so let me do that now. My wife tells me you've come well recommended. We're glad to have you with us."

The cheerful, pleasantly appointed room seemed to swim as Rose forced herself to meet her brother's gaze. It was strange to look into his face, to know this was her brother, her own kin, who had forced her from her home. His features were unfamiliar, nothing at all like the boyish blur she recalled from her earliest days. He had a strong face, lean and pleasant, with eyes a little too shrewd for comfort, she thought wildly, and a firm chin and an unexpectedly kind smile. That smile was not at all what she had imagined. Boone didn't match the hard, vindictive person she'd been picturing all these years as Pa had told and retold the story of their banishment and of Boone's vicious jealousy and hatred. Was there recognition in his face? Was he staring at her with suspicion? No. He merely smiled, his deep gray eyes holding nothing but politeness. Rose struggled to reply, though her tongue suddenly felt thick and awkward in her mouth.

"Th-thank you, sir," she mumbled.

With a jerky movement she turned aside and held out her arms for the baby. "I can take him now, ma'am, if you'd like. He . . . he looks sleepy. Should I put him to bed?"

"Yes, he's fed and ready, and his napkin has been changed." She smiled down at the smooth-skinned infant in his pleated, lace-edged gown. "Good night, my darling Adam. Cassandra, do you want to give your little brother a kiss?"

Rose stood back as the family admired and fussed over the sleepy baby for a final moment. A lump came to her throat. She hadn't expected this display of tenderness; she studied Boone surreptitiously as he stroked the baby's chin with his thumb. He looked gentle. Nice.

Tears of hurt and confusion burned behind her eyelids. Whatever Boone Walker seemed like now, it was still his fault that she'd never had a family like this around *her*. Boone's hatred had forced her to leave Ma, to spend her youth roaming the hills with Ezra. Later, after they headed west and Pa was thrown in jail for thieving in Denver City, she'd had to find work to keep herself alive. She had moved from family to family, sweeping and cooking and caring for children, lonely and afraid and always on the edge of poverty. Boone was making Cassandra miserable, too, Rose reminded herself. He was a bad man, mean-spirited and cruel, however he might be playacting tonight while she was in the room. She knew all about how people put on false fronts for the sake of appearances.

When she left the parlor with Adam in her arms, Rose hid a moment outside the door. She heard Boone's low drawl in response to a soft question from his wife.

"Oh, she seems capable enough, but—nervous. Fidgety. For some reason, she couldn't meet my eye."

"She's probably shy," Mrs. Walker suggested.

Rose didn't linger any longer. She was afraid Adam would make a sound or Cassandra would come running from the room and discover her. As quietly as she could she hastened back to the nursery. Boone Walker was already suspicious of her, she realized with a stab of alarm. She would have to be very careful until Tuesday.

During the dinner guests' arrival the next night, Rose crouched behind the upper staircase railing and watched like a child. Mrs. Walker looked serene and lovely, as always, in her square-necked gown of brocaded yellow satin with a flowering silk train and exquisite lace-cuffed sleeves. Then came the gentleman Cassandra called "Uncle Timothy," accompanied by a vivacious chestnut-haired young woman and her dignified parents, and finally, the young blond woman, "Aunt Caroline." Soft-spoken and charming in peach-colored silk, Caroline arrived on the arm of an attractive young man with well-combed red hair, a trimmed mustache, and a deep, sonorous voice that carried all the way up the steps to where Rose crouched in her gray nurse's garb. She heard the light laughter and happy voices, saw Cassandra curtsying prettily to all of the grown-ups to whom she was introduced, and then they all vanished into the hall, making their way, she presumed, through the lilac drawing room to the dining room, with its silver candlesticks and glittering table and the Sheraton sideboard heavy with priceless crystal and china. The house was filled with a delicious aroma, a tantalizing indication of the banquet that would be served; it shone from top to bottom like a polished jewel. She came to her feet slowly, realizing that by tomorrow night everything would be different.

Then this house would be a place of panic, confusion, and tears. Frantic terror for the missing children would replace the gaiety of tonight. Mrs. Walker, that nice, elegant lady, who had been so warm to her, would weep for her vanished babies. Her cries would rise to the rafters and rattle helplessly at the fine leaded windows. But it wouldn't help, Rose thought, as she closed the nursery door. She went to gaze at Adam in his crib. A shiver went through her.

It would be too late.

❦ Twenty-Five

"ARE YOU SURE I'm not interrupting something?" Caroline asked.

She was pacing about Elly's office with such restlessness that Elly wondered why she didn't collapse of exhaustion. But she refrained from pointing this out, merely replying, "Nothing is more important than you, Caro. For heaven's sake, stop pacing and talk to me. I want to know what's making you so unhappy."

A knock on the door interrupted. Jennings stuck his head in. "Mrs. Walker, there is a problem with Monsieur Jobert in the main kitchen. He is demanding to speak with you at once."

"Monsieur Jobert will have to wait. Pacify him, Jennings," Elly ordered crisply.

"But . . . have you forgotten? Mr. McAdams from the bank will be here any moment."

"I leave it to you, Jennings. Pour him a brandy or something while he waits. Or tell him he can see me tomorrow instead, if he'd prefer. But no more interruptions until my sister and I have finished."

Her firm, cool tone signaled that she would not look kindly on any more reminders of her busy schedule, not with her sister fidgeting nervously in the corner.

With a harassed look, Jennings disappeared.

Elly pulled Caroline toward the settee and sat down beside her. She took her hand. "Dr. Reeves is very nice, Caro. I liked him at once last night. He's charming and intelligent, and he seems to have a great deal of compassion. He has obviously chosen a medical career because he cares about people and wants to help them, which is admirable. And," she added with a slight tilt of her head, "he seems very taken with you. So what exactly is the problem?"

"The same as it's always been." Caroline's face was taut, her violet eyes miserable. "Panic. Fear. I can't bear to have him touch me, Elly." She made a gesture of despair. "I want to be normal, I want to allow Gilbert to court me, maybe even to get married and . . . and have children, but . . . I don't think it's ever going to happen."

"Of course it is. Your feelings will change in time. You'll find that your attraction to him will overcome the fears Jason Emmett branded you with."

"I don't know if anything is strong enough to do that. I want to love Gilbert, Elly! He is such a fine man, and when he looks at me . . ." Her cheeks glowed pink. "Well, I find I'm not immune to romantic notions, much as I thought I was for all these years. My feelings for Gilbert have brought them all back, reminding me of that summer when I . . ." She took a deep breath and continued with a flash of pain in her eyes, "When I made a fool of myself over Jason Emmett. And we both know how that romantic devotion was rewarded."

"Caroline, once and for all, you must forget it! Eleven years have passed. Our lives have changed in every way, and for the better—except in this one respect. Don't allow Jason Emmett to cripple you for the rest of your life, to stop you from loving and starting a family of your own! Caroline, you can't let him do that to you—he's already done enough."

Caroline stared at the carpet. Winter light gleamed palely on her hair. "When Gilbert escorted me home last night in the hack, he held my hand. At first, I wanted to draw it back. I was so frightened at his touch—but I got used to it. Then we alighted and went to the door of the shop. He . . . tried to kiss me, Elly. Much as I wanted him to, I was terrified. I kept remembering Jason and his friends—when they held me down. They were kissing me, touching me in the most vile way—and hurting me so!"

She started to cry. The sobs burst forth from her chest, with a pain and anguish that was horrifyingly fresh. Elly held her, and her own cheeks were wet, too. "Do you still think of it often?" she asked in a low tone, stroking her sister's hair as she had that terrible night.

"No. It only started again because of Gilbert, because I think about him and what it would be like to let him court me . . . marry me . . . Then it all comes back, and I know I could never let him touch me that way!"

"What did you do when Gilbert tried to kiss you?" A pulse throbbed in Elly's temple as she looked into her sister's agonized face. After all these years, Jason Emmett still had the power to torture Caroline. That realization filled her with helpless fury such as she had not known in a long time. She had grown used to controlling her life, to fighting battles and winning them, but this was one fray she could not win, or even enter.

"I shrank back—I couldn't help it. Oh, the look on his face was so startled, so concerned that he had offended me, it nearly broke my heart. But I couldn't even speak to bid him good night. I just ran away, up the stairs to my room, leaving him to let himself out of the shop. Oh, Elly, what must he think of me? He will never come to call on me again."

"Nonsense." Elly spoke firmly. She went to her desk and rummaged about for a handkerchief, then handed it to her sister. "If he is as gentle and understanding as he appears, he won't be discouraged. Your reaction was not so improper, after all. He was the one who made a bold advance," she pointed out. "Don't worry, he'll continue to court you, but at a slower pace, I'm sure. That will be good, for you'll have a chance to get to know him better and to feel more comfortable with him before he attempts to kiss you again." She put an arm around Caroline's trembling shoulders. "Try to remember that to be kissed and touched by the man you love is far different from what . . . what happened with Jason. There is no comparison, Caroline, except to say that one is heaven and the other hell.'' She thought of Boone and of the joy they had found together. How could she explain to Caroline how wonderful it was to make love with someone who was gentle and loving, someone you could wholly trust?

"If you love Dr. Reeves, and he loves you, he will know how to soothe you. In time, you'll forget your fear and find happiness in his arms.''

"Do you really think so, Elly?'' Caroline's wide blue eyes held such desperate hope that Elly had to swallow hard before replying.

"Yes. I do.''

But she wasn't nearly as confident as she tried to appear.

When Caroline had left her office, Elly sat at her desk deep in thought. Despite her optimistic words, a sense of gloom hovered over her. Usually, she derived pleasure merely from being here in the hotel—her hotel—seeing all that she had accomplished, keeping everything clicking smoothly along, and knowing that the Forrest was a living symbol of her own strength. Yet, for all that she had accomplished, she still had not succeeded in helping Caroline fully conquer what had happened to her. Her sister had overcome her pain in many ways and had evolved over the years into a gentle, compassionate young woman who had found a measure of peace in her life through helping others, but Elly sensed that a small part of Caroline would always remain locked in turmoil and fear. From all Elly had seen and heard last night at dinner and today in the office, she was sure that Caroline loved Gilbert Reeves. She yearned to make a home and family with him. But her past was getting in the way. Elly prayed that her encouraging words to Caroline would prove true, that her sister's love for Gilbert and her determination to have a life with him would give her the strength to overcome those crippling memories. It *was* possible, she told herself, as she rose from her desk and paced to the window. If only Gilbert Reeves would have the patience to go slowly and carefully and not to lose heart, then perhaps Caroline could defeat her past nightmare after all.

The past. Was there no escaping it? It disturbed Elly that she could not erase the pain of bygone years, that those awful events which she had struggled to leave behind could still affect the lives of those she loved. Staring out at the bleached, cloud-laden sky, which looked as if any moment it would unleash a blizzard, she felt suddenly vulnerable and afraid. She had to remind herself that in every other way, the past was done. Though Caroline might still suffer some of its effects, Timothy had grown up healthy and whole. And it was a brand-new world for her own children, for Cassandra and Adam. The old dark hatreds could not touch them. The past could not harm them. They were insulated, safe.

She pressed the buzzer on her desk, and Jennings appeared at the door.

"I'll see Mr. McAdams now," she told him, with a glance at the small gilt clock on her desk. "And you can tell Monsieur Jobert I'll be with him shortly."

Outside the window, more snow clouds were moving in across the lake. It was only eleven in the morning, but already it appeared much later. When the banker, McAdams, waddled into her office, she greeted him mechanically. A corner of her mind was thinking still of Cassie and Adam, only now she felt calm again, serene. It was endlessly comforting to know that her children, at least, were safe.

Rose fastened the wooden buttons of her plain blue cloak with fingers that trembled. She paced back and forth across her little room adjoining the nursery before opening the hall door. The house was quiet, almost eerily so, like a great, hushed cavern or funeral parlor, Rose thought with a shudder. Soon, she knew, it would be time for lunch, and Cassie would be summoned downstairs. After that, the music instructor would arrive for an afternoon of lessons before tea. Then Mrs. Coombs would return, and all manner of activities would spring up. The time to leave was now, or not at all.

As she forced herself to walk across the hall to Cassandra's room, Rose reassured herself that the plan would succeed. Mrs. Coombs had gone off on a shopping expedition, and Jeweline was busy in the kitchen preparing lunch. The upstairs maid, Dora, had passed by earlier on her way to the kitchen and was no doubt warming herself by the stove and partaking of her own midday meal at this very moment. It would be a simple thing, Rose told herself, to slip out with the children. No one would see her or notice that anything was amiss for perhaps half an hour. She would have plenty of time to walk briskly out of sight, hail a hack, and disappear into the winter's gloom.

"Are you going somewhere?" Cassandra asked in surprise as Rose inched into her room. "It's nearly time for luncheon."

"It's a surprise—a lovely surprise." Rose gave her a qua-very smile as she tried to inject hushed and cheerful enthusiasm into her voice. "Would you like to come with me for a short walk? I have something to show you. You'll . . . you'll enjoy it."

"What is it?" Cassandra's face reflected eager childish curiosity.

"Put on your coat and you'll see."

"Very well." The girl abandoned her dolls, leaving them on the carpet as she danced over to her wardrobe. "What about Adam?" she asked, as Rose helped her to don a coat of purple lamb's wool trimmed in chinchilla, a fur muff, and a hat to match.

"Oh, we shall bring him, too. He will enjoy getting out in the fresh air for a change."

Cassandra, tying the strings of her chinchilla bonnet beneath her chin, cast a glance at the window. "It's so gray. It looks like it's going to snow," she pointed out, a note of doubt creeping into her voice.

"Oh, no, it won't snow in the short time we'll be out. Don't worry, Miss Cassandra, I know what I'm doing," Rose chattered. "You and Adam will be snug inside again before the first snowflake appears in the sky."

"All right." Skipping a little at the prospect of this myste-rious outing, Cassandra accompanied her back to the nursery, where Adam was dozing in his crib, already bundled up in his little quilted cloak with the attached hood tied beneath his chin.

Rose picked up the baby and her old black satchel, which contained her few belongings as well as some of Adam's napkins and pins and three of his bottles.

"What's that?" Cassandra asked.

"Oh, nothing. Never mind. Let's go quietly now," Rose urged, "and pretend we are running away from home and don't want to be found."

Down the long staircase they went and across the gleaming oak floor of the entry hall. Muted voices came from the direction of the kitchen, but Rose dared not glance back as she fumbled with the doorknob. Beside her, Cassandra was silent, her pretty blue eyes shining with mischief and fun.

Just as Cassie pulled the door shut softly behind them, Adam let out a yelp. He was beginning to get hungry, Rose realized with a quiver of dismay. "Shh," she soothed him, hurrying along the walk, past the graceful elms and maples in their winter nakedness. "Hurry, Miss Cassandra," she said as the little girl ran to keep apace with her.

By the time they had gone three blocks, Cassandra was panting and grumbling and Rose was nearly bursting with panic over what she had done. But the die was cast; she must go through with it now and get clean away or else spend the rest of her days in prison. The thought made her quake with terror. She walked faster, nearly running.

"Driver!" she screeched, when her gaze lit upon the welcome sight of an empty hack at the near corner. She shook with relief when he tipped his hat to signal to her that he would wait.

"But, Miss Webb, why are we taking a hack?" Cassandra demanded, running alongside Rose across the street. "We're going to be late for luncheon!"

"No, no, you'll have your luncheon," Rose gasped, as she cradled Adam in one arm and with the other hand helped the girl up into the carriage. Her arms ached from carrying the baby; she was out of breath, and her thin, normally pale cheeks were bright, splotchy red. She felt very close to tears and managed to gulp them back, but her voice came out all unsteady and shrill. "This is all . . . part of the surprise."

She disappeared for a moment from Cassandra's sight, while she told the driver in a low tone where she wished to go. Then suddenly, with Adam in her arms and the satchel dangling awkwardly, she climbed into the carriage.

"There now, we're all set." Rose spoke with forced cheeriness. She sensed Cassandra's sudden unease. The child was staring at her oddly, her little shoulders very still. Traces of fright had begun to darken her eyes.

Rose glanced quickly away. "Don't worry, Miss Cassandra. Everything is fine." She couldn't look into the girl's face. Holding the fussing baby on her lap, she reached across and grabbed hold of the handle on the carriage door.

"Hurry, driver," she cried and slammed the door shut with a resounding thud.

Boone swore under his breath as he left his office on Dearborn Street, ordering his driver to take him to the Forrest Hotel. That damned telegraph message from Louis. It looked as if the bridge deal with the Mortimer Company was off, unless he could get to New York immediately and salvage it. He *would* salvage it, too, he vowed, as the carriage maneuvered its way through the heavy midday traffic. This was one of the most lucrative contracts W-and-W had gone after this year; worth a potential half a million dollars. There was no way Boone was going to allow one man's poor judgment to ruin it.

William Mortimer was a weak man who was allowing himself to be manipulated into selecting a different supplier of steel for the bridges his company built all across the country, but Boone would put an end to that. He knew that, face to face, he could easily persuade the man to honor his word and award the contract to W-and-W after all. Whitcomb and Walker had offered the lowest price and the fastest delivery schedule Mortimer could ask for. Boone knew he could point that out and steer the deal back on course once he met with the man in person. Unfortunately, he didn't like leaving Elly and the children on such short notice. They had agreed to attend a string of social functions this week, and Elly would be disappointed at having to attend them alone. But it couldn't be helped.

"Oh, how annoying," she exclaimed when he found her in her office a short while later. "How long will you be gone?"

"Less than a week. Sorry, this can't be helped."

She sighed. "What time does your train leave?"

"Three o'clock. Cooper has gone to the station to buy my ticket. I'll meet him there as soon as I've packed a few things."

"Damn William Mortimer," she said crossly. "I've had the most frustrating kind of day. First there was a problem with Caroline, and then Monsieur Jobert threw a tantrum, and now this." She put her arms around Boone's neck. "I'll miss you. These business trips are becoming far too frequent for my taste, Mr. Walker."

"For mine, too. But at least I'll escape that damned dinner party at Winnie Addison's." His gray eyes twinkled at her.

"Scoundrel," she chided, but there was laughter in her rich, husky voice.

He kissed her thoroughly before he left.

The traffic was unusually snarled as his driver, Hudson, steered the team toward Prairie Avenue. By the time Boone reached his own door he was beginning to be anxious about missing his train. It had better not take as long to reach the station as it had to reach home. He would barely have time to pack a bag and see the children before rushing off again.

He took the stairs two at a time, strode down the hall to his room, and tossed a valise on the bed. It didn't take him long to assemble what he needed for the trip: he was used to traveling back and forth between his Pittsburgh and New York offices and could at this point have easily packed his bag blindfolded. When everything was ready he went into the nursery. The room seemed unusually quiet, until he realized that it was still lunchtime. Adam was probably asleep, and Miss Webb and Cassie would be downstairs eating their soup, cold chicken, cottage cheese, and fruit. Remembering how easily his son awakened from his nap, he trod as carefully as he could across the room to the crib.

Empty.

Boone was more startled than alarmed. He turned and went across the hall to Cassie's room. It, too, was empty, and Cassie's dolls were lying on the floor.

"Miss Webb?" There was no answer to his imperative call, no voice or footstep in the hall or adjoining rooms.

He decided that the nurse must have taken the baby downstairs with her. With a glance at his pocket watch, he hurried down the steps.

"Miss Webb? Cassandra?" he called, a trickle of unease, perhaps premonition, making his voice unusually loud. A cold feeling came over him when he found the dining room empty, too. The luncheon plates had been laid, the table draped in creamy white linen, but there was no one there to enjoy its elegant simplicity.

"Mr. Walker?"

Jeweline came hurrying out of the kitchen in response to his calls. "Why, I didn't expect you for luncheon, sir. Cook

is running a bit late today. I was just going to call Miss
Cassie and—''

''She's not there. Neither is Miss Webb. Jeweline, where
is everyone?'' he demanded.

''Well, Mrs. Coombs went out for a day of shopping, but
Miss Webb and Miss Cassie are in their—''

''No, they're not,'' he repeated, a sudden dampness under
his armpits. ''Their rooms are empty. And Adam isn't in his
crib.''

''Are you sure?'' Incredulity creased her aging face. ''But
where could they all be?''

''That's what I'd like to know,'' Boone muttered as he
dropped his valise and ran back through the hall. This time he
took the steps three at a time, striding through all the rooms
with a rising sense of dread. *Stay calm, don't panic,* he told
himself as the silence about him seemed to echo with a
hushed menace. He was just about to enter Miss Webb's
room when he heard a door slam downstairs and rushed to the
landing, but it was only Timothy, come to search for a
newspaper article he had misplaced. As Jeweline hurriedly
told him what was afoot, he bounded up the steps, his face
somber beneath his mop of pale hair.

''Boone, what the devil is going on?''

''Damned if I know.'' Boone was already sprinting back
toward the nurse's bedroom, leaving Timothy to follow. ''That
damned nurse is nowhere to be found, and the children with
her.''

When he saw the note tucked in the edge of the pier glass,
he froze. Something akin to a sharp blow seemed to hit him
in the belly. He tore at the sealed paper with trembling
fingers.

''What? What does it say?'' Timothy demanded.

Boone stared at him in stunned horror. ''That filthy, evil-
minded bitch. She's taken them and is holding them for
ransom. She wants twenty-five thousand dollars to bring them
back safe.''

Boone's face was as white as the paper in his hand, and a
sick churning in his stomach had replaced the dull ache of a
moment before.

''Lord, Boone.'' Timothy grabbed the note from him and
read it himself: ''If you want to see your brats again, bring
$25,000 to the Franklin Street bridge at five o'clock today.

No police. Put the money in the shed closest to the bridge.
The one with the boarded-up windows. Then leave. If you do
everything just like you should, you'll be told where to find
your brats. If you try any tricks, they'll *both die.*''

Timothy reeled back, dazed with horror. "What are we
going to do? Elly! We've got to send word to her.''

Through the haze of shock and numbing, agonizing fear,
Boone thought frantically. Five o'clock didn't leave much
time. He had to hurry or that murderous bitch would . . .

He couldn't even finish the thought, much less contemplate
Cassie and Adam in the hands of such a woman. He snatched
the note from Timothy and shoved it in his pocket.

"You get to the hotel and tell Elly. I'm going to the police
and the bank," he shouted. He was already pounding down
the stairs with Timothy at his heels.

"Hudson!" he yelled to his driver as he shouldered past
Jeweline and Dora and sprinted toward his carriage at the
curb. It was colder outside now; his breath puffed before him,
and smoke flew from the chimneys of all the surrounding
houses. But he didn't notice anything; he was shaking all
over, shaking with rage and fear. Somehow he managed to
get himself under enough control to speak to Hudson in a low
tone, in case the house was being watched.

"The precinct station—fast,'' he said softly, between
clenched teeth. Then he flung the door open wide and already
had a leg up when a hired hack came hurtling down the street
and drew up alongside Boone's carriage. As little bits of
snow began to fly through the frosted air, he caught a glimpse
of the faces inside.

"Cassie! Adam!'' Disbelief vied with joy inside him, and
everything seemed to explode around him at once. He heard
Timothy yell and Jeweline start to cry. Like a madman, he
bolted toward the hack.

Miss Webb, pale as death, pushed open the door.

Boone scooped Cassandra into his arms, holding her tight
against his chest. She was crying, her face wet against his
coat. "It's all right, Cassie, it's all right. Don't be scared,''
he said quickly, then set her down on the walk so that he
could take his son from the nurse's arms. He was dimly
aware that Timothy had snatched Cassie up and was holding
her. Then he turned his full attention to Adam, who was
bundled warmly and appeared content. He was awake but

calm, in the innocent, unknowing fashion of a baby. *Safe*. Boone, nearly overwhelmed by relief, sent up a silent prayer of thanksgiving. Both of them were safe.

Suddenly he became aware that Miss Webb was jumping down to the curb and attempting to run off. He shot out an arm and grabbed her cloak.

"No, you don't." A dangerous fury came over him. "Come inside, Miss Webb. I want to speak with you." He said these words in a low, calm tone so as not to further frighten Cassie, but it took all of his self-control not to throttle the woman.

Jeweline rushed out to take Adam from his arms, leaving him free to propel the terrified nurse into the house.

"What about my fare?" the hack driver bellowed, as the assembly pushed through the falling snow toward the shelter of the brownstone. At an order from Boone, Hudson paid him off, though the driver was clearly baffled by all the excitement.

"Cassie, you're fine now. Do you understand? You and Adam are fine." Breathing hard with the rage that surged through him, a rage he was trying not to display before his stepdaughter, Boone managed to smile at her. He hugged her to him, wishing he could wipe away that look of terror.

"I want Mama," Cassie gulped, looking lost and wild-eyed. She put her arms around Boone's neck. "We rode for the longest time—hours and hours!"

"I know, Cassie. But you're home now."

She pulled back suddenly and glared at the brown-haired young woman shrinking in the hall. "I hate her," she burst out. "I was scared. It started out as an adventure—she said she was going to show me a surprise, but she wouldn't tell me where we were going and she wouldn't bring us home and I hadn't had any lunch and—"

"It's all right, Cassie. I'm going to have a firm talk with Miss Webb." Boone signaled Jeweline to take the baby upstairs, then turned back to Cassandra. "Go with Dora now into the kitchen and have your lunch while Jeweline takes care of Adam. I'll come to you as soon as I've finished with Miss Webb."

When Cassie finally allowed herself to be led into the kitchen, Boone took the nurse by the arm and dragged her across the hall. Timothy followed them into the library and shut the door, his face pale and grim.

"I ought to strangle you here and now," Boone snarled.

"How could anyone do anything so despicable?" Timothy added, advancing on her with barely leashed anger.

Rose flinched, darting around a heavy leather chair for protection. Tears were streaming down her cheeks, and her brown eyes looked even wilder than Cassie's had been, reflecting a terror every bit as deep as what Boone had felt a short time ago.

"Let me go! I beg you! I brought them back, didn't I? No h-harm's been done!"

"Explain this!" Boone shoved the chair aside and seized her arm, ignoring her cry of pain. He waved the ransom note before her face.

"I wrote it—yes!" she sobbed. "I didn't want to, but Pa made me! He'll kill me when I don't bring them to him, but I . . . I couldn't do it! Cassie was c-crying, and Adam looked so sweet . . ."

"You're saying that your father put you up to this? Why? Who is he?" Boone pounced on her words like a panther at prey.

The girl began to cry hysterically. "I can't tell you! He'll kill me! Oh, what am I going to do? What am I going to do?"

Boone was staring at her. Something in the small, frightened face, in those terrified peat-brown eyes, struck a chord of memory deep inside him. He said slowly, "It's true that you brought them back; we'll take that into account when the police are summoned. For that, at least, I am grateful. But you have to tell us where your father is. He can't be allowed to get away."

"He's probably gone already! I was to have been there with the children a long time ago! He must know something is wrong—I tell you, he's gone already!"

"Then we can never be safe!"

Boone shook her, furious all at once. There was no more time to lose. "If we don't find him now, who's to stop him from coming back in a month or six months or a year and trying this again?" he shouted. "He must be caught and turned over to the police! Tell me where to find him. And who he is!"

Suddenly, she gave a laugh, a shrill, hysterical laugh that was filled with hate. "You know him. You *know* my Pa, *Mr. Walker.*" Her eyes blazed at him from her mottled face. "He's yours, too, in a way. It's Ezra—Ezra Wells! Remember now?'' She was weeping as she spoke, the tears flowing fast as raindrops. "And I'm the sister you drove away!"

"Rose?" The word whistled through his teeth. For the second time that day, he felt as though someone had punched him in the stomach. The handsome, paneled library seemed to whirl about him; the paintings and books all blurred. He sucked air desperately into his lungs. Rose. Little Rose. And Ezra. Come to steal his children.

"Where is he?" he asked hoarsely.

Rose covered her face with her hands. "Near the waterfront. A shack. Behind a roominghouse . . ."

"The street, Rose! Tell me quickly!"

"Cork Street!"

Boone headed for the door.

✇ Twenty-Six

THE SNOW FELL thicker and faster as Boone's carriage reached the waterfront district. Inside, he sat hunched and tense, staring with unseeing eyes at the gunmetal gray river, the bridges and boats, the dockworkers bundled in their caps and jackets moving through the flurrying whiteness. When he passed the Illinois Central tracks, he didn't think of the three o'clock train he was supposed to catch, or about William Mortimer awaiting him in New York. It didn't matter anymore. Only one thing on this earth was important at this moment, and that was entirely in his hands. He couldn't fail.

When they reached the rat-infested neighborhood of shanties and taverns and warehouses near the docks where Rose had directed him, he felt a sickening fear in his stomach.

What if Ezra had gone?

He couldn't deal with that possibility. Ezra had to be there, or Boone would have to track him down. The feud was going to end this time for good, with Ezra taken care of once and for all.

Boone's initial fury and shock had given way to a grim realization. Seventeen years ago he had left Ezra for dead and fled his family and home, thinking that part of his life was over for good. Now it shook him to realize that the repercussions from that night were still affecting him. And they were affecting him in the deepest, most harrowing way: through the safety and well-being of his children. His face was hard and cold as he stared out the carriage window. He was thirty years old, a millionaire several times over, and he considered himself a practical, fair-minded man. Though tough in business, he had never set out to hurt anyone deliberately, only to accomplish what he considered his own reasonable goals. Unlike many men he had known on the docks and in the railroad camps over the years, he had never enjoyed violence and had never actively sought out brawls and fights—but he had never run from one, either. This time, he was running *toward* one. He was aching for the chance to use his fists and his considerable size and strength to pound the life out of Ezra Wells. Cold, savage rage gripped every fiber of his being. This time, Boone thought, his mouth twisting, he would finish this business with Ezra as it should have been finished years ago.

The moment he saw the roominghouse, he sprang from the carriage before Hudson had even brought the team to a halt.

Through the whirling snow Boone ran, skirting the house and crashing toward the dilapidated shack behind it. He burst through the door like cannon fire, then halted and swore, frustration washing over him.

Except for the insects crawling across the cracked baseboards and the lumpy, stained sofa and broken-legged table, the shack was empty. He strode across the straw matting, every muscle taut. Futilely, he glanced around the two tiny, foul-smelling rooms. Dirt-encrusted shutters were fastened across the small single window. A blanket was thrown across a chair. In the corner, several rats were squealing over a crust of cheese. Boone's stomach turned over. Rose would have brought Cassie and Adam *here?*

The stove was still warm, and a pouch of tobacco lay spilled on the table, along with three empty whiskey bottles and a tin plate covered with roaches. His skin prickled. Maybe Ezra wasn't gone yet, after all. He could almost sense his former stepfather's presence, and a drumbeat of rage pounded inside him. He froze, crouched, alert and ready. Then he heard it, a noise at the back door. He spun toward it. In the next instant, everything seemed to happen at once.

Ezra yanked open the back door, allowing Boone a fleeting glimpse of his grizzled head and squinting eyes, and of the outhouse behind the shack, which Ezra had apparently been visiting. But Boone had time for no more than a glimpse. The two men saw each other at the same instant. Then, even as Boone sprang forward, Ezra wheeled about and began to run, out of the shack, across the snow-covered yard in back, and around the crumbling shanties scattered like random debris through the neighborhood. Boone crashed after him, heedless of the snow flying in his face or the chill gusts of wind that stung his cheeks. He nailed his gaze on the darting figure ahead of him and ran him down.

The last time he'd taken on Ezra Wells, Boone had been a boy and Ezra a grown man. Now the circumstances were drastically changed. At thirty, Boone was tall, strong and powerfully muscled; Ezra's slight, wiry form had the disadvantage of age and drunken dissipation. Just before Ezra reached the iron curve of railroad track crisscrossing a deserted street of warehouses, Boone overtook him, hurling himself full-length at the older man and bringing Ezra down with a groan. Boone climbed on top of him, pinning him brutally in the snow, and slammed his fist into Ezra's nose.

Blood spurted, and Ezra screamed. He fought furiously, cursing Boone, using all his strength and every dirty maneuver he knew to throw the other man off him, but Boone held him fast. His weight and immense strength far outstripped his opponent's, and his rage was every bit as great.

"Damn you, Wells, I'll break every bone in your worthless body! You son of a bitch!"

"Let me go, boy! I didn't do a damned thing!"

Boone hit him again.

"Damn you, boy!" Ezra screamed, flailing beneath him. "I should've killed you that night in Kentucky. You've made my life a hell on earth!"

That got Boone's attention. He paused, his fist in midair. "*I* have?" he demanded incredulously.

Blood covered Ezra's face and stained his gray whiskers, dribbling down his neck. "Your ma . . . loved me . . . till you turned her against me! You're what caused it all."

"You're sick and twisted, Wells. You know what you did and why I fought you that night."

"You hated me!" Ezra gasped. "You turned her against me. All I wanted was Hannah!"

Boone stared at him in disgust and hatred. The man was crazed, wild-eyed, and twisted with hate and misplaced blame. He felt some of the anger draining from him, being replaced with contempt. Breathing hard, he shifted his weight, staring down coldly at the battered old man beneath him.

"You tried to take my children!" he snarled. "You've got no business being alive."

"I wouldn't've hurt 'em!" Ezra yelled as Boone's fingers dug into his arms. "I only wanted the . . . ransom money." Writhing, his bloody face contorted, Ezra grunted. "Why should you have so much damned money—live like a king— when I've had nothin' all my life? No home, no family . . . 'cause of you!"

"You had Rose," Boone said. He was exercising all his self-control not to slam his fist across Ezra's face again. He wanted to vent his own anger and outrage; he wanted to mash that grizzled, weathered face into bits. But he didn't. Somehow he curbed his temper, though his own mouth thinned into a cruel, hard line as he observed the man who had caused so many people close to him such grief.

Like a foul wind, the memories of that other night and that other struggle with Ezra came vividly back to him. He felt like retching. He hated the feel, the smell, the burning hate that had driven him to such frenzied violence that night and had been driving him today. He felt out of control, mad, as wild and dangerous as Ezra himself. He took a deep breath of the icy air and tried to clear his head of the anger pulsing through him. The way to solve this was not by more violence, not by more bloodshed. There had already been enough of that. And look what it had wrought—all those years of guilt and loneliness and shame, because he thought he'd killed Ezra, years and years of pain. But he was no longer a desperate thirteen-year-old boy, battling to save his mother. He was a man of thirty accustomed to wielding substantial power. And he knew there were legal measures that would ensure what he wanted. Boone felt his muscles relax, as sanity trickled back. This time he'd let the police handle Ezra. He'd use every legal maneuver at his disposal to see that Wells spent the rest of his days in prison. There were legal, "civilized," and rational ways to get what he wanted.

"The authorities will be fascinated by that ransom note left in my house," he panted, leaning back. "They'll know what to do with you."

He rolled off Ezra and dragged the older man to his feet, holding him by the collar. "Let's go. Before I change my mind and decide to kill you myself. Too bad that shot didn't do the job all those years ago."

A train was bearing down on the nearby stretch of track; the clamor nearly drowned out Ezra's shout. But his glinting, coal-black eyes were clear enough in the white winter light. "You're damned crazy if you think I'm goin' to jail, boy! I been there before, ain't no way I'm goin' back."

"Want to bet?" Ruthlessly, Boone pushed him back in the direction of the shack. Hudson and the carriage were still waiting at the curb. But the ground was uneven and slippery with new-fallen snow, and Ezra slipped on a patch of it. He would have fallen if not for Boone's grip on his arm, but suddenly, he seemed to explode with newfound energy. What happened next took Boone completely by surprise.

Ezra swung his foot back and kicked Boone's shin with the heel of his boot, a vicious blow that sent pain shooting up Boone's leg and knocked him off balance. Stunned, he loosened his grip momentarily. That was all Ezra needed. He wrenched free, elbowed Boone savagely in the midsection, then turned and veered past him like a rabbit on the run, his accompanying yelp of triumph drowned out by the roar of the onrushing train.

Boone started after him, gritting his teeth against the pain in his shinbone. Ezra had a good ten yards on him. He tried to close the distance, but each step was agony. He swore, limping across the slippery, frozen ground, running as fast as he could. But he was too slow now, pitifully slow. Ezra was lunging toward the tracks ahead, oblivious of the train only a few hundred yards away, rounding the curve.

Boone saw suddenly what he intended. Ezra planned to beat the train across the tracks, thereby cutting off pursuit, since Boone would have to wait for the train to pass before coming after him. By that time he could easily have disappeared into the wilderness of taverns, warehouses, and shacks beyond, like a hare burrowing into a hole. Boone would never find him.

With frantic effort, Boone increased his speed, but Ezra was only a dozen yards from the tracks.

He can't make it, Boone realized with a shock that penetrated the pain stabbing his leg. The train, a giant iron and steel monster hissing and roaring toward them, was too near, moving too quickly. Ezra couldn't beat it.

"Stop, you damned fool!" Boone shouted with a force that scraped his throat raw, but Ezra ran like a man possessed. Never looking to the side, he scampered toward the tracks, even as the train charged down upon him.

Nausea rose in Boone's throat at the sight he witnessed next. He fell to the ground and closed his eyes, trying to blot out the bloody nightmare on the tracks. The wet melting snow against his cheek helped; so did the throbbing agony in his shin. Presently, he sat up, sick and empty and shaken, and dragged himself to his feet.

He didn't look at the tracks again or at the little knot of people gathering. Walking slowly and painfully, he headed back the way he had come. He wouldn't have to worry about Ezra Wells anymore. That chapter of his life was finally finished for good. But as he moved slowly through the swirling flecks of snow, he knew there was another matter he'd have to face and deal with when he reached home. That matter was Rose.

She looked pathetic sitting in the library, surrounded by the massive, handsomely carved bookshelves, the leather-bound volumes stacked to the ceiling, the dark furnishings and brass gas lights. There was a fire burning against the cold, but still she shivered in her ugly gray dress, her fingers splayed on the arms of the maroon leather chair.

"Do you understand what I'm saying?" Boone sat opposite her, alongside Elly on the couch.

"My shooting him was an accident. I only meant to hit him with the gun. I ran away afterward. I was a terrified kid, thirteen years old! I thought I'd killed him. Eleven years passed before I set foot in Kentucky again." He closed his

eyes, then opened them. "It just about killed me when I went
back and Clay told me you were gone."

Boone had been talking to Rose for hours, trying to reach
her. But how could one explain a lifetime of misunderstanding? Ezra had spent years convincing her that the Walker
brothers were monsters, that she had been forced from her
mother and her home by their jealousy and hate. No wonder
she was a miserable, tortured thing, sad as a wounded little
sparrow. Boone talked until twilight fell on a crystal white
world. The snow had stopped, the wind had died down, and a
hushed stillness surrounded the house on Prairie Avenue.

"Rose?"

At last she lifted her head and stared bleakly at him.
Firelight flickered over her sallow face.

"I guess it must be true." Her voice was so small they
could barely hear it over the crackling logs. The room smelled
of smoke and leather and the quick nip of brandy Boone had
fortified himself with before this little talk began. In his
agitation, he had forgotten to replace the stopper on the
decanter, and the faint aromatic odor escaped to swirl about
them like an elusive ghost.

"I wouldn't have hurt the children," she whispered. Her
brown eyes pleaded with him to believe her.

Elly watched with a dry throat as Boone and Rose came to
their feet simultaneously and Boone embraced his sister, holding the sobbing girl in his arms. He stroked her limp hair with
awkward fingers. As Rose sobbed harder, Elly turned her
gaze to the fire.

A conflict of feelings churned inside her. Her children were
safe in bed upstairs, after an exhausting night. She had had to
stay with Cassandra every minute until she fell asleep, had to
leave a lamp burning for her in her room, but for the most
part, it seemed, the day's terror had been soothed away by the
comforts of home and family, of hearty food and a warm bed.
Cassie didn't completely understand what had happened today, and she was still frightened, but she would get over it,
Elly knew, as she had gotten over the boardinghouse fire and
Connor's and Bess's deaths. But Elly couldn't feel safe until
this woman was out of their house, away from Cassie and
Adam. Rose Wells was unstable and untrustworthy. Elly was
certain that Rose had been forced into doing what she had
done; but that didn't matter. As far as she was concerned,

they weren't going to take any chances with the welfare of the children.

She told Boone this a short time later when they left the girl with a tray of food in the library.

"I understand how you feel," Boone said heavily. He looked tired as he ran his fingers through his hair. "Lord, when I think of what might have happened . . ."

"Don't think of it." Elly shuddered, then moved into his arms, and they held each other, rocking slightly in the great domed hall. "Boone, I can't believe that awful man arranged Mrs. Woodward's accident. To think he hired a wagon to run her down, only so that Rose could get a job in this house! And her references. How . . . how diabolically clever they were to alter the writing from Rose Wells to Rosalie Webb. When I read the recommendations from those families in Colorado, I never once noticed anything amiss."

"Ezra was a sick man. Who could have guessed that after all these years he'd go to such lengths to get his revenge?" His arms tightened around Elly, his own spirit soothed by the warmth and softness of her body. "I hope you don't blame Rose too much," he muttered. "He hurt her and used her. She's never known anything different, not kindness or goodness or love."

"I don't blame her. But I can't trust her either. She can't stay in this house, Boone." She stared up at him, troubled but firm. "Not even tonight."

"No. Even though I do believe she was only confused, and that Ezra forced her to go along with the plan, I agree with you."

"Where will you take her?"

"Home. To Kentucky. We'll leave tonight. I'll arrange for a Pullman car, and I'll telegraph Clay that we're coming." He sighed. "I'll have to stay for a few days until I'm sure she's settled in with Clay and Lula Mae."

"Will Clay want her there—with his own children—after what's happened?" Elly asked doubtfully.

"I think Clay and his family will be safe. Ezra didn't poison her mind against Clay as he did against me, I guess because I was the one who shot him. Anyway, Ezra's influence over Rose is ended, Elly. That was what drove her to take Cassie and Adam—but she did bring them back. She couldn't go through with the plan, even though she risked facing Ezra's rage. Now that he's gone—well, alone, I don't believe there's an ounce of harm in her—just hurt, and loneliness. She's no danger to Clay and I'm sure he'll agree with me. Maybe being with both of us on the farm again can help heal her.''

It did help, Boone decided a week later as he watched Rose setting the table in the farmhouse along with little Hetta. In the bright yellow glow of the lamplight, amid the homey surroundings of his youth, his sister looked stronger, healthier, and happier than he had seen her before. Clay's overjoyed welcome had contributed to that, but there was something to be said for the simplicity and quiet of the farmhouse and surrounding fields, for the peacefulness of the Kentucky countryside, and for the soothing presence of Clay's little family.

Boone had persuaded Clay to let him provide a monthly sum to cover Rose's expenses. Tomorrow he would head back to Chicago, after a brief stop in New York to meet with Louis Whitcomb. The Mortimer deal had fallen through, but there were other projects in the works, always something to add to the W-and-W empire. Right now, though, the most satisfying thing was seeing his sister home where she belonged.

"Saturday we'll go to Hickoryville and buy some muslin curtains for your room." Lula Mae smiled. "What color do you like, Rose?"

"Yellow," she replied shyly. "I always wanted a room with yellow curtains, and a yellow quilt on my bed."

Watching her, Boone knew that by bringing her back here he had done the right thing. He could almost feel his ma's gratitude and relief surrounding him in the firelit parlor. After all these years, Ma could now rest in peace.

Ezra had paid for his wickedness.

And Rose had at last come home.

❦ Twenty-Seven

THE WEEKS AND months that followed Rose and Ezra's appearance in their lives were comparatively quiet ones for the Walker family. Adam grew into a bright, adventurous baby, with a curiosity that reminded Elly of Timothy when he was young. His new nurse, a stout Swedish widow with a trilling, infectious laugh, was a welcome addition to the household, and became a companion for Adelaide as well as a nurse for Adam. Cassandra continued her music lessons and dancing classes and her governess's instruction, growing daily more vivacious and beautiful—and spoiled, Boone occasionally warned—as she approached her adolescent years. And Elly and Boone involved themselves in a round of social and civic functions, which, along with their respective business enterprises, kept them busy all year long.

In the spring of 1885 they did take the time for a month-long tour of Europe, finding upon their return that the house on the North Side was nearly completed. It was a French-style mansion with a high mansard roof, and it contained thirty-five rooms, including a ballroom, a banquet room, and a rooftop terrace garden. Her new home often made Elly shake her head in wonder. Once, long ago, she had dreamed of a place of beauty and golden tranquillity. She had never expected to find it. Yet, within the exquisite walls of the Forrest Hotel and in this new magnificent house, she was surrounded by beauty. The mosaic-tiled floors, the polished marble staircase, the tapestries and paintings were almost too gorgeous to believe. Yet this home, unlike the houses of some of the other wealthy and powerful men in the nation, was marked by warmth and grace as well as spectacularly beautiful furnishings. Elly put her own distinctive touch on all of the furnishings and wallpapers and carpets. There was an abundance of fresh flowers, delicate colors, rich fabrics, and unusual pieces. Sometimes she strolled through the drawing rooms and parlors, the morning room and music room, and the cultivated jade-green gardens feeling almost dwarfed by it all.

"It's beautiful, of course, but almost overwhelming, don't you think?" she asked Boone when they were enjoying a glass of Madeira late one night in one of her favorite rooms— the private family sitting room adjoining their bedroom suite. It was small, with a pearly gray marble hearth, a rug of dusty rose, pale blue, and yellow, and comfortable chairs and sofas upholstered in cheerful rose and blue stripes.

"When I compare it to the farmhouse where I grew up, you can be damned sure it's overwhelming," Boone replied, stretching his great arms over his head. He turned to her on the cozy striped sofa and watched her sipping her wine. "But I can't live in a shack and do business with the likes of Cyrus McCormick and Everett Gantz. This is a world, unfortunately, where impressions count for quite a lot."

"And material possessions create those impressions." Elly set her glass on the rattan table. She tucked her feet beneath her on the sofa, unaware that her ice-pink satin dressing gown had come loose. When it drew Boone's fascinated gaze, she laughed, and nestled closer to him. "If anyone had told me fifteen years ago that I'd be living in this city, in this beautiful home with such a husband and such darling children, I'd have thought they were mad." She smiled and surveyed the pale rose muslin curtains, stirring softly in the June breeze. From outside the window came the chirping of crickets, a deliciously tranquil sound on this singularly peaceful night. "We are lucky to have so much. When I remember the row house where I grew up and how at times there wasn't enough food to put on the table . . ."

Her blue-gray eyes darkened as they always did when she remembered Emmettville.

Boone squeezed her hand. "That was a long time ago."

"Yes. But for so many the inequalities still exist, and they are so cruel."

"Don't let the Addisons or the Fields hear you talk like that. They'll brand you a communist quicker than you can blink,'' he chuckled, but there was a tinge of bitterness in his voice. He ran his thumb over her slender fingers. "You should see how they huff and glower and frown at the club when I speak up in favor of the eight-hour workday.''

"Do they?'' Elly frowned, her eyes hardening. "I can't understand why they are so frightened by it. Do they truly think the workers will take over the country if some of their requests are granted? That a shorter working day and better pay will rob us all of our riches?''

"Apparently. The fear of anarchy and mayhem is almost hysterical at times. Well, changes are coming, whether anyone likes them or not." Boone's voice was grave, yet it held a note of satisfaction, which was reflected also in the cool gray depths of his eyes. "Samuel Gompers's plan to unite the smaller unions could happen soon, and then nothing anyone can do will stop them.''

Elly thought back to her father and his death in the rug factory in Emmettville. Deep down, she had always been convinced that Silas Emmett had engineered the accident somehow because of Papa's efforts to organize the workers. There had been no proof, of course, and there would have been no way to force Sheriff Greeves to prosecute Silas, even if any evidence had turned up. But she still believed that the death had been an effort to stop Papa's agitation and demands. And here it was, fourteen years later and the same struggles were still going on. The violence had increased, the strikes were more frequent and better organized, but the vicious resistance to change, to shorter hours and better pay for the workers, was just as strong.

Elly condemned the tactics some of the self-styled anarchists employed, such as using dynamite and mob violence, but she could understand their frustration. She and her family had been helpless when Papa was killed. There had been nothing, nothing they could do. No recourse. No chance of learning the truth and obtaining justice if a crime had been committed. So, too, the workers of the nation today felt helpless as they watched their families go hungry, as they came home each night to poverty and filth, while the industrialists in whose plants they labored lived like kings. That feeling of utter helplessness, of being at the mercy of someone stronger, more powerful, and utterly ruthless, was the most terrifying and enraging sensation in the world. It had driven her to leave Emmettville, to build her own fortune, to make certain that her family would never be vulnerable to a rich man's greed or vengeance again. And for the most part, she had succeeded. They were all protected, all safe. Caroline was the only one who had not been able to fully overcome what had been done to her.

Elly stared at the vase of tulips on the table before her. Beside her, Boone leaned back against the couch and closed his eyes. The summer night was lulling him. He was tired. He worked hard, she thought, so hard. He was driven, as she had been, to build something so solid, so enormous and permanent that it could withstand any storm.

She turned and gazed at his strong, intelligent face, so full of good humor and understanding and steady, clear-minded purpose. How lucky she was to have him. It broke her heart to know that her sister would never have this kind of happiness, that she would never know what it was to lie in the arms of the man one loved, to be joined with him in delicious intimate pleasure, to comfort him in moments of sorrow or pain. Caroline had tried time and again to overcome the nightmare of that dark, suffocating, long-ago glade. But she had failed.

The brief courtship of Dr. Reeves had ended when he had grown tired of Caroline's skittish reactions to his slightest display of affection. Elly couldn't find it in her heart to blame the man. He was in search of a wife, someone to share the marriage bed and her husband's caresses, someone loving who could accept love in return. Caroline, by her own admission, was incapable of those things. Much as she tried, she had shrunk away from Gilbert's kisses, from his embraces, and worse, she had been too humiliated even to tell him why. After a few months of this, he had turned his attentions elsewhere, and last month had been married to the plump, black-eyed nurse who assisted him in his practice. Caroline had hidden her heartbreak well, but Elly recognized the misery in her eyes and the defeated droop of her shoulders. She had genuinely wanted to overcome her fears and to let herself know the love of a man, but the memories were too strong, too ingrained in her now, and she was their prisoner. Elly could only imagine her anguish each time she encountered Dr. Reeves and his new bride, for their happiness together only pointed up all the more her own loneliness. The work she did in the secondhand shop, the teaching and helping, along with her friendship with Roberta, only partially filled the void inside her. Unfortunately, Elly concluded, as she sat listening to the crickets' song, it was a void that would never be filled. Jason Emmett had seen to that long ago.

The long, steamy days of summer passed, and autumn came. On Timothy's birthday in October, he announced that he was going to marry Miss Delia Storm, a suffragist he had interviewed for the *Tribune* some months back. Delia was astonishingly beautiful, with coils and coils of russet hair, deep brown eyes, and fragile, finely molded features, all of which masked a will as strong as steel. She traveled about the country making speeches in behalf of women's rights, published a feminist newsletter from a tiny cubicle on Dearborn Street, and supported herself by giving piano lessons. Timothy, accustomed to the breezy artificiality of Chicago's wealthy young heiresses, had been stunned by her outspokenness, her fresh ideas, her boldness and fire, as much as by her beauty. It was a match of which Elly delightedly approved.

"Delia is the most amazing female," Timothy exulted when he introduced her that evening at his birthday dinner. "I've never met a woman with more energy, Elly—except you, that is."

Delia had grinned impishly across the oval dinner table. "What he means, Mrs. Walker, is that I've led him a pretty chase. He was accustomed to pursuing women who flitted around their parlors waiting for him to call. That was not the case in our courtship."

"No, she's been gallivanting about the country making speeches every time I've tried to see her," Timothy put in. But he was glowing, and the exchange of glances between the two bore all the marks of a couple in love. "I finally had to propose in order to guarantee that I could see her more than two nights in a row."

"I am still committed to giving talks in Ohio, Nebraska, and Missouri over the next six months," she explained. "But I gave Timothy my word that I would refocus most of my efforts on the newsletter instead so that the traveling will not interfere too much with our home life once we're married."

"And when will that be?" Elly inquired as the serving maid removed the first course and another uniformed girl brought in the second. The dining room with its Oriental carpet, pale blue-gray walls, and magnificent Sheraton side-board seemed to sparkle softly in the prisms of the crystal chandelier overhanging the table, but no more so than her brother's animated face. She didn't remember when she had seen Timothy look so happy.

"Next month," he replied, with a firm nod toward his fiancée. "I want us to be married by Thanksgiving."

And so they were. Life, reflected Elly over the course of that winter, was a series of surprises. Who would have expected Timothy, so fond of squiring an endless parade of giggling, light-headed girls to operas and plays and balls, to settle down so quickly and devotedly with an ardent feminist who delighted in arguing with him and challenging him and who insisted on having an equal say in every decision they made? It was good for him, she thought, for Delia Storm matched him in inquisitiveness and determination, and they would doubtless have a lively, exciting marriage, one that would be happy for the rest of their lives. . . .

"Louis and Victoria are celebrating their fortieth wedding anniversary this month," Boone told her, glancing up from the morning mail on a drizzly day in March. "They're having a ball in honor of the occasion." He told her the date, still perusing the stack of letters.

"Oh." She stared at the invitation he handed to her across the breakfast table. The delicately poached eggs and buttered toast on her plate were forgotten. "Are we . . . do you want to go?"

"Yes, of course. Don't you?" Boone raised an eyebrow quizzically at her unenthusiastic tone. She had always gotten on wonderfully with Louis and Victoria when they'd seen them in New York or when the Whitcombs had come to Chicago. In fact, he'd had the impression she was quite fond of them. Suddenly, understanding dawned. "It's Pittsburgh, isn't it? You're still reluctant to return to Pennsylvania."

"I had made up my mind when I left that I would never return there."

"Because of what happened all those years ago?" He was startled. "What are you afraid of?"

What indeed? Silas and Jason Emmett couldn't hurt her any longer. And she wouldn't be going to Emmettville, anyway. Only to Pittsburgh. "There's nothing to fear, Boone," she tried to explain, only partially understanding it herself.

"Only . . . the memories. The terrible feelings of despair and bitterness I had when we left. But . . ." She hesitated, her eyes clouded. "But I suppose it's foolish to let the memories keep me away from the party." She moistened her lips. "Of course we must go."

"You're sure?" Boone was watching her carefully. Despite her words, she still seemed uneasy. He didn't know all the details of the past—Elly hated talking about it—but he was aware of the crucial facts: Caroline had been raped by a mill owner's son, and the Forrest family had been run out of town to avoid a scandal. He could understand the bitterness she felt toward those who had mistreated her family, but after all these years, it seemed pointless to avoid Pittsburgh. It was a large city, his company's headquarters were there, and they had an important reason to travel there this month. Yet he didn't want to force her. "If you don't want to go . . ."

"It would be ridiculous not to go. I could never hurt Louis and Victoria by refusing."

"Are you sure?"

"I'm positive." She picked up a slice of toast and bit off the corner of it, then took a sip of her coffee. "I'm not going to let the past interfere with how I live my life. It's bad enough that Caroline still bears the scars from what happened. I refuse to do the same—even for one more day. In a way," she added, gazing at him across the table, her features taking on the determined look he knew well, "it will be a liberation. Proof that I've overcome my fear and bitterness. And do you know what else, my darling? Going back to Pennsylvania now will help me put the past behind me once and for all. In every other way, I have—except this one. I'm beginning to think I should have done it long ago."

So it was that, a little more than two weeks later, she and Boone stepped off the train in the crowded Pittsburgh station and were taken by hired carriage to the Monongahela House, the city's finest hotel. It had felt so strange to see the steep emerald hills of Pennsylvania again, particularly now that she was so accustomed to the flat Illinois plains.

The following night, she drifted restlessly about in their suite, unable to relax. There was no reason for this damned skittery feeling in her stomach, no reason why she couldn't sit still. Tomorrow, she told herself, she would tour the W-and-W steel works on the Monongahela and see the iron foundry that

Boone, Louis, and Connor had started together so many years ago. The tour would be fascinating, and it was long overdue. She should have come back to Pittsburgh long before now.

So she shed her pale green taffeta day dress, washed, and changed into a gold sequined ball gown, ignoring her own nervousness. "I'm ready," she told Boone brightly when he picked up his cane and hat. But instead of her usual serenity and self-assurance, she felt an increasing sense of unease. Much as she tried to shake it off, to reason with the emotions governing her, she could not.

Yet once inside the splendid house on Penn Avenue, Elly nearly forgot her turmoil. The Whitcombs' ballroom was vibrant with music, ablaze with candlelight, brilliant with flowers. One hundred fifty select guests in Worth gowns and evening suits drifted about, drinking champagne, dancing, and partaking of a sumptuous supper. Waltzing with Boone, wishing Louis and Victoria well, and enjoying the glittering surroundings and warm air of festivity that marked the occasion, she was soon caught up in the lighthearted atmosphere. Until, as she lifted her second glass of champagne to her lips, she saw the unmistakable face of a man only ten feet away, dancing with a blue-gowned blonde. They danced stiffly together, as if they disliked being in such close proximity, but it wasn't their posture that made Elly stare or that made the color fade abruptly from her cheeks. It was the man's face and the familiar arrogant set of his shoulders, and the smoothly brushed, glossy chestnut hair. It was everything about him that was so dreadfully, sickeningly familiar, even after fourteen years.

Jason Emmett.

She spilled her champagne all across the bodice of her gold sequined gown.

She smothered a cry and hurried to a table to deposit her glass. As she picked up a linen napkin with which to blot the champagne, she tried to clear the panic from her mind.

She had been uneasy about returning to Pennsylvania, but never, never had she actually expected to encounter Jason. Especially not here, in this house. She scanned the ballroom for Boone. He had gone off a few minutes earlier to confer with Louis about some business matter, and there was now no sign of either one of them. She guessed that they had secluded themselves in the library for an uninterrupted discussion. A clamminess came over her. She glanced back in the direction where she had seen Jason dancing, but the floor had cleared, the music had stopped, and there was no sign of Jason Emmett. Unnerved, she grasped the napkin along with her fan and reticule and headed for the carved doors of the ballroom. She had to find a private place in which to tidy her gown and compose her thoughts. Whatever happened, she must not lose control of her temper or her emotions. It wouldn't do to cause a scene here at the ball.

Inside the music room she found the peace she desired. Silence. Cool, calm silence. She went past the rosewood piano and the tall vases of ferns and flowers and seated herself on a blue velvet bench by the damask-draped windows. Slowly, gradually, the cold shaky feeling left her. All that remained was one thought: Jason Emmett was in this house. What was she going to do about it?

Nothing, that was the answer. She would do nothing. To confront him, to upset herself further and cause a scene, what would that accomplish? It would only set tongues wagging, and she would make a spectacle of herself. And nothing that she could do or say now would change the past. Was she afraid of him? she asked herself, her fingers clenched on her silk fan. No. She had never been afraid of him, only afraid of what his power could do. He had no power over her now, except the power to fill her with rage, to devastate her with a flood of ugly memories. If she did not see him again, if she could only manage to forget his presence here, she could at least control the sickening emotions roiling within her. Then the evening would not be spoiled for Boone, or for Louis and Victoria. For their sake, she would try to be calm.

When she had composed herself and blotted up the champagne from her bodice as best she could, she rose and made her way across the flowered carpet. Just as she opened the door and stepped into the brightly lit French-papered hall, a figure rounded the bend from the ballroom and came toward her. She could not mistake who it was.

It is meant to be, she thought blindly, her gaze fixed on Jason. He looked the same, only older, more dissipated, yet still filled with that smug, arrogant pride. *Fate means for me to confront him,* she told herself as she froze outside the music room, watching him advance with a rolling awkwardness which hinted that he was on the verge of being drunk.

"Evening," he said with the smirking grin she so well remembered. "I'm looking for my wife."

Elly could only stare at him. The frigidity in the depths of her eyes must have startled him, for he halted as he drew abreast of her, and peered into her face.

"How d'you do? Have we met?" he began, then broke off, faltering at the expression on her face.

"We have met," Elly replied, her tone so chilly and hard that he blinked. "Much as I regret to say it."

His pale blue eyes narrowed upon her. He was taking in her tall, slender figure in the sequined gold-brocade gown. She was elegant, graceful, a vision of superb self-assurance from the tips of her beaded satin slippers to the diamond combs in her hair. Around the white column of her throat was a magnificent gold and diamond collar, and matching earrings enhanced a face that was exotically beautiful, with delicately sculpted bone structure and wide-set flashing eyes. Her intricately curled and coiffed hair was a lustrous black, dramatic and bold against the creamy whiteness of her skin and the rich burnished gold of her gown. She was a spectacular vision, Jason acknowledged, with a quickening of his pulse, a grand lady through and through. But she was regarding him in the oddest, coldest way, as though those lovely blue-gray eyes of hers were frosted with ice. "Beg pardon?" he muttered, in a tone that had lost a little of its bland civility.

Elly's lips tightened. "As well you might."

Jason gaped at her. "Who the hell are you?" he demanded, the liquor and her hostile attitude causing him to abandon his veneer of politeness in a rush. "Come to think of it, you do look . . . rather familiar."

"My name is Elinore Walker." Her eyes glittered at him in the marble-tiled hall. "But you may remember me as Elinore Forrest."

"Elinore Forrest?" She could see him struggling through the fog of liquor and years, trying to place the name, to remember. All at once, he did. "Elinore Forrest—you?" He gaped at her, then gave a scornful laugh. "The pathetic mill girl my father ran out of town. How could I forget? You've improved your station in the world, from the looks of it."

Elly ignored his taunting tone and the insolent, appraising way he was studying her, his glance roving over her with undisguised crudity.

"How is your father?" she asked softly.

"Dead." He sounded coldly indifferent. "Father died years ago, not long after my mother." Jason's eyes lit suddenly with a flicker of malice. "How is your sister?" He chuckled, showing even white teeth. "Catherine, wasn't it? No, Carrie."

The rage poured through her then. This man had ruined Caroline's life, had choked the spirit and joy out of her and left her desolate and fearful of men forever. And he had forgotten her name. She had meant so little to him, except as an object to be abused and humiliated, that he didn't even remember her name.

"Caroline," she said in a voice that was so icy, so deadly cold that it could have frozen a sunbeam. "My sister's name is Caroline."

"Ah, yes, Caroline. A pretty little thing, but rather hysterical, as I remember." He was jeering at her, his handsome, dissolute face filled with a malevolent mirth. His brown hair was tinged with gray now; he wore it brushed straight back, a style that accentuated the cruel lines of his mouth and the flinty hardness of his pale blue eyes. How well she remembered that aquiline nose, and the mocking tone of his voice. None of that had changed. She saw no indication that the man facing her had ever felt an ounce of remorse for what he had done to Caroline or her family—or for anything else, for that matter. Watching him, her gloved hands clenched and her chest tight with anger, Elly was certain that he was as unscrupulous, cruel, and self-serving as he had been in the past.

"What are you doing here?" he demanded suddenly. The smell of liquor on his breath was repulsive. "You said your name is . . . what?"

"Walker." A strange, calming quiet came over Elly. She answered his questions with deadly softness. "My husband is in business with Louis Whitcomb."

"Boone Walker?" He practically shouted the name. When she nodded, something else entered his pale blue eyes. A glint of uneasiness, perhaps, or fear. Or maybe dislike. Elly couldn't be sure.

"You *have* done well for yourself," he added with a mocking laugh that echoed up and down the hall. "Yes, indeed, the gawky mill girl has become quite a lady. If I had guessed you'd turn out to be so damned attractive, maybe I would have paid a little more attention to you back in those days. Maybe I should have followed *you* home through the wood instead of your slut of a sister—''

Elly's hand flew up before he could react. She struck him a stinging blow across the face with her fan. The impact turned his cheek bright red and made rage leap into his pale eyes.

"Why, you little bitch!" Jason gasped. He thrust her back against the French-papered wall with a ferocity that jarred her teeth. His hands dug painfully into her shoulders. "Don't you remember what happened the last time you tried to win a battle with me? I ought to send you flying through those stained-glass windows!"

"Take your filthy hands off me!"

Elly felt blood on her lip where she had bitten it when he had thrown her against the wall. Her knees were trembling, and her shoulders ached where he was holding her. Damn him, damn Jason Emmett and his filthy mouth and vile soul! "Let me go this instant or I swear I will kill you," she cried. "And if you ever even speak my sister's name again—"

Jason laughed cruelly, his features contemptuous. "Enough of your stupid threats. You may be married to that bastard Walker, and you may be dressed like a lady, but you're nothing but a mill girl to me," he hissed at her. Spittle clung to the corners of his lips. "A filthy, worthless mill girl," he repeated, "just like your idiotic little sister. Where is she, anyway? Not here tonight? Too bad. It might be amusing to see her again. Where does she live? Tell me! I just might pay her a visit someday. Think she'll remember me?" He laughed viciously, pinning Elly against the wall. "Do you, you filthy bitch?"

At that moment, a couple departing early rounded the corner of the hall. At the sound of their voices, Jason glanced up and froze, then abruptly released Elly's shoulders.

"You're lucky, you bitch." He spoke in an undertone. Elly pushed him backward with all her strength.

"Get away from me. You're a loathsome piece of scum!" Heedless of the approaching pair, she glared at him with a wild, burning hatred. "You have made a very dangerous mistake!"

"Going to send your husband after me?" he taunted, his voice low but full of mockery. "That big dumb reb who happened to get lucky and hook up with my uncle? I'm not afraid of him. Or of you, a tramp from the mills," he muttered, straightening the lapels of his evening suit. With a final, jeering smirk and a shake of his head, he moved back down the hall from where he had come, toward the ballroom and the gorgeous, lilting music. The couple he passed stared curiously at him and then at Elly as they strolled by.

Elly felt as if she might collapse. Somehow she found the strength to push open the door of the music room. She staggered over to the settee and sank down as great, gulping sobs overtook her. She was trembling all over, sick and dizzy with the fury pounding within. She covered her face with her hands and wept, the tears streaming through her fingers.

Jason Emmett was as disgusting, as low and despicable as he had ever been. All the feelings of that night in Emmettville when she had fought him over her father's gun came rushing back. The rage, the helpless fury, the white-hot hatred that had the power to consume her, to rock her and tear her apart with its intensity, flooded through her again, every bit as powerful as before. Her hands shook, her whole body quaked with the memories—and her wrist, the wrist he had snapped all those years ago, once again began to ache with the old familiar pain.

She never knew how long she huddled there, shuddering, crying for all the old hurts as much as for the fresh wounds of this latest confrontation. But a small voice inside Elly gradually began to speak. It broke through her anguish, penetrated her grief, reminded her that times had changed. Circumstances had changed. She was no longer a powerless mill girl, and she no longer had to endure Jason's insults, his cruelties, or his threats. Gasping, she suddenly took several deep breaths, forcibly steadying herself. Her hands fell away from her face, and she lifted her head. In the solitude of the beautiful room, her anguished expression changed. Her face lost its tear-streaked misery and grew hard, cold. She sat up straight. Perspective returned, and with it came a great soothing relief accompanied by a new and powerful determination.

She rose, surprised to find that her knees were steady now beneath the flowing folds of her gown. Her hands, too, had lost their shakiness as she held them out before her, but her wrist still throbbed, and the ache in her shoulders was a dull reminder of Jason's grip on her. Alone in the cool, silent room, her eyes narrowed. Her heartbeat slowed. There was a small mirror over a table in the corner, and she went to it with slow, deliberate steps.

For a moment she stared at her reflection. Who was she? A mill girl? No. A woman of means. A lady of influence, wealth, intelligence, and power.

The scuffle in the hall had caused a few of her curls to loosen from her chignon and to wisp slightly about her face. She tidied them automatically. Still holding the linen napkin with which she'd cleaned up her gown, she dabbed at her face and at the dried blood on her lip. She intended to go back to the party. To dance with Boone, to toast the Whitcombs. But all the while, she would be thinking. Thinking and planning. Because she knew now what she had to do.

It had suddenly become very clear to her why she had been so reluctant to return to Pennsylvania and to encounter Jason Emmett again. Not because she was afraid of *him,* but because she had known deep down that once she faced him, she would be taking an irretrievable step. It was the direction her life would take on if she confronted him that had made her hesitate: the course she must and would take as result. She would be setting out on a path from which there was no turning back, and she had been uncertain whether or not she truly wanted to embark upon the journey.

But now she had taken that first step. She had seen him, and all the old hatred had come roaring back. The path was clear; there was only one direction she could go. Her route was as unalterable and prescribed as the daily rising and setting of the sun.

She was going to destroy Jason Emmett. Permanently, wholly. Whatever it required—whatever resources, money, time, or effort was necessary—she would do it. He would mourn the day he had ever touched the lives of the Forrest family. For deep down, she was still Elly Forrest and always would be. And it was finally time to seek her family's long-delayed revenge.

❦ Twenty-Eight

"NO. I DON'T believe you," Boone said with brutal honesty. "There's no good reason why you're not going on to New York with me today. At least, if there is, you haven't mentioned it yet."

Elly busied herself packing toiletries into her trunk. She didn't want to have to look into his face. It was too perceptive, too knowing. Beyond the window of the Monongahela House suite, the bridges and soot-covered smokestacks of Pittsburgh marred the pale blue spring sky. It was going to be a beautiful day, mild and balmy, though there was so much soot and smoke in the city's air that it might be difficult to tell. "You're making too much of this," she replied, trying to sound brisk and reasonable. "I simply feel I should get back to the hotel. Monsieur Jobert has a new assistant, and if he doesn't work out satisfactorily, you know perfectly well Jobert will throw a tantrum. And you also know that no one can handle him except me. Not to mention the fact that we are expecting the duke of Grieskirchen from Austria next week with a considerable entourage. I want to be certain everything is handled smoothly."

"Your staff can handle ten dukes, a prince, and a dozen senators with their eyes closed," Boone retorted, and strode to where she stood at the dressing table, fingering a collection of jewel boxes and embroidered handkerchiefs. He spun her around so that she was forced to look at him, and stared intently into her eyes.

"This has something to do with Jason Emmett, Elly, doesn't it? Tell me the truth."

She repressed the urge to do just that. Memories of Jason's

328

taunt about sending her husband after him still rang in her ears. No, though she had told Boone after the ball that she had encountered the man who had caused all the trouble for her family years ago—and that it was Jason Emmett—she wasn't going to involve him in her plans to ruin Jason—at least, not yet. She wanted the satisfaction of engineering that completely on her own.

"I have no intention of contacting Jason Emmett or of seeing him," she said truthfully. "I'm taking the train tomorrow for Chicago, and you are boarding the one for New York this morning. But if you don't hurry, my darling, you shall miss it, and then you'll have good reason for such a sore temper!"

She laughed and stood on tiptoe to press a light kiss against his lips. He fought against the grin her words were meant to coax from him. Damn it, Elly could always make him smile, and she knew it.

"I'm not convinced." He pulled her close against him and laid his hand against her hair. His fingers slid through the silken strands, then slipped beneath the heavy fall to caress the nape of her neck. She was still in her dressing gown, her hair loose and soft about her shoulders, her fine-boned face luminous in the morning light. Suddenly, he felt a surge of love and protectiveness so sharp that it almost made him cancel the New York excursion, simply to keep an eye on her. "What are you really up to?" he asked again, an urgency in his voice.

Elly recognized his concern. She reached up to rub his fresh-shaved jaw. He looked so handsome and strong and formidable in his gray morning suit and bowler. She knew he could thrash Jason Emmett to a bloody pulp and be done with it, but that wasn't what she had in mind. "I can't tell you," she said at last, responding to the anxiety in his gray eyes. "But I can promise you that I know what I'm doing, and I won't be in any danger. Boone, this is something I simply must do myself."

He stared at her for a long time, his arms slipping down to encircle her slim waist. "To think that that scum, Emmett, is the man who raped Caroline and ran you out of town," he mused at last. "It's amazing—but not surprising in view of his character. I never could stomach the fellow."

Boone had told Elly last night that Jason was Louis Whitcomb's nephew and that he had been involved in the first iron foundry Boone and Connor had persuaded Louis to invest in. He had also told her that the three of them had never gotten along. "Why don't I simply take tomorrow's train to New York and spend today breaking every bone in Jason Emmett's body?" he suggested. "Then the matter will be settled, you can come to New York with me as we originally planned, and that will be the end of it." His grin widened with growing pleasure. "Yes, the more I think of it, the better I like it. It's settled."

"No, Boone," Elly cried. She sensed he meant what he said, and felt a rush of alarm. "This is my fight—it was from the start—and I mean to finish it. Don't you think I can?" she challenged, stepping back out of his embrace.

Boone regarded her in his grave, thoughtful way. "I think you could marshal forces against all of Great Britain and win," he answered steadily. "But you don't have to. And you don't have to pit yourself against Jason Emmett alone, either. I'm your husband, and it would give me great pleasure to fight this battle for you."

"No." She moved past him, picked up his cane and gloves, and thrust them at him. "Stay out of it, for both of our sakes. Why is it men always use their fists first and think later? I have something much more interesting than a mere beating in mind for Jason Emmett. Now go ahead to your train and your meetings, and then hurry home. I'll see you in a few days, darling."

Boone frowned. He accepted the items she handed him, hefted his valise, and strode toward the door, still framing an angry reply. But as he turned and looked back at her, slender and determined and lovely, his face softened.

"Come here," he invited from the door of the suite, and Elly, all resolute femininity, marched toward him.

He was both amused and alarmed by the martial light in her eyes and by the determination he perceived in her face and in her whole bearing. "Do you know—I almost feel sorry for Jason Emmett," Boone murmured. He kissed Elly so warmly, so tenderly, that the tight, purposeful knot inside her nearly came completely unwound. His lips molded to hers, shaping them, pressing against them with a lover's ardor, making her temporarily forget everything else.

"I love you. Don't take any chances," he said between kisses.

"I won't—I won't. I love you and the children too much for that," she breathed, clinging to him as all of the love she felt for him spread through her like a surge of fire. Their kisses deepened, and his hand slipped inside her dressing gown to caress her breasts and stroke her back and hips, while she gave herself up to the tender feelings enveloping them, holding him close, so close, their bodies half entwined. All the while, their lips met in deep, wildly surging kisses until, reluctantly, and flushed with passion, he drew back.

"I'm going to miss my train unless I leave right now," he said regretfully, gazing down at her sensuously closed eyes and reddened lips.

"There's always another train," Elly murmured.

"So there is." He kissed her again, backing her against the door, but this time, it was Elly who stopped, her senses returning with a jolt.

"On second thought . . . will you really miss your train?"

"Umhumm."

"Boone . . . Boone, I'd adore making love with you all day long, but . . ."

His eyes narrowed at her as he sensed her passion fading. "But you have other plans," he drawled.

A tiny, apologetic smile. She was summoning her composure, letting her heartbeat slow, getting her emotions under control. "Yes," she said.

She traced the outline of his lips with one slender finger. "Darling, please try to understand," she pleaded. "This business of Jason Emmett . . . I've made up my mind, and I won't rest now until it's under way. I've got to get started today."

As he released her, she suddenly threw her arms around him again and kissed him quickly, with a yearning tenderness.

"Think of me while you're in New York. I'll be missing you every day," she said softly. "And please hurry home."

"You'll take the train to Chicago tomorrow? And you'll be careful?" he demanded.

"Yes."

Boone glanced at his watch. He swore. "I want you to tell me everything about this plan of yours when I get home," he said. Then he kissed her again, grabbed his valise, and left. She could hear his footsteps pounding down the hall. He'd

have to get to the depot in a hurry, or he really would miss
that train, she realized.

She paced up and down the suite, feeling guilty about not
telling him her plan just yet. But she was only getting started,
and she hadn't quite worked out all the details. She still
needed time to think and organize her strategy. Elly poured
herself a cup of tea, her brows knit in concentration. She
couldn't afford to make any mistakes, and neither did she
want to delay. The ideas she had already begun developing
must be set into motion today.

A short while later, dressed in a midnight-blue spring faille
gown, she put on a plumed hat and picked up her cloak and
parasol. As the morning sun rose over the hilltops, she set all
thoughts of Boone, of the hotel, even of her children, out of
her mind. What she required now was concentration—and
determination.

Fortunately, Elly thought, as she left the hotel, *I have a
great abundance of both.*

A strange feeling came over her as she set out. All those
years ago Silas Emmett had forbidden her ever to set foot in
Emmettville again. Today she meant to defy that order.

She was going back.

It was midafternoon when her hired coachman steered the
carriage horses across the outskirts of the town. The day was
balmy, mild, and clear with precious little breeze to ruffle the
new spring leaves that were just beginning to sprout on
the trees. As she traveled the bumpy road, she peered out the
window in tense fascination. A light blue mist softened the
outlines of the surrounding hills, much as she remembered.
Spring flowers bloomed along the road, fragrant clumps of
wild columbine, buttercups, honeysuckle. The woods, the
trees, the hills, and the scampering of an occasional rabbit
through the undergrowth—all brought back familiar childhood memories. Then, from inside the carriage, Elly watched
as the ugly buildings of the mill town sprang up in greater and
greater density, spoiling the peaceful beauty of the countryside. That aspect, too, was painfully familiar.

Emmettville had grown in the years since she'd left. There
were even more factories now, more coke ovens and blasting
furnaces and railroad yards sprawled along the river. More
tenement houses and taverns. More smoke and thick, choking

fumes. More grayness. And, she guessed, based on what she knew of Jason Emmett and what Victoria Whitcomb had told her this morning, more despair.

But not for long.

The town hummed with activity and would soon thrum with even more, when the evening whistle blew and the workers' shift ended and all the men and women and children streamed out of the factory gates, hungry for their long-awaited supper.

Her driver suddenly pulled up at the crest of a little slope alongside the wire works plant. There was nothing to be seen for miles around except rows and rows of drab brick buildings, smokestacks, and dirt. He came back to consult with Elly through the window.

"Where to, ma'am?"

"Stop at the post office. I need to purchase a newspaper there and to make inquiries about the man I'm seeking."

She told him how to reach the commercial section of town. With a nod, he resumed his seat atop the coach, and the jolting motion of the carriage began anew.

Elly soon found that the main section of the town had been built up as well. First Street and Washington Avenue were crowded with shops and bakeries and wagon works. She spotted a three-story department store, two banks, a theater, and several small hotels. And, of course, there were a good number of saloons. She drew out paper and pen from her reticule and made meticulous notes of the name and location of every business establishment added since her departure. Her mind was whirring and clicking along far more rapidly than the wheels of the coach.

In the post office she recognized no one, and no one appeared to recognize her, though many people threw her startled glances. She could understand their surprise. In her blue faille gown, parasol, gloves, and plumed hat, she looked exactly what she was: a lady of means and social position, costumed in a toilette far more elegant than anything the local women were bound to wear. And she was clearly a stranger in their midst. Not many strangers came to Emmettville, except on business, so who was she and what did she want? She ignored all the curious stares as she coolly obtained the newspaper and the information she wanted from the ogling postal clerk. Then she departed, with a swoosh of bustled skirts. Though her face betrayed none of her emotion, inwardly she was tingling with excitement over what she had just discovered.

By the time the day's shadows were lengthening, her carriage was rattling toward the familiar section of town where the Forrest family used to live.

The row houses and muddy yards of her girlhood looked even more dilapidated now. Gloom seemed to cling to the rotting porches, the broken planks of the walk, the very air, which was thick with factory dust. The wailing of a baby, drifting in through the carriage window, hurt her ears. It reminded her not only of her days in Emmettville but also of the time in the Rat's Tail, when that sound had rent the air night and day. It was always the children who suffered most from poverty. They were the ones who went hungry or cold or without loving comfort because their parents were too frightened and despairing to have time for gentle words or hugs. How ironic, what Victoria had told her this morning about Jason. He and his wife, the former Sarah Rhodes, with whom Elly had seen him dancing at the ball, had never had any children. Jason was as barren as the ugly scraped walls of his quarries. Even from his loins he could not bring forth anything vital and good and whole.

The address she had been given by the postal clerk was in a somewhat newer section of row houses than the one in which she had lived, but the conditions were not much better. Small frame buildings, surrounded by mud and weeds, were crowded together. Ragged children played on porches; stray dogs skulked about the rear alleys, nosing into crates of garbage. And pervading everything were the dinginess and the odor of coal fumes. The house before which the carriage halted was no different from the others, except that the lace curtains at the windows looked remarkably clean and white in the fading afternoon light. After instructing the driver to return for her in three hours, Elly went up the cracked porch steps. She introduced herself to the startled woman who answered the door, a baby in her arms. Three other children scampered underfoot as she was welcomed, somewhat hesitantly, inside.

By the time the front door opened again three-quarters of an hour later, Elly had helped lay out the supper dishes, given over her reticule, parasol, and hat to the fascinated children for a rapt inspection, and learned a great deal of what she

needed to know from the stout young Swedish wife who had
overcome her shyness and skepticism under the reassuring
warmth of Elly's smile. When the girl's husband crossed the
threshold in his sweat-stained clothes and stopped short in
surprise at the sight of her, Elly handed the plump-cheeked
baby back to its mother and came forward with her small,
strong hands outstretched. Her voice was rich with warmth
and affection.

"Billy, it is so good to see you. What a lovely family you
have."

Billy Moffett just stared at her, his hands at his sides.
"Who . . ."

In the little kerosene-lit parlor, Elly laughed. "Don't you
recognize me, Billy?"

He looked more confused than ever. "No, ma'am, I . . ."
Suddenly he leaned forward, peering into her face. He had
grown from a stocky boy into a broad-shouldered man, with a
thick neck, springy red hair, and whiskers, yet he still had the
same kind, round brown eyes she remembered. "Is it . . .
Elly?" The doubt in his face made her nod slowly. "Elly
Forrest?" he breathed in astonishment, which caused her to
laugh again.

"The same as ever."

"No." He shook his head. "Not the same. If I were to see
you on the street, I would have walked on by without ever
thinking that I knew you—Elly Forrest! I can't believe it!"

"It's Elly Walker now," the Swedish girl corrected him in
her thickly accented voice. She herded the children toward
the table. "Elly's going to stay to supper."

"But what are you doing here?" Billy blurted, taking in her
rich gown and carefully crimped hair as well as the ravishing
beauty of her delicate face and glowing eyes. "I can scarcely
believe you've come back to Emmettville. I never thought I'd
see you again once I set you down at the Union Depot."

Elly spoke over her shoulder as she followed Gerta and the
children to the round wooden table, gay with a flowered cloth
and neatly laid out plates and flatware. Despite the Spartan
furnishings and tiny rooms of the narrow row house, everything in it was immaculate, gleaming, spotless with care and
attention, much as her own childhood home had been. Perhaps that was why she had felt so comfortable immediately
with Gerta. "I've come on some very important business,

which will be of great significance to both of us," she said. Then she smiled at the children, who were well behaved and as clean and tidy as everything else in the house, but they were listening intently to every word. "However, let's talk about it after supper for it is both important and private," she said meaningfully, meeting Billy's thoughtful eyes. He nodded his understanding as they took their places at the table.

When the children were all put to bed and Gerta had come wearily down the stairs and brought tea into the parlor, Elly told them both why she had come.

"You must hear this, too, Gerta, every word, because it concerns you. Nothing will be the same, if you and Billy agree to my plan."

Billy shook his head. "What plan?"

"First, tell me something. Is it true that you are the principal organizer of the workers in Emmettville these days?"

"Yep. How'd you know that?"

"I picked up a copy of the *Gazette* in the post office today. Your name was splattered across it, in not very complimentary terms." She grinned. "You can imagine my surprise. I originally went to the post office to learn your address, Billy, intending to seek you out as a source of information. I was hoping you could introduce me to the local union leaders. And here you are, the very person I need to see." She clasped her hands together excitedly. "I consider this a good omen for my plan. It's puzzling, though." She regarded him intently as Gerta shifted in her chair. "I recall you telling me a long time ago that Emmettville wasn't so bad. You were content with your lot here, Billy. Remember?"

He met her gaze squarely. "Well, times change, Elly. A man changes. I've learned and grown some since I said those things."

Gerta in her faded gingham dress sent him a look of shared sorrow. "Billy only wants what's fair," she said quietly. "Shorter hours, decent pay. Sometimes we feel like . . . like slaves to Jason Emmett," she muttered. She peered at Elly, her clear, crystal-blue eyes bright with unshed tears. "He owns these houses, the stores where we buy our food and clothes and furniture, everything. *Everything* goes into his pockets, but he keeps prices up and wages low, so we are always in debt. The men, they are scared to complain for fear they will lose their jobs and not be able to make payments.

But Billy is not like them. He has courage. . . . He tries to make the others brave like him, but no.'' She was sputtering in anger and distress, shaking her head. ''Mr. Emmett is too strong.''

''That's what we're going to change,'' Elly said, looking at them both. ''If we work together.''

Billy studied her in the modest little parlor as she took a small sip of tea. ''What do you have in mind, Elly?'' he asked. He scratched thoughtfully at his red whiskers.

Her voice was steady and clear in the warm, airless room. ''I'm going to ruin Jason Emmett.''

Billy gave a guffaw, which quickly faded under the glittering hardness in Elly's eyes. ''Are you serious?'' he demanded. ''How in the name of heaven do you plan to do that?''

''I'll tell you. I'll need your help to do it. But if you work with me, I promise you that, in the end, Emmett's stranglehold on this town will be broken. In the meantime,'' she warned quietly, ''there will be months of difficulty ahead— maybe even of danger, although I hope not.''

Billy shrugged his broad shoulders. ''Unfortunately, neither of those things is exactly new to us.'' With a somber glance at his wife, he continued: ''Ever since I started working with the men, trying to organize a union, there's been trouble. Threats against Gerta and the children . . .''

''Billy was beaten once, and someone threw rocks through this window,'' Gerta put in, nodding toward the drawn lace curtains.

''It's not surprising, considering what we know about Jason Emmett.'' Elly nodded. ''But he's not undefeatable. I made some inquiries of a close relative of his earlier today, and I learned that his mills are losing money because of poor management. Jason is lazy, and he's self-satisfied. His complacency makes him vulnerable. But now, Billy, I want you to tell me about the union you've formed. How many men do you have? Who are they? And what exactly are your demands?''

She listened closely to Billy's account. Every once in a while, she made notes on paper of what he was saying. The rest of the time, her gaze was fixed intently on his face as he spoke.

It was a typical and frustrating story. Billy had been trying for several years to get Jason to shorten the work shifts from twelve hour days to eight—or even ten—but to no avail. Though at least two hundred men in Emmettville were anxious to support a union—hundreds more favored reform but were too intimidated to speak up—progress was at a virtual standstill. Every time the men started protesting and muttering about a strike, Jason would cut their wages and abruptly fire enough men to scare the rest into dropping their demands.

"It's pretty useless—that's the conclusion I've reached." Billy slumped back in his hickory chair. "We're at Emmett's mercy, like we always have been. Most of the workers are too scared of the poorhouse to risk standing up to him."

The lace curtains stirred in the cool March breeze. Elly's eyes gleamed in the lamplight. She leaned forward, tense, watching Billy's rough, discouraged face. "What if money were no longer a factor?" she said slowly. "What if every member of your union had a decent income—guaranteed— that would support his family comfortably for the duration of a strike, whether it lasted two months, six months, eight months, or even a year?"

Billy shook his head at her. "That's crazy, Elly. How could we ever guarantee something like that?"

"Would the workers support a strike then?" Elly insisted.

"Well, sure, if they could still manage to feed their families and keep a roof over their heads. But . . ."

"Billy, I am prepared tonight to write your union a check for ten thousand dollars."

Billy was gaping at her as though she had just spoken to him in fluent Chinese. Gerta Moffett clutched her teacup between her big fingers as if she would crack it with her grip.

"And there will be more funds—a great deal more. If you can organize the men, we can plan a boycott of Jason Emmett's businesses that will bring him to his knees. Also," she added, leaning forward on the sofa, "I need to know about the newspaper, the *Gazette*. I've already seen from reading it today that it is still violently anti-union. Does Frank Bremen still own it, and is he still in Jason's pocket?"

"Yes, Frank *is* one of our worst opponents. Emmett does a lot of advertising in the *Gazette*, so Bremen is more than eager to use his newspaper to keep the lower classes in their place. But he hasn't been well lately. There's talk he needs a change in climate. My guess is it's all the coal dust getting in

his lungs. Doc Chapman says he should go out west some-
wheres, where there's no factory smoke to make him cough.''

She nodded and made a notation. "Don't worry about that.
I'll take care of Frank Bremen. But I also need to know about
all of the businesses in town. Jason Emmett doesn't own or
control them all, does he? Who are his competitors? I need a
complete list of their names and their businesses, and I want
to know which ones are most likely to be sympathetic to our
cause.''

Billy held up his hand, obviously stunned by all of her
plans and the matter-of-fact way she was taking charge of the
situation—almost like a general preparing for battle, he thought.
"Elly, hold on. Are you sure you know what you're getting
into here? It sounds like you're planning an all-out war
against Jason Emmett!''

"I am.''

He stood up then and started pacing up and down the little
parlor, his shoulders stooped with weariness and fatigue. Yet
there was an underlying excitement in the depths of his eyes.
"I don't mean to sound rude or anything, but . . . Elly,
anyone can see you've become quite a lady. Your . . . your
husband must have a lot of money and all that, but the things
you're talking about, they'll cost a fortune. Do you realize
that? Are you really ready to invest so much in a plan to
break Emmett's power over us?'' He took a step closer,
shaking his head. "Why?''

She regarded him through smoldering blue-gray eyes. "Two
reasons, Billy,'' she replied. "I hate the Emmetts because of
what they did to my father and to Caroline and the rest of my
family. You know all about that,'' she remarked in a low
tone. "But it's even more than that. I also hate them because
of what they are, because of how they use—or should I say,
abuse—the money and power they possess. You mentioned
my husband, Billy. I haven't said much about him yet. Do
you know who he is?''

He shook his head, pausing behind Gerta's chair to rest his
hands on the high carved back.

"He's Boone Walker.''

"The steel tycoon?'' Billy's mouth dropped open, he slowly
shook his head back and forth.

"Yes, Boone has made a fortune in steel. He owns an
empire that makes Jason Emmett's holdings here in Emmettville

appear insignificant. But he is a fair man, Billy, decent and honorable in every sense of the word. Boone started out working in an iron mill, and he worked his way up to where he is now, but along the line, he has kept in mind the needs of the workingmen and their importance to his business.'' She edged forward on the old sofa, with its creaking springs and worn, stained cushions. ''Boone's workers have enjoyed an eight-hour day since he first opened the W-and-W steel works. His men earn top wages, and he is one of the few steel magnates who enjoy good relations with the labor unions. It hasn't always made him popular with the Carnegies and the Fricks of this world, and it's probably cost him some profits along the way, I'll tell you that, but Boone has always done what he thinks is right.''

''He sounds like a good man, Elly.'' For a moment, she thought she saw a wistful look flit across his broad features. Then it was gone and he was continuing: ''And he's willing to let you give us all this money—just to destroy Jason Emmett? It's kind of hard to believe.''

Gerta nodded, not moving on her chair.

''No, Billy, he doesn't know yet what I'm planning to do. The money I will invest is my own.'' She smiled, and her face sparkled as she continued, ''You see I, too, have learned how to work hard, and to plan well, over the years. I own a hotel in Chicago—a very beautiful and very profitable hotel. I can well afford to spend a great deal of money to destroy Jason Emmett, and I am completely committed to doing so.''

From upstairs came the sudden crying of the baby. Gerta, recalled to her duty as if from some dream, started, and hurried toward the stairs.

''Billy . . .'' she said hesitantly, as she paused halfway up. She looked down at them both. ''All this talk . . . I'm scared.''

''I can understand why, Gerta,'' Elly said softly. Again the baby's cries intruded, louder than before, and Gerta lingered no more, clambering up the rest of the steps. From upstairs, they could hear her soothing the baby, talking and singing in a softly lilting voice. In the parlor, a small silence fell.

Billy glanced dazedly around the small neat room with the white curtains and braided rug. Then he stared at the elegant woman before him.

"Are you scared, too, Billy? I don't blame you if you are," she said gently.

To her surprise, he shook his head and bolted around the chair to sit opposite her. There was suppressed vitality in his large frame as he gripped the arms of the chair and leaned forward, his eyes alight. "No, I'm not scared. I'm excited. More damned excited than I've been in a long time. We can do it, Elly, can't we? We can break Jason Emmett."

The glow in her eyes matched his. "I believe we can."

He smacked his knee with one large red hand. "That's good enough for me."

"Things may get rough, you know," she warned. Suddenly she felt tired. "I know from experience that when Jason is feeling cornered, he strikes out, very often in a violent and despicable way."

"That won't be anything new," Billy observed.

"Nevertheless, I'm going to take steps to protect you. I have a few things in mind. . . ."

Another hour passed before she left.

When she did, she had a distinct feeling of satisfaction. Sitting in the darkened carriage as it rattled back toward Pittsburgh, she could almost taste the sweet, potent wine of victory. If she was careful, thorough, and vigilant, no one would get hurt.

Elly smiled to herself in the carriage. No one, that is, except Jason Emmett. And that suited her just fine.

❧ Twenty-Nine

SO BEGAN THE systematic destruction of the Emmett financial empire. The day after Elly returned to Chicago she began marshaling her forces with the skill and relentless cunning of a general. The lawyer, Whetherby, and her clerk, Jennings, served as her lieutenants, but it was Elly who directed the campaign, who plotted each foray into enemy territory, and who pored over lists and figures and correspondence, analyzing the results of each skirmish with cool-headed precision.

Her first move was to arrange the purchase of the *Emmettville Gazette*, an aquisition that proved not very difficult at all. Frank Bremen was one of those oily little men whose eyes glazed over at the sight of crisp green money, and Elly, through Mr. Whetherby, offered him a tidy fortune, enough to permit him to follow his doctor's instructions and leave Emmettville for the more healthful climate of California. The first thing she did was to change the name of the paper to the *Emmettville Union*, and then she appointed a new editor, hand-picked by Billy Moffett to be sympathetic to the workers' cause. It was all done secretly and swiftly. The stupefaction and then wrath all this must have caused Jason she could only imagine: she was too busy organizing her other offensives to dwell on the details. But there was no doubt that the extensive and favorable reporting of the union's activities could only benefit her cause, giving the workingmen and women of Emmettville a tremendous boost to their morale and also helping to spread enthusiasm for the strikers' cause throughout the town.

Within a week of her visit to Emmettville, Billy had called a general union meeting, announced that all strikes and other union activities would be funded and supported by an anonymous backer, and drummed up enough support for a strike at four Emmett factories. The ensuing weeks brought an influx of workers to the meetings; it also brought a rash of rock-throwing incidents, small fires, and beatings by Emmett's paid thugs. The violence disturbed Elly greatly, even though she and Billy had both been prepared for it. She quickly set into motion the other component of her plan. By the middle of April, she had bribed Angus McLeish, the general manager of the iron works and Jason's closest confidant, into spying on his employer and reporting directly to Jennings. She also hired two Pinkerton detectives to keep an eye on the Moffett house and to provide secret protection to Billy and his family. With all of Billy's speech-making, strike-organizing, and saber-rattling, there was no doubt he would need it. Word reached Elly on April 23 that Jason Emmett was fit to be tied.

"Increase the pressure," Elly instructed from behind her desk.

Whetherby raised an eyebrow. "I assume you mean to widen the boycott of Emmett-owned enterprises," said Jennings, who for all his slight appearance and mild manner had a quick and crafty mind. He also seemed to particularly enjoy the brutal game that his employer had embarked upon. "Should we send word to Mr. Moffett that the townspeople should stop patronizing the shops and businesses owned by Mr. Emmett?"

"At once." Elly nodded, chewing the tip of her pen thoughtfully. "Tell Billy that from now on, he and his supporters should do business only with those establishments owned by independent businessmen who are sympathetic to our cause. You have the list I gave you?"

Jennings nodded.

"Excellent. If any products or services are needed that aren't available from companies besides Emmett's, see that they are shipped in at my expense from Pittsburgh." A cold gleam entered her eyes. "Let Jason's goods rot on the shelves."

Elly checked her notes. "And I want Billy to make certain that all the strikers are out surrounding their factories. Whenever possible, they must make it difficult for strikebreakers to get in or out," she added. "Emmett's mills must stand idle."

Both men nodded.

"Is there any indication that he is considering giving in to the strikers' demands?" she inquired at last.

Whetherby shook his head. "According to McLeish, Emmett is dead set against giving in so much as an inch. He claims he'd rather burn all the mills to the ground than turn them over to a bunch of anarchists. He's furious, and taking it out on everyone within two hundred yards." He cleared his throat, then regarded Elly through his shrewd dark eyes. "Another point. Emmett's wife appears to have left him for good. I gather there were some problems in the marriage before, but his recent financial difficulties and all this storm surrounding him now have precipitated her flight."

"To where?"

"Europe, according to the Pittsburgh gossips. With, ah, another man. Apparently it was a long-standing affair, but she was always reluctant to pursue a divorce. Mrs. Emmett comes from a very fine Pittsburgh family and wished to avoid a scandal under any circumstances—or almost any circumstances. Jason's late troubles have, it seems, changed her mind.''

''Such touching loyalty is no doubt well deserved,'' Elly observed dryly. She felt no enmity toward Sarah Emmett, never having known the woman, and could only wonder how anyone could have borne marriage to Jason for so many years. ''Well, everything seems to be progressing smoothly,'' she continued, glancing from one to the other of them with cool satisfaction. ''Unless something goes badly awry, the cogs of the Emmett empire will soon come to a screeching, grinding halt.''

The one thing that most concerned her, but which she couldn't fully control, was the safety of Billy and his family and of the other townspeople joining in the struggle. She knew it was Jason's way to strike out viciously when he was crossed, and she feared what he might do to stop Billy's all too successful activities, but she was forced to rely upon the precautions she had already taken: the detectives and the inside information provided by Angus McLeish. The man was being paid most generously to provide advance warning of any countermove Jason might attempt. Elly could only hope that the warning would come in time and with enough detail to prevent anyone's getting hurt. She reminded herself again and again that Billy had wanted to take on this fight, that he had been waging it unsuccessfully on his own before she ever returned to Emmettville. But it was only through her financial backing and organized strategy that the efforts to unite the town's laborers were working. Under her direction and Billy's leadership, the ironworkers and the cotton mill workers, the railroad men and the boot makers, the unskilled immigrants and the highly skilled Anglo-Saxon craftsmen were all joining together for the first time to force acceptance of their demands.

On May 3 and 4, a series of events occurred that made Elly's blood run cold: Chicago exploded with labor violence that rocked the city and the nation and brought home to her just what kind of powder keg she was sitting on. In Haymarket Square, between Halsted and Desplaines streets, on a drizzly Tuesday night, a crowd gathered to hear August Spies, Albert Parsons, and Samuel Fielden decry police violence against strikers at the McCormick Harvester Works on Blue Island the previous day. In that demonstration, one striker had been killed, six more seriously hurt, and at least fifty others injured. The seething labor unrest always simmering in the city reached the boiling point when word of the brutality spread, and the next morning August Spies, editor of the German workers' newspaper, *Arbeiter-Zeitung*, had distributed handbills calling for a mass meeting in Haymarket Square and a general calling-to-arms of all the laboring men in the city. On Tuesday night, May 4, the meeting in the Haymarket began peaceably enough, with the usual fiery speeches, cheers, and applause, and even an appearance by Mayor Harrison who was deemed a friend to the workingman. The mayor had judged everything to be under control and had already departed when anarchist Samuel Fielden began his remarks. Disastrously, everything fell apart after that.

A column of policemen from the Desplaines Street station, led by Captain John Bonfield, suddenly appeared and marched through the gathering. Without orders or approval from his superiors, Bonfield ordered the meeting to disperse. Fielden broke off his concluding remarks, called out that the gathering was peaceable, and began complying with the order by coming down from the platform. Then suddenly a bomb exploded in the midst of the police ranks. Seven policemen died as a result of the explosion, which set off a riot of gunfire and beatings in which more than two hundred people were wounded and an indeterminate number of additional men died. And Chicago quaked with turbulence and fear as the workingmen confronted a shocked and outraged society.

"Have you thought of what could happen in Emmettville?" Boone asked Elly the night following the explosion, as they readied themselves for bed. "Those men are stirred up as they never have been before. With your backing, they feel strong, indomitable. And they're going up against a man who is financially desperate, who is committed to maintaining absolute control. It's a violent brew if ever I saw one."

Elly was brushing her hair and watching him remove his shoes through her dressing-table mirror. "I didn't start this fight, Boone. Those men have been stepped on for years."

"Yes, that's true; they've been exploited all their lives! We both know that, but you've enabled them to do something about it for the first time. And I only hope they don't get carried away with their newfound sense of power. And I hope Jason Emmett doesn't massacre the bunch of them or do something equally horrible. Look what happened in Haymarket. The mood of the city, of the whole country, is one of outrage. I think the workingman will suffer as a result of this violence, Elly. It casts a pall over the entire labor movement. And I only hope it doesn't give Emmett the idea that he can get away with anything he pleases, that the workers are fair game now, more so than ever." He came to stand behind her chair, and in the glow of the lamp, his face was troubled. "Billy Moffett is at the center of this thing. You put him there. And if anything happens to him—"

"Don't you think I'm concerned about that, too?" Elly threw down her brush and jumped up to face him. "I'm worried sick about Billy. I'm doing my best to protect him, but you have to remember, Boone, that he volunteered to do this. He was already trying to unite the men when I sought him out. I didn't force him to do anything."

"No." He met her defensive gaze steadily. "But you made it possible for him to agitate Jason Emmett beyond all expectation. And if anything should happen to Moffett, Elly, it'll be you I worry about. I don't think you could live with that."

A shudder ran through her at his words, yet she maintained a calm facade. "I pray I won't have to. I don't think I will. I've taken precautions."

He grimaced. "Mayor Harrison took precautions, too. He told the officers at the Desplaines Street police station not to break up the Haymarket meeting, that since it was orderly, he didn't want to interfere. But somehow things went wrong."

Elly felt a cold quivering inside her. Maybe Boone was right. Maybe all her plans would ignite into a terrible inferno, an explosion of violence that would shake Pennsylvania just as the Haymarket bomb had shaken Chicago. Maybe people would be hurt or killed. Billy . . .

"I can't stop it now," she said quietly, but her arms came up to encircle his neck, and she moved closer, wanting to feel his arms around her, wanting comfort from the disturbing points he had made. "I'm not sure that I would try, even if it were possible—but it isn't. Jason must either recognize the trade unions and their demands, or be ruined. He's brought this on himself."

Holding her in his arms as the night sounds murmured outside their open window, Boone brushed his lips across her hair. He knew Elly was right: the Emmettville workers' struggle was just and probably inevitable, and there was no longer any turning back. He only hoped none of them would live to regret the course of events she had set into motion.

He had an uneasy feeling that they would.

That same night, Jason Emmett walked into a dinner party in a splendid neighborhood in Pittsburgh and was greeted by silence. Dead silence, which descended abruptly the moment he entered the room. He flushed and began to fidget unconsciously with his tight stand-up collar. A moment before, everyone at the table had been engaged in gregarious conversation. Now . . .

Was it because he was late?

Or because he and his troubles had been the main topic of conversation?

"Please accept my apologies, Louisa," he said to the hostess as he glanced nervously about the bountiful candlelit table. "An unavoidable delay—"

"Oh, not at all, Jason." Airily she smiled at him and watched him cross the walnut-paneled room. The company was half finished with the soup course. "We're delighted you could join us, however tardily."

There was a slight pause as he took his seat, and then, all at once, conversation swelled again around him. He stifled his uneasiness. His nerves were frayed, his stomach in a constant churning state. He didn't feel he could eat a bite of anything set before him. It seemed that the whole world knew of his business woes and had an opinion about them. To his chagrin, most of the opinions faulted him, for some reason, as if he were allowing those damned communists to take advantage of him, which wasn't at all the case. He was doing everything he could to bring an end to the situation. Everything. But so far, nothing was going right.

Damn them all.

At that moment, he wished all of the residents of Emmettville and all of the pompous snobs at this gathering to be burned in hell—together! Wouldn't that be a sight?

He gave a snort of laughter, which caused the lady on his right to glance at him in alarm. He didn't care. He reached for his wineglass and gulped down the contents. He was immediately thirsty for more.

After dinner, when the ladies had retired to the drawing

room and the gentlemen lingered over their brandy and cigars, John Arlington nudged him in the ribs. "Heard about your troubles, Emmett. Letting those strikers get the best of you, eh?"

"They're making a lot of noise, that's all." Jason waved his cigar with a show of unconcern. "They can't keep up the strikes for long. Never fear, Arlington, I've got everything under control."

He heard a snicker and glanced about, coloring. He couldn't tell who had made the offending sound, but Albert Morley leaned across the table with a fiery glint in his bright blue eyes.

"That's not what I heard, Emmett. 'Course, it's none of my concern, but word has it you're on the ropes." He shook his shaggy white head. "Now, if your father were alive, he'd know how to put a stop to this rabble-rousing. Silas would never allow—"

"I told you *I'm* going to put a stop to it!" Jason exploded. For a moment, it looked as if he might lean across the table and hit Morley, and there was a sharp collective intake of breath around the room before he got himself under control enough to say, "Save your worry for the communists, sir. When I'm finished with them, they'll be begging me for jobs at penny wages. I can promise you that!"

Yet, for all his denials, Jason sensed the doubts of the men gathered in the smoky room. He also sensed their disapproval. His fury mounted. He was a laughing stock. They considered him weak, a failure, not only because of his problems with those damned trade unionists but also because of Sarah's scandalous desertion. It was all tied in together, one great big hellish mess. His chest began to hurt. So did his head. It ached like hell. Miserable and half drunk, he gulped down another brandy as the conversation flowed around him.

The whole world seemed to be rising up against him. Whispering about him. And enjoying his streak of bad luck. He felt trapped, isolated, like an animal being cut off from the pack. He licked his lips over his third brandy of the evening in between puffs on his cigar. It didn't help to steady his nerves, though. Only one thing, Jason reflected dourly, would do that.

By the time he reached Hyacinth House late that night, he had made a decision. He sent for Angus McLeish, and fortified himself in the study with a bottle of port until his manager arrived. Tilting the bottle to his lips, he drained the last of it with a great, sucking gulp. Then he began to pace, wondering why in hell McLeish hadn't shown up yet. Damn the man. Damn all men conniving, greedy bastards that they were. And the women were no better, he decided, as a belch emanated from his liquor-coated throat. Take Sarah, for example. Now, there was a woman who deserved the title of bitch.

He remembered the first night she'd had dinner in this house. He had thought her a goddess, the epitome of female perfection. Hah! If she was the highest embodiment of the female species, they were all in trouble. Beneath that angelic face and petite, tempting body he had discovered a cold, calculating woman chiefly interested in the material possessions he could provide for her. Their marriage had been a convenience for her, a partnership instigated by her father and acquiesced to by Sarah with dutiful resignation—and a not disinterested awareness of the Emmett fortune. But he'd never known a day of happiness with the bitch. One way or another, she'd always managed to make him feel inferior. With cool, artificial sweetness she had criticized him before his friends and associates, demolished his pride, and needled him in her own distant, well-bred manner until he'd so sickened of her that he never even sought her out in the marriage bed anymore, preferring to find his pleasure elsewhere, with women he could control and intimidate, who wouldn't dare stick their noses in the air when he came near them. But even that didn't stop him from despising them. While Sarah was cold and superior, the others were all sluts. Sniveling, pathetic sluts worthy of his contempt—and abuse. Being abused, he had decided long ago, was the only thing women were good for.

Jason belched again, then mopped the perspiration from his brow. It was too damned hot in here. Stuffy and confining as well. He stalked to the study window, threw it open, and inhaled deeply of the balmy May air. But the faint fumes drifting up from the factory section of the town clogged his throat and made him cough. Disgusted and feeling faintly nauseated from all the port he'd consumed and the factory air carried on the breeze, he reeled back toward his desk.

Thinking of Sarah had reminded him of something he meant to do. He was going to change his will. After all, why should she get a penny of Emmett money when he was gone? She'd run out on him, hadn't she? Humiliated him by running off to Europe with that smarmy Italian bastard. And she had filed for a divorce. So why should she get one damned cent?

The answer was clear: she shouldn't. And as soon as this union trouble was settled—and settled it would be—he would have his lawyer draw up a new will and cut her out completely. The emptiness and loneliness of the huge, glossily beautiful house seemed to echo about him, reinforcing the rightness of his decision. He slumped forward at his desk, his fingers splayed upon the piles of letters and account books there. They were a sharp reminder of the unpleasant situation he was in. If he didn't do something fast, there wouldn't be much to leave behind for anyone.

He was in trouble, desperate financial trouble, and it was that, combined with the humiliating tone of the dinner party earlier, which drove him to such an angry restlessness this night. Jason felt on fire with despair. He glanced resentfully up at the gold-framed oil portrait of his father, which hung over the black marble mantel. He'd always hated his father so much that he'd never listened when Silas lectured him about business, about the need to devote innumerable hours to his work, about the importance of touring the factories regularly and meticulously inspecting all books and records—for years he'd been careless. He'd neglected the management of his properties, jaunting off here and there and leaving the day-to-day operations to a bunch of no-good, imbecilic louts. Now he was paying the price, and it was a steep one. His companies were in serious trouble—and this rash of workers' strikes, the boycotting of his retail businesses, and the mood of rebellion in the town added to his sense of impending disaster.

"Damn you, Father, you always *did* have to be right," he snarled, then glared down furiously at the grim tally sheets before him.

At that moment the doors opened and Duncan appeared.

"Mr. McLeish, sir."

On his heels came the tall, angular Scotsman, his narrow green eyes darting around as he entered the study, obviously impressed with the plush display of leather and brass and black marble, the gold-framed oil painting of Silas Emmett hanging over the mantel, the massive clawfoot desk from behind which Jason Emmett glared at him.

"It's about time," Emmett snapped. "Sit down."

He stared in contempt at the man with the bristly brown beard and scraggly brows. He felt scorn for McLeish's obvious ogling of his house. It was the first time Jason had ever invited the man to meet him here at Hyacinth House, true, but what had he expected? A hovel? Jason took the grandeur of his family home for granted. He didn't give a damn what Angus McLeish thought of it, and he certainly didn't want to waste any time listening to idiotic compliments.

He didn't give McLeish a chance to speak. "I'm fed up, McLeish. I've had it to here"—he indicated his chin—"with Moffett and his rabble-rousing. Have you seen the latest production figures for the iron mill? And there are department stores all over the East Coast yammering at me for their boot shipments. Not to mention the cotton mill . . . Oh, the devil take it all, McLeish, I won't stand for it another moment!"

Jason slammed his fist down on the sheaf of papers on his desk, the ones containing all those blasted unpleasant figures. The impact made a loud thud, but it didn't fully release his frustration. He picked up the empty port bottle and hurled it at the mantel. Glass shattered, flying everywhere about the room.

"I'm going to put an end to it—one way or another!" he shouted. Sweat glistened on his wrathful, highly flushed face.

"Do you mean negotiate with the men? Settle the strikes?" Angus inquired, scratching at his beard. He kept a wary, thoughtful eye on his employer all the while. He'd never seen Emmett quite this upset before. Angry, impatient, unreasonable, yes. But not with the kind of murderous rage that now seemed to shine from his face. Angus felt the sweat on his own palms. If Emmett ever suspected that he was spying for the people behind all the strikes . . . well, he didn't want to think about that. He didn't have a chance to, either, for Jason Emmett exploded like a stick of dynamite.

"Negotiate? Settle? You're out of your damned mind!" In two strides, he was around the desk and grasping McLeish by the lapels of his coat. "I'll go to hell before I give in to riffraff like Moffett. No, my father taught me how to deal with scum like him."

Still holding the manager's lapels, he turned his head to stare up at the portrait. His gray-haired, hard-eyed parent seemed to glower down at him with disapproving ferocity. He wet his lips and turned back to McLeish, releasing the man as abruptly as he'd grabbed him. He paced to the glass-enclosed cabinet near the door and gazed at the battered Colt displayed on one of the shelves. "Yes," he said, with a bit more self-control. A hard smile twisted his lips as he studied the gun. "My father knew how to handle the lower classes, how to keep them in their place. He gave me a few splendid lessons on that very point."

"It does seem peculiar, their sudden interest in these strikes. I can't imagine how they're scraping by. Those men need their pay, Mr. Emmett."

"Mark my words, McLeish, someone's behind this, helping them, supporting them. Moffett's too weak and dumb to do all this alone." Jason spun about to face him, his expression vicious. "I'll wager it's one of my competitors—Van Wyle or Crittenly, perhaps—trying to ruin me so he can buy up my properties for a few pennies, or so he thinks. But I'll be damned before some scheming snake and a bunch of communists get their hands on any of *my* holdings." He paced the study, a smirk spreading across his face. "You see, I know exactly how to put a stop to it, McLeish: Billy Moffett."

McLeish cocked his head to one side. "What about him?"

"Get rid of him," Jason returned shortly.

He wheeled about, sat down in the chair behind his desk, and gazed at the other man with a slyly calculating look. His narrow face and high-bridged nose emphasized the aura of natural arrogance that characterized him; even the liquor he had consumed tonight didn't lessen his air of self-importance. He seemed to be waiting with smug expectation for the manager's response.

"I'm not sure I understand you, Mr. Emmett. . . ."

"Damn it, man, do I need to spell it out for you?" Jason gave a harsh bark of laughter. "I want Billy Moffett dead and out of the way. And I know just the way to do it, too."

McLeish shifted in his chair. A gleam had entered his shrewd green eyes, and he scratched his chin thoughtfully. "What might that be, sir?"

"Arrange a meeting with him. Tell him that I'm ready to give in to his demands, that I want to discuss terms—but just the two of us, privately, before we make announcement of a formal agreement. Say whatever the hell you have to say,

McLeish, just be sure he meets me at . . ." He considered a moment, then nodded to himself. "Have him meet me at the shed behind the livery stable at the edge of town. First of next week. Let's say Monday, eight o'clock in the evening. That ought to give you enough time."

"Time, Mr. Emmett?"

"To get the dynamite." Jason leaned back in his chair and put his feet up on the desk. He studied the startled expression on his manager's face, feeling more pleased with his idea by the moment. "The fewer people who know about this, the better, McLeish. Understand?"

The manager wet his lips. "What exactly do you want me to do?"

"When Moffett gets to the shed, expecting only to see me, you'll join us, armed, of course. We'll force him to tell us who's really behind this strike business, and then you can beat him senseless with your rifle or a brick or whatever the hell you choose, so he won't put up any more fuss." Jason shrugged. "After I've gone, you light the fuse on the dynamite and run like hell." He chuckled thickly, then began to cough. It was obvious he enjoyed the scenario. "The beauty of it is that it will look as if Moffett blew himself up while he was making a bomb. Greeves will have no problem giving that as the official explanation of his death. And no one will be the wiser, except you and me. And you'll be well compensated for your efforts, McLeish, believe me you will."

He opened a drawer, withdrew an envelope, and tossed it on the desk. "Here's two hundred dollars, McLeish." He didn't mention that it was damned close to the last available cash he had left. His bank account was nearly dry, but once Moffett was out of the way, his enemies would find damn few people eager to oppose him further. Fear and panic over the circumstances of Billy Moffett's death would divide the workers and shatter their false courage. The strikes would collapse, and the factories and mills would hum busily again. And those who were avoiding his stores in Emmettville would lose heart, tired of limiting themselves to the competition's goods. In no time, all would be restored to the status quo. After that, Jason promised himself, he would pay more attention to things. He didn't ever want to sink this far into debt again, or have to fight off these mangy packs of trade-union anarchists, either. Once Moffett was dead, he'd keep a tight

lid on any organizers who even tried to open their mouths.
And he'd crack the whip over his factory bosses to seal in
every last profit.

"Take the money," he told McLeish. "Spend what you
need on the dynamite, and keep the rest as payment in
advance. Just don't talk—or bungle the job."

"I won't, Mr. Emmett."

Angus McLeish reached eagerly for the packet of money.
He stuffed it into his pocket, looking suddenly much happier
than he had all along. "There's only one thing, sir. Moffett's
no fool. He might be suspicious. He might not follow orders
and come to the shed alone."

"What the hell do I care?" Jason was growing impatient
with the company of the Scotsman. And he was thirsty. He
wanted to open another bottle of port, but without sharing any
with McLeish. "Let him bring a few of his dirty little friends
along—the more anarchists we get rid of at once, the better.
You'll have your rifle. We can knock them out one by one or
tie them up—I'll leave the details to you, McLeish. You can
handle that, can't you?" he snarled. He swung his booted feet
to the floor with a thump, then stalked to the door, throwing
it wide.

The Scotsman assured him that he could, touched the brim
of his hat, and left.

Jason heaved a sigh of relief, went to the liquor cabinet,
and opened a fresh bottle of port. He didn't bother with a
glass. Holding the bottle by the neck, he sank into the deep
olive-green armchair in the corner. A smile of satisfaction
flitted across his handsome, dissolute face. Thanks to those
damned socialists in Haymarket Square in Chicago, the whole
nation was up in arms. It was perfect timing. No one would
think twice about a small-town labor leader blowing himself
up with a bomb he meant to use against his employer. No one
would shed a tear.

Except the man's wife.

He gave a small shrug, then took a deep, belly-warming
slug of the port and smacked his lips. For the first time in a
long while, he felt confident and in control. By this time next
week, his troubles would be over. He would be back on top
where he belonged—for good.

❧ Thirty

THE THREE FIGURES stood on Sheriff Greeves's front porch just before seven o'clock. Twilight lay over Emmettville, deepening the drab grayness of the town. The uniformed officer tapped twice on the wooden door.

"Who're you? And what do you want?"

From the threshold of the flickering gaslit interior of the large frame house, Greeves peered suspiciously out at the two police officers and the dark figure of the woman. He had aged over the past fourteen years, Elly noted. His dirty gold hair and drooping mustache were now gray, his cheeks were sunken, and his neck was so thin and scrawny it resembled a turkey's. He looked smaller, too, his wiry body shriveled and puny, but his eyes were the same beneath their spectacles: tiny, blue, and pugnacious within that brown weathered face. He looked none too pleased at the disturbance.

Farther down the hall, a large-nosed, heavy woman stared around a doorway.

"Sheriff Greeves?" The younger of the two officers spoke. "I'm Officer Mayburn, and this is Officer Flynn of the sixth precinct in Pittsburgh. May we come in?"

"What fer?"

Flynn answered in a deep, rolling brogue reminiscent of Connor's. "To discuss a criminal matter, to be sure, Sheriff. But we don't have all night, you see."

Greeves stood aside, letting them pass through into the olive-green- and red-papered hall. Of the three visitors, Greeves stared most curiously at the woman as she glided forward over the red ingrain carpet, graceful and composed in the sheriff's darkly somber home.

355

A greasy smell wafted in from the kitchen, increasing the churning feeling already present in Elly's stomach.

"What's this all about?" he complained, glancing in quick irritation at the two policemen. "I was just about to set down to my supper."

Elly regarded him icily. "Unfortunately, Sheriff, your supper will have to wait."

Her voice, rich and husky and melodious, had an oddly familiar sound to it, but Greeves couldn't place it. He glared at her, taking in her simple but elegant black traveling dress and shawl, her impeccable chignon beneath a dark, plumed hat. Lord, she was handsome. Too snooty for his taste, though, he decided with a stab of contempt. He didn't like the high-handed way she was staring at him.

"Sheriff, we've come to ask that you accompany us to the shed behind Emmett's livery stable. We have reason to believe that a crime is going to take place there shortly," Officer Mayburn said.

Greeves scarcely heard him. He was still studying the woman, trying hard as hell to place her. Something about her was familiar but . . . "Who are you?" he demanded suddenly, unable to stand the uncertainty any longer. "You're not from these parts are you?"

"Not anymore."

"What's your name, then?"

"Elinore Walker." She watched his face as she added in a dry, cool tone, "It used to be Elinore Forrest, Sheriff. I'm certain you recall my family."

Another time, Elly might have enjoyed the shock that registered on Greeves's face at her words. Tonight she was impatient to get on with the purpose of this call. She was nervous almost beyond endurance. Billy would face Jason Emmett in the shed in less than an hour, and she was terrified that something might go wrong.

"What're you doing back here?" he demanded, hostility making his voice shrill. He half turned toward his wife, who was still hovering near the kitchen doorway. "This gal was always trouble! Damnation, if she hasn't got gall to show her face after all these years—"

"Sheriff, that'll be enough out of you," Officer Mayburn cut him off harshly. "Mrs. Walker is here as a concerned citizen. Word reached her that a murder is going to be committed here tonight, and she brought the information to our precinct.''

''It seems,'' the Irish policeman broke in, with a hard gaze directed at Greeves, ''that she doubted your ability to prevent the crime and to prosecute it.''

''She what?'' Greeves screeched. His tiny eyes sparked hate in the yellowish light of the hall.

From outside, Elly heard the noisy chorus of crickets, the whistle of a distant train. It seemed to her that she could also hear the ticking by of the seconds, and with each one's passing, her uneasiness increased.

''Officers, perhaps we should explain all this later,'' she interrupted, her gaze sweeping toward the two uniformed men in urgent appeal. ''We're losing a great deal of time here, and it is imperative that we be in place before Emmett gets to that shed.''

''Emmett?'' Greeves's face was beet-red with fury now.

''Come along, Sheriff, the lady's right. We'll explain afterward.''

''I'm not goin' anywhere till I know what this is all about! You men have no jurisdiction here,'' Greeves shouted, which made the husky young Mayburn grab him by the arm.

''We've got all the jurisdiction we need.''

''The hell you do!''

''Mrs. Walker's husband is an important man in this state, Sheriff. When she came to us, our precinct captain decided this was a special case. He thought she deserved our full cooperation. Captain Knox, he telegraphed the governor and got special permission for us to take over on this one.''

''Special permission? The governor?'' Open-mouthed, Greeves stared at Elly. He looked like a man who had just swallowed a hornet.

''That's right,'' Flynn continued easily. ''Providing we informed you of the situation and let you help with the arrest. Sure and we're doing that now, Sheriff, aren't we? So let's step lively here before we're too late.'' He whistled cheerfully as the two officers nearly dragged Greeves with them to the porch and down the steps into the night.

''Now, ma'am, shut your door and don't open it or speak to a soul until your husband gets back,'' Mayburn advised Greeves's wife over his shoulder. ''You wouldn't want any trouble with the governor now, would you?''

Ashen-faced, the old woman slammed and bolted the door.

Elly walked alongside the men in the darkness, her shoes clicking on the planked boards, her heart pounding. They had wasted a great deal of time with Greeves, she fumed. What if Jason came early and saw them going into the shed? She shook at the very thought. The entire plan would collapse. They had no actual proof of what was to happen, and Jason could not be arrested merely on McLeish's word. Jason would get away and figure out who had betrayed him—and their chance to stop him for good would be ruined. . . .

Horrible misgivings filled her as the little group climbed into the carriage she'd hired in Pittsburgh and drove to the outskirts of Emmettville's commercial district. There was the livery stable looming out of the darkness, and there, behind it, was the shed.

She had underestimated the quickness and stealth of the officers accompanying her. Within moments, they were all in place, hiding behind barrels in the gloom of the shed. Waiting, listening, and, in Elly's case, praying.

Angus McLeish was the first to arrive. He whispered into the darkness, "Mrs. Walker?"

Mayburn went forward and spoke to him conversing in low tones. Their voices washed over Elly like ghosts in the darkness. She glanced across at Sheriff Greeves. If the circumstances had been different, she might have felt sorry for him. He looked terrified. Thin, bone-pale, his scrawny neck quivering. As well it might, she reflected coldly. He was lying in wait, with honest policemen and a woman Jason hated, to seize the man who had so handsomely lined his pockets all these years. And there was nothing he could do to prevent the arrest. Officers Mayburn and Flynn had made it very clear to him in the buggy that if he made any sound or signal or interfered with them in any way, he would himself be hauled up on charges of obstructing justice and could expect to spend a long time in a Pittsburgh jail. Greeves was in a well-deserved tight spot, Elly acknowledged, but she felt only contempt, not pity, for him.

While she waited for Jason Emmett to arrive, her thoughts turned anxiously to her family in Chicago. Boone hadn't wanted her to come here after McLeish informed them of Jason's plot. He had wanted her to let him or Jennings or Whetherby handle it. Against his wishes, Elly had insisted. It would have been cowardly to stay away when she was at the core of all the goings-on, she had argued. And besides, she had told him, her features hardening, she wanted the satisfaction of seeing Jason Emmett put behind bars. It was something she had waited a long time to do. No one—not even Boone—could persuade her to give up that singular pleasure. She could still see in her mind Boone's grimace of resignation, the way he had run his fingers through his sandy hair. Then he had insisted on accompanying her, to which Elly had raised no objection. At the last moment, though, there had been an accident at one of his quarries in southern Illinois, with three men hurt and one dead, and Boone had had to get down there in a hurry to take care of things. One last time, he had urged her to send Jennings or Whetherby in her place, but she had kissed him, smoothed his cheek with her hand, and refused. Now, as she crouched in the dusty gloom of the shed, she thought of him, of Cassandra and Adam, and of how they would all be affected if something happened to her, and she thought about the dynamite. . . .

Little worms of apprehension wiggled through her stomach as the seconds ticked by. When she heard the click of the shed's door latch, Elly started. *Jason.* Her palms were wet with perspiration. She rubbed them on the folds of her skirt. Then quick footsteps sounded on the gravelly floor.

"Where the hell are you, McLeish? It's dark as hell in here."

She caught her breath as Jason's voice whipped out of the darkness. Only when McLeish answered as planned did she begin to breathe normally again. A match scraped, and a lantern flared, sending eerie yellow light dancing around the walls of the shed.

"I'm here, Mr. Emmett. Just as you told me."

Footsteps across the floor. "Moffett should be here any time now. You have your rifle? And the dynamite?"

"Yes, sir." To Elly's straining ears, McLeish's voice sounded a little too breathless, an indication of his tension. She could only hope that Jason would attribute it to the edginess a man might feel before committing murder.

"Ah, Mr. Emmett . . ." McLeish's tension seemed to reverberate through the musty shadows of the shed. "You're sure now? You want me to knock Moffett senseless and then, ah, set the fuse to this stuff?"

"What did you think I set this up for—a theatrical entertainment?" Jason sneered. "But keep that dynamite away from the lantern, you jackass. And don't you even go near it until I'm well away from this place, McLeish!" The sound of his boots scuffing the floor echoed through the low-ceilinged shed, which smelled of leather and saddle soap and, faintly, of manure. "And don't knock Moffett unconscious until we've questioned him about this strike business. I want to know who's really trying to ruin me so that I can get to the source. Moffett is only the pawn—but now he's going to be a dead pawn," Jason growled.

Elly glanced questioningly at Officer Flynn beside her, wondering if they couldn't arrest Jason now on the basis of what he had just said instead of waiting for Billy to enact his role in the dangerous charade. In answer to her unspoken words, the policeman gave his head a little shake. Apparently he thought it prudent to see the entire plan through to the end, so as to trap Jason Emmett as securely as possible in the web of his own making. Grimly, Elly accepted his decision. She had no objection to making the trap escapeproof. She was merely anxious, dreadfully anxious, to snare him in it and eliminate the danger once and for all.

Jason's low, excited voice broke into her thoughts. "I think he's coming, McLeish. Hide yourself and that rifle of yours until we see how many men he's brought with him."

But Billy was alone, just as he and Elly had planned. He shut the shed door behind him when he entered, then crossed to where Jason lounged on a stool. Beside him on the floor was the lantern, sending up its flickering arrows of light. Elly, unable to resist peering out from behind her barrel, could just make out Billy's broad back in the flannel shirt and patched trousers. Tension mounted in her as he spoke, as he played out his part, and Jason Emmett played out his.

"McLeish says you're ready to come to terms."

"Does he?"

"It's the reason I'm here."

Jason let out an arrogant laugh. "You're here because I wanted you here, Moffett. You've been duped. Did you really think I'd give in to you and your scum communist followers? I'd sooner burn down all my own mills."

"It might come to that, Emmett." Elly heard the hardness and contempt in Billy's voice. She marveled that this was the same man who once had claimed to be satisfied with his lot in life, who had seemed content with the tyrannical system against which Samuel Forrest had struggled. Billy had grown into a strong man, a man toughened and embittered by the poverty and injustice all around him, but in no way defeated by it. She had underestimated him all those years ago, much as she had overestimated the charms and talents of Connor Maguire. It brought home to her clearly in that instant the scope of her own ability to make mistakes. Yes, she had misjudged in the past. Like everyone else, she had made mistakes, at times very damaging ones. She watched the two men squared off against each other in the center of the shed, hoping with every ounce of her being that she hadn't made a mistake in setting this trap. That she had been right to lay siege to Jason Emmett's empire and to involve Billy in her battle. That this evening would not somehow culminate in tragedy.

Billy continued, his thumbs hooked in the pockets of his trousers. "The men are encouraged because they know you're losing money and contracts fast, Emmett. Face it. You can't hold on much longer. The day of the bosses is coming to an end."

"Tell that to those anarchists in Chicago who took matters into their own hands! They're in jail, the lot of them, and they'll hang for throwing that bomb."

Suddenly Jason laughed, and out of the darkness, a cold shock struck Elly. She remembered that laugh well, the harsh tones, the completely self-assured sound of it, which grated on the nerves and chilled one to the bone. No doubt he had laughed just like that when he had thrown Caroline to the ground and raped her. She had to force her mind away from the dreadful image and back to the conversation in the shed.

"But I've got a more suitable fate in mind for you," Jason was saying. At that point he called on Angus McLeish to come out of hiding.

Elly tugged at Officer Flynn's sleeve.

He nodded, not taking his eyes off the scene in the center of the shed. She noticed, though, that he was fingering his billy club, as if in readiness to spring forward.

"You're going to be remembered in Emmettville as the bungler who blew himself up while preparing a bomb to be used against society," Jason went on, his tone gleeful. "But

first, you're going to tell us who's really behind all this
anarchist rabble-rousing. Who's giving you money and orders? Talk to us, and quickly, Moffett, or McLeish here will
start bashing in your skull," Jason warned. He sounded
smug, utterly confident. He was enjoying every moment of
the power he thought he held over the other man, just as he
must have enjoyed his power over Caroline in the glade that
night, Elly thought. The hatred within her burned; it licked
through her blood. Through the pounding in her ears, she
heard Billy's steady voice.

"He's welcome to go ahead and try."

"Jackass," Jason hissed through his teeth. "McLeish, maybe
you ought to shoot his foot off. That might loosen his tongue."

"But, Mr. Emmett, you said you wanted it to look like an
accident. If I shoot him—"

"Fool! Once the dynamite explodes in this place, there
won't be enough left of him to tell he ever had a foot, much
less that there was a bullet in it! Shoot him, I said!"

Officer Flynn stood up and strode forward. "I think that'll
be about enough out of you, Mr. Emmett. Mr. McLeish, you
can hand over that rifle now." Mayburn hurried over and
took charge of the rifle—and the dynamite—while Jason
Emmett's face drained of all color.

"Who the hell . . . ?" he sputtered, sounding suddenly
hoarse. He looked both stunned and terrified. "Greeves!" He
lashed out at the sheriff, who shuffled reluctantly from behind
the barrels. "What the hell is going on here? Answer me, you
old fool!"

The sheriff was too upset even to speak. Surrounded by a
circle of grim-faced men, Jason saw Elly emerge from the
shadows. He spun toward her. His jaw dropped. As she
approached and the light touched her hair and the delicate
bones of her face, he let out a string of curses. "What has
this whore been telling you?" he howled, wheeling toward
the two police officers. "She's a damned liar!"

He didn't have a chance to continue. Billy Moffett sprang
forward and knocked him down, the sound of his fist striking
bone making a dull thud in the silence of the shed. Mayburn
yanked Billy backward, snapping: "That'll be enough of
that!"

Officer Flynn dragged Jason to his feet. "Mr. Emmett,
you're under arrest."

"Damn you, you little tramp!" Clutching his jaw, already purpling with a bruise, Jason seemed oblivious of the police officers, of McLeish standing uneasily in the shadows, even of Billy Moffett's bristling animosity. He was staring at Elly, his pale eyes almost maniacal as they fixed upon her with undisguised hate. "I ought to have taken care of you long ago! That night when you dared show your face in Hyacinth House to plead for your sister! My father and I showed you leniency then; we let your whole stinking family leave Emmettville—and look at the reward I've gotten for that! This proves what happens when you try to be fair and generous with low-life garbage like you and Moffett here."

"You still don't understand, do you, Jason?" Elly's voice had steel beneath it, despite its relative softness. In contrast to his hysterical, purple-faced rage, she looked composed and deadly calm. She met his maddened glare with an icy detachment. Now that he was in custody, and Billy was safe, Elly felt drained. She was relieved that it was over, satisfied with the outcome, but exhausted by the intensity and strain of the battle. "You've lost, Jason."

In the silence that fell, where all she could hear was his heavy, frantic breathing, she studied for a moment his disheveled coat and trousers, dirt-smeared from the sprawl he'd taken in the dusty shed. His hat had been knocked off and lay forgotten on the floor. Perspiration shone on his brow and temples and on his nose. In the leaping lanternlight, he looked rumpled and disreputable, which was precisely what he was. "The greed and arrogance and selfishness that you and your father have flaunted over the years has been your undoing," Elly continued softly. "These officers are taking you to jail in Pittsburgh where you'll stand trial for conspiracy to commit murder." She allowed a thin, cold smile to touch her lips, though it did not reach her eyes. "You've deserved to be locked up in a jail cell for many years now, and it is finally going to happen. You're disgraced. And you're ruined. The reporters I've summoned—"

"Reporters!" he gasped in fresh alarm.

She continued without acknowledging the interruption. "—will be at the precinct house when you arrive. Billy and Angus will give them all the details of your case and by tomorrow the entire county—maybe even the nation—will know exactly how greedy, desperate, and vicious you are.

I'm certain the newspapers will enjoy a story as fascinating and scandalous as this one," she added thoughtfully. "So will all your friends and business acquaintances, who will come to see how you desperately tried to arrange a murder and botched it, as you botch everything else you touch!" Contemptuously, she lifted her hand. "Officers, I think it is time to take this man away." In response to her words, the two Pittsburgh policemen grasped Jason's arms. She watched without expression as they marched him outside.

"So," Billy said, as Angus McLeish and a pale, shaking Greeves followed the policemen from the shed. "I guess it's over." They had all agreed that Billy would accompany her back to Pittsburgh in the carriage, while Emmett, McLeish, and the officers were to travel in Billy's wagon, which he had ready nearby.

They heard the crunch of the wheels on the cobblestones outside, and then silence, except for their own quiet breathing, the chirrup of a few thousand crickets in the night, and the rummaging of an unseen rat in a corner of the shed.

Billy picked up the lantern from the floor.

"Yes," Elly said with a wan smile as she looked into his calm freckled face. She felt enormous relief and a surge of pure, sparkling triumph. It was as if a tremendous burden had been lifted from her shoulders. Caroline's image flashed into her mind for an instant, the way she had looked many years ago: golden-haired and violet-eyed, her lovely face glowing, innocent, vibrant with the gay bloom of youth. She held to the image for a moment, closing her eyes, before opening them to smile again at Billy. "Yes," she repeated softly. "At long last it is over."

The next morning Elly called at Penn Avenue and was received by Louis and Victoria in the sunny morning room overlooking their manicured grounds. She had come to explain what had happened and to apologize for any grief or embarrassment the scandal might cause them as Jason's relations.

"I'm only glad that my sister isn't alive to see what kind of creature her son has become," Victoria said after a pause. She looked away, out the window at a fountain that splashed in the bright May sunshine. The burnished light reflecting off the yellow and peach tones of the morning room revealed all too clearly the deep lines etched around her eyes. In her seafoam morning gown with its high ruffled neckline, she looked older and more careworn than she had appeared at the anniversary ball last March, but she was still a handsome and dignified woman, Elly thought with admiration. And a strong one. Victoria glanced back toward Elly without any hint of blame a moment later.

"We'll get through it, my dear. Just as we have gotten through other trials, far more serious than this one."

Louis, standing behind the peach satin sofa where his wife was seated, dropped his monocle and blinked. "Right you are, Victoria. Right you are."

Elly wondered if they were thinking of their son, Philip, who had died at Gettysburg. She was certain of it when she saw Victoria's glance stray to the oil portrait of the solemn brown-haired young man, which hung over the mantel. Elly, perched in a brocaded wing chair, spoke gently, her tone full of heartfelt regret. "I am so sorry to have caused you any pain. I can understand it if you feel differently about me from this day on. Only I hope you won't let it affect your close feelings and friendship for Boone. He is so fond of you both. I would never forgive myself if you were to hold this against him."

It was Louis who answered her. "Nonsense. Put such thoughts out of your head, Elly. We've no ill will toward you, my dear. You did what was necessary, and my rascal of a nephew ended up exactly where he belongs, and through no one's fault but his own! And as for that husband of yours . . ."

Victoria smiled. "Nothing could change our feelings toward Boone, my dear. Over the years, he has become . . . like a son to us." She turned her head and gazed at her husband, and her sky-blue eyes were soft with affection. "Over the years, Boone has been a stimulating and loyal companion to Louis, far more than a business associate alone. Louis's affection and respect for him, and mine, kept us from becoming too involved with our own grief and loss in the long years after Philip died, which was something that was happening, little by little, day by day. Until Boone came along. He's added years to both our lives. He is a part of us. As are you, and your children. I want you to know that."

Elly felt the sting of tears in her eyes. "Thank you, Victoria." Then she lifted her gaze to Louis, who seemed patently embarrassed by his wife's words, though he made no effort to dispute them.

"Well, I'll leave you ladies to your morning tea," he said, clearing his throat noisily. He moved around the sofa toward the door. Despite the warmth and humidity of the weather, he looked crisp in his gray business suit and starched collar, with his red whiskers and mustache neatly trimmed. "When does your train leave for Chicago, my dear?"

"Two o'clock."

"Then you must stay to lunch with Victoria, and Briggs will drive you to the station."

"That would be lovely—" Elly began, but broke off as the morning room door, which Louis was approaching, suddenly flew open.

Jason Emmett burst into the room.

He was filthy, unwashed, and unshaven, and a foul musty odor clung to the clothing he had worn the previous night.

Behind him, the Whitcombs' butler bobbed in dismay. "Sir, I tried to detain him but he pushed past me—"

"Summon the footmen, Humphreys, and have them evict Mr. Emmett immediately." Louis planted himself before his nephew, bristling with anger. "How dare you come in here like this, Jason? Leave this house at once!"

Jason shoved past him. Only when he saw Elly, rising from her chair in pale-faced shock, did he slide to a halt. Hate shone from his eyes. "I knew you'd be here. As soon as they told me at the hotel that you'd gone out, I guessed it."

"Why aren't you in jail?" Elly demanded. Her heart was skittering like a runaway train. Jason looked almost demented, the way he was staring at her, shaking, and shouting.

"Greeves," he told her triumphantly. "Greeves brought my bail money early this morning. He did some checking on your whereabouts. He also brought me this!"

He pulled from his rumpled coat pocket the old Colt revolver that had once belonged to Samuel Forrest.

"Oh, my Lord," Victoria shrieked from the sofa.

"Humphreys!" Louis shouted and took a step toward his nephew. Jason swung the Colt in his direction and clicked the safety.

"Back up, Uncle Louis. You old bastard, you'd side with this tramp before you'd defend your own nephew! Get back where I can keep an eye on you." He chuckled wildly as Louis reluctantly obeyed his command.

"Don't worry, Aunt Victoria. I'm not going to hurt you or your precious husband. It's this bitch I'm going to kill."

Elly couldn't speak. Her gaze was locked with that of the outraged man before her as the barrel of the gun shifted, pointing directly at her chest across the sunny morning room.

She thought of Cassandra and of Adam, and of the void they would always have in their lives after growing up without a mother. Her body was paralyzed with grief and terror, icy cold from head to toe.

From a great distance, she heard Louis and Victoria pleading with Jason, heard the stamping of feet in the hall and, incongruously, the shrill song of birds outside the tall, silk-curtained windows.

From a great distance, she heard her own voice. "Don't do this, Jason."

"That's it. Beg. Plead with me to show you mercy, like that other time when you pleaded for your sister." He was crying and laughing all at the same time. Tears streamed down his unshaven cheeks, a curious contrast to the jubilant quirk of his mouth. "Aren't you going to beg?" he taunted, bringing his other hand up to level the gun.

Her throat was too dry to speak again. She tried to swallow, tried to form words, and couldn't.

"Bitch!" he cried.

She read in the sudden glitter of his eyes that he was about to pull the trigger.

An instant later, he did.

There was a tumultuous explosion, a thundering boom that knocked Elly off her feet and shattered the vases on the mantel. Through her numbing shock and the wisps of gunpowder smoke, Elly saw Jason's bloodied body on the floor. There was a great cavity where his chest had been; there were membranes and blood and gaping flesh. . . .

Gagging, she rose, then sank back in her chair. Victoria was screaming. Louis yanked up an Axminster rug and threw it over Jason's ravaged body, and the house was suddenly alive with frenzied activity.

Elly, through a fog of shock and horror, realized one thing. Her father's gun, which had probably not been cleaned or oiled since the day Jason took it from her, had misfired. It had killed the man who pulled the trigger.

"Thank you, Papa," she whispered, too dazed and weak to move anything but her lips. "Now it is truly over."

✥ Thirty-One

Chicago, 1887

MAY SUNSHINE SPLASHED through the window and warmed the silk-papered walls and ruffled organdy coverlet on Cassandra's four-poster bed. Lace-embroidered pillows and satin-gowned dolls and picture books were everywhere, yet the girl before the brand-new ivory dressing table, a birthday gift from Boone and Elly, was no longer a child. Tall, slender, with luxuriant dark hair and magnificent blue eyes, Cassandra Maguire at age twelve was a graceful, self-assured young lady—one who was alarmingly grown up, in her mother's opinion. As Elly dressed Cassie's hair with the enormous pink satin bow that matched the girl's new silk dress, she thought back to the baby she had held in her arms, to the two-year-old who had toddled around the boardinghouse with her doll, Daisy. Daisy still held a place of honor on Cassandra's bed, but she was surrounded by a host of finer, more splendid companions. Yet it was Daisy who still lay in the crook of Cassie's arm when she slept, and Daisy to whom she still whispered her troubles. But no one knew about that except Cassandra herself.

"You look beautiful, darling." Elly stood back and admired her handiwork. "Perfect."

Cassie jumped up from the dressing table, her young face eager and lovely in the May sunlight flooding through the windows.

"Is it nearly time? When will they be here? Oh, I wish

Mayor Harrison would finish his silly meeting with Uncle Boone. His carriage is blocking the street!''

Elly laughed. ''There is plenty of room for your friends' arrival, Cassie,'' she soothed. ''Calm down. The first guests won't come for nearly an hour.''

''I'm going to check on the gardens and make sure everything has been done just right,'' the girl said suddenly. A word from Elly, though, made her pause in her flight toward the door.

''Have you forgotten, Cassie?''

She turned, looking blank. ''Forgotten what?''

Elly shook her head. ''You promised to look in on Aunt Adelaide and show her your dress before the party started.''

''Oh, yes.'' A guilty look banished the excitement from Cassie's face for a moment. ''I guess I did forget. I didn't mean to, Mama, but . . .''

''I understand.'' Elly smiled and crossed to the bedroom door with her characteristic grace. ''You've never had such a grown-up party before, with ten of your friends coming to luncheon. And you've never been a young lady of twelve before, either. That's something,'' she said, tweaking one of her daughter's dusky curls, ''that we'll both have to get used to.''

Together they walked down the long, spacious hall and entered the sickroom where Addie lay propped up in her bed.

For the past three months, she'd been unable to leave this room, and Elly had hired a nurse to care for her. The family gathered around daily to entertain her with stories or to play cards, and she was comfortable if she didn't try to move too much. Her hair was thinner and whiter than it had been, and there were deep sagging pouches beneath her fading blue eyes, but she was still the chatty, warmhearted woman who had welcomed Bess Forrest and her children into her home years ago. Elly gazed at her with affection, thinking of how much she owed to this woman who had taken them in, who had nurtured and supported them in her own way after Bess had died in the fire. She felt a swelling of love. As Mrs. Brown, the nurse, removed a silver tray of cookies and chocolate from the room, Elly slipped into a chair beside the bed.

Aunt Adelaide's beaming gaze was fixed upon the enchanting young girl who sailed across the room and twirled before her, showing off the silken cloud of her dress.

"Cassie, my love, aren't you splendid? Oh, Elinore, aren't you *proud* of her?" She clapped her hands together. "She's grown into a beautiful young lady, if I do say so myself, and you're going to have to watch out for all the fortune hunters who are going to want to marry her for her looks as well as her money. Yes, indeed," she exclaimed happily. Then she drew breath, grasped Cassie's hand in her own, and went on. "Oh, if only your grandmama could see you today. You have a look of her about you, my love, do you know that?"

Cassie perched on the edge of the bed. She shook her head. "Everyone always says I look like my father."

"So you do." Addie's double chin bobbed as she nodded. "But every once in a while, in the way you turn your head or move across the room, you look like your grandmama. Your mama has it, too. That lovely grace and elegance that was peculiarly hers. It's a special quality, my love. You should cherish it."

Addie's eyes filled with tears suddenly, and Cassandra looked embarrassed. She glanced toward Elly for help.

"Oh, now, it's nothing," the elderly woman babbled on, as Elly handed her a handkerchief from the rosewood bureau. "Just a silly, emotional old woman. I was thinking about my brother, dear Samuel. He never even had a chance to see you, child, or Adam either. But he'd be proud of you both, so proud. Ah, well," she sighed and blew her nose. "I suppose from somewhere he is smiling down on us all this day, don't you think so, Elinore?"

"I'm certain he is, Aunt Adelaide." Elly leaned forward and kissed her cheek. "It's time for us to go down. Will you be all right?"

"Oh, fine, of course. Helen will be back any moment. Run along now, both of you. Oh, but I do wish I could see all the young ladies and watch all the fun!"

"I'll come up the moment the party is over and tell you all about it, dear."

"So will I," Cassandra vowed. The girl had bounced up from the bed and was nearly skipping about the airy, cheerful room with its pale blue coverlet and bed hangings, its crisp curtains of white dotted Swiss, and the abundance of cushioned chairs, settees, and couches, all adorned with numerous pillows, shawls, and antimacassars. In light of Cassandra's obvious impatience, Addie gave a tremulous smile and waved them both away.

"Go, go to your party, my loves—but do send some of those lovely pastries up to me, Elinore, I beg of you. Especially those raspberry tarts. You know how fond I am of sweets."

Promising that Jeweline would bring some up directly, Elly followed her daughter from the room.

Downstairs, while Cassie ran out to survey the festive tables set up in the garden, Elly found that Boone was just returning from showing Mayor Harrison to the door.

"How does it look?" she asked, as he met her in the hall.

"Not good, I'm afraid." Boone sighed. In the sunlight streaming in through the slender windows flanking the door, his bronzed face showed signs of strain and fatigue. "Sentiment is running high in favor of the execution, as of this morning. Even with the mayor's sympathy and that of a few other local men, I doubt that Governor Oglesby will agree to commute the sentences."

A chill touched her at his words. Last June, Judge Joseph E. Gary had imposed the death sentence on August Spies, Albert Parsons, Samuel Fielden, and four other men who had been convicted of murder in the Haymarket bombing, although no link had actually been found connecting them to the unknown person who threw the bomb. Another man, Oscar E. Neebe, whose only crime seemed to be that he owned stock in Spies's *Arbeiter-Zeitung*, had been sentenced to fifteen years in jail. The city, indeed the entire nation, were demanding vengeance for the policemen's deaths, despite the fact that those arrested hadn't actually committed the murder. They were convicted of inciting it through the political beliefs they advocated, and many people seemed to believe that that was enough to warrant the death sentences. Though there were some in Chicago, Boone and Elly among them, who felt it was a grave mistake and a dangerous injustice to hang seven men for murder without showing any direct connection to the crime, the spirit of hatred for the anarchists seemed to have blotted out reason in the matter. Even men like Lyman Gage of the First National Bank and Henry Demarest Lloyd called for clemency, but from the grim look on Boone's face after his meeting with Carter Harrison, Elly realized that a merciful decision seemed unlikely.

Boone leaned down and kissed the tip of her nose when he saw her distressed reaction. "Don't let this spoil Cassie's birthday," he said firmly. "Who knows? Perhaps clemency will somehow be granted after all. We'll see what can be done. At any rate, this is a special day, and you, ma'am"—he inflected the words with his Kentucky drawl and his warm smile—"look especially lovely."

As always, his arms around her helped the problems in her mind to recede, even if only for a little while. As they smiled at each other, she thought how truly lucky she was. Boone and the children and their surrounding family were the most important things in her life. After them came the Forrest: her monument to hard work and determination, that long-sought place of beauty and tranquillity that she had built for herself. It had taken a long time to reach this point, but she finally felt at peace. Her family was secure and happy, and the hotel was so well run and managed that she could afford to stay away more often than she had used to do. Life had taken on a leisureliness and peace that she hadn't previously known and that she cherished all the more for its previous absence. Yet she had already decided that she ought to enjoy her leisure while she could, for soon her children would grow up and face their own challenges and problems. She couldn't protect them forever, much as she might wish it otherwise, and once their own life's choices and difficulties lay before them, she knew she would hurt and fear for them as she had for herself, but this time she would need to step back and let them go to fight their own battles and find their own solutions, their own strengths. For Elly, accustomed to controlling and protecting, that necessary detachment might prove difficult, even agonizing. She recognized that, just as she recognized its necessity. Eventually, she would have to let them go. . . .

But not yet.

That was why, for now, she gave herself up to Boone's kiss, tightened her arms about his neck, and decided to enjoy every moment of this rich, blessed happiness while she could.

"There you are! Kissing again!"

Their son's impatient voice broke in on them, evoking laughter. Adam Walker, four years old, was the image of Boone, and every bit as forthright. Small for his age, as his father had been, he had the same sandy hair, keen gray eyes, and, in miniature, the strong, stocky build. He ran in through the garden, his knickerbockers grass-stained and his shirt ripped, but a wide smile brightening his sun-browned face. "I've been waiting for hours, Father," he complained to Boone. "When are we going to the baseball game?"

"As soon as you change into a decent set of clothes," Boone replied, trying to sound stern, but his eyes held more amusement than anger as he took in his son's disheveled and distinctly boyish appearance.

"Adam, what in the world happened to you?" Elly scolded, kneeling beside him in the hall.

"I was chasing a squirrel in the garden. It almost jumped on one of the party tables—you should have heard Cassie scream!" the little boy exclaimed. He laughed jubilantly, the sound echoing through the sunlit hall, where the gleaming mosaic tiles seemed to glow and the perfume of lilacs filled the air. Boone and Elly exchanged glances, both trying hard not to join in his laughter.

"And?" Elly prompted, brushing dirt from his cheek.

"And I fell over a tree root and my shirt got torn and the squirrel went under a bush and got away," he finished, spreading his hands in a gesture of finality.

Boone shook his head. "Better get upstairs and change. The game begins shortly, and now that your sister's party is nearly under way, I think we'd best leave before all the young ladies arrive."

"How long will it take to get to White Stockings Park?"

"Not long. Now, hurry," Boone ordered, and Adam scampered up the broad marble staircase, as nimble as a squirrel himself.

In the next few moments, everything seemed to happen at once. Cassie's guests began to arrive, as did Caroline, Timothy, and Delia, and Elly hurried out to the garden to greet everyone. Shortly after, Boone, Timothy, and Adam departed for the baseball game, where Boone had arranged a special surprise for his son: an introduction to Cap Anson, who had led the White Stockings to several National League championships over the past few years. This was to be Adam's first baseball game, and he had been talking of little else for days. Cassie, in turn, had been unable to think of anything other than her party, and it was Elly's job to see that everything ran smoothly.

It did. From the gaily decorated garden to the dainty luncheon to the opening of the elaborately wrapped gifts and the playing of croquet amid much giggling and arguing, all of the girls seemed to enjoy themselves. By two o'clock, with Delia animatedly supervising the girls, Elly sank down on a lawn chair in the shade and reached for a glass of icy lemonade.

"Next year, she will want a dancing party," she remarked to Caroline, beside her on a comfortable wicker chair. "With, heaven help us, boys to serve as partners, and to giggle about from the opposite side of the room."

"She's so carefree, so alive," Caroline said lovingly. Her gaze rested on her high-spirited niece who wielded the croquet mallet with considerable skill. "She reminds me so much of Connor, with all of his energy and charm and enthusiasm."

"Yes, I always think of Connor when I look at Cassie," Elly mused. She went on quietly: "The best aspects of Connor, that is. Cassie seems to have inherited all of those bright, sparkling qualities that first endeared him to me."

"She also has your drive and determination," Caroline said quickly, lest Elly begin to worry that her daughter might resemble Connor in less favorable ways as well. "You have nothing to worry about regarding *her* character—or her future."

"Perhaps only that she is a little spoiled." Elly sipped the cool lemonade, relishing its tart refreshment in the heat of the May afternoon. "Boone has told me that for some time, and I paid little heed, but I sometimes see that he is right. She'll grow out of it, though, Caro. She is a good-hearted child."

"And she and Boone? They get on better these days?"

"Yes." Elly was glad to be able to tell her sister that Cassie at long last showed signs of truly accepting Boone. Sometimes she even displayed real affection for him instead of mere tolerance. Elly was confident that things would only improve.

She glanced over at Caroline, so calm and placid in her yellow muslin gown, with the wind lightly ruffling her hair. Today even Caroline seemed especially tranquil. She had recently enrolled in a series of nursing classes so that she could learn to instruct the women in the Rat's Tail neighborhood on how to better care for their young and infant children. She was busier than ever, and yet, though she worked hard and though the hours in Roberta's shop were long, calling for her to deal with situations that were often sad and upsetting, she seemed to have found satisfaction in her work, in looking beyond herself. She gave every appearance of being content with her life, and for that, too, Elly was thankful. "What have you heard from Billy?" Caroline asked suddenly, as if reading the direction of Elly's thoughts.

Elly shifted in her chair and smoothed her spring gown of white lace adorned with violet satin ribbons. Her voice was full of pleasure as she replied, "He's well. Boone says he is doing a grand job. And Gerta is expecting another child."

"That's good."

Silence fell between them in the soft, golden radiance of the afternoon. Except for the laughter of the girls and the low murmur of Delia's voice above the fountains, there was no other sound. They were both thinking of Emmettville, which was no longer called by that name. As a final blow to Silas and Jason Emmett's corrupt empire, Elly had seen to it that the name was changed. The mill town outside Pittsburgh was now officially known as Forrestville, in honor of her father.

Jason had apparently never had an opportunity to change his will. Thus, in the weeks following his death, Elly and Boone learned that everything the Emmetts owned had been left to Sarah. Boone located her in Europe, where she was involved in an affair with an Italian aristocrat. She was more than happy to rid herself of her husband's problem-beset holdings. Whitcomb and Walker Steel bought all the properties from her, including Hyacinth House, which was converted into a school for the workers' children. The trade unions had to find themselves a new leader, though, because Boone hired Billy Moffett to supervise his new Forrestville holdings. Under Billy's management, and with Boone's approval, conditions had drastically improved in the town. Roads were being paved; sewage and plumbing facilities were being updated, and new, decent housing was being constructed. The eight-hour workday had been established in every mill and factory in the town.

It was a good beginning, Elly reflected with satisfaction. All traces of Jason's and Silas's oppressiveness would eventually be erased. Well, perhaps not all, she thought now, with a quick glance again at her sister. But most. Most wounds did heal, and most scars became less noticeable with the passing of the years. . . .

"Caroline?" Elly leaned over suddenly to take her sister's hand. "I'm proud of you." Her eyes sparkled in the afternoon sun, reflecting depths of love and admiration. "I may have never said this to you before, but I'm very proud of you. The work you do, the way you've overcome what happened to you . . ."

"I haven't overcome anything. I've just survived," Caroline interrupted quickly. She lifted her face to Elly and gave her a quiet, simple smile. "The same way others who have been hurt or abused or tormented have survived. That's all."

"But you've found happiness, a measure of contentment," Elly insisted. "You didn't let Jason Emmett destroy your life."

"No, that's true." Caroline nodded. "I found important work to do, and that has been my salvation. But I never completely overcame what Jason did, Elly. You know that. If I had, I would have a husband and children beside me today. I would know the pleasure you must feel every time you look at Cassandra and Adam."

Suddenly blinking back a mist of tears, she smiled. "You are the one to be admired, Elly. You fought back—and won. Not many people can say that."

Elly thought of the blood splattered everywhere in the Whitcomb morning room, and spoke slowly. "Fighting has its time and its purpose, that's true. But only if there are people and ideals worth fighting for. You were right when you said that the important thing is to survive. To survive and go forward. To find and give love where you may. Maybe that is what the struggle is really all about."

Cassie ran toward them then, her hair streaming behind her, her face indescribably lovely with youthful innocence and joy.

"I won, Mama—Aunt Caroline! My team won!" she cried.

"Wonderful, darling," Caroline exclaimed, offering her a quick, tight hug, and then Elly came to her feet and for a moment held her daughter in a lingering embrace.

She felt supremely peaceful as she looked at the vibrant, animated girl before her. Life itself was a victory, and so was the extraordinary gift of love.

"I hope you always win, my dearest Cassie," she said softly.

"Look, Mama, here come the others. Is there more lemonade? And cake?"

Then they were surrounded by laughter and youth and the shimmering, airy joy that is found on an afternoon in spring when the world looks new and the possibilities of life are endless.

Elly breathed deep, and smiled. She would savor every day, every hour, every rich and golden moment.